W9-BMT-109

A TIME FOR LOVE

Wind Dancer gazed into her eyes before he murmured in a voice made husky with deep emotion, "I trust you, accept you, and want you as my wife. I hunger for you as a man hungers for a woman; I have desired you since the first sun I saw you in the Brave Heart forest and did not know if you were flesh and bone or spirit come to help me. I did not wish to force you to lie with me upon my sleeping mat, but I yearn for you to do so. I wanted you to come to me of your own free will, not out of duty."

Chumani was thrilled and relieved by his stirring words. "When we joined in my camp," she began, "I did not know you and wished for us to get closer before we mated on the sleeping mat; in the past nine moons, we have learned much about each other and have become friends. I have never felt this way about a man, but I know what we share is strong and special, for the Great Spirit put us together and knows all things."

"That is wise and true, *mitawin.*"

Chumani savored his touch as he caressed her cheek. "I did not mean to make it hard on you, *mihigna,* and you have kept your word of honor to be patient. When you are ready to lie with me, I am ready to lie with you."

Almost afraid to trust his hearing, Wind Dancer took a deep breath and asked, "Do you mean on this moon? Here? Now?"

Chumani smiled and nodded, assured they would not be disturbed with a fierce storm raging outside the cozy cave. "It is time we become mates in more than words spoken before our peoples."

JANELLE TAYLOR

LAKOTA WINDS

Zebra Books
Kensington Publishing Corp.

http://www.zebrabooks.com

ZEBRA BOOKS are published by

Kensington Publishing Corp.
850 Third Avenue
New York, NY 10022

First Kensington Hardcover Printing: March, 1998
First Zebra Printing: May, 1999
10 9 8 7 6 5 4 3 2 1

Printed in the United States of America

Walgreens

Healthcare Plus   **REFILL REQUEST**

8350 S. River Parkway Tempe, AZ 85284

REFILL MAY BE REQUESTED ON OR AFTER: 11/27/2000

BY PHONE (with credit card): 1-888-858-2951   or BY INTERNET: www.whphi.com

(en espanol 1-800-778-5427)

BY MAIL: ENCLOSE THIS REQUEST WITH YOUR ORDER

THIS PRESCRIPTION EXPIRES ON: 03/04/2001

Cust ID: 478-70-9931

RX#:   7287570   PLAN: HNET

St#:   03397   Refills: 1

DIXIE YODER   PUREPAC

LONAZEPAM 0.5MG TABLETS

Dedicated to:

My husband, Michael, and mother-in-law, Betty Taylor,
my fantastic research assistants on this novel.

My daughter, Melanie Taylor,
for her research assistance.

And,
Dick Griebe
Pony Soldier RV Park
a generous and kind man who opened his campground
in the wintery off-season to allow Michael and Betty
to camp there to do additional research at Fort Laramie
and in the surrounding area, and who gifted them
with a bottle of wine to warm their chilly bones. A big
thanks from me!

Chapter One

APRIL 1851
PAHA SAPA (THE BLACK HILLS)

As the brave knelt by the fallen doe, a blade in his hand ready to skin and butcher the animal, Wind Dancer crept forward until he was close enough to prevent the stranger from having time to retrieve a bow and quiver of arrows from near a tree, and he cautioned. "It is not safe or wise to steal the hunt of another. Put away your knife and go in peace while I claim what is mine."

The brave leapt to his feet and whirled to face Wind Dancer, whose eyes widened in surprise, for it was a woman—not a man—who stood before him. Long black braids hung over her shoulders. She was clad in a buckskin shirt, fringed leggings, and a breechclout—a man's garments. But she was the most beautiful female he had seen, and for a short time, he simply stared at her in amazement. Her dark brown eyes studied him from head to foot, then she raised one brow slightly and looked directly into his gaze as she pointed her knife toward him. He wondered if she recognized him. He also wondered to which band she belonged, as nothing upon her unbeaded and unpainted garments and weapons gave him a clue to her tribal identity. She narrowed her gaze and glared at him as if its flames of anger could sear away his life force. Then she spoke, her voice, the sound of soft and slow moving water, her words as hard and stinging as a thrown stone.

"It is not safe or wise to prey on another band's hunting grounds. Why do you risk trouble by stealing an ally's game? There is no coup to be earned by such reckless theft. Have your people slain or driven all creatures from your grounds? Is that why you encroach upon another's?"

Wind Dancer did not know if her behavior resulted from shame, courage, arrogance, or ignorance but he was disappointed and vexed by her rudeness and apparent lack of training. He was a famed warrior, a man, son of a chief, a future chief himself. She should not speak such words to him. "The deer was not slain on your people's grounds," he explained. "A wounded animal roams where it wills; a hunter must track it and find it to end its suffering. She is mine, for my arrow lodges in her body. Look, it bears my markings." He watched her eye the feathered shaft which he withdrew from his quiver and held before him, then half-turn to compare its painted symbols to the arrow's which was embedded in the doe's chest. Despite viewing that proof, she shrugged, frowned, and insulted him again.

"It is a long way to another's hunting grounds. If your arrow had flown true, she could not have run so far before she halted to die. It is wrong to make the Great Spirit's creatures suffer so much and for so long."

Wind Dancer was astonished by her rebuke. He concluded that her parents and people had failed to teach her respect. He did not even want to imagine how his family and people would react to his sister if she dared to speak to a man in this offensive manner. His wife had never belittled, shamed, or scolded him. "My arrow missed its true mark when I was attacked by an enemy," he said in his defense. "I could not track the Great Spirit's creature into your people's forest until that danger was past."

Chumani noticed that he had received no injuries from that fight, and the fact he stood before her proclaimed him as its victor. Yet, he did not boast of his triumph. And he mistakenly assumed she was of the Brave Heart band since this was their wintering section of the Paha Sapa, an area upon which she also was trespassing.

"I am Waci Tate of the Red Shield band of the Oglalas," he identified himself. "My people's winter camp is almost one sun's ride from this place, but our hunting grounds travel closer." If she recognized his face or name, it did not show in her now stoic expression, but he had seen her gaze roam his face and body for bloody signs of his recent struggle and markings of his tribal identity. He wondered if she was impressed by the fact there were none, or if she believed he was speaking falsely to her.

Chumani knew who the tall and muscular warrior was, but she was the daughter of a chief and a skilled hunter and fighter in her own right, and she did not fear him. Following a deadly attack on her people by the Crow two seasons past, she had trained every sun to master warrior skills and increase her stamina, strength, and wits until she could defend herself and help protect her people. She had seen this warrior of awesome prowess at a distance on the grasslands on several occasions when the many bands gathered for seasonal trading. As a woman, she had been compelled to remain at her people's chosen camp site; it was the White Shields' way of keeping their females away from the temptation of being drawn to and mating with outsiders, Indian and White. But she and her best friend had sneaked near the men's location one night and spied upon them. After Waci Tate arrived, she had been unable to look away from him and thoughts of him had tormented her for many moons. Now, here he stood before her, over-filled with pride and scolding her as if she were a bad child!

As one who tried his best to practice the Four Virtues—Bravery, Generosity, Fortitude, and Wisdom—Wind Dancer

doused his hot irritation. "If your family is hungry and
you search for food, the deer is yours," he offered.

"There are three skilled hunters in my family," Chumani responded. "The deer is yours to take, but do not
roam these hunting grounds again. If I had known you
pursued her, I would not have tried to take her."

As she sheathed her knife and collected her bow and
quiver, showing she either trusted or had no fear of him,
he nodded. "That is wise. Now, tell me, who are you and
where do your people camp?" Before allowing her time
to respond, he added, "Rest while I prepare the deer and
I will carry you to your camp on my horse. It is not safe
for a woman to walk the forest alone when enemies are
restless."

Chumani's wits cleared and she realized she was behaving badly, especially since he had offered her the doe and
an escort home. Yet, she felt compelled by shame and
another unknown feeling to deceive him. "I am called the
morning mist. I know this forest and will be safe. Grandfather's creature awaits your prayers and preparation." She
wanted to leave fast, as she, too, had unwittingly
encroached upon the Brave Hearts' territory so deep were
her thoughts as she enjoyed the forest during the rebirth
of the land after a long and bitter winter.

Wind Dancer watched the stubborn female vanish into
the dense woods. She was beautiful and shapely, he admitted, but her ways were unappealing. Yet, he experienced
a strange attraction to her, more than a physical one, and
that baffled and piqued him. He walked to his kill and
knelt to thank it for its sacrifice and to praise its prowess.
This was one of the few times he had ridden alone to
either hunt or battle enemies. Usually his best friend, Red
Feather, was at his side; and often, so was his younger
brother, War Eagle. He did not know why he had wanted
to travel alone on this sun, but the feeling within him had
been too great to ignore. He was glad no one else had
witnessed the woman's bad behavior, as reporting it could
have caused trouble with her band if she were mated to a

great warrior, trouble he wanted to avoid at this busy time when Mother Nature changed her face and while a large group of men from their band was at Fort Pierre for trading. He had not gone with them to the enclosed village which was called a fort but was only a trading post, as he did not like or trust those with hairy white faces, the *wasicun.*

As he loaded the game on his horse, his body stiffened and his mind came to intense alert as if something warned him of imminent danger. Perhaps, he reasoned, the enemy who had attacked him had not been traveling alone. His gaze was drawn—as if by a mystical force—toward the direction in which the woman had disappeared, and a voice within his head ordered him to ride quickly that way.

It did not take long for Wind Dancer to hear ominous sounds coming from a clearing beyond him. He dismounted and told his horse, a smart and loyal animal, to remain there. He sneaked to a location where the woman was encircled by three Crow warriors, their identities unmistakable from their garments and markings. Anger filled him at the sight of his enemies encroaching on Lakota hunting grounds and taunting the beautiful creature. No doubt the daring warriors intended to take her captive and steal her innocence. His fury increased as he saw them darting in and out as they played a cruel game with her. There was no way she could escape their human enclosure, though she held a knife at the ready in her right hand and appeared agile and alert. She moved quickly as she whirled about and slashed out with her blade to keep the three foes at a safe distance, threatening and insulting them with her shouts. He noticed there was no fear in her brown gaze, only sheer hatred and coldness. She looked as though she wanted to slay them barehanded.

The men began taking turns with their sport, one resting and laughing while the other two continued dancing around her and thwarting her strikes with their lance points, their clinking contacts sounding loud in the forest's quietness. He assumed she would soon exhaust herself, making her vulnerable to seizure and worse. With all of the stealth and skills he could summon, Wind Dancer approached the resting man.

With a loud yell and knife brandished, the oldest son of Chief Rising Bear leapt into the clearing and challenged his enemies, determined to rescue the woman even at the risk of his safety and survival. He had confidence in his prowess, for he had battled more than three foes at a time in the past, and he still walked unharmed and alive to chant those coups.

Wind Dancer sent his blade into the heart of the startled Crow. Without delay, he set upon the second enemy, who charged at him like a raging buffalo during mating season, as the woman was fighting the third with skills which both impressed and astonished him. Though he was concerned about her safety, Wind Dancer was forced to focus his attention on his own battle, as his larger responsibility and duty were to his family and people as their future leader. He needed to use his strength, and skills to best his foe, which he could not do if his thoughts were on her.

The Oglala and Crow warriors exchanged taunting grins, both assessing his opponent's weaknesses and strengths. They stepped sideways in a circular pattern, each seeming to await an unspoken signal from the other to begin their struggle for victory. In the flicker of an eye, Wind Dancer fell backward to the ground and delivered a stunning kick into his competitor's groin, causing the man to shriek in pain, double over for a moment, and then retreat with haste for recovery as he himself laughed at his successful maneuver and sprang to his feet with ease.

With lightning speed and hopes of benefiting from the man's brief vulnerability, Wind Dancer raced forward and hurled his lowered shoulder into the man's abdomen, bringing forth a rush of air from his lungs. As the Crow stumbled backward and gasped for air, Wind Dancer used his knife to slice across the man's right side. His gaze flickered to the gaping wound and he thrilled at the knowledge he had brought forth the first-blood in what had to be a life-or-death encounter. He saw the Crow's gaze darken and glitter with outrage and pain, then narrow in determination that this would be his first and last injury.

Both warriors shoved with powerful bodies, kicked with nimble feet and legs, and struck with hard fists as their battle continued at a fast pace. They grunted and taunted and sucked in air to aid their labored breathing as their physical conflict stirred up moist dirt, dead leaves, and small stones. The Crow slashed out in an attempt to carve a path across the Oglala's stomach and chest, but Wind Dancer darted to his right and opened up another gushing red wound on the man's arm which wielded an equally sharp weapon. Wind Dancer read fury in the man's gaze and tried to keep his own impassive to prevent exposing his strategy.

A few feet away, Chumani knew her edge was in a mixture of her opponent's annoyance at being the one to battle a female while his friend challenged an elite warrior, of his arrogance in underestimating her skills, and of his belief he could defeat her quickly and easily. That he could not win quickly and was receiving cuts from her blade and blows from her left fist and feet visibly increased his vexation and made him careless during his ensuing attacks. Her gaze never left his, as she knew his next move and the timing of it would be revealed there first, a lesson Fire Walker had taught her well. She also had learned that even a brief delay in reaction could cost her her life. She kept her feet apart, her arms and hands controlled, and her knees bent.

As the enemy lunged at her, she dodged his approach and whirled to send her blade into his heart from behind. The Crow arched his back, grunted, and fell to the ground, soon dead from the lethal blow. She withdrew her knife and gazed at his body, her generous heart unable to pray for his departing spirit after what his people had done to hers two seasons' past. Unlike the Crow war party who had attacked her people, she and her band did not slay women and children, even for revenge. For every Crow warrior slain by her or another, she wondered if he was the one who had taken the lives of her loved ones.

Chumani forced her anguish aside, retrieved her other weapons, and hurried into the forest. She dared not take victory prizes with her or reveal this glorious incident upon returning home or the men in her family would refuse to allow her to leave camp alone again. To do so was a rare action for her, but her best friend had been busy with other chores when the urge to roam the forest had overwhelmed her.

Now she recalled how the Crow's knife had almost nicked her arm when she was startled by Wind Dancer's sudden arrival and her brief distraction by him. It was unlike her to lose her wits over a man and to allow her attention to stray at a perilous moment, but, indeed the Oglala warrior had stolen her thoughts for a time. She could not stay to thank him, even if she should; to do so would compel him to escort her home, and that would expose the peril she had encountered. Shielded by trees, she paused to take one final look at him. Though annoyed with him and his unwanted assistance she could not help but admire his looks and respect his great prowess. She frowned and scolded herself for allowing herself to linger, then left to find her beloved Cetan and return with him to camp before darkness blanketed the land.

Wind Dancer cautioned himself to be patient and vigilant, as a lack of those qualities often meant defeat. Sweat glistened on his face and dampened his garments, as the air was unusually mild for this time of year. His breathing was ragged, but his energy was heightened by the excitement of the battle and the coup awaiting him. He realized the Crow's stamina was lagging. He ducked as the Crow tried to ram him in the chest to knock him off balance. He licked his lips in anticipation of impending triumph and with a few more clever strikes and evasions, the man lay lifeless on the ground.

He turned to look at the woman, knowing her battle was over from a brief glance toward her earlier, but she was gone. His keen senses scanned the surrounding area, but he neither sighted nor heard anything to indicate her location or direction of retreat.

Wind Dancer walked to the third slain enemy and let his ebony gaze examine the man's injuries. The woman had fought with amazing skill, strength, and cunning—and had won. He could not imagine why she had sneaked away or why she had not thanked him. And she had taken no prize of her glorious victory, which astonished him. He selected those possessions of the slain warriors he wanted, summoned his horse, and loaded them. He concealed the bodies of the Crow with rocks and thick brush, a few branches in the shade still dusted with the last of the rapidly melting snow. He did not want them found before Mother Nature could dispose of them.

After everything was prepared for his departure, Wind Dancer left his horse there and followed the woman's trail until it, too, vanished as she had. Her tracks on the soft earth simply halted and no hint remained of where she had gone—no leaves, rocks, or limbs were overturned or moved or broken. He knelt and studied the damp surface with confusion. His troubled mind filled with questions. Who was she? Why had their paths crossed two times in one sun? Where had she gone? How had she vanished without leaving a trail? Was she the "morning mist" as she had told him?

Chumani observed Wind Dancer from high above him in the tree. She made certain to remain silent and still. She did not even flinch when a bug crawled over her hand and bit it. She prayed Cetan would not return from his hunt and give away her position or attack Wind Dancer. She remained there until the bewildered man shrugged, took a deep breath, and returned to the clearing, where he mounted, took the tethers of the Crow horses, and rode away, out of her life forever.

When she was assured he was gone, she scampered down the tree with the agility of a squirrel. She walked to where her horse awaited her, with Cetan perched on a nearby branch, watching her with his keen eyes.

"There you are," she murmured to the beloved hawk she had kept since she was ten winters old. "Come, Cetan, we ride for camp," she said, holding out her arm with a wide leather band now secured around it. After the bird settled himself there with his tawny gaze on her, Chumani reprimanded in a playful tone, "I may have needed your help if Wind Dancer had not appeared and rescued me from our enemies. But it was not a good sign to meet him up close, Cetan, for he stirs strange feelings within me. I must make certain our paths never cross and our eyes never meet again."

As soon as those words escaped her lips, Chumani frowned and scolded herself once more for having such forbidden feelings and thoughts. She kneed her mount and headed southward to her village.

As Wind Dancer approached his people's winter encampment the next day, the shaman of their tribe halted him before he reached the numerous tepees which were set up amidst tall green pines and still-barren hardwoods in a northern sheltered valley of the Paha Sapa. He smiled at his mother's father, as he loved and respected the wise and powerful man. Despite the clouds within his grandfather's eyes, which whitened more with every circle of the seasons, he noted an odd gleam in them and an unusual expression on the old man's heavily creased face.

Nahemana rested a wrinkled hand on the warrior's muscled thigh, locked gazes with him, and said, "Remember the past sun, he who dances with the wind, for your feet have touched the path to your destiny."

"I do not understand your words, Grandfather. I have battled and defeated Crow many times. Their horses are a gift to you for trade. Their belongings will be given to those with loved ones slain by our enemy."

"Your heart is good and generous, *micinksi.*" Nahemana praised Wind Dancer, calling him "my son," since he had helped rear this man as was the people's custom. "Wakantanka will reward you on the hunt and in battle. Soon, the words the Great Mystery put within my head will become clear to Nahemana; this is not the sun for Him to reveal their meaning or for us to speak of them. Walk with me, *micinksi*. Tell me all your hands did, your ears heard, and your eyes saw since you left camp on the past sun."

Wind Dancer was eager to go to his family's tepee to show them he had returned safely. He also wanted to share his exciting news with his best friend, Red Feather, and his younger brother, War Eagle. Yet, he always obeyed his grandfather, so he slid off his horse's back, secured four sets of leather thongs to bushes, and followed the slow-moving shaman to a small clearing surrounded by black boulders. As with Nahemana, he sat on the ground cross-legged, facing him and with little space between them.

"The air grows warmer each sun, *micinksi,* but a strange coldness attacks within me." Nahemana revealed his concerns in low tones. "I have not felt such trouble in my heart and mind since my firstborn daughter vanished many seasons ago. I fear danger rides toward us at a fast pace and great suffering lies ahead for our people if we do not find and defeat it. My daughter's safe return was a great victory over our enemy, but soon we must seek an even greater victory over them."

Wind Dancer remembered the painful time when all believed his mother was dead for two circles of the seasons. That had been twenty winters past when he had lived to four marks on a growing stick. It was during that tormenting time when his father had felt and shown his only weakness, but that was not something either he or Rising Bear wanted to recall. It was strange, he reasoned, that the number *two* played another agonizing part in his life, for two winters' past, it felt as if his heart had been torn from his body when his son and wife were slain by a Crow band. At times, Wakantanka worked His will in mysterious and cutting ways, yet, an honorable man accepted those challenges, without anger and a loss of faith in Him. "When will you seek answers about me and our danger from the Great Spirit, Grandfather?" Wind Dancer asked.

From his grandson's expression, Nahemana knew his mind had visited the past once more, and silently grieved with him for a while. "I will do so on the next full moon," he finally answered, "as He told me in a dream when I last slept. The ice which chills my thoughts and body comes from the direction of the rising sun and from where the winter winds are born and blow toward us."

"You speak of two different perils, Grandfather?"

"Yes, *micinksi,* but the two threats will melt into one force as the ice arrows on the trees melt into a stream and mix with its waters. If we do not control it and keep it within its banks, the new water has the power to flow over us and destroy our people and camp."

Wind Dancer felt his own heart chill and his spirit tremble at the use of the number *two* again. "Do not worry, Grandfather," he tried to assure the shaman, "we will keep it within its banks."

Nahemana's weakened gaze locked with Wind Dancer's. His grandson's eyes contained a contradictory mixture of confidence and uncertainty, as did his own heart. "That task will be yours, *micinksi,* for you also walked in my dream when I last slept. You have been chosen as the Great Spirit's weapon against our enemies. As has another who is a stranger to us, but will become our ally and your helper. I will pray for your courage and skills to help you walk the path He will set before you."

Wind Dancer wondered who that "ally" and "helper" would be and when he would come. "What words must I speak and what deeds must I do to save our people and our land, Grandfather?" he asked with great curiosity.

"The Great Spirit did not allow me to hear and see them at this time. Soon He will speak them in a loud voice for my old ears to hear and He will uncloud my eyes so I may see them and reveal them to you and others. I will go to Mato Paha for my vision quest on the next *Wi minbe.*"

Wind Dancer's heart filled with anticipation and he

prayed he could meet the unknown challenge which loomed before him. But what, he wondered, did his coming duty have to do with what had taken place on the past sun? Did his task and destiny involve the fallen Apsaalooke warriors, or the spirit woman who still haunted him, or both? He had no choice except to live through twenty-one suns until the next full moon at their sacred Bear Mountain where his grandfather, their shaman, would be granted his answers.

Chapter Two

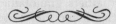

Following their daily morning prayers and meal, Wind Dancer and Red Feather sat on rush mats near a pine tree while working on their weapons. Beside each man lay a pile of shafts from the chokecherry, gooseberry, and willow. Already those slender limbs had been measured and cut for the proper length, bark peeled away, straightened of any curves, shaved with a knife to make them as identical as possible, notched on one end for fletching, and grooved on the other for a piercing head. Strong sinew and glue made from buffalo hooves for securing the points and feathers to the shafts lay nearby. Though some of the other warriors used iron obtained from trading with the *wasicun*, both men preferred to use stones they found and chiseled into arrowheads, a task done often during the long winter.

"Where does your mind roam, *mitakola*?" Red Feather called Wind Dancer "my friend" with great affection and respect. "You wrap the sinew around the tip and shaft many times, only to remove it and do the task again when it was right the first time. I have made ten arrows while you play with one."

Wind Dancer laughed as he laid the chokecherry shaft across his lap and looked at Red Feather. "It thinks of the

woman I met in the Brave Heart's forest three suns' past,"
he confessed, as the truth had always been spoken between
them. One of the greatest honors and enjoyments in life
was a friend—a *kola*—who loved and protected another's
life as much as his own. It had been that way between them
since they were small boys. They had played and trained
together with their fathers, grandfathers, and other males
in their family circles. Later, they had ridden together on
hunts and into battle, their bond as close as blood brothers.
"There were many enemies in the forest that sun; I wish
to know if she returned home safely as I did."

"You speak of the wit-stealing *wicagnayesa*,"Red Feather
jested as he recalled what his friend had told him about
the mysterious woman upon returning to camp.

Yes, Wind Dancer's mind concurred, she was a "trickster" who had eluded him and bested his tracking skills,
a beautiful woman who invaded his thoughts when awake
and his dreams when asleep. He did not understand this
powerful pull toward her, but it could not be denied,
though he made every attempt to do so. He did not want
a woman to become special to him, another woman who
could die at an enemy's hand, and at a time when a dangerous and unknown challenge loomed ahead. Yet, it was as
if she called out to him, and he could not seem to resist
that summons.

After Wind Dancer whispered those thoughts to him,
Red Feather said, "The Brave Heart camp is within a sun's
ride. We can say we come to see when they break camp
to head for the grasslands to hunt buffalo."

Wind Dancer refuted his best friend's suggestion. "It is
too soon to hunt the buffalo; the females are bringing
forth new life at this time. And the great hunt always takes
place after the growing and mating season."

"We can say we come to see how they survived the cold
season."

"That would not sound true, and we must not speak
false to those we may need as allies or they will turn against
us."

"We can say we come to ask if more Crow have encroached on their hunting grounds or attacked their camp in the night."

"That would reveal I have done the same," Wind Dancer pointed out.

"But your reason was a good one, to spare Wakantanka's creature from suffering; they will understand and accept it. Or you can speak the truth."

Wind Dancer shook his head at his friend's playful hint. "I must not ask about a woman who may have a husband, a warrior who would not like my interest in her. Perhaps she was not supposed to be in the forest alone and that is why she sneaked away and took no battle prizes. To seek her out would expose her disobedience."

"That could be true, *mitakola;* you told me of her bad ways. The women of our band would be punished for such behavior toward a warrior."

"Perhaps there was a good reason for her mean words and manner."

"Perhaps the fierce and powerful Waci Tate frightened her into a loss of wits. Or perhaps she was angered and shamed because you filled her body with desire when her husband is ugly and selfish and does not give her pleasure upon the sleeping mat or he is too old to do his duty there."

Wind Dancer chuckled at his friend's jests. He called to mind her beautiful image and how she had looked at him with interest, a remembrance which sparked fiery hunger within his loins. The thought of her being captured and abused by a Crow enemy sent quivers of fury throughout him. He even felt nibblings of envy and jealousy toward a possible husband, a man who could enjoy her body every moon and enjoy her beauty, smiles, and laughter every sun. Why, he wondered, had his wife never made him experience such potent feelings? But he knew the answer as he asked himself the question: she had been chosen by his father, not him, after he had reached manhood and it was time to mate and bring forth children. Even so, following her death, he had not wished to repeat that experience. No woman had tempted him until—

"It has been over two circles of the seasons since you lost your wife and son, *mitakola*. Do your heart and body hunger to replace them?"

Wind Dancer's fading smile vanished fast at Red Feather's serious expression. "I had put such longings away until I saw Morning Mist," he revealed. "She stirred my body as no woman has, and I yearn for another child. I love and respect my family, but it was strange to return to their tepee and to remain there after mine was gone, as if doing so shouts loudly of that defeat by the Bird People. At times, it is as if I walk two life trails. When my moccasins roam one, it is as if they never lived; when they travel the other, it is as if they still live and I will see them that sun or moon."

Red Feather understood well: following the deaths of his wife and son, Wind Dancer, as was their custom in the *ituwahan*, gave away all he owned except his weapons and horse which he needed for hunting and for battling enemies. He also kept his Wicasta Itancan shirt which was half blue and half yellow and decorated with hairlocks, a symbol of his rank in that powerful group of men who carried out the orders of the council. Homeless and alone afterward, he returned to his parents' tepee, there to stay until he took another wife, who owned the family's tepee and its possessions. Their physical bodies had long ago been reclaimed by nature's elements from their burial scaffolds, their spirits—*wanagi*—now living with Wakantanka.

"That is the way it is meant to be, *mitakola*,"Red Feather said. "The Great Spirit dulls those memories so peace can come and pains be healed. The time for Ghost-Owning is past, so you must release them forever and travel a new and happy path."

As he stared at the unfinished arrow across his thighs, Wind Dancer briefly reflected on the loss of his cherished son. He recalled the *wanagi wopahte* which had contained his son's second finest garments, favorite playthings, and hairlock; that leather spirit pouch had hung on a short *huyamni* for a year following the boy's death. Food had been placed before that three-legged stand at meals for one full span of the seasons, until those possessions were placed upon his son's scaffold after the *ituwahan* ceremony of feasting and giving away of almost all of his belongings, thus ending the Ghost-Owning rite for his beloved child. He recalled how he had sung the death chant for two suns and moons until he was exhausted and hoarse. He recalled how his heart had ached and felt empty of emotion for a long time. Then he had accepted his fate and the reality his son traveled the "spirit trail." Yet, he had never gotten over loving and missing the boy or hungering for revenge on the Crow, one in particular.

Not wanting to reopen that wound, Wind Dancer changed the subject, "Grandfather says a war is coming, one like a lance with sharp points at each end, each facing a different direction. I do not fear death, my friend, only dishonor and being denied the ranks of hunter and protector for my family. I am certain Morning Mist was not a woman who would bend like a willow to become a supple bow. I do not need a woman with skills and prowess to match mine; I need a woman who gives joy, warmth, and obedience."

"If the Great Spirit crossed your path with the one of Morning Mist, is it not wise to find it and walk it?" Red Feather speculated, "Come, let us ride to the Brave Heart camp to seek word of her fate and to learn if she has a mate. We need only to say we come to visit our allies, words which are true."

"Your words are wise, my friend; let us seek enlightenment."

The following evening, Wind Dancer and Red Feather camped at the edge of their hunting grounds after leaving the Brave Heart's camp.

The oldest son of Chief Rising Bear said, "I do not understand, my friend. How can it be they do not know and have not heard of a woman who dresses and battles as a man and is called Morning Mist?"

"It is strange, *mitakola.* Perhaps she was a spirit helper sent to guide you to the Crow so you could defeat them before they scouted our camp or the Brave Heart's. As with the coming of White Buffalo Maiden long, long ago, after her task was done, Pte Skawin disappeared and has not returned."

"It is as if she vanished as did my mother and half-white brother many seasons ago. We do not know why either was taken away or why only one was returned to our family. Perhaps it will be the same with Morning Mist. Perhaps our paths will cross again as they did with my mother, or perhaps she is gone forever as happened with my second brother. Until her truth is revealed to me, I must push away all thoughts of her and think only of the perils before us," Wind Dancer concluded aloud, and his best friend agreed with him.

Ten days had passed since Wind Dancer encountered the mysterious woman in the forest when bad news arrived at their winter encampment which was nestled in the protective foothills of the Paha Sapa. The two sons of Chief Rising Bear along with several other men had just returned from a successful hunt when they heard someone approach and call out to them.

Wind Dancer turned and saw a rider slide from his horse and slump to the ground and surmised one of their tribal members was injured. Before he and others could reach the fallen warrior, the man called out a warning in a weakened voice.

"Hiya! Lila makujelo! Lel mayazan!"

Wind Dancer halted everyone's approach when Badger said, "No! I am sick! It hurts here," and touched his stomach. He asked where the rest of the trading party was and Badger told him they would not be returning.

"Upi kte sni yelo."

Sighting no wounds, Wind Dancer asked him why not. *"Toke sni?"*

"Come no closer; I am bad medicine; I carry the white man's sickness within me. All others are dead. This evil will leap upon you and slay you as it did with us. I must tell all before my spirit leaves my—"

Wind Dancer grabbed one man's arm and halted him from going to their friend's aid when the warrior clasped his arms over his abdomen, groaned in agony, and dry-heaved so hard he shuddered. Liquid ran down his thighs from beneath an already soiled breechclout. His heart ached at Badger's torment, but they could not risk bringing him into camp and infecting others with a lethal disease. He still remembered the *mikosica*—the smallpox epidemic—which ravaged many tribes when he was ten winters old. That was only one of the *wasicun's* evils, along with his false tongue, firewater, and thundersticks. Many reasons abounded to reinforce his feeling that his people should avoid them. Yet, others wanted to trade with them, as with those who had taken pelts and hides to the post at Pierre which was built along the mighty river a few suns' travel away.

After Rising Bear and Nahemana joined them, the chief asked what was wrong, and his eldest son explained the grim situation. When others began to talk, the chief requested silence and told Badger to continue his report and to take his time. *"Inila. Wociciyaka wacin. Hanheya."*

"It feels as if the grizzly's claws rip at my belly. My skin is cold and strange like a dead featherless bird. The blood walks as a turtle within me. I shake as the leaves in a strong wind. I can keep no food or water within me."

By that time, most of the Red Shield Band had seen or heard the commotion and had gathered near the group of hunters and their leader. They listened in horror to their friend's story, one told with great difficulty.

Following another spell of shivers, the weakening man continued. "The sickness the white man calls cholera came on the boat which spits smoke into the air. All who went near those who were sick were struck down by this evil. I could not save the others in our party; the medicine in our bundles did not help us. I rode like the wind to warn our people not to go near the trading post on the big river to look for us. It is too late for me; I will die soon, as the others did."

Badger sat bent over on the ground and clutched his horse's foreleg for support. "All I am is leaving me. Even the white men have no medicine to save them; many die there and their bodies are burned to slay the sickness on them and their garments. You must throw limbs on me and shoot a fire arrow at mine to do the same. It is bad to touch even a dead body whose spirit has left it, for the evil remains on it. Do not wash me, put on my finest garments, and place me on a scaffold. Do not keep my belongings or horse; all must be eaten by flames. If you do not obey, the peril which comes from the direction of the rising sun will destroy you."

Wind Dancer exchanged glances with Nahemana as those last words were spoken. "That is the same warning given to Grandfather in a recent dream which he revealed to me. Grandfather said we would be attacked by two perils, one from where the winter winds are born and one from where the sun rises. The dream told him they have the power to destroy us. One has come to be." As night closed in around them, and although he knew the answer to his question, he asked, "What must we do, Father?"

A troubled Rising Bear looked at the elderly shaman upon whose heavily furrowed face light flickered from a freshly lit torch and asked, "What did Wakantanka say we must do to battle such evils, Wise One?"

"Follow Badger's warning," Nahemana replied in a solemn tone. "Our friend and brother has seen the power of this evil and knows he cannot be saved from it. He is brave and ready for his spirit to travel the Ghost Trail. Wakantanka will seize it from the flames and guide it along its journey."

Nahemana looked skyward. "See, the moon's face is dark so she will not have to witness this sad deed. No one must go near Badger. He must walk his final steps upon Mother Earth alone. After his spirit leaves his body, his horse must be slain so Badger can ride him along the Ghost Trail. Wood must be gathered; it must be light enough to be thrown over our friend and brother from where we stand. Wind Dancer is skilled with the arrow, so he must shoot one with a flaming tip into the wood. After all is eaten by the fire, dirt and rocks must be piled atop the ashes."

"It will be as you say, Wise One," Rising Bear said before he assigned a group of men to guard Badger's safety until his spirit departed.

Mothers with babies and small children left to feed the infants and to lay the little ones upon their sleeping mats, and other women returned to their tepees with heavy hearts, but most of the men remained there for a time to give their tribesman comfort.

More torches were lit and jabbed into the ground in a large circle around the fallen warrior as the guards began their vigil against predators attacking the vulnerable man. As time passed, the night air grew chilly but the wind remained calm as if in mourning. The only sounds were those of mumbled prayers, soft chanting, nocturnal creatures and birds creeping about in the forest nearby, and the burning of the torches. All witnesses noted that Badger bore his torment in brave silence. His wife and two children observed the tragedy in a mixture of pride at his courage and sadness at his sufferings and impending loss; they wanted to tend him to ease his agony, but that was forbidden. Everyone knew the good and safety of the tribe came first. All they could do was watch, wait, and pray in shared anguish and utter helplessness.

At last, Badger lay still and quiet in a merciful stupor, yet, the vigil continued by the guards, friends, and family as death sneaked closer to him.

* * *

By the first rays of sunlight at dawn, Badger was dead. Many hunter-warriors gathered limbs and tossed them into a pile atop their fallen companion. War Eagle, the youngest son of Rising Bear, ended the horse's life with speed and mercy, requiring only two well-placed arrows to complete his task. Red Feather lit grass secured around the tip of Wind Dancer's arrow before it was shot into the heap which quickly caught flame.

As the fire burned and dark smoke rose skyward, Badger's coups were chanted by his best friends and members of the Sacred Bow Society to which he belonged. Afterward, the Sacred Bow song was led by fellow member War Eagle to honor Badger as he made his way to the Ghost Trail.

Soon, Wind Dancer thought, another great warrior—probably Swift Otter if he could pass the rigorous tests required—would take Badger's place as one of four Bow Carriers. He was proud and happy that his own brother had succeeded with those awesome tests of skills and endurance.

Before the sun loomed overhead on a warm spring day, the sad deed was completed. As was their custom, Badger's family and friends would save, make, and collect items for the *ituwahan*, the ritual giveaway, following the passing of one circle of the seasons. That was one experience, Wind Dancer thought, that he did not want to repeat.

It was late afternoon when a call went out through the camp for an important meeting: *"U wo omniciye!"* the messenger shouted in passing.

All males who were or had been hunter-warriors halted what they were doing, gathered certain items, and headed for a large clearing surrounded by verdant evergreens and slowly renewing hardwoods.

The Red Shield leaders—*Naca Ominicia*—sat together on either rush mats or folded buffalo hides. The members of the Big Belly Society included Rising Bear, Nahemana, Strong Rock—the brother of Rising Bear's wife—and other older men of great worth and wisdom; they were the ones who made the important decisions for their band. Although all directives were voted on by each man and it required only one to disagree and have that matter set aside, usually they followed their chief's wishes. Another group—the *Wicasta Itancans*—sat nearby, warriors who had been chosen by the *Nacas* to carry out their orders, which included selecting the Shirt Wearers from among them who were responsible for the survival of the tribe and the peace amidst it. Next were the *Wakincuza,* Pipe Owners, who carried pipes in beaded bags for performing a Peace Ceremony, the "Making of Brothers." Members of certain warrior societies sat together. The rest of the Oglala males—mostly younger men who had not yet joined a society and youths still in training—took places around the outer edge of the large circle.

As Nahemana prepared the sacred pipe to begin the smoking ritual before their talk, he told of how it was brought to them by White Buffalo Maiden. "Long ago, Pte Skawin appeared to two hunters and told them she had come with a message from the Buffalo People. She was so beautiful that one warrior quivered in hunger for her. When his ears refused to hear his companion's warning and he approached her in lust, a crash of thunder roared across the sky and a white cloud enclosed him. When the wind blew away the cloud, nothing remained of him except his bones. Pte Skawin told the second man to prepare a place for her in the center of their village. When all was ready, the people awaited her appearance on the next rising of the sun. She came and walked around a circle of buffalo skulls, each facing one of the directions of the four winds. She carried a pipe of sacred red stone from the flesh and bone of our ancestors from the Great Flood."

Wind Dancer, who sat with the Shirt Wearers, gazed at the pipe in his grandfather's gnarled hands. As with the legendary one, a red stone bear was carved atop its bowl. Twelve eagle feathers were attached to its stem to represent the sky and moons. It was secured together by grass from the Plains where the buffalo roamed and fed, the greatest necessity for their survival, since it provided food, shelter, clothing, and tools.

"Pte Skawin told our people to use the pipe and its smoke to make peace, to make good medicine, and to send word to Wakantanka for the good of our people. She said that honoring and using the pipe would make our nation strong. She gave it to the chief to protect and respect, since through the pipe our nation survives. She also gave them the Seven Sacred Ceremonies which include Purification, Vision Seeking, Making of Brothers, Sun Dance, and Owning a Ghost. She lit the pipe and offered smoke to the Sky, Earth, and each of the Four Winds. After she left singing, she turned at a distance, looked at the people, then transformed into a white buffalo which vanished amidst a white cloud. She who is also called Whope, daughter of the Sun and Moon, had come to earth with those sacred gifts."

Nahemana stood in the center of the human enclosure and prayed: "Great Spirit, see us and hear us. We come to honor You and all You have created. We come to speak what dwells within our hearts. We come to seek Your guidance and protection. Great Mystery, see us and hear us." The elderly shaman lit the tobacco, lifted the pipe upward, lowered it toward the ground, then turned several times to face each direction to honor Father Sky, Mother Earth, and the Four Winds. He sat down and sucked upon the stem to inhale smoke deeply into his body. As he slowly exhaled, his wrinkled hand wafted the gray haze around his head to bathe it in the breath of the Great Mystery. When his part in the ritual was done, he passed the pipe to Rising Bear to draw upon it before the chief gave it to the man beside him to continue the ceremony for those of worthy ranks to partake.

After taking his turn, Wind Dancer watched the pipe pass from man to man. His gaze paused on his best friend who sat with their society, the Strong Hearts. His gaze lingered longer on his brother, War Eagle, who sat with the Sacred Bows and was one of the four Bow Carriers, as he himself had been before he was chosen as a Shirt Wearer and Strong Heart, as a Sacred Bow member—whose society goals were making successful war, and peace when possible—left that society only by death or for an honorable reason. As a Shirt Wearer, his group helped settle disputes between band members, made sure no person went hungry or unsheltered or unclothed, sought the best camping grounds during travels, planned travel paths and guarded the people during journeys, led the annual buffalo hunt, and carried out any commands of the *Nacas*. The Strong Hearts Society was comprised of fearless and skilled warriors who were first to confront any unforeseen peril, to help and protect those in need and alone—the old ones and families of braves who had been slain or injured or died and could no longer provide for their loved ones— and to do nothing to dishonor himself and his rank. That first goal had taken him away from camp two winters ago when a second band of Crow pulled a sneak attack on the village and claimed the lives of his wife and son while they were out gathering wood in the foothills. But he did not want to think of that great loss which still troubled his heart. Since the smoking ritual was over, he focused on his grandfather's words.

"When the men with pale skin and hairy faces came to our land many seasons past, our fathers and grandfathers smoked the *Wakincuza*'s peace pipe with them and let them hunt on our grounds and trap along our rivers. We have done the same with those called Spanish, French, and American. We traded with them and called many friends. It was the same with most bands and tribes. We were told they would not remain in our land for many seasons, but their words were false. Many stayed and others came to take the place of those who left; with each passing season, more come and stay. Eight trading posts sit along the great river; four are only a few days' ride from our camp. They have many trade goods, but we can live without their knives, kettles, cloth, beads, axes, and such. The Great Spirit and Mother Earth provide all we need for survival. If we turn from the old ways, grow lazy and weak, we will be destroyed.''

Nahemana paused as many men nodded or verbally concurred. "They build wooden tepees and places with standing trees to hide within. They cut into the face and body of Mother Earth to plant strange seeds and grow their food; they do not seek it from the land as we do. They do not believe in and respect the Great Mystery; they bring words of a God unknown to us and say He made all things. The Lakota know Wakantanka made all things. The words of peace and sharing on the white man's lips do not match his actions. We honor the spirits in the Four Winds, grasses which give life to the buffalo and other creatures, trees, Mother Earth, Father Sky, two-leggeds and four-leggeds. Wakantanka gave each creature special colors or markings to help it hide from its enemies, and a means of defense against them. Now, the white man craves their hides and pelts; those in the land of the rising sun send for more buffalo robes and tongues. The white hunters slay our brothers for them and leave their meat and bodies to rot and waste on the Plains. They bring fire-water to make our wits dull, our minds crazy, and our bodies weak. They bring strange illnesses to slay us, such as the one which took the life of Badger and others. They bring thundersticks that kill with loud and small stones, hard stones which travel a great distance. They cross our lands in wagons and use them at will in passing. Many have come on long journeys to draw the face of our lands, to learn its secrets and where our strengths lie. They have taken bones of the ancient creatures from the sacred Paha Sapa and Makosica. Others take old or pretty stones and shiny rocks which reflect the sun's golden light which the white man craves.''

Wind Dancer remembered the tales his father and grandfather had told him about what happened in the Black Hills and Badlands when those strange whites collected old bones and rocks and made "maps" from twenty to two summers past. He believed the whites should not be allowed to enter those sacred regions again to steal Wakantanka's possessions.

Nahemana continued. "Soldiers follow or make permanent camps to protect the *wasicun* from people they call 'savages' and 'hostiles.' Our fathers spoke of a big thunderstick which spit forth many powerful stones in a hurry, a weapon the whites called a 'howitzer.' It roared across the land and sky when treaty was made with those at Fort Pierre. Nineteen winters past, the post was destroyed when fire touched the black powder in a keg, powder the white hunters use in their thundersticks. Their weapons are powerful and evil, my people, and can destroy us."

Wind Dancer wondered if defeating such powerful weapons was part of the challenge which loomed before him and his people. If so, how could such an awesome deed be accomplished?

"Such times and events have been painted upon our tribal hide by the Story Catchers so we will never forget them. The whites crave all that was given to us by the Great Spirit. If we do not send them away while their numbers are few and their powers grow stronger than ours, all is lost. They will steal or slay the companion of the Old Woman Who Quills At The Edge Of The World. If the dog does not unravel her work each sun when she adds wood to her fire and stirs her soup, she will complete her quilling upon the sacred buffalo hide and our world will cease to exist. If we do nothing, the whites will become as another Great Flood and their evil waters will flow over us and destroy us. Already they seek to make allies with our worst enemies, the Crow; together they will be stronger than we are. We must find a way to plant the war lance between them so no truce is possible." He took a deep breath before concluding. "On the next full moon, I will go to Mato Sapa to seek a sacred vision to ask Wakantanka how and when we can defeat such enemies, for surely the time has come when the whites must be called and viewed as great perils to us."

A long distance away in the White Shields' camp, Chief Tall Elk of the Brule Lakotas said to his daughter, "Come, sit, my child. Sees-Through-Mist has words to speak to you."

Chumani could not surmise the reason why her father and their shaman had summoned her from her chores when she needed to complete them before night blanketed the land. She took a seat on a rush mat and allowed her dark gaze to shift from man to man as she awaited the answer.

"On the last full moon, an owl appeared to me in a dream," Sees-Through-Mist revealed. "The messenger from Wakantanka said I was to bring this garment and moccasins to you as a gift. I waited until Snowbird made them from the sacred white buffalo skin which was given to me during the last cold season. The owl told me you will wear them two times in the coming seasons and both will be big medicine. They are yours, Dewdrops, so you may help the Great Spirit save our people from our enemies. They are not beaded so the enemy will not read our tribal markings upon them."

Chumani accepted the dress and moccasins, each beautiful and soft and unadorned. The lengthy fringes on the end of the sleeves and bottom of the dress tickled her arms and calves as she placed the garment in her lap with the moccasins atop it. After she thanked him and told him to tell his wife the same, she said, "I do not understand your meaning, Wise One. How will these gifts help me save our people from evil? And why was I chosen?"

"I do not know, Dewdrops. The messenger owl did not tell me, but the Great Spirit has been at work in your life for the passings of twenty-four circles of the seasons to train and prepare you for these challenges. The owl said you will take another mate and together you will ride away and do great deeds for us. I saw you standing in our camp dressed in white, but the face of the warrior beside you was kept hidden from me. Then I saw you dressed in white and standing on a high hill with a hawk upon your arm.''

Chumani felt apprehension shoot through her body like swift and deadly arrows as she heard those awesome words. Why had she been chosen for that great honor? How could only two people defeat their enemies? She knew the white garment was made from a sacred white buffalo who appeared and died near their camp, but what great magic did it possess? Who was the man she must be bound to before meeting that challenge together? Would she find him desirable or repulsive? Would she bear another son to replace the one she had lost? Before she could ask more questions, a shout was heard outside the tepee, whose flap was closed to signal privacy, then a familiar voice called out to the chief.

Chumani put aside the gifts and followed them to observe the action when Tall Elk and Sees-Through-Mist joined the four men who were standing there, sweaty and almost breathless from an apparent swift ride. Their attention focused on the chief's only son as he spoke first, and members of their band gathered around them.

"Great evil walks in the white man's village, Father. It came on the boat which breathes fire and smoke. All who went near it or tended those who became sick fell prey to its power. We did not go to trade, so we camped a short distance from the post and waited for our friends to return. After they became too weak to ride or walk to our campfire, we did not go near them. One of the hairy faces warned us it was certain death to touch those whose bodies spewed forth watery evil. The hairy face said it was the same danger even after their spirits left their bodies, so we could not bring them home with us. We must not go near the white man's village again."

"What Fire Walker says is true, my chief," Gray Fox concurred. "Many of the whites and those of other bands and tribes were struck down by the evil. The hairy face said any man who returned to his camp while sick would spread death among his people. We camped a sun away until we were certain we did not carry the sickness with us, for the hairy face said the sickness rears its head in one to three suns. We are fortunate to be untouched by it."

"Many seasons ago, the white man brought another sickness to many bands," the shaman reminded everyone who had gathered around to listen, "a sickness which brought forth ugly marks upon their skin. This is a sign to us to avoid the white-eyes or they will bring more evils to us. Long ago, the whites were few and offered us friendship and trading. With each new season, more come, and those who do will never leave our lands unless we drive them away. Those who call themselves trappers, traders, peddlers, soldiers, and homesteaders roam our lands and claim them as their own. Our grandfathers and fathers allowed many to hunt and trap and travel our land; it was wrong and foolish, for they hunger to stay, for more land and furs. They make paths they call roads across our hunting grounds. They cut trees in our forests. They shoot buffalo, deer, and elk. They dig into the face of Mother Earth to plant seeds to grow their strange foods. They make wooden tepees with trees lashed together around them; they make villages they call trading posts and forts for soldiers. They bring weapons which spit fire and thunder. They bring water which burns the throat and steals a man's head and causes him to act foolish and to fall asleep. We grow smaller and weaker from attacks by our Crow enemies and this white man's evil while our two enemies grow stronger and larger."

While the shaman continued to speak, Chumani recalled the fierce Crow attack two summers ago when she lost her husband and son. Now, the Bird People were leaning toward becoming allies with the white men, which would make a great force against them. If the Great Spirit had chosen her to help defeat either or both forces, she was ready and willing to do so, eager for revenge, especially upon one particular Crow whom she would recognize if she saw his face again. If Wakantanka heard and answered her prayer, she would be guided to him. But why must she take another husband, she wondered, and who would that man be? There was none among her people who caused her heart to sing and her body to warm; nor had her first mate. Surely she deserved such happiness this next time.

"When Grandmother Earth was a young maiden and Wakinyan, the Thunderbird Spirit, was angered, he hurled great thunderbolts across the sky and made rips in it. The rains came for many seasons until the world was almost covered with water by a great flood. The two-leggeds and four-leggeds fled to higher and higher ground, but could not outrun the waters. The People perished; their flesh and blood created the sacred red stone from which our sacred pipe is made. When the waters flowed to the edge of the world and mourning songs were sent skyward, the Great Spirit sent a giant eagle to pick up a special maiden who was trapped on a tall peak. He carried her to the last tree on the highest peak, to the Center of the Hoop of the World. There, he changed into a mighty warrior and protected her until the waters returned to the banks of their streams and rivers. Then they left the mountain and gave birth to our nation. Wakinyan is angered again by the coming of the white man and the attacks of our enemies. He has the power over life and death to people, creatures, and the land, but he does not wish to destroy all who live upon it. We must seek a way to defeat our enemies so the sacred hills will not shake with the thunder of his voice again."

"How will we defeat such powerful enemies, Wise One?"

Sees-Through-Mist glanced at Chumani and smiled before he replied to her brother, "Soon, Fire Walker, Wakantanka will give us a sign to guide us to that path. It will come like the morning mist which blankets the face of Mother Earth on a new sun. Long ago, when the Great Spirit painted the flowers and they lowered their heads and asked where they would go when the White Giant came from the north and they were slain by his cold breath, Wakantanka said they would travel to the Happy Hunting

Ground on the rainbow which steals some of their colors in passings. If we do not follow His message to us, we, too, will travel that beautiful trail. Return to your tepees and work, my people, and prepare yourselves for what lies ahead while we await the sign from the Great Spirit."

Chumani headed for the forest to finish gathering wood with her mother, her best friend, and other women. As they worked a short distance away from the others, she whispered with Zitkala about what the shaman had said and given to her, as the two shared even the innermost secrets in their hearts. "What if I fail in my dream task, my friend?"

"You will not fail, Dewdrops. Your skills are as great as any warrior's. Your wits are keener than those of most men. Wakantanka would not have chosen you if you are unworthy of your challenge."

"But what of the man I must bond with soon? I do not wish to take another husband not of my choosing. Why must others pick them for me?"

"This time, Wakantanka does the picking, Dewdrops," Zitkala reminded. "He knows and sees all; He will not make a bad choice for you."

"I hope not, my friend. Would you not feel worried in my place?"

Zitkala laughed softly. "No man has touched my heart in such a way. That is good, for no man wants me and I am happy to remain alone on my sleeping mat and in my family's tepee. Since I have no brothers, my father and mother need me there to hunt for them and protect them."

Chumani knew why her friend believed herself undesirable to men: Zitkala was quite masculine in appearance and manner. Yet, beneath that misleading outer shell, she was very much a woman. Surely, Chumani reasoned in hope, a great warrior would come along one sun to steal Zitkala's heart, just as Wind Dancer had—*No, Dewdrops, you must not think of him!* She chided herself.

"Soon, we must go to Mato Sapa so you can hang your

son's hairlock upon a prayer tree there; it is time to say a final farewell to him and the past, for a different destiny shines before you."

Chumani's fingers touched the leather-bound hairlock she had worn around her neck since her son's death. She vowed to never part with it until his slayer was dead by her hand. How could she ever forget a child she had carried within her body and reared to two winters old, a son she had loved with all her heart despite a lack of similar emotion for his father? Was it time to place this remaining reminder of him in the hands of the Great Spirit? That was a decision to make later, but for now a visit to Bear Butte to make offerings and send up prayers was good.

Their chore finished, Chumani looked at her other companion on the branch of a pine tree. "Home, Cetan," she instructed the hawk. "Night approaches." *As does my destiny.*

Chapter
Three

Wind Dancer and Nahemana sat cross-legged in the sweat lodge which had been constructed by their helpers and protectors, Red Feather, War Eagle, and Strong Rock. Perspiration poured from their bodies, clad only in breechclouts and moccasins. No fresh air entered the turtle-back-shaped dome made of thick buffalo hides thrown over the bowed limbs. It was stuffy and oppressive in there, but neither man complained about the ritual which would purify their bodies in preparation for their impending visionquests. For the previous two days in their small camp on the northern side of Bear Butte, they had fasted and prayed before entering the sweat lodge. Their three helpers—without talking and in a reverent manner—heated rocks in a campfire outside, exchanged them with chilled ones in a shallow pit in the *initipi*, and poured water over the new additions which sent forth sizzling steam inside the darkened enclosure.

Soon it would be time to sit upon a high location in Wakantanka's view, eat the sacred peyote, and allow the Great Spirit to speak to them in separate visions. They would remain there—exposed to the elements—until their task was completed. Afterward, they would purify themselves again, partake of food and water to replenish their strength, rest for a while, and return to their camp. Once back with their people, either their visions would be kept secret in their hearts and minds, or would be shared with others if so commanded by Wakantanka.

Chumani and Zitkala approached the southern side of Mato Sapa which sat upon the face of Mother Earth as a tall tepee, a short distance from the Black Hills. Both knew that the Cheyenne, and most Indian tribes, viewed the site as a spiritual one. *Noavosse* in the Cheyenne tongue was where Sweet Medicine and Erect Horns of the Cheyenne received their *Maahotse*—Four Sacred Arrows—the power of *Esevone*—the Sacred Buffalo Hat—the Sun Dance, the war shield, and other rituals and commands. People of many tribes, bands, and nations visited Bear Butte to pray for guidance and protection, to give thanks for their blessings, and to present offerings to Wakantanka. Even some white men had encroached on this peaceful and powerful setting over a hundred winters past and continued to do so on occasion. Yet, rarely did an Indian attack another Indian, as most believed it was bad medicine to battle and slay on sacred ground or to interrupt a sacred ritual. For that reason, the females felt safe in journeying together and being there without the presence of men.

The women dismounted and made their way up a gently rising slope to where other short trees and bushes were decorated with bits of cloth, feathers, beaded objects, and leather pouches of special belongings. Some areas were barren rock and others were dotted by evergreens and small hardwoods and various grasses. Two streams crossed the surrounding Plains near the base of two of its sides, opposite of each other, and provided water for weary and thirsty travelers. The first flowers of the new season mingled with verdant grass, their colorful heads and the numerous blades swaying to and fro in a strong breeze. The day was exceptionally warm, the sky was clear and blue, the sun was sinking toward the heart of Mother Earth, and all snow had melted. Birds, animals, and insects now flourished and feasted and roamed upon the new growth. Those sights and sounds and smells filled the two women's hearts and souls with the serenity of the Hoop of Life.

Zitkala—her hair secured by two thick braids with leather thongs—was attired in a buckskin shirt, breechclout, and leggins, but, Chumani wore a fringed dress. For her communion with the Great Spirit, her garment was simple and unadorned, and she wore no beaded wristlets or choker. Even her long black hair was unbound and held no decorative ties or rosettes.

After praying to Wakantanka to keep the spirit of her lost son close to His side, Chumani removed his leather-enclosed hairlock and secured it to a branch. She closed her dark brown eyes and said a final farewell to him. As she reopened them, her gaze locked upon the two scars on her left arm from cuts made there during the mourning of his death. Those were two memories—one representing each winter of his life—she could never remove. The thought of joining with another man and bringing forth another child was both elating and frightening to her. It would be wonderful to hold another son in her arms, but it would be an even worse torment to lose him to an enemy. Since her child's death and her return to her parents' tepee, she had lived from sun to sun without giving thought to any changes in her life.

Now, Chumani admitted, since her talk with the shaman and her meeting with Wind Dancer in the forest, her thoughts roamed continuously to that matter. She told herself she should be concentrating only on the words of Sees-Through-Mist from his contact with the Great Spirit and on practicing her skills to be ready to meet that unknown challenge, yet, dreams of that enchanting warrior haunted and distracted her. There was no way their paths would ever cross again, at least not as they did in her dreams. Soon she would be compelled to join to another man, so she must forget him. Besides, he did not seem to like or respect her and he would not make a compatible mate for her. If the son of the Red Shields's chief did not already have a woman in his tepee, which was doubtful at his age and rank, he would want one who was silent, modest, and obedient; not someone like her. If she joined to a man like that, she reasoned, it would not take long to be swallowed up by him and to lose herself completely and forever, which did not appeal to her.

Chumani took a deep breath. "Come, my friend," she said, "let us go before my heart begs me to defy the will of Wakantanka."

"What do you mean, Dewdrops?" Zitkala asked in astonishment.

Chumani revealed what she had been thinking and her best friend empathized with her fears and doubts. "Do not be afraid or uncertain, Dewdrops. The Great Spirit will guide and protect you."

"Yes, but into the arms and tepee of a man I do not and cannot love."

"Perhaps Wakantanka will place love in your heart for him."

How can that be when another man already lives there? Chumani's troubled mind refuted, for the first time not sharing an important worry with her best friend. "Come, let us return home and await His will for me."

Wind Dancer and Nahemana reached the location they had chosen for the next part of their spiritual journey, a place on the southern side of the butte away from the sight of their temporary camp and three helpers, a spot where they would face the setting and rising suns. As Nahemana spread out his own blanket, upon which he would sit in its center, Wind Dancer gazed out across the Plains and saw the woman from the forest mounting a horse, accompanied by a man. Their garments were unmarked, so there was no way to determine which tribe or band she belonged to, but he knew it was not to the Brave Hearts. Surges of desire and jealousy swept through his body and mind, already dazed by fasting and sweating. For a short time, he was tempted to race down the slope or to shout her name, but it was wrong to do either, for one person did not intrude upon the sacred rites of another, or halt his own without an important reason after his body and mind had already been prepared for his visionquest. He must put all thoughts of her and other earthly matters aside and dwell only on his purpose for being there in order for Wakantanka to speak to him. Yet, it was strange that she had appeared to him for a second time.

Chumani did not know what force drew her gaze upward, but it was a powerful, irresistible one. She sighted Wind Dancer with an elderly man, both clad only in breechclouts and their dark bodies outlined against a vivid blue sky. It was the younger warrior who captured her attention and caused her heart to race with excitement as her gaze roamed over him. His raven-black hair was unbound and blew about his head in a brisk wind. His tall body was virile and enticing. His shoulders were broad, his Sun Dance-scarred chest was otherwise smooth and hairless. His arms were muscular, his waist trim, and his legs long and lithe. His stance revealed high rank and great strength and prowess. Never had she seen a more handsome man. His dark and potent gaze was fixed upon her, and she quivered despite the warmth of the late afternoon. But as quickly as she experienced that strange reaction of chillbumps splashing across her arms and legs, a fierce heat assailed her flesh. She felt her nipples grow taut and her loins ache. She knew she must break his visual hold over her and leave in a hurry, as he was a formidable temptation and forbidden desire. Yet, that seemed impossible. Perhaps the Great Spirit had brought him there so she could also say a final and necessary farewell to him.

Zitkala's gaze traced the path of her best friend's and saw what held Chumani transfixed. She noted the flush on the other woman's cheeks and fretted over the hot desire clearly revealed, a fire which could never be fed and appeased, one which she must help extinguish. "Come,

Dewdrops, we must leave before evil medicine attacks us,"
she suggested gently.

Chumani looked at her friend and confessed, "It has
done so already, but I will defeat it. Let us ride as swiftly
as the deer flees an enemy."

Nahemana had already consumed his peyote and his
mind was reacting to its potency, but he noticed his grandson's distraction and asked, "Who seeks to steal your eye
and wits, *micinksi?*"

As he rubbed sweet sage and other ceremonial herbs
over his upper body, Wind Dancer disclosed, "It is the
woman from the forest, Grandfather; she who called herself Morning Mist and eluded my tracking skills. Is she
flesh and blood or spirit, Wise One?"

Nahemana squinted to study the woman, but his eyes
were too clouded by age and his wits too ensnared by the
peyote, along with her hasty retreat, for him to see her
clearly. "I do not know, *micinksi,* but we must continue
our quest. You must forget all else at this time."

As Wind Dancer saw her ride away with her companion,
perhaps her husband, he took a seat on the center of his
blanket and placed the peyote in his mouth. He chewed
and swallowed it, then awaited its effect. The last thing he
remembered was seeing a hawk swoop down from the sky
and land upon her outstretched arm as she headed for
the Black Hills and out of his life once more. His swirling
thoughts vowed, *One day I will find you, beautiful mist of the
morning, and I will make you mine, even if I must steal you from
another and hold you captive.*

Nahemana sat on a mat in the tepee of Rising Bear to
discuss his vision with the chief. Also present were his
two grandsons, his daughter, his wife, and his thirteen-
summers-old granddaughter. The three women—his
mate, Little Turtle, his eldest daughter and the chief's
wife, Winona, and his granddaughter, Hanmani—sat apart
from the four men to observe the event. They, like all

Indians, were firm believers in sacred visions. They were allowed to hear about matters which affected the family and band, but—as females—they would not participate verbally in the meeting.

The talk between the men would not include the seventeen-winters-old War Eagle; he was present only to listen and learn. The younger man knew and accepted the fact that his older brother was the one being reared and trained to become their next leader. Their family had a tight bond and were fiercely loyal to each other, their kin, their band, and their nation. As was their custom, the children and relatives of a chief were the band's most important members, and leadership journeyed through his bloodline, passing from father to the oldest son unless there was a reason to ignore that practice. War Eagle was certain his beloved brother would never do anything to dishonor himself, his family, and his people. He was proud of Wind Dancer, and no jealousy or envy lived in his body against him; to become their next chief was Wind Dancer's birthright, destiny, and duty. True to his name, Waci Tate "danced with the wind" as he lived and rode in pride and freedom, heeded to the "four virtues," honored the land and animals and Great Spirit, challenged the powers and perils of the enemy, and soared upon Father Sky's currents as a man above other men.

"Speak, Wise One," Rising Bear said, "tell us what Wakantanka revealed to you in your vision."

Nahemana nodded and began his enlightenment. "In the directions from which the sun rises and the winter winds are born, I saw our enemies gathering as storm clouds to attack and destroy us, to claim our hunting grounds as their own. The Great Spirit was angry. He sent the Thunderbird to flap its great wings to scare them away, but they did not hear its message. He sent fiery lances into their presence, but they did not see His message. He sent Spirit Warriors to challenge them; they did not flee; they only retreated to grow stronger to try again. The Great Spirit sent a powerful wind war-dancing across the sky; it swooped down and gathered dewdrops from the face of Mother Earth and returned to the sky. Together they challenged our enemies and frightened them away. A glorious rainbow appeared. The sun blazed in joy. Victory was ours. That powerful force and duty lies in the hands of he who dances with the wind, your oldest son and our next chief. He must get Dewdrops, live and ride with her, and let her heal his heart; only then will the Red Shields know peace."

Respectful children and wives remained silent as Rising Bear asked questions that came quickly to his mind: "We have not heard of such magic and big medicine. Those who lived before us did not pass along such words to us, and that story is not painted upon our tribal buffalo hide. Where will my son find the sacred Dewdrops, Wise One?"

"In the camp of the Brule White Shields," Nahemana answered. "She must become his mate. That union will make him even stronger, wiser, and more generous."

The baffled chief glanced at his oldest son before asking Nahemana, "Dewdrops is a woman? He must take a Brule as his wife?"

"I know the names of the children of most Lakota chiefs; Tall Elk's are Fire Walker and Dewdrops. Wakantanka showed us many things separately, and together they tell us what must be done. We must ride to Tall Elk's camp and ask for an alliance, and for his daughter to bond it to ours."

"Why the White Shield Band, Wise One?" Rising Bear asked. "We have never allied with them in the past?"

"The Brules are members of the Seven Council Fires of the Lakotas. Though the seven major tribes are divided into many bands and all live and ride separately, we meet for seasonal trading fairs and unite for big wars. But in the past when we allied with other bands from the Oglalas or other tribes, we did not ride and work as one war party. Each side wished to show superiority and to gather the most coups and prizes; it cannot be so in our next conflicts with the Crow and Whites." Nahemana breathed deeply before continuing. "I see and speak with many chiefs and their warriors when we meet to talk or trade; it does not appear the White Shield Brules think and ride as our past allies did. But there is another reason: In his vision, Wind Dancer was told to make a new shield to carry in the challenges before him; it was painted white. Upon its surface he saw a yellow dewdrop and a large bird."

"The eagle, the ruler of the sky?" Rising Bear ventured.

"No, the hawk, a new spirit helper for his tasks ahead."

"What are those tasks, Wise One?"

"I do not know, for they have not been revealed to us. First, my grandson must take another mate, one who will become his companion in the challenges ahead. Wakantanka has chosen the daughter of Chief Tall Elk to join with him and ride with him. If we are to obey the Great Spirit's command and if we are to survive and become stronger, it must be so."

As he heard the interpretation of his and his grandfather's visions, Wind Dancer was troubled. What if this Dewdrops was unappealing, barren, dull-witted, or already taken? But surely she could not be any of those things or she would not have been chosen for him. But why did Wakantanka select his next wife? Why could he not pick the woman—one he desired and who had the skills to help him meet and defeat his challenges? A woman like Morning Mist, his near defiant heart whispered, if she were flesh and bone. Even if the Great Spirit's choice was a female warrior, how would a mere woman become his successful companion in the face of such danger ahead? What, he wondered, could only two people do to obtain glorious victory? But, Wakantanka had spoken in the visions, so they must be obeyed.

Wind Dancer sat alone on a flat top boulder of black rock. Items to be used for his task set nearby. Three suns had passed since his visionquest began and he saw Morning Mist for the second and final time, one sun since his grandfather had interpreted the visions to him and his family. It was time to prepare for his coming journey. First, he must make a new shield to carry with him and to use during his imminent challenge, one such as both he and his grandfather had seen during their spiritual quests.

As a sign of his virtue of generosity, he had given his old shield to a warrior who had lost his own during a conflict with the Crow. At the end of the last buffalo season, he had made a new hoop from a supple sapling—as that shape showed that all things traveled in an unending circle. From the sturdy hump section of six buffalos, he had tanned and stretched those hides over the frame, then put it away until the Great Spirit told him what symbols to place upon it. He would use paints obtained from rocks, dirt, plants, and animals which lived upon Mother Earth to show his eternal connection to and dependency upon Her. The yellow came from buffalo gallstones and from ocher, as did red and orange. Blue was from the *wanhu* and pokeberries. Other red came from vermilion; black, from charcoal; green, from grasses; and many more colors from clays and flowers. Sometimes the extracts and particles were mixed with water, and other times, with grease or oil from animals or plant stems. Usually those gathering and mixing chores were done by females; his, by his mother and sister Hanmani, whose name meant "To-walk-in-the-night."

As this was a reverent occasion, he had sought privacy away from his friends and people. He lifted his gaze skyward and prayed, "Sun, Moon, and All You Above Ones, listen and watch me as I work. This shield I am making, give it of your sacred power so it will keep its owner safe in his encounters with the enemy who is seeking to destroy Your People. Give its owner the skills and courage and wisdom to carry out the will of Wakantanka. Charge it with strong medicine. Bless it and the warrior who sits before You."

First, he painted the entire surface white, as if it were a cloud. Around its edges he painted black grizzly paws from which strength and courage were drawn, and black deer tracks to draw from the speed and agility of that animal, and red tracks of the buffalo upon which their survival depended. He attached a fox tail to the lower right side to inspire cunning and stealth. Four eagle feathers were added near the leather shoulder band, the ruler of the sky where the wind danced, one for each of the directions from which it blew. He secured a tiny bundle of red stones on the lower left to show his forever-ties to his ancestors. Another small bundle, which held blue flax and green sage to represent the earth and sky, was attached to the lower right side. He painted on a yellow lightning bolt and several blue hailstones across the lower half to gather their power and speed.

Wind Dancer rested for a short time before finishing with the two sacred signs from the visions, symbols painted across the top half, one in yellow and one in brown. *Two,* his mind echoed, that number having a calming—yet stimulating—effect on him this time. He gazed at the completed, still wet shield and smiled. Yes, the Great Spirit would make his dreams come true and would show him how to defeat the threats against his people.

He returned to the camp and hung the shield upon his three-legged *huyamni* to dry. The wooden legs of the stand allowed the renewing power of the earth to travel into his possessions. It stood outside so his belongings could soak up the warmth and light of the sun, the shining power of the Great Mystery above. His gaze passed over his other weapons suspended there: his decorated bow, a beaded quiver filled with arrows and painted with his markings, a wrist guard, a war club, war lance, coup stick, and sheathed knife with an elk antler grip. His personal pipe rested in a beaded bag and his medicine bundle was suspended as well; from it dangled several grizzly claws and it contained special stones, bones, feathers, and good-luck charms.

In an elated mood, the oldest son of the Red Shield chief headed to tend his three horses before night blanketed the land. One was used only for carrying items, for riding during journeys, and for hunting. Another was a buffalo horse, which was agile, swift, and trained to race with the great dark beast while avoiding its sharp and lethal horns. The last was his war horse, upon which a warrior's survival and success depended, and Wind Dancer's favorite mount, who he had trained and ridden for eight spans of the seasons. That would be the animal he rode to face his coming challenges. When the next sun rose, he would paint his victory and medicine symbols upon its hide and journey with a chosen party to carry out the first step along his destiny trail.

Nahemana joined his grandson shortly after dawn on what he expected and prayed would be a momentous time in their lives. His gaze roamed the white-and-black horse with its numerous markings which exposed Wind Dancer's high rank and glorious exploits. The shaman's gaze drifted to the war shield in his grandson's grasp and read the meanings for its many colorful symbols, including two new ones: signs of his spirit helpers from the sacred vision.

"It is good, *micinksi,*" the old man said. "You will enter their camp as the great warrior and future chief you are. Are the joining and friendship gifts ready?"

"Yes, Grandfather; War Eagle and Red Feather will bring them to us. They will come soon; they gather supplies for our journey and task. Father is preparing himself to leave with us."

"Are you ready and willing to face the tasks before you, *micinksi?*"

"Yes, Grandfather." Wind Dancer prayed he would not fail in his duty, once it was revealed. He had vowed to do his best in those impending challenges, to sacrifice his life if necessary. And he had vowed to never again think of or crave another woman in his future wife's place. The symbols of his two new spirit helpers were painted upon his shield, and he hoped they gave him the strength and courage to do what he must, including forget Morning Mist, if she was real. He must not go chasing a foolish dream, a woman out of his reach.

"Do you think they will hear our vision words and

believe them, Grandfather?" he asked. "Will they agree to our plan?"

"They must, *micinksi*, for they are the will and commands of Wakantanka. He will open their eyes, ears, hearts, and minds to the truth. Now it is time to go; your destiny awaits you and your chosen one."

Wind Dancer saw his father, brother, and best friend heading toward them with five choice horses trailing behind them and with many gifts secured atop their backs. He took a deep breath, and closed his eyes. *Farewell forever, my beautiful Morning Mist, for our paths must never cross again,* he thought in great sadness. *If they do, I must resist your powerful pull, for I will soon be joined to another for the rest of my suns and moons on Mother Earth.*

Chapter Four

Chumani left the forest and approached her parents' tepee with a bundle of wood resting across her back. As she did so, she noticed the group of horses tethered outside their lodging and surmised they had visitors. She paused to study one animal in particular, a large black-and-white creature with alert eyes and a sleek hide. It was not his beauty and size which captured her attention, however; rather, its markings and decorations were so startling, they drew her astonished gaze and caused her to walk around the horse several times to read their meanings. A yellow life-circle was painted on its left shoulder. Many white coup slashes were on its forelegs, and red ones were across its broad nose. Wide yellow circles enclosed the animal's eyes to aid its vision. Four red handprints upon its chest indicated four enemies had been slain in weaponless fighting with bare hands, telling her the man whose horse it was possessed great prowess and courage. A black square revealed its owner had been a past war leader in at least one battle, so he was highly respected and admired. Many upside-down black tracks told her the man had been on successful horse raids. Also included in the markings were blue dots of hailstone from which the animal and rider sought its power to rain a terrifying force upon his enemies. A lightning bolt to summon that element's speed and power seemingly flashed across its left hindquarter in brilliant yellow, and blue lines on the right one said he was a member of a warrior society. Attached to both sides of the thong which passed through the animal's mouth were two eagle feathers to total four in all, and beaded strips for other coups and decoration, and the same decorated the creature's dark tail and mane.

Chumani had seen many horses painted with their owner's medicine signs and accomplishments, but never one with so many. It was evident to her that its owner was an important man, a warrior of enormous prowess. Her curiosity was piqued about him and his reason for being there.

She hurried to the tepee entrance to gather information and to serve refreshments to their visitors, as her mother was still in the forest gathering wood and spring plants. Since the flap was thrown aside, it was acceptable for her to enter without asking permission first, as was the custom if the flap was down to indicate a desire for privacy. In the center of the large tepee, five men sat facing her father, their backs to her. From the flowing bonnet upon his head, one was obviously a chief. Another was older, from his white hair and bent shoulders. The other three were young males, all with dark hair cascading down their backs and with feathers attached to gathered strands.

The warrior who sat between the elderly man and chief wore a Wicasta Itancan shirt with a blue top and yellow bottom, fringed in tiny hairlocks. In his raven-black mane were three eagle feathers and one hawk feather dangling down the back of his head. One had three dots on it to indicate he had slain three enemies in a single battle. Two others had red, blue, black, and yellow bands on their shafts to reveal how many enemies in all he had slain, which were numerous. The fourth, a hawk's, she assumed was to signify his spirit helper. No doubt, Chumani reasoned, he was the owner of the much-decorated black-and-white horse.

Tall Elk, chief of the Brule Lakotas, noticed his daughter's arrival when he looked up from some of the gift items across his lap, a pile of sleek and shiny pelts from various creatures. He nodded and smiled at her.

"Do you wish me to serve water and food to our guests, Father?" Chumani saw the Shirt Wearer stiffened his back when she spoke, but did not turn toward her as the other men did as she finished her query. Yet, that was unnecessary in order for her to guess his identity when she gazed upon the faces of Chief Mato Kikta, Nahemana, Wanbli, and Wiyaka Lute of the Red Shield Band of Oglala Lakotas. What, her panicked mind shouted, was Waci Tate doing there? What would he do after he recognized her? Perhaps her voice had already exposed her identity, the reason for his odd reaction to it. Would he betray her past mischievous exploits? Should she apologize for them or remain quiet and hope he did, too?

Tall Elk rose as he said, "I must speak with my daughter alone. Stay and rest and we will return soon to seal our bond of alliance with the pipe."

"*Alliance?*" Chumani's mind echoed in dread. The last thing she needed or wanted was to have Wind Dancer around in the suns ahead when she must forget his tempting existence, when an undesirable joining to another man loomed before her like a dark cloud, and she had a great and unknown challenge to meet and conquer! As she turned to depart, her gaze was snared by a war shield amidst other weapons near the entrance; it widened as she sighted the yellow dewdrop and brown hawk painted upon a cloud-white surface. Somehow she knew to whom it belonged, and its symbols caused apprehension within her. Without even glancing back at the men, she sensed their keen gazes upon her as she followed her father, her heart drumming in panic and her mouth suddenly gone dry.

Before reaching the forest, they encountered her

mother, and Tall Elk told her to see to their important guests while he talked with their daughter.

Magaju nodded, confused by the strange occurrence, as it was unlike him to leave visitors alone. Magaju could not help but wonder if Chumani had committed some terrible misdeed, but prayed she had not. Their child was not intentionally disobedient or overly headstrong, but Chumani had changed since being compelled to join to a man she did not love and especially since the loss of her baby. Following that awful sun, her daughter had not wanted to join to another mate or bear another child, in fear of enduring their losses. All Chumani had concentrated on was obtaining warrior-hunter skills and honing them to perfection with the hope of finding and slaying the Crow who had caused her such grief. Magaju said another prayer that someone and something would come along to change her daughter's mind, and Sees-Through-Mist had vowed that would happen.

In the edge of the treeline, Tall Elk halted and leaned against a pine. He watched his daughter's eyes widen and stare at him as he revealed the reason why the Red Shields had come to their camp. He finished his task by saying, "The number of our warriors was lessened by the Crow attacks two winters past and following the buffalo hunt last season, and with the white man's evil sickness. We must unite with the Red Shields, my child, as the Bird People and white-eyes are many and strong, stronger if they form a truce and ride against us. That bond will be sealed with a joining between the children of Tall Elk and Rising Bear. You must do this for our people."

He wanted her to give herself to Wind Dancer . . . "But, Father, he is not Brule; he is not White Shield."

"That does not matter in perilous times, my child. He is a worthy man; he has the skills to protect you and to provide for you."

"But who will do those things for you and Mother if I leave camp? My brother cannot do so, for he has his own tepee and family to care for."

Tall Elk laughed. "I am still young and strong enough to defend my mate and hunt for our food," he said. "I only allow you to do so because it pleases you and gives you practice with your skills. This is the meaning behind Sees-Through-Mist's dream and his gifts to you." *And it will take you off of danger's path.* "You will be the wife of a powerful chief when Rising Bear walks the Ghost Trail; your son will be chief when his father is gone. Those are great honors, my child, and our bond to them will last forever."

At that difficult and shocking moment, a tribal alliance between Brule and Oglala was not foremost in her mind, though she told herself that was selfish and wrong. Both tribes were members of the Seven Council Fires of the Lakota, but why had the Red Shields picked the White Shields to ally with, and why at this particular time? Why not select another Oglala band, such as Red Cloud's or Black Hawk's? Or another Brule Band, such as Spotted Tail's? Any of those bands were larger and more aggressive than her people's desirable qualities to help defeat the Crow and Whites, especially if those two enemy forces banded together. Had Wind Dancer—she mused in a rush—lusted for her as the brave had for White Buffalo Maiden, Pte Skawin, discovered her identity and location, and was using this deception to lay claim to her? A strong and irresistible man like him would devour her, would try to change her. On the other hand, she might have offended him during their first encounter and earned his dislike and disrespect, and perhaps he felt challenged to prove he could conquer her, or punish her. And no doubt a man like him was already taken by another woman, if just one would be enough!

The patient and astute Tall Elk had waited in silence while his daughter meditated on the serious matter before them. He had mixed feelings about asking his child to make this sacrifice of herself. On one side, he was proud and happy she had been chosen for the sacred task ahead and for a union with a great warrior. On the other side, he felt guilty about the past torment she had endured. He had been the one to persuade her to join to Dull Star when she reached twenty-one winters, was mateless and childless; and Dull Star had proven himself a warrior and had asked for her in joining. That mistake in judgment had cost him the lives of his grandson, his parents, his wife's parents, along with many others.

Dull Star had been left in charge of their camp two winters past when most of the men were out on hunting and scouting parties, but he had been distracted from his lookout duty while playing *tapa* with a group of boys. When a small party of Crow were sighted nearby, the foolish and arrogant man had summoned other braves and led a chase to drive the enemy away. But that pursuit had been a trick to lure the guards out of camp so another and larger raiding party could attack, and they did so. He could not convince himself he was not partly to blame for what happened, as those loved ones might still be alive—and his daughter would not have experienced such anguish and resentment—if another warrior had been in charge. But that was in the past, and it must be the present and future which concerned him. His daughter had been chosen by Wakantanka and must obey Him.

"Does Waci Tate have a wife? Perhaps two or three?"

Tall Elk chuckled again. "No, my child, his mate and son were slain two winters past by the Crow, as were yours. Like you, he still seeks vengeance on the Crow to blame, but their paths have not crossed. His time for ghost-owning has passed. He performed the giveaway ritual last winter, as did you and our family. He lives in the tepee of his parents with his brother and sister."

Chumani was sad about his matching losses, but was relieved he was alone. "Why has he taken no wife to replace her?" she asked.

"Why have you taken no mate to replace yours?" Tall Elk reasoned.

"I have not found one among us who steals my eye and

heart. After my son's loss, you said I would choose my next husband when I was ready."

"I am happy you speak the truth to me on this sun, my daughter. The same is probably true for Wind Dancer."

"He is a future chief and must have a son to follow him. Such is not so for me. The child of Fire Walker will be chief after my brother is gone."

"I do not pick your next mate for you, Chumani." He reminded her of what he had said earlier, "Their shaman saw dangers coming from two directions, and you were in their visions as Wind Dancer's helper to defeat them; it is as Sees-Through-Mist foretold. Wind Dancer rode to our camp with your symbol painted upon his cheek and with a dewdrop and hawk painted upon his shield. Nahemana's vision and Sees-Through-Mist's dream are commands from Wakantanka, my child; do not dishonor yourself, your family, and your people by refusing to obey them. You are strong, my child, but you must bend like the willow. To all four-leggeds and all two-leggeds, the Great Spirit gave a song, a costume, a life ritual: powerful medicine to share with His people. This calling will be your song, garment, and ritual, Dewdrops, and you will make powerful medicine with Waci Tate. Many winters ago, the Whites made Pike's Treaty and Prairie du Chien Council, but they did not keep their word; they took the Nakotas and Dakotas lands and drove them away. Now, the Whites cast their eyes upon Lakota lands, as have our Crow enemies since before my grandfather was born. If we do not form a strong alliance with others, our hunting grounds will be stolen and we will be destroyed and driven away. Our destiny lies within your hands."

Chumani realized a heavy burden rested on her shoulders, and wondered if she could truly carry out those duties. "Return to our tepee, Father, and I will come soon. I must have time to think upon all you have told me and to calm myself."

"Will you obey the command of Wakantanka?"

"Yes, Father, but it does not make me happy. Pray to

the Great Spirit that I am worthy of this task and can meet this challenge.''

Tall Elk embraced his daughter. ''You are wise and good, my child,'' he said, ''and your skills are many and large. Wakantanka will reward you greatly for obeying Him.''

Following Chumani and Hehoka Hanska's departure, Wind Dancer's thoughts spun wildly and swiftly from the reality of his discovery and what it might mean to him. He could hardly believe Morning Mist and Dewdrops were the same woman. Was that, he pondered, a good or bad sign? How could he master a woman who lived and thought as a warrior, a woman who had shown stubbornness, defiance, and rudeness at their first meeting? Surely she would be trouble for him, but he must find a way to tame her wild spirit and improve her ways. Would she agree to unite with him? Had her dislike and disrespect of him in the forest been real or faked? Did she love and desire another man and he was stepping between them? In spite of all his questions, he could not deny his desire for her, nor doubt her great prowess, though he doubted she would have a large role in the tasks looming before them. Would she surrender to him or would she scorn him as she had done in the forest? No matter, she was the Great Spirit's choice for him, so he must obtain her.

Chumani knew she could not delay her return much longer or Wind Dancer and his party would take it as a sign of insult, but she had not settled down and still paced in the cover of the trees, her emotions in a turmoil. Dread mingled with assurance; resistance, with compliance; desire, with repulsion; elation, with sadness. She wished Zitkala was there to advise and comfort her. But her best friend and constant companion had gone hunting with others for a few suns and to scout for the buffalos' seasonal movement toward the Plains. She had not gone with them because her mother had been ill and had needed her help with the chores. Now, she must face this test of her beliefs, sense of honor, and courage alone.

Chumani could not help but worry that Nahemana's and Wind Dancer's visions at Paha Mato six moons past had been controlled or altered by seeing her before or shortly after they consumed the revelation-inducing peyote. Or that an evil *wicagnayesa* had tricked the two men only to lure her from the sacred path she was to walk, the one in her shaman's dream. Would all be lost if she yielded to temptation and was misled by the evil spirit?

Since her heart still ached over the loss of her son and his death had not been avenged, why did a stranger stir it to life and longing? Why did she feel weak, afraid, and uncertain, qualities so foreign to her? Why did he cause confusion and distress within her? That, she deduced, was the center of her troubled heart and mind; she feared she would lose herself in him and his life. She feared the power of her irresistible pull toward him, as such feelings could make an awesome weapon against her in the hands of a cruel foe. She feared relenting, becoming happy for a time, and losing all again. *But you must go, Dewdrops,* she urged herself, *and face your destiny, whatever and wherever it may be.*

Magaju joined Chumani. "I have heard of what lies before you, my daughter," she said. "This is good for you and our people, so what troubles you?"

"Is it truly good for me, Mother?" she asked. "Why must I join to a stranger, an outsider? To another man I do not love and desire?"

"If you possess the four virtues of the Lakota and the warrior you try to be, you will make this sacrifice for the survival of your people while our forces are weakened." Falling Rain reasoned in a gentle tone. "You must show courage, strength, insight, and kindness; this will be your greatest coup."

"A man such as Wind Dancer will not accept a female hunter-warrior as his wife. He will try to cower and weaken me as he would a captive. He will halt my search for the enemy who slayed my son and people. Have you forgotten his raiding party killed the families of my parents and many old ones while our men were away from camp?" *Have you forgotten the man my father chose for me was in charge of the guards left behind that day and he failed in his task?* "If I must leave my people and end my vengeance quest, all remaining joy will leave my heart and life."

Falling Rain had not forgotten that agonizing time or what it had done to her beloved child. "You will become a wife and mother again, as it is meant to be for a woman."

"I do not wish to bear and lose another child; that pain is too great."

"Another child will heal your heart and bring much joy, my daughter."

"Who will share such feelings and suns when I am in a camp far from my family, best friend, and people?"

"You will share them with your husband and your new people. Wind Dancer's mate and son live with the Great Spirit, as do yours. Go with him, my daughter, and allow the Great Spirit to heal your hearts and help your peoples. If we do not ally with them and seal our bond with your joining, we will suffer under the lances, arrows, and fire-sticks of the Crow and Whites. A union between the children of two chiefs will form a powerful bond. Now come, we must return to our tepee; there is much to do and say."

That time, Wind Dancer turned and looked at Chumani when she arrived in the tepee. Though she appeared to attempt to keep her expression void of feeling, he sensed gleams of anxiety and uncertainty and a hint of defiance.

Chumani forced herself to lock gazes for a brief time with the Red Shield warrior, to show him she was unafraid. Then she sighted the yellow dewdrop on his left cheek as if he had already staked a claim of ownership on her, and her jaw tightened in annoyance. Here before her stood the legendary warrior Waci Tate, son of a chief, a future chief, the man who too often sneaked into her dreams at night and into her thoughts during the day, the man from her shaman's dream whom she was to join. How would it feel to be held in his arms, to feel his lips and hands upon her body, to lie with him on a sleeping mat, to—

"Dewdrops, come and sit with me," Tall Elk summoned her.

Wind Dancer turned and faced the Brule chief as the woman sat beside him, her gaze lowered to the clasped hands in her lap. He had noticed her irritated reaction to the symbol on his face, and had seen that emotion vanish and her cheeks warm with color. Her eyes had made a swift pass over him from head to feet, and a glow had danced across her beautiful face and in her dark eyes. Yes, he decided, he was appealing to her, but that reality disquieted her. Now, all that remained to be learned was her reaction to his shocking news.

"Will you honor the words of the Great Spirit?" Tall Elk asked her.

"Yes, Father, I will obey the commands of the Great Mystery, though I do not," she began in a deceptively calm voice, then locked her stoic gaze with Wind Dancer's equally stoic one, "understand them."

When she paused and stared at him, Wind Dancer feared she was about to shame him before his family and best friend by saying she did not want to join to him but would force herself to become his wife and do her duty. He was relieved when those words did not escape her lovely lips. She showed great courage and wisdom in the face of inner turmoil.

Tall Elk smiled and nodded. "It is good, my daughter, and soon their meanings will be revealed to us. While you prepare yourself for your joining and departure, we will smoke the pipe for the Making-Brothers ritual. Come," he said to his guests, "we will seek another place to do so."

Chumani and Magaju watched the men leave before they started to get ready for the *wakan kiciyuzapi* ceremony and her journey. As Chumani bathed and dressed, and while her mother packed her belongings and other gifts, she thought about what lay ahead for her. She would be far away from her family, best friend, and people and would see them only on two occasions—the annual trading fair and the annual buffalo hunt—unless something important arose to cause a visit. She would live among strangers, in a tepee with a stranger, be possessed by a stranger. Yet, she must be doing the right thing, especially since the awful news of the white man's sickness had reached their ears; two hundred fifty *wasicun* trappers and traders and others, along with hundreds of Indians from many bands and tribes, had died from what they called "cholera." The only good news was that the "epidemic" had ceased to attack either side. News had also reached them that the Crow and Whites were getting friendlier with each other, implying a truce was wafting on the spring winds. If that—

Falling Rain interrupted her thoughts when the older woman smiled and hinted, "The face and body of Waci Tate are good to look upon, yes?"

Chumani selected a careful answer. "They are not repulsive, Mother."

"He is a warrior of high rank and great skills; his coups are many."

"So the stories of his deeds tell us."

"Do you fear him, my daughter?"

"No, Mother," she said, as she did not, in the way Magaju meant.

"Do you fear the unknown and dangerous challenge before you?"

"No, Mother, for it will save our people and lands."

"Do you fear lying with him upon the sleeping mat?"

Following a short silence, Chumani admitted, "I do not know." She decided not to explain her troubled feelings, things she did not grasp herself which might worry and sadden her mother.

"It was not good for you upon the sleeping mat of Dull Star?"

Chumani was a little surprised by that query. "No, Mother." She hoped Magaju would leave that trail of thought, as she did not want to discuss sex with her mother.

"It is because you did not choose him; you did not love or desire him."

"Can the same not be said for Wind Dancer?" reasoned Chumani.

"It will be different with him, my daughter. His looks and ways are good. He was chosen for you by the Great Spirit, Who is never wrong."

"I pray those words are true, Mother."

"They are, my beloved child. The Great Spirit would not bring sadness and distraction into the heart and mind of one He has chosen for a great and sacred duty. Allow Wind Dancer to heal your pain and bring you joy. Give him the opportunity to win your love and acceptance; it must be so for you two to work together for the good of our peoples."

"What if Wind Dancer does not feel the same way, Mother? What if he does not want my love or care about my acceptance? What if he is not pleased with the Great Spirit's command to join to me?"

"It will be your task to change that. Only by forming a powerful bond between you, or at least a truce, can you two achieve glorious victory. You are a beautiful and desirable woman, my daughter; you have many good traits and skills. Use them, use all you are, to create the needed bond between you two."

"I will do my best to grasp victory for our peoples, whatever it takes," Chumani vowed.

Magaju embraced her, and with misty eyes and hoarsened voice said, "That is good, my daughter. My love for you is great."

Chumani's emotion matched that of her mother.

"My love for you is larger than the sacred mountain," she whispered. "I will miss you."

"As I will miss you, my child. Be safe and happy, Dewdrops."

"I will try, Mother," she promised. Then she heard a shrill call from outside. "Cetan has returned," she said. "I must go tether him to his post while strangers are in camp. I would not want him to see them as a threat and attack our honored guests."

Chumani and Waci Tate stood in the center of the group of people gathered around them; close by were members of their families. The son of the Oglala chief was clad in his finest array of garments and high-ranking Wiscasta Itancan shirt. The daughter of the Brule chief wore the fringed but unbeaded white dress and moccasins made by Snowbird and given to her by her shaman, a kind and wise man whom she loved and respected deeply.

"We come to hear Dewdrops and Wind Dancer make a joining bond," Tall Elk said, "as we have made an alliance bond with his people. Beneath the eyes of the Great Spirit, they will become mates. Soon they will ride together on a great quest for victory for our two bands. Until that sun rises, we will meet and travel together to the grasslands to hunt the buffalo; there, we will camp nearby and will unite to battle any enemies who challenge us. Wind Dancer, you have brought many gifts to me and asked for my daughter as your wife and sacred task companion. Is that not so?"

Wind Dancer kept his gaze on the chief, as looking at the beautiful and tempting woman beside him would be most distracting. "That is true, Tall Elk. I will become her mate, hunter, protector, and father of her children."

"Dewdrops, my daughter, you agree to become Wind Dancer's mate, mother of his children, and sacred quest companion?"

Chumani was all too aware of the handsome and virile male beside her, and she dared not even glance at him and risk exposing her mixed feelings for him. "That is true, my father; I will obey the Great Spirit's commands."

Tall Elk smiled. "It is good. We will feast before you go into the forest to seal your bond."

As the group ate food provided by many White Shield families, the joyful people mingled and talked and placed gifts for the couple in a pile near the chief's tepee entrance: blankets, clothing, work and decorative items for their new tepee in the Red Shield camp, beaded jewelry for both people, pelts and hides, rush mats, pemmican and other foods for their journey home, leather pouches of healing and cooking herbs and plants, and adorned parfleches in which to carry their belongings.

As Wind Dancer roamed amidst the crowd and Chumani stayed near her parents' dwelling to accept and give thanks for the gifts, Rainbow Girl—wife of her brother, Fire Walker—joined her.

Rainbow Girl looked at the hawk nearby. "He is uneasy."

"Yes, he does not understand why strangers come near me and why he must be tethered to protect them from his sharp talons and beak. Soon he will learn to accept them." Chumani stroked the anxious bird's head and neck with the backs of her fingers and spoke in a gentle and loving tone to him. As if the creature understood her words, the large hawk rubbed the top of its head against her open palm many times, its round and shiny eyes focused on her face.

"You will take him with you?"

"Yes, he is my friend and we have been together since I was ten. He has not chosen to leave me and take a mate. Perhaps one sun he will do so."

"Your new garments are lovely, Dewdrops. Are you uneasy about what lies ahead on this moon and during the suns to follow soon?" the other woman asked in a whisper.

She nodded, but did not explain, as two people halted within hearing range as they admired Wind Dancer's horse and its markings. "I will not be here to see the face of your first child when it takes its first breath of the Great Spirit's air, my sister," Chumani said, as the mates of siblings were often called "sister" or "brother." She touched Rainbow Girl's protruding stomach and sighed. "I will not be here to tend you while you grow strong again or watch the baby while you do chores or help you teach your child. I will miss you and my brother and such special events."

"We will miss you, Dewdrops, my sister. You will be in our thoughts each sun. We will pray for your happiness and safety."

"As I will pray and work for yours. It is good my brother chose you for himself; you will be a good chief's mate."

"Your words are kind and your heart is good, Dewdrops."

"As are yours. When my brother and the hunter-warriors are out of camp, keep your child close and watch over it with eagle eyes, for the Crow and Whites grow bold this season."

"I know this, my sister, and I will guard my child each sun and moon."

Fire Walker joined them. He embraced his sister. "My love and pride are great for you, Dewdrops, and I will miss you. Wind Dancer will be a good mate for you. When the time comes, I hope I will be riding with you two on the sacred task."

"If that is to be, my brother, it will make me happy. You are brave and skilled; you would drive fear into the hearts of our enemies."

"Soon we will see each other again when we hunt the buffalo."

She touched Fire Walker's arm. "That sun cannot come fast enough for me, my brother. I will miss my family, friends, and people."

"You are sad because Zitkala is not here to share this sun with you?"

"That is true, Rainbow Girl."

"I will tell her all that happened when she returns to camp."

"Thank you, my sister."

Wind Dancer arrived then. "It is time to seek privacy," he said.

"I am ready to go," Chumani responded with faked

courage. "See to Cetan until my return," she asked her brother, who nodded agreement.

They mounted the prepared horses, waved farewell to the still-celebrating group, and rode out of the White Shield camp to spend the first night of their new life together.

Chapter
Five

While riding slightly ahead of her in silence so he would not become distracted from his guard duty, Wind Dancer guided Chumani over a gently rolling terrain of grassland which edged the Paha Sapa and traveled toward the rising sun. That verdant landscape was dotted with solitary trees and scrub bushes and with scattered clusters of intermingled pine, spruce, and hardwoods. Multicolored wildflowers and other plants wafted amidst the lush green covering and added beauty to the serene setting. They sighted buffalo, deer, and pronghorn grazing, and two wolves loping across a low hill, though none took much notice of them.

In one area, they had to skirt a prairie dog village where countless furry creatures fussed and scampered into their burrows and a few stood tall and brave while staring at them. Both knew the perils of entering such a location, as stepping into an unseen hole could cause serious injury. In addition, those underground dwellings were often inhabited by deadly snakes and other creatures which could strike out with no warning. As the *wakankiciyuzapi* journey continued, their movements flushed out startled doves, quail, and rabbits.

Small birds flew and larger ones circled overhead,

reminding her of Cetan and of the brown hawk painted upon his new war shield. She was nervous about what lay ahead tonight and wondered where he was taking her, but she refused to ask him. She wished she were riding in the lead, as it was a constant struggle not to watch his loosened black hair blowing in the breeze, to seek glimpses of his profile when he turned his head in either direction to check their surroundings, and to quell the unbidden desires which crept into her body.

Wind Dancer fought the same battle against irrepressible passion as he wondered what she was thinking and feeling, as he sensed her potent gaze on him. It was difficult, impossible at times, to keep his mind on his guard duty. Just knowing she was close by and she now belonged to him ignited a hungry fire in his loins.

They passed through tranquil meadows, near-dense forests, and beside mountains with tall pinnacles and steep sides in a shade as dark as a moonless night. They crossed several streams and one winding river. As dusk neared, they followed the latter's banks until they reached the canyon Wind Dancer had chosen for their campsite, a place with towering jagged cliffs on three of four sides so no enemy could sneak easily up on them.

Before Chumani could dismount, Wind Dancer grasped her by the waist and lifted her down. As her moccasins touched the ground, their gazes fused and they stared at each other for a short time. Her hands, which had gone reflexively to the tops of his shoulders, slowly slid down his chest and halted near his heart.

Wind Dancer trailed his left forefinger across her cheek and over her mouth. He found even this light contact with her stimulating. It had wounded his pride when his first wife never reached out to him of her own volition, only yielded to him out of submissive duty. He had taken her as his mate out of a similar sense of duty, thinking and being told it was time for the future chief to seek his own tepee and begin a family. He did not want to repeat that unpleasant experience. He had to discover if passion for him dwelled within Chumani's body, however deeply concealed. He wanted her flesh to burn with the same fiery desire which scorched his. He slid his finger under her chin to raise her head when she lowered it; he was glad she did not jerk away from him. His thumb drifted over her parted lips and felt her warm breath upon it, then his hand roamed into her dark and shiny hair.

The yearning to respond to this stranger was so great it almost overwhelmed Chumani. Yet, those urgent longings for him alarmed her. He seemed to take possession of her soul and emotions just as he claimed her mouth and ruled her destiny. The kiss was both intimidating and exciting. Never had her first husband evoked such feelings within her. If Wind Dancer continued to tempt her so, it would be impossible to resist him. Had it been only this morning, when he appeared in her camp and declared a bold and shocking claim to her? So much had happened since the sun arose that it seemed much longer. Soon darkness would blanket the land and they would . . .

When Wind Dancer felt her stiffen in his embrace, he separated their lips and gazed down at her. He read disquiet in her dark eyes, and felt her tremble. "Do you fear me?" he asked gently.

"No," she forced herself to say. It was true she was not afraid of him as a man, only of his enormous effect upon her and her life.

"Does contempt for me fill your heart?"

"No."

"Do you fear what happens between a man and a woman on a sleeping mat? Do you scorn such touching with me?"

Chumani felt her cheeks grow warm at those unexpected and intimate questions. "You have not touched me in such a manner, so how can I speak of that which has not happened?"

"If all you say is true, why do you shake as a leaf in the wind? Why does your gaze reveal such sadness and unrest? If a kiss and embrace so repulse you, how will you endure the union of our bodies?"

"We are strangers, and such touching is special. It should take place between a man and woman who know and love each other. We have not shared walks or been around each other for many seasons. You have not played the flute for me or ridden me upon your horse. We have not shared the talking blanket. We did not choose to join each other."

Wind Dancer knew if they were to have a peaceful tepee and to accept each other, he could not force or trick her into surrender, or allow her to learn this soon how much he hungered for her, as that powerful secret could tempt her to take advantage of him. Even male birds and animals courted their chosen ones, and the female would not accept a mating until she was ready; so, should he not, as a man, do the same? "That is true," he answered bluntly, then sought a change of topic. "While I tend the horses, gather wood for a fire," he instructed.

Chumani watched him unload their belongings and lead the horses away to where the two animals would graze and drink. She was confused, and relieved by his restraint. She had sensed his hunger for a union and felt the hard proof of it against her body. Yet, that need might be nothing more than physical, as with Dull Star.

As she gathered wood and arranged rocks in a circle, she told herself it was good fortune her woman's blood flow had ceased two moons before his arrival so she would not have to deal with it for a long time. As was her people's custom, she had spent three suns and moons in the separated shelter—the *cansakawakeya*. Following a purifying sweatbath, she had washed herself in the river, donned fresh garments which had been smoked by her mother over a fire of evergreen leaves and wood, and returned to her parents' tepee. That thought brought forth unhappy memories from her past.

When they first joined, she recalled, Dull Star rolled atop her to thrash wildly and grunt out his needs almost every moon until she was soon with child. Then he had ceased until long after their son's birth; and she had rejoiced in that lengthy reprieve. When he returned to taking her upon the sleeping mat, it was only for one time between each blood cycle and on the first night immediately following her stay in the *cansakawakeya* and ensuing purification, as if it were the only time she were pure and clean enough for him to enter her body. She had been glad he reached out for her so rarely, as those unions were unpleasant and sometimes almost painful. Yet, with Wind Dancer, her body urged her to respond to his touch. She could not help but hope it would be different, be good, with him, as she did not want to spend her nights being invaded by a rough and selfish mate.

Chumani forced those worries to leave her mind as she knelt by the stone enclosure and withdrew two sticks from a thong-bound bundle of them. She poured sand from a pouch onto the larger one with a depression cut into one side, placed dry leaves and grass atop it, and used the smaller round one to roll between her hands until sparks ignited a tiny blaze. She blew upon it as she slowly added more leaves and sticks. When it was burning sufficiently, she added wood.

After Wind Dancer returned, they sat together on a thick hide, ate leftovers from their joining feast, and drank water from a buffalo bladder bag. Darkness was approaching at a swift pace as the last rays of sunlight faded on the western horizon and a half-moon made its presence known in the eastern sky. Each was aware of the other's close proximity and seductive allure. Neither could imagine what lay ahead for them on this momentous night.

As he eyed two scars from mourning cuts sliced upon her forearm, he said, "Your father told me about the loss of your husband and son two winters past. It was the same for me. Perhaps those who killed our families will fall prey to our knives or arrows during our sacred quest."

Chumani touched the faint lines which represented the two circles of seasons of her child's short life. "That would please me, for my son has not been avenged unless that Bird warrior has fallen prey to another's arrow."

"How did you capture and train the hawk who lives with you?" he asked, her words reminding him of that feathered companion. "I have never known another to have a giant bird of the sky as a friend."

"I found Cetan injured when I was a child. I took him to our tepee and tended him until he was healed. We came to love each other, so he did not leave me. He often flies away for one or two suns to hunt and search his territory, but he always returns to me. He has never taken a mate, but surely he will do so one sun, for hawks mate for life. Sometimes he brings me rabbits, squirrels, or other small animals he has captured. I cook part of his gift and he feeds on the other. It pleases him to hunt for me and watch me eat his offerings. He endures the presence of others, but no one can touch him except me. He does not claw or bite those close to me, but he attacks when I battle enemies. Many times he has swooped down on concealed foes and warned me of their approach. He has grabbed bows, knives, and lances from the hands of enemies. He is very smart and wise, and very protective of me. He was hunting when the Crow attacked me in the Brave Heart forest, or he would have helped me defeat them. I will take him to your camp with me unless you forbid it."

"There is no reason to forbid it, Dewdrops, unless he becomes a danger to the children of my camp. They will be told not to approach or touch him, and will be punished if they do not obey. But he will not be allowed to attack without reason. If he cannot accept his new surroundings, you must release him for the safety of others." He watched her nod in agreement. "Since he is well trained and loyal, perhaps there is some way he can help us on our sacred quest." He looked deep into her eyes before seeking an answer important to him. "Why did you speak false words to me in the forest? You are not called Morning Mist and you are not a Brave Heart."

Chumani noticed that he changed the topic. She surmised he was not ready to discuss their coming challenge together or perhaps did not want her to ask about the vision hawk he had painted upon his war shield. "I am Dewdrops, which is the morning mist; and I did not say I was of the Brave Heart Band. I did not intrude upon their land to be bad. My thoughts had roamed as I enjoyed the rebirth of Mother Earth and I walked too far before my mind cleared. I did not tell you my name and band or accept your offer to escort me, for I did not wish for you to ride to my camp with me. To hear of my bad deed and danger would not please my father and brother. I thank you for not exposing such things to them."

"How did you vanish?" he asked, and listened in amazement while she explained her actions that day. "Your skills are many, Dewdrops. We have walked the same path many times. We were both born of a chief's seeds. We have both lost our mates and sons. We have fought the Crow together. Perhaps that reveals we are well matched as mates and quest companions."

Chumani allowed his last statement to pass without her remarking on it. "What is the task which lies before us and why were we chosen for it?"

"I do not know; the Great Spirit has not revealed those answers to us. When the time comes, He will tell our shaman and perhaps tell yours."

"How will we defeat our enemies? We are only two people."

"I do not know," he answered frankly. "That lies in the mind of the Great Mystery."

"Why do we not plant the war lance between the Bird People and the White-eyes? There are many ways we could do so. That would halt a truce or alliance between them, then each force alone would be easier to defeat."

"How would you cause trouble between our enemies?"

She was surprised that he asked her opinion, and was pleased he had done so. "There are many cunning ways to cause trouble between them. Do you not possess Crow war prizes in your camp?" After he nodded, she said, "They could be left behind when we harass the White-eyes to lead them to believe the Bird People are to blame. We could steal the white man's horses and picket them near Crow camps. The hard moccasins their animals wear will leave tracks even the *wasicun* or their Bluecoats can follow. When we attack Crow hunting parties, we can leave behind possessions we have stolen from the White-eyes. Such things will cause suspicions and hostilities between them."

"Your words are wise, and I will not forget them." He looked to the sky. "Night has come and it is time to rest. I will return soon."

Chumani wanted to get past the impending awkward moment fast. While Wind Dancer went to check on their horses, she unrolled the sleeping mat, undressed, and lay on the soft buffalo hide, naked. "I am ready," she told him upon his return in a voice hoarsened by apprehension.

He looked down at her and, though aroused by the sight of her naked body and almost aching to possess it, said, "There is no need to rush."

"There is no need to move slowly. Do as you must to seal our joining bond, just as you smoked the pipe to seal the alliance bond with my band."

"Such matters must not be done in haste. First, we must talk more."

"There is no need for words when such a task must be done."

Wind Dancer could not suppress a grin at her own words, but as suspicions soon filled him that she had not enjoyed her nights with her first husband. Perhaps Dull Star had never given her pleasure on the sleeping mat; perhaps the foolish man had been neither gentle nor generous with her.

"It is unwise and unkind to laugh at another in pain."

"Why does it pain you to become my wife? Am I not worthy of you?"

"I did not wish to join with you and leave my people. I will do my duty, but it brings sadness to my heart."

"I will do my duty soon, but our tepee will be a happier place if we become friends first. To do so, we must learn much about each other."

"What more do you desire to know about me?"

"All things," he responded as he held a blanket out to her.

Chumani wrapped it around her. "Why does a great warrior, a future chief, like Waci Tate choose a woman he does not know?"

"I did not choose Dewdrops to become my wife," he reminded her. "The Great Spirit chose you. If we are to love each other, He will put such feelings in our hearts. If not, we must find our happiness in obeying His command, for He knows all things and has a purpose for our union. Since you had a mate and child in the past, you know how to tend a tepee and do a woman's work. But you also possess warrior-hunter skills, so I will not fear for your safety or that of our children's when I am away from camp. I know it is hard for you to leave your family and people, but you will see them again soon. Sleep, Dewdrops, for on the new sun we will return to your camp, gather our possessions and my family, and ride for my camp. After we have come to know each other and have become friends, we will become mates."

"Your words are wise and your heart is kind. It will be as you say."

"That is good, *mitawin*, for we must have trust and acceptance between us to face the dangers and challenges which loom ahead for us."

After Wind Dancer was lying beside her and they were covered by a warming hide, Chumani listened to the pops and crackles as new wood caught fire and feasted in delight. She heard nocturnal birds, creatures, and insects as they foraged and spoke with their mates, or warned rivals away from their territories. A shiver passed over her, as if she were lying naked in the snow; yet, her flesh itched as if she were staked over an anthill. The nights were still chilly and the wind was brisk that moon, and she was enclosed naked in a blanket, so she tried to blame those conditions for her sensations, though she knew they were not at fault. Her heart and body had warmed when Wind Dancer gave her the blanket, gave her a mating reprieve, and called her, "my wife."

Chumani admitted to herself she was a little disappointed that he did not lay full claim to her, as doing so would answer many of the questions about him, their new life, and the contradictory emotions which troubled her. She got little sleep, too aware of the temptation nearby and the numerous uncertainties in her future.

As was the custom, Wind Dancer sought a private place at the river for his morning ritual of bathing and greeting the Great Spirit. Clad only in his moccasins and breechclout, he stood straight and still as he faced the rising sun and mutely prayed to the Creator of all things. He gave thanks for his blessings and asked for guidance and protection in the days to come. He closed his eyes for a moment as he ended the holy communication, then took a deep breath of invigorating air and knelt to finish his daily task.

As he splashed water upon his face and torso, he noticed the flecks and small nuggets on the shallow river's bottom which glittered like the golden sun. He knew he could pull up clumps of grass which edged its banks and find the same shiny *mazaska zi* clinging to their roots. He also knew the white man would trade his very soul to collect them and would encroach on this sacred site at any price of warfare to lay claim to it. So did other bands and tribes, and all had agreed not to reveal its presence in the sacred Papa Sapa or to use it for trade with the *wasicun*. Yet, somehow and some day, he recalled with a resentful heart, the enemy would make that discovery and a fierce war would ensue, for his grandfather had seen it happen in a vision long ago; and Nahemana had never been wrong.

The Oglala warrior heard the splashing of water beyond a section of dense bushes on the bank where the river curved behind them and did not have to be told his wife was there bathing. As he closed his eyes again and summoned her image to his mind, his loins sprang to life with desire for her. He warned himself he must learn to control his urges or they would consume him and he would seek her out on the sleeping mat before she was ready to reach out to him. Patience was a virtue and he must practice it, no matter how hard or how long his quest for her required.

Chumani bathed in a hurry, as the water was still chilly even if winter was past and the snow was gone. The sky was blue and almost clear of white clouds. The winds from all directions were calm, and the day was warm, warmer than it normally was for this time of the rebirth season. Mother Earth had renewed her face. The grass and trees were green. Flowers had bloomed. Nature had called out the birds, animals, and insects who were busy with the mating and reproducing season. Perhaps, she mused, that was the reason behind her discontent; no, her yearnings. Female urges and instincts buried within her were straining to burst forth when she must hold them captive. Since she was so well trained and well practiced in deceit and self-control, surely she could dupe Wind Dancer about her feelings. If not, how would that influence her future?

Chumani could not answer with accuracy, so she pushed those thoughts aside to return to their campfire.

After sharing embraces and final words with her loved ones and people, Chumani mounted to leave with her new family and to take the next step along the path of her new destiny. The gifts had been loaded upon two of the horses Wind Dancer had brought to her father, who had given them to her to transport her possessions to the Red Shield camp and to the grasslands for their summer encampment there. She had warmed when Wind Dancer had smiled and thanked Tall Elk for his generosity, and had thanked her people for theirs. She recalled she had told her mother during a private moment together upon their return, that Wind Dancer was a good and kind man and a great warrior, that the Great Spirit chose well for her. She had said those things to give her mother joy and comfort; in her deepest heart, she hoped they were true.

Their farewells finished, the couple departed with the other four Oglala men riding slightly ahead of them and with Cetan flying high overhead, his keen eyes on the strange sight below him.

As they journeyed in silence, Chumani thought about her best friend who had not returned before she had to leave, so Wind Dancer had not met Zitkala. She could not help but wonder if her husband would like and respect her best friend in spite of her masculine demeanor. She knew that even if she had been away with Zitkala instead of in camp tending her ill mother when Wind Dancer arrived, he would have awaited her return to claim and take her away. Despite her doubts, she knew the inter-tribal alliance was necessary. She could not help but feel proud to be the one chosen to seal it and to be a part of the sacred visionquest. No matter her uncertainties in many areas, she must not do anything to dishonor her parents, people, and herself; she must make the best of this challenge and sacrifice.

Besides, Chumani told herself as she stole a glance of him, Wind Dancer was being understanding and patient. Still, she worried that his behavior might be nothing more than a trick or a gentle ploy until he got her away from her loved ones and under his control. Perhaps, she fretted, his heart belonged to another woman whom he had been compelled to sacrifice in order to obey the sacred vision. Or perhaps he did not find her desirable, and mating with her would be a chore for him. Maybe *that* was the true reason why he was delaying their physical bonding. *Do not think such foolish thoughts,* she chastened herself. *You are smart, brave, and strong. The Great Spirit chose you for an important task, so He will guide and protect you.*

When dusk approached, the small group halted to camp. As was the custom, while the men tended the horses and talked, Chumani gathered wood, built a fire, and fetched fresh water from the nearby river. As she waited for the men to eat before she consumed her own meal and put everything away for the night, she listened to their talk and observed their actions.

"It is good the Great Spirit chose Dewdrops to become the wife of my son," the chief said. "He has told me of your courage and skills in the forest with the Crow. My heart is proud to look upon you and to call you my new daughter. You will be a good sister for Hanmani and War Eagle."

Chumani was touched by his comments, but surprised that Wind Dancer had exposed their past meeting to his family. "Your words are kind, Rising Bear, and I thank you for them. I will do my best to be a good wife, daughter, and sister to my new family." She looked at War Eagle as he spoke. At seventeen winters he was a handsome and virile male and a skilled warrior, who had great pride in his family and older brother.

"You will have a place of great honor in our camp and upon our tribal buffalo hide. Our people and my family will rejoice at your coming, and sing happy songs that my brother has finally taken another mate. He will become a great chief as our father is. It is good to have you in our family."

"Your words are also kind, War Eagle, and I thank you for them."

"All he said is true, Dewdrops," Nahemana concurred with his young grandson. "Your coming was foretold in my sacred vision and soon you will ride a glorious trail with Wind Dancer to save our two peoples and lands."

"I pray I am worthy of that challenge, Wise One, and I will not fail in my duty to the Great Spirit, my husband, and our peoples."

Red Feather grinned. "Do not worry, Dewdrops, for my best friend has seen your skills and courage and has boasted they are a match for any warrior's. I pray to be chosen to journey with you two on the exciting task ahead."

"As do I," War Eagle added to Red Feather's remarks. "When will the Great Spirit reveal what that task will be, Wise One," Chumani asked the shaman, "and when we will depart to begin it?"

"Soon, Dewdrops," Nahemana told her, "for the signs I saw in the vision are close to those which cover the face of Mother Earth this sun."

"Will the hawk who lives and travels with Dewdrops be a part of the sacred quest, Grandfather?" War Eagle asked.

"I do not know, but a hawk was in the visions and Wind Dancer was told to paint one upon a new shield to carry."

After Red Feather questioned her about Cetan, Chumani answered him with the same details she had revealed to her husband last night. She glanced at the large bird who was perched in a pine tree nearby, smiled, and finished with, "He is my friend and he will obey any commands Wakantanka gives him."

"We have far to ride on the new sun, so you must eat before we rest."

Chumani did as Wind Dancer suggested while the men continued their talk about past battles with the Crow, then put away the remaining food and added more wood to the lowered flames. When she returned from excusing herself in bushes cloaked in shadows, she took her place beside her husband upon their sleeping mat. Her feelings were mixed when Wind Dancer cuddled up to her from behind, arranged a blanket over her shoulders, and allowed his arm to rest over her waist. Between the cover, his body heat, and her reaction to contact with him, she was warm and cozy in many ways. Yet, she was tense from suppressed desire and from wondering if his gentle behavior was genuine or only a pretense before his family to dupe them about their relationship being a happy one. She prayed another sleepless night would not follow the previous one, and to her delight, it did not.

The five men and one woman approached the Red Shield camp late the following afternoon.

Chumani's heart began to drum within her chest at the thought of meeting the rest of his family, relatives, and people. As if he sensed her apprehension, Wind Dancer moved his horse closer to hers, looked at her, and smiled as if to encourage and comfort her. For a moment, she felt lost in his captive gaze. Then she returned his smile before focusing her eyes on the large encampment spread out before her where her new home, new people, new life, and unknown destiny awaited her.

Chapter Six

⚜

Chumani was elated by the genial welcome she received, as War Eagle and Red Feather had ridden ahead to announce their approach. It was as if the entire band enclosed their horses to greet them, to study her, and to gaze in fascination at the large hawk which sat upon her shoulder on a wide and thick leather strip to guard her flesh against accidental pricks from his sharp talons. Several times she lifted her hand to stroke Cetan's chest and to speak soothing words to him as he flexed his claws and jerked his head about, as he was uneasy amidst the unfamiliar crowd. As their gazes shifted from her and Cetan to the two symbols—a yellow dewdrop and brown hawk—painted upon Wind Dancer's new shield, she overheard several of the Big Bellys remark on the accuracy and "big medicine" of the sacred vision. She met countless people in a rush and realized there were many names and faces to learn: his family of five, his mother's parents, Winona's brother and his family and her sister, the sister of Rising Bear and her family, and their many friends. It appeared to her that she was accepted and respected as the mate of their chief's son and future leader, and as the "vision woman." She told herself that even if she had lingering doubts about what their shaman and her husband saw during their peyote-induced dream quests and how Nahemana interpreted those signs, they, his family, and his people believed they were messages from the Great Spirit; and she, a part of them.

Wind Dancer had expected his new wife to get a warm reception, but he was overjoyed when her arrival went better than anticipated. Surely that event would please and calm her, draw her closer to him.

"Come, we will show you your new home, my second daughter and my first son," Winona said. "Then, Hanmani and I will help you unload the horses. Many helped with the tepee and many brought gifts to fill it with your needs. Later we will have a great feast to celebrate your joining and to welcome Dewdrops to our camp and family circle."

Before the crowd dispersed to return to their chores, Wind Dancer and Chumani thanked the people for their generosity and hard work.

Afterward, they followed his exuberant mother and sister to a location near the edge of the forest which traveled into the foothills of the Paha Sapa. Numerous other tepees were scattered amongst evergreen and hardwood trees and huge black rocks and in small clearings between the deep and swift-moving Spearfish Creek and backdrop of mountains and canyons; they were not placed in ever-widening circles as on the grassy Plains where a tighter set-up was required for self-defense.

Chumani knew from her camp far to the south near the Cave of the Spirit Winds that such sites were chosen for seasonal encampments because the sacred hills provided rear protection from enemies' attacks and protection as well from the worst winds and snows of the cold season. The sheltered valleys were filled with grass and water where horses could be kept in safety and grazed.

As they stood before a large conical dwelling where the band's Story Catchers had painted his coups on its exterior, the couple was amazed and delighted by its size and beauty, and the quality of the hides and work. With enthusiasm and pride, Hanmani hurriedly told Chumani about several of the glorious and successful exploits colorfully recorded there.

Many scents filled Chumani's nose as they entered the dwelling: recently cut and debarked pine, whose finished poles had been rubbed smooth using rough sand; the smell of tanned buffalo hides which covered those poles; upward-drifting smoke from a low-burning fire enclosed by a circle of rocks in the dwelling's center; and various other familiar or unknown scents. Twenty-six tall poles made a sturdy framework for it. A fifteen-foot pointed cluster seemingly reached for the sky, which was exposed through the open ventilation flap. The buffalo hides had been laced together to prevent them from being blown apart or off during a violent storm or brisk winds. Above the entrance flap, numerous wooden lodge pins held the two sides together. She noticed that the tepee's interior was clean and neat and everything was well organized, thanks to Winona and Hanmani.

She continued to scan the area. A colorfully painted dew-cloth, an added layer of brain-tanned hides stitched together to form a lengthy roll, was suspended from a height of five feet to the ground where it was pegged securely in place; that strip discouraged drafts at the base, provided added warmth in winter, and beauty during all seasons for the simple home. It also diverted to the outside any rain that ran down the poles and created an air flow to force smoke upward and out the peak's flap. The dew-cloth's numerous top ties were secured to a lengthy rope that went from post to post and was attached to each to hold it in place.

Possessions—which Hanmani delighted in pointing out and telling their giver's name—hung from the strong rope: a sewing pouch with an awl and sinew; two buffalo bladder waterbags; two backrests made of willow and interwoven reeds; large pouches for holding horn spoons and cups and wooden plates, along with a pounding stone and wooden bowl for crushing nuts and dried berries and corn obtained through trade from distant tribes; an open topped bag which held a flesher and a scraper; a furry kneepad for doing chores; parfleches for holding clothing and such; a medicine bag with healing herbs and plants; a wood sling; and many other gifts.

A thick sleeping mat had been placed near the tepee's base, rolled and tied into a tight ball until needed at night. A three-legged stand held the weapons Wind Dancer had left behind; she knew some man had placed them there, as females were not allowed to touch them or to touch a man's prayer pipe and personal medicine bundle. Her husband's other belongings, which the two women had moved from Rising Bear's tepee, were there as well.

"My heart overflows with joy for all you have done for me," Chumani told his mother and sister, her eyes misty with emotion. "You and your people are kind and generous. I am proud to join your family and band."

"We are happy you have come to live with us and be my son's wife."

"It will be good to have a sister," Hanmani added with a smile.

"Yes, it will," Chumani concurred with a smile in return as she placed her hawk atop a backrest, "for I only have one brother in my camp."

While she unpacked the possessions they had brought with them with the help of the two women, Wind Dancer and Red Feather dug a deep hole and placed Cetan's T-shaped post inside it. They used many rocks to hold it steady and straight before replacing the dirt and adding more rocks around its base for added strength. Afterward, they took their bows and headed into the forest to hunt something fresh for the creature to eat, as Chumani did not want to release him until he became familiar with the area.

When everything was in its place, Winona and Hanmani left to give Chumani privacy to rest after her long ride and chores and before the feast, scheduled to start at dusk, began.

Chumani washed her face, arms, and legs of trail dust. She changed garments and moccasins, brushed her long black hair, and decorated it with a beaded rosette with short fluffy plumes. She also adorned her neck and wrists with beaded bands, gifts from her mother. As she did so, she talked with Cetan in low whispers. "This is our new home, my friend. Soon you will learn its sights, sounds, smells, and people. Then I will allow you to soar the sky in freedom and to claim this territory as your own. I know fear does not live in your heart and mind, but they do within me. I fear I will fail in the sacred task set before me. I fear the new feelings that stir within me. I fear this new and unknown life, and I miss those I love in my camp. Will I come to love this man and his people?" she asked her beloved hawk. "Will I be happy here with him?"

Chumani smiled as Cetan chattered when she finished, as if he was responding to her words. "I wish I could understand you, my friend, as I am sure your answers are filled with wisdom and comfort. I—"

Chumani stopped talking when she heard Wind Dancer outside saying good-bye to Red Feather. She watched him enter their tepee, halt, and scrutinize her from dark head to moccasined feet, a smile steadily broadening on his handsome face.

"Your beauty is large, Dewdrops; it gives me pleasure to look upon you and pride to have you as my wife." After she smiled and thanked him, he said, "I brought Cetan a small rabbit to eat. Do you wish him to feast inside or upon his new home?"

"I will secure him to his post to enjoy the fresh air."

As she attached a leather thong to one leg and then to the post, she noticed Wind Dancer had secured the furry covering around the top section, one with scents well known and calming to the large bird. Also secured to one end was a horn cup which he filled with water. "You must offer the rabbit to him so he will learn to accept you and one sun to obey you. Place it over your palm, lay your hand across mine, and let me guide it to him."

After their hands were in contact, Chumani raised them toward the hawk. Cetan studied the rabbit and two people for a short time, then lifted his unfettered leg and grasped the gift with its talons. The bird placed the animal across his perch and held on to it as he eyed their touching hands.

Chumani smiled. "It is good you give him food and water. He accepts your presence and soon will accept your touch and commands. It warms my heart that you allowed me to bring him and to keep him."

It warms more than my heart to hear you think and say such words and to look at me as you do. Wind Dancer thought with great pleasure. He noted that the tips of her fingers had curled between his spread ones and her hand remained in contact with his as they were lowered to the space between their bodies. "Perhaps the Great Spirit will use him during the sacred quest and that is why he was given to you many seasons past and why I saw a hawk in my vision. Now we must go, *mitawin,* it is time for our feast."

Or perhaps it was because you saw him with me before you entered the dream world and your mind or an evil force played tricks upon you, her mind could not help but reply. Even so, she was pleased by his acceptance of her feathered friend and his good opinions of her. "I am ready, *mihigna.*"

After they had eaten, eight men sat around a large drum made of willow with a tanned hide stretched across the top hoop. As they pounded upon its taut surface with sticks, they sang tribal songs to entertain the couple and the crowd. At one point in the evening, Wind Dancer joined other men to dance around a campfire while they sang songs to praise the Great Spirit and to summon His protection and guidance in the days to come.

Chumani watched her husband as he moved around the glowing flames with great agility. No man she had ever seen had looks to match his enormous ones; and few, if any, could chant more coups than he could. His body was strong and nimble, his rapid steps were confident and accurate, and his expression was joyous and serene, as if he were caught in a spiritual trance. Her heart seemed to catch the beat of the music and keep time with it. Despite her excitement, she felt relaxed amidst such friendly people, proud to be Wind Dancer's wife and to be sitting with the family of the band's leader, and aroused by the sight of the virile warrior whom she would lie with tonight.

As he danced and chanted with his eyes almost closed, narrow slits allowed Wind Dancer to snatch glimpses of Dewdrops each time he moved before her position with his parents and sister. She looked breath-stealing and peaceful, as if she was enjoying herself and the event, not just pretending to do so. He knew the heat and moisture on his flesh came from more than his exertions and the nearby flames; most of it resulted from blazing desire for her. How he yearned to scoop her up, race to their lodge, and bond slowly and blissfully with her on their sleeping mat. He craved to taste her lips and body, to caress her soft skin, to feel his erect shaft buried deep within her woman's core. He knew it was too soon to mate with her; first, he must win her trust, acceptance, loyalty, and love; and do so before they began their sacred task. He wished the Great Spirit would reveal their challenges soon, as he was eager to get started on them. Perhaps, he reasoned, the Great Spirit was waiting until he and Chumani became as one before sending his grandfather the next message. He longed for her to reach out to him, so he decided he must tempt her at every turn to desire him and make her feelings known.

When it came time for couples to dance together, Wind Dancer joined Chumani and extended his hand to her. His heart leapt with elation when she did not delay in placing hers within his, and he assisted her to her feet. They faced each other with little space between them and with his back to the campfire as they took sideways steps and made other movements to the slower and softer music. Both felt it was important as a recently joined couple to gaze tranquilly into the other's eyes to show acceptance and affection for a new mate. Yet, what began in part as a charade became much more. Each was aware of the other's nearness, of the growing passion between them, and of the knowledge they had been matched by the Great Spirit Himself.

After the stimulating dance ended, Wind Dancer rejoined his family while Chumani, who needed to regather her lagging poise and wits, went to excuse herself in bushes near the edge of camp. A young woman whom she had seen observing them many times since their arrival followed her.

"I am called Wastemna, daughter of Buffalo Hump, our war chief. It is unwise for the wife of our next leader to leave the safety of camp alone. You would make a valuable war prize for our enemy, the Crow."

"Your fears and warning are kind but unneeded, Wastemna. I have my knife with me and I am skilled not only with it but also fighting with bare hands."

"That is good, but it is rare for a female to be a hunter-warrior. A great warrior and chief needs a wife who is skilled with woman's work and shows him much love, respect, and pleasure in his tepee."

Chumani wondered if she detected barely concealed hostility in the female's voice. She had seen Wastemna watching them, especially her, several times during the evening but assumed it was out of curiosity. "I am the daughter of the White Shield chief, so I must know how to help feed and protect our people and lands. I have ridden on raids and hunts many times, but I also was well-trained in women's chores and behavior."

"Wakantanka smiled brightly on you when He chose you to become Waci Tate's wife. Many females among our band desired to mate with him. No other man among our people has his great courage and prowess. And his face and body are good to look upon. Are my words not true?"

"He is certainly skilled and brave. But I do not know about the desires of other women."

"They would not matter now; Wakantanka commanded Waci Tate to join to you and he was compelled to obey. Was it the same for you?"

Chumani thought the female was being too inquisitive as they did not know each other well enough to speak of such private things. Yet, she did not want to offend the war chief's daughter or make an enemy of her. She smiled and jested, "As you say, Wastemna, Waci Tate is not a man to be scorned or refused. It pleased me to join to him."

As they returned to the feast in chilly silence, Chumani suspected that Wastemna was going to be anything but "sweet-smelling" as her lovely name alleged, and dreaded to discover if her instincts were accurate.

As Wind Dancer and Chumani settled down to sleep for the first night in their new tepee, they shared the same buffalo hide mat but did not unite their bodies as both desired without the other's knowing. Each had enjoyed their welcome feast and hoped to close the gap between them, but both were reluctant to make the first romantic move.

Chumani did not ask Wind Dancer about Wastemna or any other female who had longed to join to him as the female had alleged. She wondered again if he did not truly desire her for herself or could not bring himself to make love to her, a woman he had not chosen and one who had no doubt made a bad impression on him at their first meeting. Out of pride and not wanting to suffer anguish and loss again from a mismatched love, she told herself she must continue to control such desires. Also, she reasoned, as long as they did not bond on the sleeping mat, he could not plant his seeds within her body, which she feared would prevent or halt her participation in the sacred task. She prayed for the strength to deny her urges and for the cunning to avoid insulting him while doing so. She knew that task would be difficult since her husband was so tempting in many ways.

* * *

The following morning while the men were hunting game, Chumani gathered herbs and plants and collected firewood with Hanmani, her best friend Macha, her grandmother Little Turtle, Rising Bear's sister Pretty Meadow, Winona, Songbird, wife of Winona's brother Strong Rock, and Little Deer, sister of Winona who had never joined to a man and who still lived in the tepee of their parents Nahemana and Little Turtle. As they talked and laughed while they worked together, her affection and respect for his family and people increased and she learned more about them and the events which had bonded them as a close band. She was delighted and relieved to discover that the family circle of Rising Bear and Winona was loved and esteemed. She was proud that her second father was the son of a reputable chief and her second mother the daughter of a revered and beloved shaman. There was no denying that her husband's bloodline was a good one, just as their future son's would be.

Chumani's father did not come from a long and honored bloodline of chiefs. When she was three winters old, Tall Elk had been chosen as chief by their council and accepted by the entire White Shield Band after their last leader and his two sons were slain in a fierce battle with a joint war party of Crow and Pawnee where her father had taken charge following their deaths and led his warriors to a glorious victory. Her brother would become their next chief, unless Fire Walker did something to dishonor himself and his rank or was slain. Since her brother was a good man and renowned warrior, she must not imagine either ever happening.

That afternoon, Wind Dancer asked her to take a doubleback ride with him in the Spearfish canyon to one of its water falls, the largest in that area.

Chumani was elated when he suggested Cetan go with them so the hawk could exercise his wings and hunt fresh meat, but mostly by the implication he was courting her with a romantic ride together. A private outing also would reinforce his people's belief in their intimate relationship, which should please him and cause him to continue his restraint.

She quickly put away her tasks, released Cetan, and accepted Wind Dancer's hand to be pulled up behind him on his brown riding horse. She sensed his pleasure at her willingness to comply, and she smiled to herself for her fast thinking and cunning. Perhaps, she mused, this pursuit game would be fun.

At first, the canyon was shallow and wide and filled with radiant sunlight as they traveled near a rapidly flowing stream whose water was cold but refreshing. The setting was lovely and peaceful. The day was clear and warm and without even a hint of a thundercloud. Vegetation was abundant and green, especially spruce and tall grass which swayed to and fro in a gentle breeze, and wildflowers flourished amidst the verdant covering. Their arrival flushed a variety of birds and animals from or near their path and spooked them into temporary concealment.

As they continued along a well-worn trail, the black cliffs on both sides of them rose higher and steeper and more jagged. When the canyon narrowed, less sunlight entered that lovely domain, yet, a strip of blue sky was overhead and made a vivid contrast with the greens and blacks.

After they reached the falls and dismounted, Chumani was amazed by the loud noise of water rushing over the towering cliff occasionally spraying a light mist on them. "I can see why your people chose this location for your winter camp," Chumani observed. "It is well protected from the cold and snow, and the water moves too fast to freeze. I am sure there is always something growing here for your horses to eat, and animals lingering to furnish you with game. Those are the reasons why my people camp near the place where the warm springs bubble from the face of Mother Earth far away. See," she said as she pointed upward, "Cetan likes this place and soars in freedom as he seeks his prey."

"I am glad this journey makes you both happy. Many suns past you said we had not shared rides, so we must do so many times to bring us closer. Tonight I will play the flute for you, for I did not do so before we joined."

Chumani smiled at him. "It is good to share such things before we become as one. I thank you for your patience and generosity. You have much respect for the Four Virtues and practice them well."

Wind Dancer smiled in return. "It stirs my heart to hear you speak such words to me." He yearned to caress her cheek, to kiss her lips, to hold her in his arms, to lie upon the grass with her, and to make love. But first he wanted to pull her closer and tighter to him.

"It stirs my heart to have a husband who is good and kind to me," Chumani said in response. "It also stirs my heart to see the beauty of Mother Nature and the work of the Great Spirit's hands. He has created many things for us to use and enjoy."

"That is true, and I thank Him each new sun for doing so."

"As do I, *mihigna.*" She sighed then before speaking. "I wish we could stay longer, but I must return to our tepee to prepare our evening meal. I thank you for this good deed."

"It is only the first of many, *mitawin,*" he vowed.

En route to camp, Wind Dancer ached with desire as she rode with her breasts pressed against his back with her arms laced around his waist. He enjoyed the sound of her laughter, the soothing tone of her voice. His wife was a heady mixture of strength and softness in mind and body. Her pleasing scent was already familiar to him. Even her breath whispered of fragrant dried herbs when she spoke or they kissed. The only scars on her sleek flesh were the two mourning cuts on her forearm, which were signs of great love and courage and a tragic loss. Since their joining, she had done nothing to disappoint or shame him; her behavior in private and public had been perfect. His family and people liked, respected, and had accepted her. His brother and best friend had told him how fortunate he was to have her. Yes, he concluded, she was the best choice for his wife, quest companion, and mother of his children; for which he silently thanked Wakantanka.

After placing a shaft-skewered rabbit over two end Y-shaped posts to cook slowly, Chumani went inside the tepee to fetch tenderizing and flavor-enhancing herbs to sprinkle over the meat. After that task was done, and from pouches hanging on the dew-cloth, she retrieved elk antler spoons, chokecherry plates, and buffalo horn cups with their points driven into blocks of pine for balance. Knowing she had plenty of time before the rabbit was done, she walked a short distance to the river to fetch fresh water. As she did so, she realized she felt aglow in heart and body from the outing with her handsome and virile husband. He was so enticing and—

"Your fire is too large and the meat burns past eating."

While kneeling to fill the bladder bag, a distracted Chumani turned and looked up at her tall husband and asked him to repeat what he had said.

As quietly as possible for privacy, he warned, "The flames of your cookfire are too high and hot and burn the meat; it will soon be ruined. It is not a man's place to do such work, so I came to alert you of trouble."

Chumani hurried to the site beside their tepee. She was astonished to discover he was right; lofty flames licked greedily at the meat and were charring its sizzling flesh. She quickly hung her water bag on its post, pushed most of the high pile of wood aside, and doused their roaring flames with water she had just fetched. As she studied the meat to see if it was past saving, she murmured almost to herself, "There is mischief at work here; I did not make my fire so high."

Wind Dancer moved closer to her to ask in a whisper, "Do you say a trickster lives in my camp or one has sneaked into it?"

Chumani understood his concern. She knew it was reckless to accuse an unknown member of his band of this wicked trick, but—to avoid appearing careless—she was compelled to say, "I do not know, but I did not make a bad fire. I used only a small amount of the wood I gathered this morning and the rest is piled nearby. I also do not use the dried wood of the pine for slow cooking, as it burns too swiftly."

Wind Dancer did not want to believe one of his people had done such a thing on purpose; nor did he want to believe she was lying to him to cover her carelessness. Either way, he was worried about the strange incident. He felt it was wisest to advise her in her low tones: "It is best if we do not offend others by asking if someone did such a bad deed or to cause fear by saying an evil spirit sneaked into our camp to play a trick on Waci Tate and Dewdrops."

"It is agreeable to me to walk that path to prevent trouble," she concurred, but added to herself, *I will use the eyes of the eagle to watch for more trouble.*

"I will sit here and guard our lodge and meat while I play the flute for you." He assumed others would think he was only entertaining them, but she would know from his earlier words that he was courting her.

As he played music and she worked, Chumani's mind whirled with questions about the cooking fire. Even the type of wood used was not what she had gathered. She wondered who disliked her so much and wanted to make her look bad to her husband, and to cause him to think even worse of her for accusing one of his people of such a foul deed. She knew if Cetan had not been tethered inside the tepee out of the bright sun, he would have sounded a warning to her about the encroacher; and if he had not been tethered outside, he would have attacked the person responsible, and his injuries would have exposed the guilty one. She realized that with the placements of the tepees, as many—like theirs—were backed up to the forested hills and all entrances faced the rising sun for spiritual reasons, it was easy for a clever person to sneak up to her site and create such mischief. Also, each woman's cooking and working area was to the left of her dwelling to prevent one's smoke from blowing into the next woman's face as she did her chores.

Then, another and more irritating speculation crept into Chumani's mind. She wondered if Wind Dancer had created the event to see how she reacted. Perhaps he wondered if she would display bad temper, or panic and cry in helplessness. Would he do such a sneaky thing? Had their outing been nothing more than a means to relax and dupe her before he tested her character and skills? She did not know, but in time she would discover if he was fooling her.

Both were a little guarded since the disruption earlier. After the evening meal was ready and as they ate it, they talked about many things as they sought to get to know each other better. It was the custom for men to eat first when in a group of them or with male guests present, but if they were with only their families, everyone ate at the same time.

Neither Wind Dancer nor Chumani commented on the places where she had scraped away burned sections on the meat or remarked on its slight dryness from excessive heat. They also had camass bulbs which she had found that morning and roasted in the still-glowing coals, along with bread made from corn, nuts, and dried berries. Wind Dancer did smile and tell her how good the bulbs and bread were, and she thanked him.

Afterward, they took a short walk through the camp, stopping several times to speak with friends, his grandparents, and family. Neither noticed anyone watching them or behaving oddly since the fire incident, though both kept a sharp and furtive eye out for such a person.

Later as they lay on their sleeping mat, Wind Dancer suggested they practice kissing and touching to make their behavior appear more natural and convincing in public. He said, which was true but not his sole motive, that he was concerned that his people might worry about the sacred visionquest if it appeared they were not well matched in their joining and feelings. To his delight, his wife agreed.

Even so, Chumani told herself she was cooperating only to safeguard the secret of their unconsummated relationship, and to dupe the trickster—who might be a jealous woman—about Wind Dancer's feelings for her and commitment to her. Yet, it was a fierce struggle not to lose herself in the passion and pleasure of her husband's lovemaking. His mouth was skilled and delicious upon hers. His hands were gentle and arousing upon her body, though he did not touch her intimately. His mood was tender and caring, and he seemed to enjoy their game. Her previous doubts about him vanished for a while as he enchanted her entire being. It was exciting and flattering to have a great warrior and future leader pursue her, and to do so with persistence and without a great rush to seek his own appeasement. She liked viewing this side of him, the gentle and sensitive man. It gave her the chance to become more relaxed around and with him before they united their bodies. She also wanted to delay their bonding for as long as possible because, if it was not enjoyable or was painful to her, that would breed resentment in her, and problems between them. It was best to move along this path slowly, even if she was tempted to race along it in wild and wonderful abandonment.

Wind Dancer struggled to retain control of his overtures and her effect on him. She was so tempting, so beautiful, so responsive that it evoked a fierce yearning in him to possess her fully. But, he was not certain she was ready to take that step. For now, he must be satisfied just to hold her, taste her lips, caress her arms and face, and heighten her awareness of him as a man. He realized he had to halt their stimulating behavior soon or stopping would be impossible for him. With reluctance, he dragged his mouth from hers and said, "It is good to work on such skills, as they will strengthen our bond for when we are alone and for when we are with others."

"Your words are true and wise, *mihigna*. We get closer

each time we are together in this way, and soon no space will exist between us. I am happy you wish us to become friends and learn to trust each other before we bond as mates. It is a good thing we do for our future life together."

"Your words also are wise and true, *mitawin*. It is good we wait and move closer, for our bond will be stronger and more satisfying when we join together as friends than if we had done so as strangers. Now it is time to sleep, for we do not know what tasks or dangers lie before us on the next sun."

The romantic game, which served to increase their mutual attraction, ended too soon to suit either one.

The next morning, her husband's young sister entered the tepee and said to Chumani, "We go to wash garments, Dewdrops. Come with us. Macha, my mother, and Pretty Meadow head for the river now."

"That is good, my sister. I will come as soon as my soup is cooking."

After Hanmani left, Chumani tethered Cetan to his post outside so he could guard her fire and the kettle suspended over it, a trade item from the white man's world and a gift from one of his people. She collected their dirty garments and joined the other females at the river.

She liked Hanmani, who was thirteen winters old, and her best friend Dawn, who was two winters older. Watching the girls laugh and talk and work together caused her to miss Zitkala even more than she had since their four-moon separation, six moons if she counted the two before Wind Dancer's arrival and their joining. She could hardly wait to see her best friend and to talk with her about the many changes in her life. She knew Zitkala missed her terribly, too, and would have difficulty finding another very close friend, as Chumani had accepted the differences in Zitkala's looks and manner without any reservations. Unfortunately, the males of her tribe viewed Zitkala as an unattractive and unfeminine woman, while the females viewed her a man. Surely the Great Spirit had a good reason for creating Zitkala that way, and some sun or moon it would be revealed to them and all others.

Chumani realized how much she also missed the exciting hunts and challenging raids with Zitkala. Now that she was confined to camp in a wife's role, she missed the freedom she had come to enjoy in her camp. She also was aware that many of Wind Dancer's people seemed to watch her whenever she was outside. She understood they were curious about her and wondered what part she would play in the coming quest. She yearned for a visit with her best friend and with her family, so the seasonal move to the grasslands after the next full moon would be a favorable event. But that would not take place, she counted up, for another twenty or more nightly moons.

That afternoon while Chumani was speaking with his sister near their tepee, Wind Dancer joined them and asked his wife to go for a short walk in the forest and suggested Cetan go with them.

"I cannot do so, *mihigna,* for I must watch the fire and soup."

Hanmani smiled. "Go with him, Dewdrops," she said, "and I will watch them for you. I have beading to be done. I will sit nearby and do both."

"You are kind, my sister. Come, *mitawin,* and share a walk with me," he entreated again, extending his hand to her.

Chumani realized she had no choice except to go with him, as to protest would not look good before his sister. She untethered Cetan and allowed him to fly upward, knowing he would keep his keen eyes on her and follow wherever she went.

After they returned, Hanmani left to help her mother with their evening meal and Wind Dancer went to play toss-the-hoop with Red Feather and his brother, War Eagle. Although it was a game, it was also training to enhance their hand-to-eye coordination, flexibility, and target accuracy skills. She would like to see if he could ring the Y-shaped sticks—far and near, tall and short, or either chosen branch—with the various-sized willow hoops each time he flung them from a measured distance. She wished she could go with him and even join in on the fun and show him how skilled she was at it. But she was not invited: the other men could object if she were, and she could not leave her soup and tepee unguarded.

Instead, Chumani sat beneath a shade tree on a furry hide to do beading on a shirt given to Wind Dancer in her camp. She allowed Cetan to stay untethered so he could enjoy freedom for a while longer.

As she sat down on a sitting mat inside their tepee, Chumani noticed the scowl on her husband's face as he stared at the soup in the wooden bowl which she had served him. "What is wrong, *mihigna?*" she asked.

Wind Dancer looked at her, took a deep and decisive breath, and said with reluctance but in a gentle tone, "The soup is not good."

Chumani filled her spoon, sipped from it, and frowned. She lifted the bowl and sniffed its contents, but detected no foul or unusual odor. She eyed the ingredients as she stirred them but sighted nothing strange. She tasted the soup again and tried to determine what caused its odd flavor, which teased too lightly at the back of her mind to grasp it. If the same trickster had put something in the kettle, it had been ground too fine to be visible. But with Hanmani working nearby during their absence, she mused, how was that possible? It was possible, she answered herself, if the trickster was watching the young girl and she left for a short time to excuse herself in the bushes. She knew she must not ask Hanmani any questions, or speculate about her new suspicion to her husband. There was no doubt in her mind that someone—the unknown trickster, Hanmani, or Wind Dancer—had ruined the soup. But, Chumani worried, who and why? As a test or a spiteful deed?

"I do not understand why it is so bitter," she deceived

him by murmuring. "Its looks and smell are good. Perhaps an evil spirit possessed the creature who provided its meat. Or dwelled within the plants I gathered," she quickly added to prevent her prior words from sounding like an insult to the family hunter or as if she were passing the blame to him. "Perhaps one or the other is tainted. We must not eat it or we may become sick or even die. Perhaps that is what the harmful spirit desires, so it can stop us from going on the sacred visionquest."

Wind Dancer observed how she kept her gaze lowered to the bowl in her hands as if denying him a view of her eyes, and he listened to the tone of her voice which sounded strained. From those clues, he suspected she was not being fully honest with him and wondered why. Was she responsible for the two strange occurrences, either by accident or on purpose, and was grasping at anything to use as an explanatory excuse, or was an evil hand truly at work in their lives as she had proposed? There was that almost hated number *two* again; first, the oversize cookfire and burned meat, and now, bitter inedible soup. But if it was not Dewdrops or a *silwaecon*, he reasoned, who was behind such wicked mischief and why was it being done? He had no enemy or rival in his camp, and he had seen no member treat her as either one. Yet, something bad was afoot, as he was convinced that a cunning instigator was behind the two matters.

"Until this mystery is resolved, *mitawin*, we must keep it a secret to prevent insults and trouble," Wind Dancer suggested. "But we must keep our eyes and ears alert for another trick. We do not want anything or anyone to stop or damage the sacred challenge before us. Do you not agree?"

"That is true, *mihigna*," she responded as her gaze locked with his. "I will stay alert and near our tepee so I will not be tricked again. I do not want you or your people to think I am foolish and careless."

She looked as if she was being truthful that time. But her action would deny them of any future walks and rides

... Could that be the motive behind the two puzzling incidents? Did she dislike those romantic outings? Was she repulsed by him, only enduring his touch? There were a few questions he could ask and a certain request he could make which might expose her feelings. Tonight. Now.

Chapter Seven

After serving Wind Dancer some of last winter's pemmican, *wasna*, leftover bread from that morning, and dried fruit from the last hot season, Chumani carried the kettle into the forest. She dug a hole, emptied its contents there, and replaced the dirt. She piled rocks atop the location to prevent Wakantanka's animals from eating the bad soup and becoming sick, or worse. Afterward, she went to the river to scrub the kettle. All the while, she had the sensation that she was being watched, but could sight no one.

Later, as she unrolled and spread their sleeping mat, Wind Dancer lifted an item, grinned, and said as he shook it between his fingers, "Why do we not play Share-The-Blanket before we rest? We still have much to learn about each other to strengthen our bond." He watched her as she looked up at him, smiled, and nodded. That told him she had no objection to the courting game of talking privately under that cover, which was usually done outside by couples who were getting acquainted or in love. When they did so, everyone was supposed to pretend they did not notice them.

Instead of going outside where it was cool and they

would be noticed by others or standing inside the tepee, they sat down cross-legged and face-to-face on the sleeping mat. As soon as they were positioned for a cozy talk, he tossed a Cheyenne trade blanket over their heads. It settled around their shoulders and halted near their hips, which, added to the loose weave of the material, allowed for light from the campfire to sneak under its edges and to penetrate its tiny holes to prevent total darkness from encompassing them. Their hands rested in their laps, and their knees touched. In the dim light, their gazes locked as they readied themselves for the game.

"Do our joining and friendship bring you joy and pride, *mitawin?*" Wind Dancer asked.

That question was unexpected but she responded without hesitation, "Yes, *mihigna.* We have a good match and alliance for us and our people. You are a man of many superior skills and traits. I am honored to be your wife."

"As I am honored and pleased to have Dewdrops as my wife. Your good skills and traits are too numerous to count. We would not be mates if the Crow had not attacked our two camps long ago. Does love still live in your heart for your first husband? Do you still long to see and be with him?"

Chumani gazed at him for a short time, surprised by those serious queries. "No, *mihigna* and *mitakola,* and such feelings for him never lived in my heart. Dull Star was chosen by my father and I joined to him to obey Father's wishes." She divulged how Dull Star's carelessness was to blame for the tragic Crow attack on her camp. "I was respectful and obedient as a chief's daughter and as a warrior's wife, but I did not love or desire him."

"It was the same for me, *mitawin:* I joined to my first mate to give joy to my parents and people. I did not love and desire her, but I was a good husband and protector for her and our son." He took a breath before he disclosed, "There was no enjoyment with her on the sleeping mat, only duty and release. I believe it was the same for you, as great pleasure comes only to those who share true love and a unity of spirits."

"Your words are wise and true, *mihigna*. I did not like sharing the sleeping mat with Dull Star and was happy he claimed me there so rarely. He was not patient, understanding, or gentle; as you are, *mihigna*. Perhaps it is wicked of me to feel and say such words, but I am not sorry Wakantanka took him away. I only suffered over the loss of my son."

Wind Dancer was elated by her revelations. He was thrilled to hear her speak so highly of him and his behavior and relieved to learn she not only did not have lingering anguish over Dull Star's loss but also had never loved him. "Perhaps in a season to come, Wakantanka will give us another child, a son to become Red Shield chief after I walk the Ghost Trail. When the right time arrives for us to join our bodies, it will be different between us. I will never harm, dishonor, or reject you, *mitawin*, for you were given to me by the Great Spirit Who sees and knows and created all things."

Wind Dancer cupped her face between his hands, closed the distance between them, and sealed their lips. That kiss was slow and gentle, but almost as entrancing as a peyote button. His mouth left hers to travel over her face for a while, then, his lips returned to hers with a firmer and swifter kiss. As his flames of desire burned brighter and hotter with her response, he separated their mouths so he could keep his promise of restraint. He gazed into her eyes, smiled, and murmured, "Yes, it will be good between us when that special moon rises and we become as one."

Chumani was tempted to say "that special moon" had risen tonight, as her entire being yearned to unite their bodies. But if she did so and he was agreeable, that would not reveal his true feelings for her, as he might only react out of physical cravings. They both needed more time and more closeness. Yet, waiting would be difficult since he aroused her so highly.

"Do you not agree?" he asked when she remained silent and watchful.

"Yes, *mihigna,* that is true."

Wind Dancer smiled and caressed her cheek before he removed the blanket, drew fresh air into his lungs, and lay down.

Chumani glanced at the low fire to be sure it was all right, then took her place beside him. She closed her eyes, and before she slept, imagined what it would have been like if they had not halted their actions.

"I go to bathe and pray. I will return soon," he said, upon arising.

"Your shirt hangs on the rack outside. It is dry by now," she told him as she prepared to do the same before starting their morning meal.

Wind Dancer left to fetch the garment but returned shortly and said in a somber tone, "I cannot put on a shirt that is not clean. I will wear the other one again this sun."

Chumani took the shirt and stared at the dirt and stains upon it. She grimaced. "I do not understand," she explained. "I washed it well on the last sun. It was clean when I hung it there."

Wind Dancer was certain she spoke the truth. "Perhaps the evil spirit sneaked into our camp while we slept."

"Perhaps, but I will wash it again for you, for I should not have left it there with an evil-doer working amongst us. It will not happen again."

Wind Dancer heard the frustration and anger which bubbled within her. He knew it must make her uneasy and unhappy to know she was the target of someone's—or something's—spiteful mischief. He felt those same reactions and emotions simmering within him. He did not want this wicked game to cause problems between them, to make her wish she had never come to live in his camp and tepee. "Do not worry, *mitawin,*"he tried to assure her, "I will find a safe way to uncover the guilty one and halt these mean tricks."

"That will be good, Waci Tate, for it is wrong for me to have to guard our food and possessions in the camp and tepee of a great warrior and the future Red Shield chief. Now I go to bathe and pray. I will return soon and serve your meal." After she ducked and left the dwelling, she looked at her hawk on his post and said, "Guard, Cetan, for an enemy stalks me."

Wind Dancer winced at hearing her parting words. He reminded himself Dewdrops had called him by his name rather than by the endearment she had used since arriving in his camp. He had to solve this mystery fast, as damage was being done daily to his bond with her. How could she accept and respect him as the family protector when she was being attacked so many times by mischief, and in *his* camp?

When he returned from his solitary ritual, Wind Dancer found his meal ready, which told him she had rushed her tasks and communion with the Great Spirit so their dwelling would not remain vulnerable for very long.

She looked at him and said, "My words and mood were bad and I ask you to forgive me for them. I do not blame you for the workings of a trickster or evil spirit. I know you are a man of great honor."

"That pleases me, *mitawin,* and things will be good for you soon."

Yes, for I will make certain of it, she vowed silently. *I have been challenged to a battle, and I will find and defeat that enemy soon.*

Later at the river as she knelt to rewash her husband's shirt, Chumani was joined by Wastemna and her mother. She stole a sideways glance at the pretty young woman who knelt nearby to do the same task for her father. She could not forget her encounter with the war chief's daughter in the forest during her welcome feast. She wondered if Wastemna desired Wind Dancer and was the one behind the malicious episodes. If so, did the woman hope to make her miserable enough to drive her away from him? Had Wastemna forgotten about the sacred vision and impending quest? Did she not fear the wrath of Wakantanka for her misdeeds? What if it was another woman? Or a real evil spirit? Or her husband for some reason?

Wastemna looked at the garment Chumani was scrubbing between her folded fingers. She smiled and said, "This will do better work, Dewdrops; it is called 'soap' and comes from the white man's world. Rub it on the dirty spots and they will come clean quickly and easily."

Chumani forced herself to return the woman's smile. "You are generous to share such magic with me. These dirt and stains do not wish to leave."

"Give it to me, Dewdrops, and I will work on them for a time. Your hands are red and must hurt from your difficult task."

"You are kind, but I will do it," Chumani said as she flexed her fingers.

Wastemna laughed as she quickly seized the fringed shirt from the rock and rubbed a large square of soap upon the spots. "You must not be too proud to accept the help of another, one who is a new friend."

After those words, spoken in a gentle tone, Chumani felt it would be rude to yank her husband's garment away from the smiling woman, especially with Wastemna's mother watching and praising her daughter's skills. She watched Wastemna scrub the shirt, but noticed nothing in her manner to imply she received any pleasure from handling Wind Dancer's garment. When the woman held up the rinsed shirt, Chumani was delighted to observe it had come clean.

"See, the white man's soap has much magic and power. You may keep this one, as I have several more in our tepee. You must not refuse a gift."

"I thank you for the gift and your help, Wastemna."

While Chumani was busy with other chores, Wind Dancer, who had witnessed the river scene, sneaked a walk with his sister in the forest. After swearing her to secrecy and revealing the recent occurrences, he asked, "Did you remain near my tepee on the last sun while we were gone?"

A dismayed Hanmani shook her head. "No, my brother, but I was away for only a short time. I left to fetch more beads from our tepee and to excuse myself in the forest. While I was near your lodge, no one approached her cookfire. I am sorry I did not keep my word and aided the trickster's or evil spirit's mischief. It will not happen again."

"Do not feel bad, my sister. You did not know of the problem. If it did not exist, leaving for a short time would not have mattered. But do not forget to keep your promise of silence. I do not want to offend others with my suspicions or alert the evildoer to my watch for him, or her."

"I will keep my ears and eyes open in search of the wicked person."

"That is good, my sister, but be careful and silent as you do so."

That afternoon, Wind Dancer looked at his wife as she smeared a coneflower and plant oil substance on her hands. He noticed the many scratches upon her fingers. "What injured you, *mitawin?*" he asked.

Chumani was startled by the sound of his voice, as she had not heard him approach. "I quilled a new garment this sun and was careless while I worked. I have tended my wounds and they will heal soon."

"What so distracted you, *mitawin?*" he asked, dreading to learn of another, perhaps more serious, incident.

As she put aside the small wooden bowl in which she had mixed the plant oil and wildflowers, she shrugged and said, "Women's thoughts."

That evasive answer worried him, as did the aura of sadness which surrounded her. "Things you would not speak of to your husband?"

She looked at him and forced a smile. "That is so. Do you not also think things you wish to keep private?"

"That is true," he said, matching her smile. "Now I go

to shoot arrows with Red Feather to practice for the great hunt. We will be at the end of the camp if you need me," he told her before his departure with his bow and filled quiver.

What I need, you cannot give to me, her troubled mind retorted, *I need to leave on the sacred quest to be gone from my enemy's reach. I need to see my family and best friend, to speak with Zitkala about the secrets in my heart. I need to be convinced the vision was real and from Wakantanka.*

What you need to know most is if he can truly come to love, trust, and accept you, her heart refuted. *I must discover if this is my true destiny or if it is only another trick by an evildoer.*

"Grant me the answers I need, Great Spirit," she whispered, "and help us to find each other amidst the shadows which surround us."

That night, Chumani was worried when Wind Dancer did not ask to practice their kissing and touching. She wondered if her prayers of that afternoon had been answered and she was being shown he did not love and desire her as she did him. Yes, she admitted to herself, she loved him and wanted him as she had no other man. Little could make her happier than for him to feel the same way about her.

Wind Dancer lay curled on his left side, his back to her. He sensed her sad mood and assumed she wanted to be left alone. She seemed to be battling doubts and fears, and experiencing loneliness for her loved ones. He had ridden into her life as a whirlwind, and changed her existence forever. He had drawn her into a perilous quest against awesome forces. He had thrust her into a situation which stole her joy and serenity, and forced her to retreat from him just as he was breaking down the last few barriers to total surrender to him and their new destiny. No matter how much he wanted to hold, kiss, and comfort her, he restrained himself. He knew from past experiences that a person had to depend solely on himself for strength and on Wakantanka for guidance and solace. He also knew that love filled his heart for her and soon she would know it, too.

The next day as he was returning from tending his horses in a nearby canyon, Wind Dancer encountered the war chief's daughter as she left the forest with a sling of firewood. When she halted to speak, so did he.

"How is Dewdrops on this gift of a beautiful and warm day?"

"She is fine. She works on beading at our tepee."

"Perhaps I should visit with her, as she seems sad and in need of a friend. Perhaps that is because . . ."

Wind Dancer studied the woman's face. "Why did you halt your words, Wastemna?" he asked.

"Perhaps it is wrong of me to speak them about your wife."

"Speak them," he encouraged.

"It seems she has trouble with her chores. Perhaps that is because she lived more as a hunter-warrior than a woman in her camp. I saw the wild campfire she made, but I did not come to help with it for fear it would shame and anger her. I also saw her bury her soup in the forest. Her hands had many wounds from quills when she fetched water this morning. I would help her learn such tasks better but I fear an offer would insult her. I helped her rewash your shirt on the past sun and gave her the white man's magic soap to make that task easier next time. Does she not like our camp and people?"

He wondered if the female truly had only witnessed those three strange incidents or had instigated them. If it was the latter, why? "What do your last words mean?" he coaxed.

"When many women work together, she holds herself apart and does not smile and talk with us. When she thinks no one is watching her, she eyes us with suspicion, as if we are the enemy and she is only a captive here. Will it help her to accept us if I try harder to become her friend and teach her the things she does not know well?"

Wind Dancer was intrigued by the woman's words, for they contradicted what his mother and sister and others had told him. Was the female lying or was she only mistaken? Was she trying to be helpful or hurtful? "I did not know such things, Wastemna, for she is happy around me. If you speak to her of friendship and help, do so out of the hearing of others. It is unkind to do so while others are nearby."

"Your words are wise, Waci Tate, and I will obey them."

After Chumani halted her exit and remained concealed inside her tepee, she observed the encounter between Wind Dancer and Wastemna. She could not overhear their words at that distance, but she took note of their expressions and body movements. She had made friends with some of the Red Shield women, with Wind Dancer's mother, sister, grandmother, others in their extended family circles, and Hanmani's best friend Macha. Yet, no one could take the place of Zitkala in her heart or could share the confidences and companionship they had. She suspected Wastemna was only pretending to become a friend, as she had glimpsed how the woman watched her slyly. She also saw how Wastemna grabbed every chance she could to be around Wind Dancer, who appeared to be flattered by the woman's attention. Nibbles of jealousy and insecurity flooded her, but she could never reveal those feelings to anyone there, especially to him. She could not help but think that if she were his wife in all ways, she would not experience such foolish worries and his eye would not be roving in another woman's direction. Yet, she did not want to be the one to suggest they mate, or to do so only to obtain his allegiance.

She retrieved her wood sling and untethered her hawk. "Come, Cetan, I have work to do and you must hunt for food." If Wind Dancer or Wastemna noticed her departure, she did not know, as she refused to even glance in their direction.

* * *

Upon his wife's return with a load of wood, Wind Dancer summoned her inside and asked, "Did you move my weapons?" Had she, he worried, seen him with Wastemna and become angry and jealous?

Chumani stared at him in confusion and disbelief. It also pinched her heart for him to even ask her such a doubting question. "No, I did not touch them; that is forbidden."

"They are not as I left them, not as they are always positioned on the *huyamni* outside where they soak up the powers of Mother Earth and Father Sun. Did you bump against them as you did your chores? Do not fear to speak the truth, *mitawin.*"

"If someone touched them, *mihigna,* it was not me. Perhaps an enemy, evil spirit, playing children, or the trickster is to blame."

He tried to keep his voice gentle and his expression tender as he reasoned, "Red Shield children are taught from their first steps not to go near another's tepee or a warrior's weapons, and little ones are never left alone to get into trouble or danger. If it was a cunning foe, he would have stolen them. If it was an evil spirit, he would have broken them or tossed them to the ground. If it was not you, the trickster must create more mischief for us."

It appeared to her as if he doubted her honesty when he uttered the words, "If it was not you." "I did not touch them either on purpose or by accident, *mihigna;* that I swear is true." Anger and disappointment surged within her.

Wind Dancer grasped her negative reaction to his words, but he had been compelled to ask her, as the weapons would need purifying if they had been touched by a female. As a strong gust of wind suddenly and wildly flapped the entrance cover and tugged at the buffalo hides covering the cluster of poles, he said, "Perhaps the wind shook them loose, for it blows hard this sun. Now I go to hunt with Red Feather and my brother. I will bring you meat for your kettle and a hide for a new garment."

"That is good, *mihigna*," she said, taking those words as an apology for his near accusation. Even so, his doubts of her honesty lingered in her mind for the remainder of the day.

That night when Wind Dancer asked if she wanted to kiss and touch, she told him, "I am tired and need sleep to tan the lovely hide you brought to me, *mihigna*; we will do so on the next moon."

On the eighth sun since joining to Wind Dancer, Chumani worked outside her tepee to tan the hide of the deer he had slain on the past one.

She knew the procedure well. A hide or pelt was either pegged fur side down or was stretched taut and secured to a wooden frame. Fat and bits of meat were scraped off with a sharp tool. Afterward, it was rubbed with animal grease and brains to soften and condition it. Tanning was done with sumac and with buffalo brains, liver, and fat. Then it was stretched out to dry as snugly as possible so it would not curl at the edges or pucker along its surface. Last, it was twisted, pulled, and rubbed for a lengthy time to soften it even more.

It was late afternoon when she went to fetch water and wash up at the river. As she did so, she glanced skyward to see if she sighted Cetan who had been released to hunt fresh prey because she was there to guard her dwelling, and he had learned the area from many past hunts.

Chumani entered her lodge to find Wastemna preparing to leave it. As both women halted in midstep, Chumani noticed how nervous the intruder was. "Do you sneak into my tepee to cause mischief again?" Chumani raged. "Were the other tricks not enough to appease your bad feelings for me?"

Through the open flap, Wastemna saw Wind Dancer

approach and stop nearby. "I did not come to cause trouble for you, Dewdrops. Your words are cold and cruel, and your heart is not kind. I came to bring fruit bread and a *wanapin* I beaded for you with your name symbol as a show of friendship. I do not understand your hostile words and feelings for me and my people."

Chumani glanced at a place near the campfire and saw the items the woman had mentioned, the bread and necklace with a yellow dewdrop in its center. "Why did you not leave your gifts outside, as it is not the custom to enter another's tepee when they are gone or the flap is closed?"

"I wanted to surprise and please you, to show you I accept you into our band and wish to become your friend. Why do you treat me so badly? What have I said or done to offend you?"

"If I spoke in haste and wronged you, Wastemna, I ask your forgiveness and understanding. A trickster or evil spirit has done wicked things to me," Chumani said more kindly, then detailed the four evil actions.

"You think I am to blame for such mean things?" Wastemna asked when Chumani concluded her explanation.

Chumani observed her look of astonishment, but believed it was faked. "I did not know why you entered my tepee without permission, so I thought you might have come to do more mischief while I was gone."

"I have not done such wicked things, Dewdrops, and I would not do such things, for you are the wife of our next chief and you are the vision woman. Since our tepee is nearby, I will keep alert for the one who is to blame. Can we not bury the knife between us and become friends? I will tell no one of your bad words to me, for I understand why you spoke them, and they would cause trouble for you with others."

Since the female had a logical excuse for her presence, Chumani felt it unwise to call her a liar. She decided it was best to pretend she believed her. "Your words please me and your heart is kind. We will become friends. And I thank you for your gifts and generosity."

Wastemna smiled at Chumani's words. "I must go and do my chores. My eyes and ears will remain open at all times for trouble. Do not worry, Dewdrops, such evil will be exposed soon, for your husband is a man of great skills and wits. If you have not done so, you must tell him your suspicions so he will not think badly of your actions."

"My husband knows of such troubles and knows I am not to blame for them." For a brief time, Chumani was tempted to claw the feigned smile from the woman's lips, and was surprised to experience that dark urge.

"That is good. If there is anything I can do or say to make things better for you, ask it of me or of the women in your new family circle."

After the war chief's daughter left the tepee and Wind Dancer entered, he asked his wife, "Why do you mistrust Wastemna? I overheard your talk."

"Her words roll sweet as honey from her lips, but I do not believe them. I have seen how she looks at me and . . ." She halted before saying *you.* "And I have not forgotten her action on my first moon here."

"What do you mean, *mitawin?*"

Chumani disclosed the encounter with Wastemna in the forest during the welcome feast. "Her lodge is close to ours, so it would be easy for her to be the culprit. You are right; I do not like her or trust her."

Wind Dancer wondered if his wife viewed Wastemna as a rival for his affections, but thought it best not to pose that query to her. If Dewdrops was right about Wastemna being to blame for the mischief, how could he ensnare the woman in the act?

Midmorning on the following day as she was about to head into the forest to gather wood, Chumani heard Winona give forth a muffled scream. She flung down the wood sling and returned to her tepee, where she grabbed her bow and two arrows. One arrow she placed between her teeth and the other she nocked in readiness for trouble. As quietly as possible, she hurried to the tepee beside hers and peered inside. Her scanning gaze locked on Winona as the older woman stood petrified near the dwelling's rear. Winona nodded toward the peril located between them; that and the ominous sound of rapid rattling drew Chumani's gaze to the coiled and agitated snake.

"Do not move or speak," she cautioned in a whisper. The creature obviously had sensed her arrival and repositioned itself to face her. Chumani froze in place until it was still again except for the swiftly moving clattering rings at the end of its tail. Its fat size and number of rattles told her it had been around for many circles of the seasons. Slowly and while keeping her gaze fastened to the viper, she stepped sidewise near the tepee's base. When she was between Winona and the snake and had backed her up as much as possible, she tried to force the creature to wriggle out the entrance by tossing several objects at it and then by throwing two toward the open flap to draw its attention there. The creature not only refused to be lured to escape but also made it apparent he was going to advance and strike.

"Forgive me, Great Spirit," she murmured sadly, "for I must take its life to save my second mother." She drew back on the bowstring and let the first arrow fly, striking the snake in its largest section and pinning it to the ground, though it thrashed wildly for freedom. Without delay, she nocked her second arrow and pinned its head to the ground. She hurried forward, withdrew a knife from her waist sheath, and ended its life. She cut off the length of rattles and gave them to Winona, who embraced and thanked her.

"I did not want to kill him, but he would not leave and was preparing to attack," Chumani explained. "I will feed him to Cetan so his sacrifice will not go to waste."

Hanmani returned from gathering wood and was told the frightful story in haste. She, too, embraced and thanked Chumani for her brave deed. She rushed outside to fetch her father and brothers, as she had seen them approaching with the game from their morning hunt.

The three men joined the women and listened to the same tale as an excited Hanmani told.

As Chumani was being embraced and thanked and praised by Rising Bear and War Eagle, Wind Dancer looked around to make certain no mate or offspring was lurking about to cause trouble later and made a shocking discovery. Until he could speak with his wife privately, he secreted the item beneath his shirt. He moved closer to the group, told them no other creature lurked inside, then observed his wife furtively.

"I thank Wakantanka for bringing you to us, Dewdrops, for you have saved the light of my eye and warmth of my heart," the chief said in an emotion-choked voice as he handed her an eagle feather he had retrieved from a pouch nearby. "This is your reward for such a great coup."

"You are kind, my second father, and I shall wear it in honor. I, too, thank the Great Spirit for slowing my body this sun. If He had not done so, I would have been in the forest gathering wood and not heard her cry."

They talked for a short while longer before Chumani left to finish her daily tasks, taking the snake with her to give to her hawk to devour.

Wind Dancer followed her into their tepee and asked, "Why did you take your bow and two arrows when you rushed to Mother's lodge?"

Chumani was baffled by his odd tone and expression. "When I heard a scream, I sensed trouble or danger must be nearby. I did not take the creature's life quickly or easily, *mihigna,* and I asked Wakantanka's forgiveness for doing so. Did you not hear how I tried to force him to flee, but he would not go? Was there another path I should have walked? Did I displease you?"

"I am happy you saved the life of my mother, and you showed great skill and courage in doing so. Soon, all who live in our camp will hear of your good deed and prowess." Was that, he worried, a possible motive for creating the perilous situation? No, surely she would not endanger his mother.

"Perhaps that is why the Great Spirit guided him there, to show your people I am skilled and worthy to be your companion on the sacred quest." When he continued to look at her strangely, she asked, "What troubles your heart and mind about this deed, *mihigna?* It is in your voice and gaze."

Wind Dancer withdrew the item from beneath his shirt, held it up before her, and queried, "Is this your *wazuha?*"

Chumani looked at the beaded pouch. "It is mine," she said. "Why did you take it and hide it beneath your garment?"

"I found it in my mother's lodge behind a backrest. Signs within the *wazuha* say the snake was kept there for a long time and crawled out of it." As he spoke, he opened the pouch and dumped the dark droppings into the palm of his hand. He watched her stare at the small black balls, then lift her gaze to look at him questioningly.

"Do you ask if I captured the snake and put him there?"

"I only ask how and why your *wazuha* was there?"

"I do not know. I have not missed it. I did not take it there. Who would want to frighten or harm your mother?" Chumani's gaze darkened and narrowed. "Or perhaps it was used to make me appear to blame? It is another wicked trick of the *silwaecon* or *wicagnayesa.* Who was found in our tepee on the last sun?" she reminded him.

"Do you say Wastemna stole it, captured the snake, and placed it in my mother's lodge?" After his wife half-nodded, he considered the accusation before concluding. "She lacks the courage and skill to do so."

Chumani knew he referred to entrapping the viper. "When one's heart and mind are controlled by evil thoughts and feelings, one can do and say many things we find hard to believe and accept. It does not require much skill or courage to kneel upon a high rock and use a stick with a thong loop to slip over a snake's neck. Do you forget this is the season when they leave their winter holes and lay about in the sun, making them easy prey?"

"I have not forgotten."

"Why did you not show the pouch and question me about it before the others? Did you fear they would also doubt me and wish to punish me?"

"No, I did not want them to know of the mischievous intent. I did not wish to frighten and sadden my mother or to worry my father. Until we learn the face of the trickster, I do not want such matters known to my family or my people. I must go speak with Grandfather in private and ask him to seek answers from Wakantanka."

"That is good, *mihigna*, for these tricks could cause much trouble if not halted soon. I will do my chores while Cetan guards our tepee and you seek guidance from the Wise One and Great Spirit."

Distracted by her troubled thoughts, Chumani walked very deep into the forest as she gathered wood there. After the sling was filled and she straightened, she gasped in surprise to see she was not alone, and that person was heavily armed and close by.

Chapter
Eight

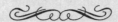

"Where have your skills and instincts gone in such a short
time, Dewdrops, for you did not sense my presence?"

Chumani smiled and playfully scolded, "Zitkala, you
must not sneak up on me and tease me unfairly." She
knew why Cetan had not sounded a warning—for her best
friend's face and scent were familiar to him.

The two women hugged and laughed in elation.

"I have missed you and my heart soars with joy to see
you," Chumani murmured as she grasped Zitkala's hands
and held them as they faced each other. "You must tell
me all that has happened in our camp since I left my
family's tepee," she coaxed, eager for the news of her
loved ones.

"Your parents did not want me to visit too soon; they
feared it would make you more lonely for us. I was sneaking
close to camp only to see how you are doing here and I
was not going to show my face to you, but I saw you enter
the forest alone and sensed you needed me. Was I wrong?"

Chumani's smile faded as she shook her head and admitted, "No, my friend, and I am glad you came. My heart
aches at our separation. I did not know our shaman's
dream meant I would be taken away from our people and

mated to a stranger in another band, and so far from my camp."

"I am sorry I was gone when you were forced to join him and depart. It was hard to face such tasks alone, was it not?"

"That is true. I needed you there to give me strength and guidance. Such big changes in my life have been difficult."

"Your parents told me of the Red Shield shaman's vision that took you away from us. It is good to have an alliance with a strong band during such troubled times, but I wish it had not been your duty to bond us together. When and where do you ride to face that dangerous challenge?"

"I do not know."

"What must you do on the sacred journey to defeat our enemies?"

"I do not know."

"Are you happy in this camp and with your new husband?"

Chumani took a deep breath and released it swiftly. "I do not know. At times, things are good; at others, they are bad and strange."

Zitkala perceived her best friend's sadness and confusion. She placed her arm across Chumani's waist and guided them to a large rock where they sat down. "What do such words mean?"

As they had never kept secrets between them, Chumani told her about Wind Dancer's astonishing arrival and the talks with her father and mother. She related the details of their joining ceremony, their first night together, her welcome into his camp and family, the many deeds of mischief, and all the indications that her husband doubted her behavior. She also divulged the truth about their lack of intimacy and the alleged reasons for their long restraint.

Zitkala reminded Chumani of her desire for Wind Dancer when she saw him at the annual trading fair, in the Brave Heart forest, and at Bear Butte. "Why do you resist becoming his wife in all ways when your heart and body have yearned for his many times in the past?" she asked. "Did you not say his touch and kisses are pleasing? Did you not say he is gentle and kind?"

"That is true, but something stops me from yielding to him. It is hard to trust a stranger who raises wariness within me. I fear his unknown power over me; I fear it will change all I am and must be to face our challenge. What if seeing me in the forest and before his visionquest are what placed me in it, not Wakantanka?"

"Even so, that does not change Sees-Through-Mist's dream. The owl messenger told him you would mate soon and would do a sacred task to save our people. Is that not what the Red Shield shaman also saw in his vision? Did you and your parents not tell me Waci Tate saw a dewdrop and hawk in his vision and painted those signs upon his new war shield and his face?"

"That is true," Chumani reasoned, "but what if Wind Dancer is not the man from our Wise One's dream? What if an evil force has tricked me and them to lure me away from my rightful mate and our task together? What if Wakantanka is warning me of a mistake through those incidents and they are not the spiteful work of Wastemna or a *silwaecon*? Do not forget Wind Dancer and his grandfather saw me and Cetan at the sacred mountain during their ritual; that could have placed us in their minds before they entered the Spirit World and some force kept us in them. Even though they believe in their visions, what if they are not the true words from Wakantanka?"

"Perhaps Wind Dancer only joined to you to honor his shaman's vision," Zitkala speculated, "but he thinks you are unworthy of his touch or he desires another woman among his people. It is unnatural for a man not to take possession of such a beautiful wife after sharing a tepee and sleeping mat with her for so many moons. Is that not true?"

"I do not know."

"If his shaman's vision is real, do you think your husband tests you with mischief, or the war chief's daughter or another woman tricks you?"

"I do not know."

Zitkala placed her arm across Chumani's shoulder. "You have answered me that way many times, Dewdrops. It is unlike you to be so doubtful and uneasy, or to lower your guard so far. What if I had been an enemy?"

"Cetan sits in the tree above us and would have attacked you or given me a warning as you sneaked up on me."

Zitkala glanced upward, smiled, and greeted the hawk who kept cocking his head and blinking his tawny eyes as he observed them and guarded Chumani. As if he understood, the hawk sent forth a shrill cry and fluttered his wings before he flew off to hunt. "Is he happy here?" Zitkala asked.

"He has accepted his new home and territory and no one bothers him, which I wish was true for me. It is good Waci Tate did not force me to part with him, for it would be easier to cut off a finger than to lose him, just as it pained my heart to lose you."

"You have not lost me, Dewdrops. We will remain best friends until we walk Mother Earth no more. Then we will travel the Ghost Trail together. Soon we will be together again on the grasslands. But it troubles me to see you so unhappy."

"Do not worry, Zitkala, the Great Spirit will protect and guide me. I will keep alert for more mischief, and Cetan will watch over me. Do not tell Mother and Father how you found me; it would make them sad. Besides," she added with a smile, "it calms me to see and speak with you. This is good medicine for me and heals my troubled spirit."

"It is good medicine for *my* suffering heart and spirit."

"Why do you not return to the camp with me where we can talk while I do my chores? You can sleep in our tepee and leave on the new sun."

"Since there is trouble between you and your husband, it would not be wise to have me stay there. It would look as if I was sent to check on you and them. It is best I come and go in secret."

"Your words are wise, my friend. Now, tell me all that has happened in our camp since my departure," Chumani coaxed again, then listened with great enjoyment until it was time for Zitkala to slip away.

While they were lying upon their sleeping mat without touching or speaking, Wind Dancer realized that his wife had been acting distant and unusually quiet since that morning. He assumed her reserved behavior was caused by his unintended accusation earlier that day and the continued bouts of harmful mischief. He thought it best to leave her be until she settled down and they could talk again.

The next morning after returning from an early hunt, Wind Dancer was looking for Chumani to tell her about the game she needed to prepare when he encountered Wastemna as she returned to her tepee from fetching water. He asked the smiling woman if she had seen his wife. He noticed a strange look on her face as she glanced around as if to see if anyone was nearby and appeared reluctant to respond. "What holds your tongue, Wastemna? Have you seen Dewdrops? Has more trouble struck while I was away? Speak, now," he said in a commanding tone and with a stern expression. He watched her glance around once more, then answer just above a whisper.

"Perhaps she sneaked into the forest to meet with the man from her tribe as she did on the last sun. Perhaps he stayed nearby during the night so they could see each other again before he returns home."

Astonished by that unexpected reply, Wind Dancer scowled and asked in a sullen tone, "What do your strange words mean?"

"When I saw her leave camp, I followed her, for I did not think it was safe for her to be in the forest alone. She looked sad and distracted, so I feared her guard was down and she would not hear an enemy's approach. She is the wife of our next chief and the vision-woman, so she must be protected. I also hoped it would give us time and privacy to talk so we can become friends; and if I was with her and more mischief was done, she would know it was not my doing. Before I could catch up to her, I saw her meet with a man. They embraced many times and held hands as they spoke, and the hawk knew him. I could not get close enough to overhear their words, for I feared they would see me or the hawk would either attack me as a threat or warn them of an intruder. It was a tall man with a plain face and garments, but he must have been from her band, for it was clear she knew and loved him from her smiles and touches. Yet, often she appeared sad and I saw her wipe tears from her cheeks, and the man placed his arm around her and drew her to his body to comfort her. After their talk, she returned to camp and he slipped into the forest.''

Anger and jealousy washed over Wind Dancer, reactions he struggled to conceal and to master. Surely, he reasoned, Wastemna would not speak falsely about a matter he could investigate for himself. He might believe she was mistaken if his wife had told him about the meeting and had not behaved so strangely last night. "Are you sure that is what you saw? Are you sure it was Dewdrops with him?"

"I am sure. I swear it upon my life and honor."

"Why did you not come to me on the last sun and reveal this to me?"

"I feared you would not believe me and you would hate me. I do not know how strong her love medicine is over you. I swear it is the truth."

"Have you told another of what you saw?"

"No, for it is your right and duty to deal with an unfaithful wife. Please do not hate me because I was the one who was forced to reveal this matter to you."

"Do not worry, Wastemna, for it is not our way to hate the one who brings bad news, only hate the words told to him. But I am certain it must have been a friend, not a lover, you saw with Chumani."

"If that is true, Waci Tate, why did she not tell you about him?"

"I do not know, but I am sure her reason is a good one."

"I pray your words are true so your heart will not be pained again with the loss of another wife and the Great Spirit is forced to punish her for dishonoring you and the sacred vision."

Wind Dancer took Chumani for a walk in the forest after her return to their tepee a short time later, as he did not want others to overhear his words. "When you joined to me, you did not tell me your heart and body belong to another man. Is sadness and revenge why you hold back from me and why you behave badly to Wastemna and other women here and why you create such mischief in our lives? Do you hate me and wish to make me unhappy so I will send you away so you can return home to him? Why do you betray me and the sacred vision for your lost love?"

Chumani was hurt and baffled. "I do not behave badly in your camp or to your people. I seek no revenge on you with the mischief which attacks us; it is not my doing. I am a good wife to you in all ways but one; that was your choice to make and I agreed with it. My heart loves and my body desires no other man, not my first mate or another from my camp or in any camp. Why do you think such wicked things about me? Your words are cruel and untrue."

Her anguished reaction cut into his heart, but he was compelled to ask, "Who was the man you met with and embraced in the forest on the last sun? The secret visit you did not reveal to me last night?"

"Do you spy on me?" Chumani asked in shock. "Do you not trust me?"

"No, I do not watch you, but another saw you meet him there and told me of it this sun. Is he why you were distant with me last night and do not wish to lie beneath me?"

"The person who told you I met a man was mistaken. It was Zitkala, my best friend. She approached me in the forest and we talked for a long time. She is a female warrior and hunter, as I was before you claimed me."

"It was not a woman Wastemna sighted with you." He saw Chumani's gaze narrow and chill at the name he mentioned. He watched her withdraw the sharp weapon from her waist sheath. He wondered if she was going to challenge him to a death fight or try to slay him and escape, and knew she would not be successful with either attempt. She placed the blade between her teeth and spoke around its edge as she refuted his words, her dark gaze drilling into his watchful one as she performed the swearing custom.

"I bite-the-knife, Waci Tate, and swear: I speak the truth. It was Zitkala, a woman, my best friend since we were but a few circles of the seasons old. We trained, hunted, rode, and fought together as you do with Red Feather." Chumani removed the weapon and continued to speak. "She came to bring me news of my family, friends, and people. Do you not recall she was away from our camp when you came to claim me? I did not ask her to enter this camp and our tepee; I wished to speak with her alone. Zitkala has taken no mate, for her face, body, and ways are more of a man's than a woman's. You can accept or refuse my words, but I do not speak with a split tongue. I do my best to follow the commands of my husband, father, Great Spirit, and the sacred vision. If you do not believe me or you are displeased with me, speak the parting words before our tepee flap and I will be free to return to my people." She knew all he had to do was take that position and announce she was no longer his mate and their joining bond was broken. Yet, deep inside, she prayed he would not do so.

As Wind Dancer studied her and considered her explanation, Chumani wondered if he was seeking an excuse to get rid of her and to save face while doing so by making it appear her fault. When he started to speak, she held up her hand and told him, "Do not speak while your heart and head are filled with mistrust and anger or while mine are too filled with them to listen. Think upon what you want to do; then we will talk. Now I go for a ride to calm myself; I will return before night comes. Then, this destructive and hurtful matter must be settled between us for all time."

Wind Dancer thought it was best to let her leave for a while to allow both of them time to clear their heads and cool their hot feelings. He also needed to decide how to repair the obvious damage he had done to their relationship, as he was almost certain she spoke the truth. It would be too easy for him to check out her story for her to lie to him; and by doing so, she would be dishonored in her camp and banished from it. Yet, his fear of loving, trusting, and then losing her kept a tiny doubt nibbling at his mind.

After Chumani left him standing there, Wind Dancer turned and sighted his mother and sister nearby in the bushes. He realized the two women had happened upon the scene by accident and had remained quiet to prevent disturbing and shaming him as he quarreled with his wife.

Winona approached him, placed a hand on his forearm, and said, "You must go after her, my son, and make peace with her. Time and distance can become your enemies and slay all her good feelings for you. Do you not know Dewdrops has great love in her heart for you and great pride in being your wife and vision companion? Do you not know she would not speak false words to you? Do you know the Great Spirit would not give you a bad wife? Go before you lose her forever and glorious victory is denied to us."

Wind Dancer knew those words were true, and hearing them sent a surge of joy and energy throughout his body. He quickly prayed that he had not destroyed her good feelings for him and driven her away forever. He smiled, embraced his mother, and hurried to his tepee. He realized she had taken nothing except her horse and Cetan, which he considered a favorable sign she planned to return. He gathered his weapons and other needed supplies before he headed to his horse to mount and pursue her.

As he loaded his possessions on the animal, Red Feather

joined him. Wind Dancer told his best friend of the misunderstanding and that he was looking for Chumani.

Red Feather grinned and said, "She rode that way."

Wind Dancer's gaze followed Red Feather's gesture toward the south. "I go to spend private time with her. I will not return until she is mine. Guard my family and our camp, and pray I find victory with her."

"It will be so, *mitakola.*"

In the forest, Hanmani murmured, "Love should not bring sadness and trouble, my mother. Why does it do so for my brother?"

Winona looked at her youngest and only female child whose name meant To-walk-in-the-night and said, "They are still strangers in many ways, and they endured great losses long ago which make them wary of each other and their feelings. They fear to show their love and desire; they fear the other does not feel the same way; their minds fear to accept and trust what they know in their hearts to be true. If they listen to each other with their hearts open wide, all will be good between them when they return."

"Do you think so, Mother?"

"Yes, my beloved daughter, I am certain of that, for my father, our wise shaman, saw it in his vision."

Winona's mind added, *One sun, you will learn such things for yourself, my beloved daughter, for I saw it in a dream on the night you left my body thirteen winters past. When that season comes, you will find great love, but the trail you must ride toward it will be a difficult and dangerous one, just as it is with your brother and Dewdrops.*

Chumani halted her horse and stared at the ground as her mind filled with troubling thoughts. She had spoken too quickly and harshly, for his misconception was normal, whether he or another person witnessed her meeting with Zitkala, especially since she had kept it a secret from him. By doing so, she had given him just reason to doubt her and be angry. He had never met her best friend, so he

was not familiar with Zitkala's mannish looks. She should
have remained in camp and settled the matter with him.
It was wrong of her to blame him and to leave.

As she heard Cetan's shrill cries overhead, she glanced
upward and noticed the sky was darkening rapidly and
ominously and the force of the wind was increasing in
strength and purpose. Already, limbs shook, grass swayed,
and wildflowers trembled in anticipation of the brewing
storm. She reasoned the Great Spirit was displeased with
her and was trying to warn her to hurry back to his camp.
Yet, she had noticed the signs too late. She knew the conditions would soon make it too dangerous to be outside and
she must seek shelter fast. Recalling she had sighted an
area where caves and rock ledges were located, she headed
in that direction, calling out to Cetan to follow her to seek
cover from the weather's fury.

Wind Dancer tracked and located Chumani, then left
the grassy terrain to ride into the tree-blanketed foothills
which swept upward into the sacred mountains. He
assumed she was seeking protective shelter in one of the
Paha Sapa's canyons from the approaching storm and
hoped he could catch up to her before it struck. When
the trail signs indicated she had dismounted, he reasoned
she could not be far ahead of him; her destination must
be a nearby cave or a position beneath low and wide overhanging ledges of black rock, he decided. To keep from
frightening her, he shouted her name to make her aware
of his presence.

Chumani entered a cave with a load of wood she had
gathered for a fire. Only minutes later she heard Wind
Dancer's call followed by a peal of thunder which roared
across the terrain, a dazzling display of lightning. Her heart
leapt with happiness. She tossed down the wood, rushed
to the cave's mouth, and halted there to look for him.
Lightning flashed in jagged lines and in brilliant multi-
branched forks across the ever-darkening sky, and rumbling thunder chased it at a swift pace as she sighted him

coming out of the treeline on the other side of the clearing before her. She smiled and waved as she yelled for him to bring his horse into the cave and to join her there before a deluge began. She watched him smile and wave in return, causing her heart to beat faster with excitement and joy.

Then two perils struck like a double-edged knife. Suddenly his horse snorted and whinnied, reared on its hind legs, and pawed the air with its forelegs, its eyes wide in panic as it yanked wildly on the tether clutched in Wind Dancer's left hand. That unexpected action caused her husband to stumble aside on loose rocks and fall to his knees. As he hit the ground, a strong wind gusted briskly and blew dirt into his eyes, causing him to jerk his free hand toward them. Yet, it was the threat beyond him that almost petrified her into stone, the reason for the horse's terror: a grizzly had topped the low hill behind them, halted there, and was eyeing the two targets with great interest. She knew her horse was safe in the cave, but her husband and his mount were in terrible danger. Although the massive beast appeared to be slow and lazy when it ambled along, she knew he could charge with awesome agility and speed and could slash open its prey with one swipe of those long and deadly claws.

"*E'tonwan! Matohata!*" She shouted for him to look out because a grizzly was heading his way. "*Inahni sni yo.*" She warned him not to run, as that would be considered as a challenge to the giant bear.

"*Tokahan hwo?*" he called out, asking where it was since his vision was blurred.

As he rubbed his eyes and shook his head, she realized he was temporarily blinded by the dirt and was vulnerable to a lethal attack. "*Uyelo; inila yanka yo.*" She cautioned him to be quiet because the creature was advancing on him. "*Lecetkiya.*" She asked him to come to her. She hurried into the cave and retrieved her bow and several arrows, elated she had brought them along. With one shaft nocked and holding two between her teeth, she rushed outside and made her way to the right of the entrance.

Chumani glanced at Wind Dancer as the frightened horse shifted about and kept bumping into him. She wished he had his war mount with him, as that animal was braver and more nimble-footed than his daily riding horse. Her gaze darted to the bear with its dark and sleek hide. She saw the muscular hunch between his powerful shoulders ripple with its movements. It paused to stand to sniff the air and to see better, its height and size enormous and intimidating. She knew her injured husband could not outrun the swift and keen-eyed creature or successfully battle it while hurt, though she was certain he could do so under different circumstances.

She glanced at Wind Dancer again. He had drawn his knife, but it was obvious he had not recovered his vision from his gestures. She shouted to the bear to seize its attention and hopefully to draw it away from its intended prey until her husband could see. The grizzly halted and looked at her as she continued to yell at it, wave her arms, and then throw rocks at it. He growled and made a short bluff charge at her. She repeated her actions and increased the volume of her shouts. When Wind Dancer yelled for her to cease her dangerous ploy, she made them louder and incessant so her voice would drown out his and keep the ferocious grizzly's focus on her.

Chumani fired an arrow at the bear and struck him in his left shoulder. The angered beast slapped at the shaft and broke it off near his body. When she pelted him with rocks and danced around on the canyon floor, he made a charge toward her using another brief burst of speed. His body jiggled after he made an abrupt halt about ten horse lengths beyond her. As the weather worsened rapidly, the creature stared at her, assessing her strengths and weaknesses. As she watched him extend his thick neck, flatten his ears, take a stiff-legged stance, and lock his intense gaze on her, she realized she had succeeded in becoming his new target. When he shook his body to loosen it and growled again, she knew the fierce beast

would lower its head next and race toward her in an unre-
lenting attack.

Chumani prayed for skill and courage as she whirled
and scrambled up a nearby incline toward scattered rocks
which would delay the awesome predator's approach and
give her a chance to fire her other two arrows at him, at
closer range. She doubted three would slay the animal,
but perhaps they would injure him enough to slow him
down so they could escape or would cause him to loose
interest in her and Wind Dancer.

Leaning against a black rock for balance on the slippery
terrain, she fired a second arrow into him as he reared to
his full height to get a better view of her. She struck what
she knew was a vulnerable spot at the base of his throat,
yet, he also snapped off that arrow and kept advancing as
if it were nothing more than a small insect bite, even with
blood seeping down his chest and shoulder. She scooped
up several large rocks and pelted his head with them,
hoping to strike his eyes and damage his keen vision. She
jumped as radiant lightning blazed across the darkened
setting and almost ear-splitting thunder boomed around
them and seemingly caused the cliffside and ground to
tremble. Gusting winds blew hair into her face and obstructed her line of vision, forcing her to use one hand to
grasp it and hold it behind her neck.

Suddenly Cetan sent forth many shrill cries and dove
for the grizzly's face, using his talons to slash at its eyes.
The bear bellowed in rage, swiped at the hawk with sharp
claws, and stumbled on the precarious terrain as it did
so. Still, Cetan persisted with swoops around the animal's
massive head and cleverly eluded those lethal paws. Chumani fired a third and last arrow into the bear's chest,
increasing its pain and rage. As the creature ignored the
hawk and came toward her, she tried to scramble backward
up the slope. She only covered a short distance when she
lost her footing, her rear hit the ground, and she began
to slide toward her fierce attacker's gaping mouth and

huge white teeth. *Help us, Great Spirit,* she prayed silently, *so we may live to honor the sacred visionquest!*

As the grizzly rose on its hind legs, lifted his arms skyward, tossed back its head, and roared as loud as the thunder, a resplendent lightning bolt struck it full force in its heart. The blow was so powerful that it knocked the bear backward and sent it toppling to the canyon floor. Chumani stared at the scene in amazement; it was as if the Great Spirit had slain his forest creature to save their lives. She saw Cetan alight on the fallen beast's chest as if to check it for signs of life. As if finding none, the hawk flew to a spruce and perched on a large limb while Chumani made her wobbly descent to the massive heap of deep brown fur.

Wind Dancer joined her, a bow with a nocked arrow in one hand and still rubbing his eyes with the other. He nudged the grizzly with his foot and knew it was dead. His heart still pounded within his chest from the fear Chumani would be killed or mauled. He had been desperate to rescue her and had reacted as fast as his disabled condition would allow. He had never felt so helpless in the face of such great peril, and he would have been to blame for her death or injury after driving her from the safety of their camp. His watering and scratchy eyes went to his wife to make certain she was not injured.

He smiled when she looked at him and he said, "Wakantanka did not wish us to join Him on this sun. He asked Wakinyan to hurl a lightning lance into the forest warrior's heart to halt his attack. You challenged a mighty force with great skill and courage, *mitawin,* as did Cetan. I wish my eyes had been clear so I could better witness such a great show of prowess."

Chumani hoped his pride was not bruised by her taking charge of the perilous situation and by the vulnerability his temporary blindness had caused. "Wakantanka works in mysterious ways, so I do not know why He chose me and Cetan to fight this battle for us," she said gently.

"Perhaps it was to show you a way to use that dirt trick when we challenge the Crow in the coming suns."

Wind Dancer was grateful for her words of support. "That is true. You risked your life to save me, and I thank you."

"Just as you would have endangered yours for me, as you did when you challenged two Bird warriors in the Brave Heart forest, and I thank you for saving me that sun. If you had not come when you did, I would have been slain or captured and they would have . . . done great harm to me. The storm is upon us," she remarked as wind yanked at her hair and garments, along with the greenery around them. As the lightning and thunder increased in frequency, she added, "Soon night will blanket the land. I will take your horse into the cave while you pray for the bear's spirit and sacrifice. If your eyes still suffer, I will return to help guide you there."

As he wiped away moisture on his lashes and cheeks, he said, "They are angry at the attack upon them and send forth water like a slow rain, but my vision clears slowly. I will join you there soon. There is food, water, and a sleeping hide on my horse. We will camp in the cave this moon, for we have much to say to each other and need privacy for our words."

"Yes, *mihigna*, there is much to say, for another sun must not rise before there is peace between us or we will fail in the sacred task before us."

Chapter
Nine

Chumani used water from the bladder bag to flush any lingering dirt from her husband's eyes and told him to keep them closed for a time so they could rest while she built a fire and prepared their food. As she worked, she allowed her gaze to drift slowly over him from head to feet as he remained prone on the buffalo hide which she had spread on the cave floor. She liked his bold features and strong body, and was tempted to trace her fingers over them to test their magic. She liked the way his ebony hair shone in the firelight, the gleam in his dark eyes when he was aroused by her, the feel of his flesh when they touched, and the stimulating way he had kissed her on other moons. She craved to have those full lips roving her face and body, to have him within her. Surely it was time for them to bond together as husband and wife.

Wind Dancer sensed her intense scrutiny of him and found it exciting. He heard the change in her breathing and how her hands had stilled their task. He could almost taste the sweetness of her mouth from vivid memories of past kisses. He longed to trail his fingers over her skin and longed to possess her fully. If he reached out to her, he wondered, would she yield or retreat?

Almost enthralled by his potent allure, she asked him the question which haunted her: "Does your keen mind not tell you Wastemna desires you and speaks badly of me so she can win you for herself?" Without waiting for an answer, she reiterated her innocence and honesty. "I am not to blame for the mischief in our tepee and it *was* my best friend, Zitkala, a female, I met with in the forest. I would not betray or shame you."

Wind Dancer sat up and faced her, their gazes fusing. He was convinced it was concern for their relationship which spurred her words, not feminine jealousy. "Her tricks and lies will fail to dupe and capture me, Dewdrops, for I have no such feelings for her, or for any other woman in my camp, only for my wife whose words I believe. I do not know why the Great Spirit chose us to become mates and visionquest companions, but we must obey His commands."

His words appeased her worries. "That is true, *mihigna.*"

Wind Dancer gazed into her eyes before he murmured in a voice made husky with deep emotion, "I trust you, accept you, and want you as my wife. I hunger for you as a man hungers for a woman; I have desired you since the first sun I saw you in the Brave Heart forest and did not know if you were flesh and bone or spirit come to help me. I did not wish to force you to lie with me upon my sleeping mat, but I yearn for you to do so. I wanted you to come to me of your own free will, not out of duty to the Creator and His vision. Perhaps my restraint has caused you to believe I do not desire you or desire another in your place; that is not true. Do you also trust, accept, and want me as your mate in all ways? Do you also hunger for me as a man, as a husband?" He almost held his breath as he awaited her reaction and reply.

Chumani was thrilled and relieved by his stirring words. "When we joined in my camp," she began her reply, "I did not know you and wished for us to get closer before we mated on the sleeping mat; in the past nine moons, we have learned much about each other and have become friends. I also was afraid to lie with you as your wife, for it was bad with Dull Star on the mat. I feared, if it was the same with you, it would cause trouble between us; I do not believe that will happen."

Wind Dancer's loins flamed with desire, his heart pounded with joy. "Do not worry, Dewdrops, for I will not hurt or shame you there. I hold many strong feelings in my heart for you, and I am certain more will come in the moons before us, as it should be. I did not feel this way about my first wife, and I feared your powerful pull on me if you did not feel the same as I do."

"I have never felt this strange way about a man, but I know what we share is strong and special, for the Great Spirit put us together and knows all things. As time passes, I am sure He will place great love in our hearts for each other, for desire already dwells within our bodies."

"That is wise and true, *mitawin.*"

Chumani savored his touch as he caressed her cheek. She knew that an evil force could separate them at any time, so she was compelled to have him for as long as they walked the face of Mother Earth and breathed the Great Spirit's air. He had proven to her he was a perfect match for her in all ways but one; and soon that question would be answered for her. They had to become one before more mischief occurred and put distance between them forever. "I did not mean to make it hard on you, *mihigna,* and you have kept your word of honor to be patient. When you are ready to lie with me, I am ready to lie with you."

Almost afraid to trust his hearing, Wind Dancer took a deep breath and asked, "Do you mean on this moon? Here? Now?"

Chumani smiled and nodded, assured they would not be disturbed with a fierce storm raging outside the cozy cave. "It is time we become mates in more than words spoken before our peoples."

Wind Dancer admired her honesty and courage. As if two different desert winds, they had blown into each other's lives when their hearts were frozen by great losses and

by an icy desire for revenge on the Crow warriors who had
caused such suffering; they had brought each back to life.
They must risk loving and binding themselves together
with the hope that bond would be too strong for any evil
force to break.

The flames within his loins kindled to a greater height
as he pulled her into his arms. For a short time, he did
nothing more than hold her to feel her against him and
to tell himself this was meant to be. When she looped her
arms around his waist and nestled her head to his chest,
his embrace tightened and a moan of intense need escaped
his throat. He grasped her chin with one hand, lifted it,
and melded his lips with hers.

Shared passion caused Chumani to quiver and ignite
with pleasure and anticipation. She felt unusual but wonderful all over. Her pulse raced wildly through her body.
She returned his kiss eagerly, enjoying every sensation his
nearness evoked. She was relaxed yet tense. She was unsure,
yet confident this was right for them. Despite the fact she
had lain with a man before, she hoped she would know
how to please Wind Dancer. Surely such things took care
of themselves as Mother Nature intended when such an
event occurred between two people who desired each
other.

Wind Dancer was almost spellbound by the way she
clung to him, kissed him, and cuddled against him. He
was not a stranger to sex, but he was to these emotions.
Even so, he instinctively knew he must move slowly and
gently with her, though she was making self-control and
leisure difficult with her ardent responses. He trailed kisses
over her face and down her throat as she leaned her head
back to give him access. His lips caused muffled groans to
escape from deep within her. He was elated that he could
arouse her to such feverish yearning for him. He rubbed
his smooth face against her sleek hair and relished the
feel of it against his cheek and neck. He drifted his hands
up and down her back and felt long black strands tease
over his fingers during each trip upward. He kissed her

forehead and the tip of her nose. Nothing in his life felt as good as she did in his arms. As his mouth brushed over hers, he vowed, "I have craved you every sun and moon since I first saw you. If I did not know better, I would swear I am only dreaming or I am drifting toward the Ghost Trail after a deadly grizzly attack."

Amidst their mingled breaths, she said, "So would I, Waci Tate, but we are awake and alive. That day in the Brave Heart forest after meeting you, I knew my life would never be the same. I never thought our paths would cross again but the Great Spirit works in mysterious and most unexpected ways."

He looked at her radiant face and into her luminous dark eyes. "We do not know where our twisting path will take us, but it will be together."

Chumani agreed with those heart-stirring words before she peeled a fringed shirt off his broad shoulders to expose a hairless chest with Sun Dance scars and an abdomen whose muscles rippled like rolling terrain. She freed the ties of his beaded belt and pulled it through the side loops of his leggings. As he stretched out each leg in turn, she removed his moccasins and tugged off his leggings. She folded and placed his garments in a pile beside them, then waited in suspense to see if he removed hers or if that task would fall to her.

She watched his lowered gaze as he took off her beaded belt and knife sheath and laid them aside. He undid the leather thongs at her neck, grasped the fringed hem of her dress, and lifted it over her head after she raised her arms to assist him. Then he untied the narrow laces of her undergarment, and she shifted her body to permit its removal. At a snail's pace his gaze crawled up her body, pausing on her naked breasts, until it reached her face.

Their eyes met and they simply looked at each other, as if each was making sure the other had no reservation about what was going to happen next. Her palms were flattened against his bronze chest while his hands cupped her face and his thumbs stroked the sleek skin near her parted lips. Chumani's fingers played in hair as dark as midnight and almost as long as hers, and he slid his behind her head to draw it toward his. Their mouths met in a tentative kiss which flowered into full-blown passion within moments.

Chumani slipped her hands beneath his arms to rove his broad back and felt the strength which dwelled there; his shoulders and arms, she soon discovered, held the same power. She was aglow with desire and eager to take the next step along this new and crucial journey.

Time seemed to stand still and any reality beyond the cave seemed to vanish as they explored their feelings and stimulated each other to a lofty degree. Their kisses became ravenous and greedy, and their hearts pounded as their excitement increased.

As if receiving a mental message from her, Wind Dancer eased them down to the buffalo hide with her in his arms and them on their sides. Her nipples hardened as Wind Dancer's fingers tantalized them to firmer points after rolling her to her back.

Chumani was awed by how wonderful it felt to have him touching her breasts. Her astonishment and pleasure multiplied when his questing mouth closed over one rosy brown bud. His tongue lavished hot moisture and generous attention there between light flicks and mind-spinning suckles. The sensations he created were deliriously arousing. She closed her eyes to absorb them, as the cave was almost too dark to see him in the glow of the fire's dying embers. Yet, each time lightning flashed and illuminated the interior, her lids flew open to catch even a brief glimpse of him.

Wind Dancer's right hand ventured over her bare body as far as it could reach without dislodging his mouth from its splendid location. She had a firm and agile body, and every part was an enchanting enticement. His hand drifted over her rib cage and stomach, caressing its way to the tempting region between her thighs. He rubbed the small nub there, massaging it with light and slow strokes at first, then with firmer and faster ones as her hips began to move and soft moans escaped her mouth.

Chumani squirmed and sighed as he feasted at her breasts and drove her wild with his caresses. A curious tension gnawed at her, a tension that pleased her and tormented her all at one time. She had never felt this way with Dull Star.

Wind Dancer's mouth slowly traveled up Chumani's chest and neck and at last melded with hers as he moved atop her. He hoped she was as eager to continue their bold journey as she appeared to be; he certainly was. His manhood felt like a burning torch which needed to be sated lest it be consumed by fiery flames. He had never had to use this kind of restraint before or delay his release for so long, as his first wife had not enjoyed such unions and wanted them over with as quickly as possible. With great gentleness, he eased within her feminine core. When she arched toward him, he thrust himself deeper within her, kissing and caressing her all the while. He prayed he was not being too forceful and too swift as he assumed Dull Star had been. After her ankles overlapped his calves and she seemed to open and offer herself fully to him, he penetrated her even more deeply and began a steady pattern of undulations.

Chumani was relieved she felt no pain, only pleasure. She realized every movement Wind Dancer made only increased her yearnings. Every time he entered her, it was the most wonderful sensation she had experienced, as if each new thrust was more stimulating than the preceding one. It was beautiful and natural to have their bodies meshed, to have such powerful feelings racing through both of them, to discover such joy and unity. It was a total sharing of themselves, a bonding on all levels, a consummation of their joining, an exquisite foreshadowing of a glorious future together.

Their hearts pounded in unison as they mentally and physically pledged themselves to each other. Their passions mounted, each seeking a goal only to be imagined at that point. They urged their spirits skyward and grew dizzy at the awesome heights of their soaring passion. Chumani reached her climax first and Wind Dancer soon followed her. Afterward they cuddled as their bodies cooled and their pounding hearts slowed.

"Did I ride too fast and hard?" Wind Dancer asked.

"No, *mihigna,*" a sated Chumani replied. "You did so with great skill."

"That is good to hear, and makes my heart beat with joy and pride."

Chumani nestled into his strong embrace and rested her head on his shoulder. She liked the way his fingers trailed over her arm and shoulder, and the husky tone of his voice. He seemed happy and calm and possessive; and she thrilled to all of it. Although they had not spoken of love for each other, she was certain that was what they felt; it definitely was what *she* felt. At last, they were fully bonded.

Wind Dancer savored the feel of her naked body against his, the way her arm rested over his chest and a knee over his thighs, the way she cuddled up to him, and her occasional dreamy sigh. At last, she belonged completely to him, and he would allow nothing and no one to take her away from him.

They closed their eyes and drifted into the most restful and peaceful night's sleep they had found since their joining.

Upon awakening, Wind Dancer and Chumani made love again before they bathed in a round depression in the cave where water trickled down one side and formed an ankle-deep refreshing rock pool. They ate the food they had ignored last night while engrossed in each other. As they did so, the horses grazed outside near a narrow stream where the son of Chief Rising Bear went to say his daily prayers after their meal and while his wife prepared their belongings for departure.

The storm had passed during the night. Before his morning ritual, Wind Dancer noticed that wildflowers and blades of grass stood tall with renewed energy. Tree limbs and branches on bushes hung low with water-filled leaves. Birds sang; animals foraged; and insects fluttered about to gather nectar. Despite the heavy rain, the earth and vegetation had drunk so greedily that it appeared only damp, not muddy. The sky was a clear blue and the few clouds in sight were distant and wispy. The air was warm and the breeze was gentle, promising a lovely day.

After Wind Dancer said his mental prayers to Wakan-tanka while facing the rising sun, he turned to see his best friend leaning against a rock nearby. *"Wiyaka Lute, u wo,"* he called the man's name and invited him forward.

Red Feather joined him. "We searched for you and Dewdrops after the storm halted and light returned to the face of Mother Earth," he said. "It was a hard task, for the rain removed your tracks. We waited for you to leave the cave so we would not disturb your sleep and . . ." He grinned knowingly and did not finish his sentence. "After we saw the slain grizzly and your horses feeding, I sneaked closer to be sure you were unharmed."

Wind Dancer realized he had been so distracted while making love to Chumani that he had not heard his friend's approach or departure, and that great lowering of his guard astonished and mildly displeased him, for Red Feather could have been an enemy. Yet, there was something more that baffled him. "Why do you say, 'we'?" he asked as he glanced around the area. Before he finished his query and Red Feather could answer, he sighted a woman atop the hill the bear had used, one who was holding the tethers of their horses.

"She is called Zitkala; she is the best friend of your wife."

Wind Dancer eyed the woman and wondered how Wastemna or anyone could mistake her for a man. She did have a rather plain face and tall body, but she was clad in a fringed dress, and long black hair—a beaded rosette in it—flowed around her shoulders. "Why do you come here?" Wind Dancer asked in concern. "Is there trouble in the camp of Tall Elk? Did she bring bad news to Dew-drops?''

"No. She came to visit Dewdrops two moons past, but did not enter our camp. As she returned to the White Shield camp, she saw two Crow and one Pawnee heading toward our camp in a cunning manner. She came to warn us of their approach and spoke with me. It was a scouting party; we believe they spied on the Brave Hearts first and were coming to do the same to our camp for two reasons: to learn our numbers after the white man's disease took many lives in many bands and perhaps to learn if we pre-pare to leave for the grasslands so their war party could encircle and entrap us while we were spread out and vulner-able. Together we tracked them, attacked, and killed them in fierce battles. She is a great warrior, for she fought as a she-wolf protecting her young. Her skills are many and her prowess is large. We feared other enemies had found you and Dewdrops and harmed you."

"We are safe, and we saw no one during our ride and stay here. We kept the horses inside the cave while we slept, sheltered from the storm."

"What of the grizzly?" Red Feather asked, nodding toward the bear.

Wind Dancer disclosed the exciting story to the amazed man, who kept glancing at the massive creature with lethal claws.

"Dewdrops is a worthy companion for you on the visionquest. Our people will chant her large coup for saving your life."

"As they will chant yours and Zitkala's for slaying our enemies before they could scout our camp. We will skin the bear and take its meat home to those in need. I will summon Dewdrops to see her friend. Call Zitkala to join us. I have not met her," he reminded Red Feather, "and wish to do so."

"You will like and respect her, *mitakola,* as I do."

Wind Dancer wondered if there was a special gleam in his friend's eyes when Red Feather looked at the Brule woman and an unfamiliar tone in his voice when he spoke of her. Later, he would ask about that. "Why is she called, 'Bird,' and was not given a color or more name?"

"Her mother told her she received that name in a dream during the birth process; Zitkala told me this in our camp when we talked much. She slept in your tepee, for I gave her permission. She wears Dewdrops's dress, for her garments—those of a man—were soaked by the storm before we returned to camp. I hope that does not displease you."

"It does not, for she is our ally and friend and helped save our people."

"That is true, *mitakola*. She is—"

"Zitkala!" Chumani shouted from the cave's mouth as she was leaving it. Her heart leapt with joy to see Zitkala again so soon, but her mind quickly filled with curiosity and concern about her friend's presence there.

Zitkala joined Chumani at the foot of the incline and they embraced.

"Is there trouble in our camp?" Chumani asked immediately, then realized Zitkala had lacked the time to go home and return. She also grasped that Zitkala was wearing her garment and hairpiece, was clad as a female. She looked at her husband and his best friend as the men joined them. "Why do you two come here?" she asked.

Red Feather repeated the news he had just shared with Wind Dancer, causing Chumani's gaze to enlarge with amazement. "They all walk the Ghost Trail, so they can not return to their camp to reveal our secrets. We fought well together; is that not true, Zitkala?"

"It is true, for Wiyaka Lute is a warrior of great skill and courage."

Chumani was astonished to see her friend's gaze lower for a short time and her cheeks glow with warmth. Zitkala was not normally a person of shyness; and ordinarily she would have kept on her male garments even if drenched or soiled. Chumani also perceived Red Feather's elated expression and tone of voice, which implied great interest in her best friend.

"In our camp, few men are better hunters or warriors than Zitkala," Chumani remarked. "It is good she was placed in the path of our enemies. I have not seen Wiyaka Lute in battle, but Zitkala always speaks the truth and knows when one has great prowess. I am glad you fought beside her."

"It was almost night when we finished our battle; the storm was upon us; and no moon rode in the sky," Red Feather explained. "Zitkala stayed in your tepee until morning and we came to be sure you were alive and unharmed."

Chumani smiled at Red Feather. "We are blessed to have two good friends who love and protect us," she said. "Is that not so, *mihigna?*"

"That is so, *mitawin.* After we return to our camp, Zitkala, will you stay with us until the next sun rises so our people can honor you?"

Zitkala was delighted she could remain near Red Feather for another day so she could study his strange effect upon her. "I thank you, Waci Tate, but I must not intrude on a newly joined couple."

"I would ask you to stay in my parents' tepee," Red Feather injected, "but you are a woman and not of our family circle. It is not our custom."

"She will sleep in our tepee; it is only for one night when many loom before us for privacy. Is that not true, *mitawin?*" Although he hated to sacrifice even one night with Chumani, he knew how much she would enjoy a visit with her friend, and Zitkala deserved to be honored.

"It is true, *mihigna,*" she concurred, pleased by his words.

"It will be so. We will prepare the grizzly while you speak alone."

"Waci Tate told me how you battled the bear and slew him," Red Feather said. "It took great courage to challenge a forest warrior."

"I fought him, but he was slain by Wakinyan at the

Great Spirit's command. The Thunderbird Spirit sent a lightning arrow into his heart before he could slay me."

"Wakantanka rescued you to ride on the visionquest with my friend after you saved his life. It is a good sign, Dewdrops, big medicine."

Chumani smiled and thanked Red Feather before she and Zitkala went to sit on a flat-topped boulder, out of the men's hearing range. She coaxed her friend to tell her the details of the perilous adventure with Red Feather. Chumani listened and observed closely as Zitkala gave a detailed report of their tracking episode and ensuing clash. She noticed how her best friend kept stealing sideways glances at the man in her colorful story, how her gaze and cheeks would glow for a while, and how she almost stumbled over her words during those brief distractions.

"He is a great warrior, Dewdrops, and his courage and skills are as large as the sacred mountain. I ate with his family and we talked until it was late. I slept in your tepee and I borrowed your garment, for mine was soaked from the rain. I could not return home after our battle and he would not allow me to camp in the forest alone and during the storm."

Chumani covered her mouth with a hand as she laughed softly. She could not resist jesting in a near whisper, "What do you mean by, 'he would not allow' you to do something? I have never known Zitkala to follow the orders of anyone but her parents, chief, council, and the Creator."

"You tease me unfairly, Dewdrops, as I did with you in the forest at our reunion. I cannot put it into words, for I do not grasp it myself, but I am amazed and confused by Red Feather's effect on me. It is strange, unlike me to be ensnared by a man. It is frightening to have such potent feelings. And it is foolish, for he would never desire a manwoman."

"If such is true, Zitkala, why does he look at you with such desire in his gaze and why does his voice grow soft and warm when he speaks to you or about you? I do not believe I am misguided when I say, you tug at his heart and mind."

Zitkala stared at Chumani, afraid to accept those stirring words. "How can that be? I am a hunter-warrior, not a real woman. We are strangers."

"Are those not the same questions I asked you about Wind Dancer? You could not answer them for me, and I cannot answer them for you. Love and desire are great mysteries which perhaps only the Great Spirit and Mother Earth understand. For certain, they are hard to resist or conquer."

"Even if he did desire me, we could not join. My parents have no son or other daughter to be their protector and provider; they need me."

"Your father is young and strong enough to do his own hunting and fighting for many circles of the seasons to come. When that is no longer true, your parents can move into your tepee in our camp. Do you not see, Zitkala, the Great Spirit has given you acceptance by and a place of honor with the Red Shields? He has opened the tepee flap for you to enter our band. Perhaps He crossed your path with Red Feather's as He crossed mine with Wind Dancer's. Would it not be wonderful to live side by side again? To do chores together? To speak and visit on every sun?"

"We ride this new trail too fast, Dewdrops. We have me joined to Red Feather and our future suns planned before he even moves toward me."

"If you do not slyly reveal your feelings to him, he may be too wary to approach you; and another female could ensnare him while you hang back," Chumani warned.

"What if he does not want me as a woman, only as a friend?"

"What if he does want you and you elude him out of fear of rejection? Look upon it as a challenge: if you do not risk losing your heart, there is no chance of winning such a struggle and prize. That is what I did on the past moon and found glorious victory. You must like, respect, trust, and desire Red Feather before love fills your heart for him. I did not have such feelings for Dull Star, but they flow as a powerful river within me for Wind Dancer. That is why we came here, to bond with each other, and we did so. I have never known such great love and desire for a man. Wastemna saw us in the forest and told Wind Dancer I had betrayed him with another man; we quarreled, and I left camp to calm myself and think. He realized I spoke the truth and came after me to settle our problems, and we did so."

"After we rode from the Red Shield camp, Red Feather told me you two had come here to be alone," Zitkala said. "When I reached their camp on the last sun, Wastemna was with Red Feather. She told him I was the man who had met with Dewdrops in the forest and was your secret lover. She said I should be captured so we could be punished together. Though I was wearing men's garments and my hair was braided, he knew I was a female. He scolded her and sent her to her tepee for causing trouble. Perhaps that is another reason why he wanted us to find you this sun, to show me to your husband to prove Wastemna lied or was mistaken and you spoke the truth."

"He is a good friend to us, Zitkala, and would be a good husband for you. I have seen young women in our camp approach him with the hope of winning him, but he has never looked at or behaved with them as he does with you. If you feel love and desire growing for him, do not evade his chase. Be cunning and encourage his pursuit."

"I will think upon your words, my friend, for to obey them carries a great risk and much sacrifice. I must make sure he is worth them."

"I believe he is, Zitkala, and I would not speak falsely to you, for I love you and want you to be happy. I would not send you down a wrong trail. You would like living in the Red Shield camp; they are good people. And, it would put you nearby to help us with the sacred quest," Chumani tempted.

"You are clever and greedy, my friend, for you know

my heart well. You know my strengths and weaknesses and my secrets."

"As you know mine, Zitkala."

As Wind Dancer and Red Feather skinned the grizzly and prepared the meat for transport on a makeshift travois, they talked of many of the same things which engrossed the two women. It was obvious to Wind Dancer that his best friend was enchanted by Chumani's best friend, which pleased him.

As he stole a glance at the object of his desire, Red Feather warmed and murmured, "She is a special woman, is she not?"

Wind Dancer grinned and said, "Yes, my wife is that and more."

"Dewdrops is also special, but I speak of Zitkala. The tepee and family of her mate would be safe when he was out of camp on raids and hunts. Her skills and courage are large and she could do all things for a man. She is not beautiful, but she is good to look upon and tempts a hunger in me. Is it foolish to desire a female of another tribe, a near stranger?"

Wind Dancer chuckled. "You ask that of a man who did the same thing? When my eyes first touched upon Dewdrops, I knew I must have her. She entered my heart as swiftly and powerfully as an arrow, but she did not slay me; she returned me to life with her magic. Our bond is strong and complete, my friend, as it was meant to be. Perhaps it is the same between you and Zitkala."

"What if she does not feel the way I do?"

"That same worry and fear filled me until the last moon. There is but one way to learn the truth, and that is to seek it no matter where it lies."

"What if that 'truth' is bad and cuts into my heart and spirit? She lives and rides as a hunter-warrior. Perhaps she does not wish to mate."

"Perhaps that was true until she met you, my friend, but no longer. Did you not see how she looks at you? Hear how she speaks to you? How she steals glances in your direction?"

"Do not tease me, *mitakola*, for this matter is grave to me."

"I do not tease or misguide you; we are best friends, like brothers. After we return to camp, I will find a place and time to speak privately with Dewdrops. I will learn if Zitkala is open to your interest in her."

"Thank you, my friend."

"Do not move slow like the turtle, my friend, for soon she must leave our camp and we must begin the sacred quest. Dewdrops told me clever ways to distract the Crow from our camp, tricks we must use to keep them busy in this season. We will speak of them in the meeting lodge this sun."

The two men loaded the travois which was attached to Chumani's horse, as she would ride with her husband.

As their work was being completed, Wind Dancer realized how eager he was to reach home because he had another important task to perform, no matter how much trouble it caused.

Chapter
Ten

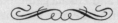

The Red Shields were awed and elated by the detailed account of how Chumani battled a grizzly while Wind Dancer was blinded by dirt in his eyes and how Wakinyan struck down that threat with a lightning bolt. As they murmured about how blessed and honored the two visionquest companions were, many gathered around them to look at or touch the long and sharp claws of the slain creature. Afterward the couple presented them to his mother, along with the bear skin, as gifts of love. Yet, only Wind Dancer, Chumani, Hanmani, Winona, Zitkala, and Red Feather knew the motive behind the gesture: gratitude for her encouraging words to her son before his departure. The meat was passed out to women whose husbands had died from cholera, as some had not yet taken another mate. People praised Chumani for saving the life of their future chief and the Great Spirit's path to glorious victory. The Story Catchers said they would paint that story on the tribal history hide so all would remember her great deed.

Zitkala and Red Feather also were praised and honored with the gifts of coup feathers for their brave and daring deed against the enemy scouting party. That stirring tale was repeated again, as most had been confined in their tepees last night when the two warriors returned.

The men were told to get their work finished quickly so they could meet with the council before dusk, where Chumani's ideas for provoking trouble between the Crow and Whites would be revealed and discussed.

While Chumani and Zitkala gathered wood and fetched water before preparing the next meal, Wind Dancer sought out Wastemna to speak with her, wanting to get the offensive task behind him. Near her tepee, he pulled her aside and warned, "Do not speak bad words about Dewdrops again or I will summon the other women to prove you speak the truth or speak falsely about her defiance and lack of skills. Say nothing of what you told me about her meeting in the forest with a man, for it was a female, her friend. Do not attempt to cause more trouble, Wastemna, for it will not be good for you."

Wind Dancer took his wife for a lengthy walk in the cool and lovely forest following the council meeting, which she was allowed to attend and speak in as the vision-woman. "Did it make you happy when Grandfather said the Great Spirit put those clever thoughts inside your head?" he asked and watched Chumani smile and nod, her gaze radiant with pride and joy. "Grandfather says the Creator speaks to us in ways other than in dreams and visions, and He spoke to you in whispers only you could hear. When the Crow garments are ready for us to use, we will begin our victory quest."

She leaned against a tree. "I did not tell Zitkala of our plan, for I must speak with her alone about it. She must learn she will face great peril if she agrees with it, and that she must remain in our camp to ride with us."

"It is a cunning trick on those at the trading post, but I fear for your safety. I would rather lose my heart than lose the one who fills it with joy."

Chumani's body warmed as her husband gazed into her eyes and caressed her cheek, and she heard the concern in his voice. "I will be fine, *mihigna*, for the Great Spirit will guide and protect me in our enemy's presence. He knew this sun would rise and that is why He prepared me with learning the Crow and White tongues. I will fool them and not be in danger."

"I hope Zitkala will stay and go with you. Red Feather says she is a great warrior, and two together will ease my fears." Wind Dancer winced inside as that dreaded number *two* leapt into his head and from his mouth. To distract himself from his apprehension, he asked, "Do you think Zitkala would stand under the Talking-Blanket with Red Feather, and ride double-back with him, and listen when he plays the flute?"

Chumani nodded. "But he must not move too swiftly, for such feelings in her heart confuse and frighten her. She has never been close to a man and did not expect to meet one who wished to do such things for her. Is Red Feather's interest good and large?"

"As good and large as mine were for you. I will tell Red Feather he can begin his journey toward her, but to ride slow and easy."

Chumani laughed and jested, "You did not ride slow and easy; you galloped into my camp and laid claim to me. I was forced to join to you."

"It was not a bad or hard command to honor and follow, was it?"

"At first, yes; but now it is different; it is good and easy."

"As good as your mouth tastes? As easy as it is to desire you?"

As he asked his first question, he nibbled upon her lips. As he asked his second one, his mouth drifted across her cheek and brushed over her ear. After many kisses, with each waxing deeper and swifter, one of his hands found and fondled a breast through her garment and the other slipped beneath it to stroke her inner thigh. Wind Dancer wondered if he should continue to tantalize her, to seek a few moments of blissful rapture in her arms. It was late evening and most of his people were busy with chores and families, so no one should disturb them if they hurried, though he craved a leisurely encounter.

Chumani was having those same daring thoughts and intoxicating desires. She loved him and wanted him urgently, so she cast restraint to the wind and let her emotions dance away with him to seek pleasure and release. As he pressed her to the large pine tree, she did not mind and hardly noticed the rough bark which nipped at her back and crackled against her hair as she looked upward so his lips could journey down her neck. As she did so, she sighted Cetan perched on a limb above them and knew the hawk would sound a shrill warning if an intruder approached. She relaxed as much as those blissful sensations would allow and surrendered fully to his possession.

Wind Dancer felt her body loosen and knew she was willing and eager to proceed with their sensual adventure. His left hand fondled her breast while his right one titillated the taut peak between her spread thighs as his lips meshed with hers and kissed her with great hunger. He felt her arms encircle his body and rove his back as her mouth feasted on his.

They kissed and stroked each other until their passions were hot and feverish and their mutual desires could not be denied. A flood of anticipation and sheer pleasure washed over them. She quivered when he nibbled at her earlobe. He did the same when her hand rubbed back and forth over the bulge in his breechclout that was almost aching to break free. They found it exciting to kindle each other to such fiery heights, knowing the force of the victory looming before them. As their mouths clung and worked magic on the other, each lowered the undergarments which stood between them.

Wind Dancer gazed into her luminous brown eyes. Her beauty and allure were so enormous that his breath caught in his throat and his pulse quickened. He grasped her by the hips, lifted her slightly, and sank his erection within her. He remained motionless for a short while as he simply savored the heat and moisture surrounding his shaft. He was thrilled when her arms clung to him, her legs gripped him snugly around his buttocks, she melded their mouths, and she rode him at an ardent pace. The defined muscles in his arms, back, and buttocks repeatedly tightened and slackened as he thrust onward and upward in his endeavor to sate her. He could barely maintain his self-control and struggled to do so, as he knew the goal he strove for was worth his best effort.

Chumani kissed his neck and her hands clasped his shoulders as she listened to his ragged breathing near her ear as his cheek pressed against her temple. The position and his erotic movements stimulated her to an ever greater hunger for appeasement. Exhilarating and wonderful sensations charged through her body as a powerful release burst upon her and warmed her skin from head to toes. She moaned in triumph and hung on to finish the wild ride.

Wind Dancer realized she had captured her goal, so he reached for his own, found it, and savored every spasm of ecstasy. On legs which now felt weak and trembly, he shifted their positions so his shirted back was to the tree. His arms banded her waist and he held her close as they calmed their breathing and heartbeats to normal. Afterward, he sealed their lips as he lowered her feet to the ground, wanting to end the enchanting episode in the same way it had begun.

Chumani felt suffused by love and happiness. She smiled into his tender gaze, trailed her fingers over his strong jawline, and teased, "You stole my wits, *mihigna.*"

"As you steal mine many times, *mitawin.*"

Chumani was filled with courage and confidence after the rewarding experience. "It is good we have the same thirst and hunger for each other."

Wind Dancer grinned. "It is more than good when we drink and eat together in this manner."

"Will it always be this way between us?"

"Always, *mitawin,* for as long as you desire me as I desire you."

She laughed and quipped, "Since you are such a skilled hunter in my forest and upon my grounds, I will never tire of this meal."

"And I will never tire of providing it for us."

Reluctant to sever the intimate movement, she nevertheless brought conversation back to reality. "We must sneak to the water in that direction to refresh our bodies, for I must speak with Zitkala before we sleep."

Wind Dancer knew she referred to a shallow stream not far away where they would have privacy to remove the signs and scents of their lovemaking before they returned to their tepee and friends. "While you speak with Zitkala, I will visit with Red Feather."

As Zitkala listened in amazement to Chumani's revelations about Red Feather's strong attraction to her and about the impending task in which they wanted her to be included, joy and suspense filled her, as did some grave concerns. "What if his heart runs in another direction after he learns more about me and my heart has already softened toward him?"

"That is a risk you must take, my friend."

"What of my parents? They need me as their hunter and provider."

"No, Zitkala, not for many circles of the seasons to come. While you await their passings, you can find happiness in Red Feather's arms and tepee. Do not allow fear to steal this prize from you. We will send a Red Shield warrior to your father's lodge to tell him you join us in the sacred quest. He will feel great pride and joy in knowing you are a part of it."

"What will I do to help? Why do you need me to go along?"

Chumani disclosed the first plan to her wide-eyed friend.

"It is cunning and will work Dewdrops. It will stir my heart and blood to ride with you and the others. But it is best if I ride home to enlighten my father and mother and gather possessions I need for living here. I can return before things are ready for us to leave."

"That is good. Why do you not take Red Feather with you? You can speak privately, become friends, and your parents can meet him."

"It is too soon to reveal my feelings for him to my family."

"Then keep them a secret until the right sun arrives."

"What will the other Red Shields say if we travel alone?"

"They will think Red Feather guards one of the sacred quest party."

Zitkala nodded in satisfaction. It was decided she would go.

The morning after Zitkala and Red Feather left for the White Shield village near the southern tip of the Black Hills, peril struck at the Red Shields on the northern tip of that sacred and wintering location. A Crow raiding party from the Powder River area attacked along the outermost fringe of their encampment. Simultaneously loud whoops from enemies, the thundering of many horses's hooves, and screams of surprise and pain rent the air as a large group of Apsaalooke swarmed on dwellings and working women with children playing nearby. Most of the men were gathered at the other end either doing daily tasks or practicing warrior skills in clearings nearby. Some were in the forest or on the grassland hunting.

At the first ominous sounds of trouble, Wind Dancer, War Eagle, and others seized their weapons and raced toward the commotion. Chumani dropped her water bag and ran to her tepee to grab her weapons to help thwart their enemies and protect her adopted band. As the Red Shield fighters converged on the scene, many already lay wounded and a few lay dead and two tepees were afire from flaming arrows. The Crow whirled on their colorfully painted mounts, many shouting or hand-signing insults to the Oglala men, and galloped away amidst a thundering noise.

"We must chase them and slay them to avenge our fallen people!" shouted Buffalo Hump, their war chief and Wastemna's father.

Wind Dancer glared at their foes' retreating backs and countered, "It is a trick to lure us from camp so another hidden band can attack while we are gone. See how they ride for the grassland rather than into the forest and hills or toward their hunting grounds. They tease us to come after them in the open where they can take us on a wild chase while others carry out their true purpose to steal, destroy, and slay here. You lead the pursuit and charge against them. The Strong Hearts will conceal ourselves in the trees and our dwellings to defeat their second raiding party."

"The first party is large, Waci Tate, so a second one is doubtful. We need all warriors to ride with us," Buffalo Hump refuted his idea.

"Do not forget the Crow have pulled that trick before, and it is one of their favorites during any raid. We must not leave our camp unprotected."

"My grandson is wise and careful," Nahemana told the gathered men. "The Strong Hearts must remain, and Buffalo Hump must lead the chase."

"Those are the same words which fill my heart and head," Chief Rising Bear concurred. "Our homes and people must be guarded."

Plans were made in a rush as the women, children, and old ones sneaked into the forest to hide during the impending clash. Then, a large party of Red Shields galloped from camp on a retaliation trail while the leading warrior body hid themselves as Wind Dancer had suggested.

It was not long before his suspicion was proven to be accurate: another and smaller band of mingled Crow and Pawnee attacked the camp from the other end, whooping and firing arrows as they charged in amongst the scattered tepees. As soon as they passed the first dwellings, the surprise trap was sprung and an awesome conflict ensued.

Members of the Strong Heart Society leapt from concealment and attacked fiercely with great prowess, as their group was made up of the most fearless and skilled warriors in their band, a group whose main purpose was defense and survival of the Red Shields.

As she had promised her husband, Chumani lingered near their tepee but had refused to go into the woods with the women, children, and elders since she was a more than capable fighter and might be needed there. She glanced at her beloved and his father as they battled enemies while standing back-to-back for protection of their vulnerable spots. She noted that Rising Bear had not lost his stamina, or talents with weapons and hand-to-hand combat. To avoid being distracted by observing her mate's abilities and possible perils, she refused to watch him. As her gaze drifted around the area where many struggles were in progress either upon horseback or on the ground, she was horrified to sight Nahemana leave his tepee, several beyond theirs, carrying a ceremonial buffalo skull which he had no doubt returned to fetch to prevent its theft. With bow in hand, an arrow nocked, and several more shafts clasped between her teeth, she hurried toward the slow-moving, dulled-vision shaman.

Chumani saw a Bird Warrior guiding his horse toward Nahemana with a lance lifted high in one hand. *"Oochia, bishkishpee!"* she shouted to seize the foe's attention. "Fight me, not an old man, if you are a worthy warrior!" The startled Crow looked at her with an expression of mingled amusement and scorn as she ordered him to stop, called him a lowly and scorned dog flea, and issued him an insulting challenge in his own language.

"I will slay the shaman first, take the sacred skull as a war prize, then capture you. I will fill your body with my man seeds before I slit your throat and cut out your tongue. Run, foolish woman, but I will catch you soon."

"You will capture and harm no one, piss of the elk!" He clearly did not consider her a threat as he refocused on the shaman who had frozen in place at his tepee entrance. As he drew back his arm to fling his lance into Nahemana's body, she released an arrow, quickly yanked another from her mouth, and nocked it in readiness if she missed her agile target.

As Chumani fired the first shaft, Cetan gave a shrill cry from overhead, swooped down in a rapid dive, and seized the lance with his strong talons. Yet, its weight and imbalance caused the hawk to drift toward the ground, despite its great strength and determination. At that slow pace, another enemy warrior fired an arrow into Cetan's left wing, which sent the large bird tumbling to the earth. She whirled to shoot his attacker, but saw Wind Dancer leap upon the man from behind, both crashing to the ground. She hurried to Cetan as the hawk flopped about with the arrow protruding from his wing. She spoke soothingly to him as she lifted him and carried him to Nahemana's tepee so she could protect both from further danger.

"Do not worry, my friend, I will remove the arrow and tend your injury very soon. Remain quiet until I can do so, for dangers surround us." To the white-haired man, she said, "Go inside your tepee, Wise One, and I will stand guard here." Without a word, only a smile and a nod, Nahemana obeyed her soft command. She placed Cetan behind her in the entranceway and faced forward. She only glanced at the enemy whom she had slain with her first arrow before observing her love's fierce battle for survival.

Wind Dancer sneered at the foe who had dared to attack his camp. He knew the other Strong Hearts and Oglala warriors had the conflict under control, but he did not want to take the time to play with his enemy, as the wounded needed tending. His gaze mocked the man who was now vulnerable in the center of his camp with no rescue or escape mount within sight or reach, so his death was a certainty. Even if he were slain during their struggle, another would take his place, and another if necessary, until this raider lived no more. *"U wo, suska,"* he taunted, motioning the Crow forward and calling him "worthless and lazy."

Though the Bird Warrior laughed and sneered in return, it was obvious to Chumani that he knew his death loomed before him, so he would fight with all he possessed to go out in a blaze of prowess. She saw her husband's white teeth gleam as brightly as the blade in his grasp, a metal one from trade with the *wasicun*. She had confidence in Wind Dancer's ability to win, but she dreaded seeing him hurt.

"Where is your honor, Crow dog? Why do you slay innocents? Why did you not ride to our camp and challenge worthy warriors to battle you? Only a coward and weakling strikes at women, children, and old ones. Where does the coup lie in such a bad deed?"

"All Lakotas must die and this land will be ours!" the Crow scoffed.

"The land belongs to the Creator. Do you seek to steal what is His?"

"Do you fear me, he who dances with the wind? Why do you wait? Do you hope to breath the Creator's air for a short time longer?"

"No more words or waiting, Crow dog. Prepare to die by my hand."

A fierce and rapid clash ensued as the men rushed toward each other with knives held high in readiness to strike the initial blow, to bring forth the first blood, to kill their enemy. Both were strong, nimble, highly trained, and experienced. They slashed out at each other, used their hands and feet as deadly weapons. Their muscles bulged and rippled as they battled, and they soon were breathing rapidly and glistening with sweat. The fringes on their shirts and leggings swayed and snapped as they whirled and fought. Their expressions had become frozen and harsh; their gazes, glaring and hate-filled.

To Chumani, it was like watching a deadly dance as they writhed, twisted, and darted about, kicking up dust and stones with every step. Despite the fact she was positive her husband would win the match of wills because he was protected by Wakantanka, she flinched each time the knife slashed too close to his body or his stalwart frame accepted a near stunning blow. When Wind Dancer's head made forceful and painful contact with the Bird Warrior's stomach, it sent the Crow tumbling backward to the hard ground. Without hesitation, the foe was on his feet again and charging her agile mate who parried his attack. It was apparent to her that Wind Dancer was the superior fighter, but the Crow's desperation and resolve made him a dangerous and unpredictable opponent. She made sure she did not shriek or move or do anything to distract her beloved, as it only took a moment's loss of focus to turn the odds against him. She was almost angered when other Strong Hearts and Oglalas gathered around the scene of the last action and cheered on their companion and friend, fearing it would distract him, though it seemed to give him a burst of energy and renewed stamina.

Using quick reflexes and cunning, Wind Dancer soon had the Crow pinned to the ground. He straddled his imprisoned enemy, knowing he had but one course of action. He must kill the man or he would return another sun to attack his people, for pride and generations of hostilities would demand it. He raised his knife, glued his gaze to the Crow's blazing one, and finished the deed. Afterward, he stood, lifted his arms skyward, and released a whoop of victory as his friends encompassed him in a tight circle.

Chumani wanted to rush to his side, to embrace him, to kiss him, but she held back to avoid embarrassing him before his society members with such a show of emotion. She stepped aside for the smiling shaman to join the excitement, turned, and gathered Cetan into her arms. She carried the hawk to her tepee to tend his wound. She knew it was not a lethal one, but could be disabling. She closed her eyes for a short time and prayed: *If he is to help us on the sacred task, Great One, heal his wing so he can fly again.*

Wind Dancer glanced around the human enclosure for

his wife and, finding her absent, asked his grandfather, "Where is Dewdrops? I saw her standing at your tepee. Was she harmed?"

"No. She saved my life when I was the target of a Crow's lance and remained nearby to guard me from another attack." He explained how the hawk had helped her in that battle but, sadly, Cetan was wounded. "She goes to tend him," Nahemana revealed.

After Rising Bear returned from the forest and joined the others, the exciting story about Chumani's and Cetan's glorious deed was repeated to him, as was the final battle nearby. "It is good my son was shown the peril of this sun so our camp would not be destroyed and our people slain," the chief proclaimed. "We must tend our wounded, build scaffolds for our dead and mourn them, and help those whose dwellings were damaged by fire. Soon the others will return and join us to chant the new coups of my sons, my second daughter, her bird companion, the Strong Hearts, and our other warriors. It is a good and a bad day for us, for we have a great victory, but suffered many losses."

"Soon we will leave on the first ride of our sacred quest, Father," Wind Dancer said, "and it will turn the Apsaalooke's eyes from us when they must battle the Whites who will hold them to blame for our coming deeds. We must post guards around our camp until we have distracted them with another conflict and our people move to the grasslands to hunt buffalo. On the next sun, we must hold the Sacred Bow ritual for Swift Otter to replace Badger, for War Eagle will ride with us to trick the Crow and Whites."

Within a short time, the rest of the band had returned to camp from the forest and were enlightened to the events. With a mixture of elation at their triumph and sadness over their losses, the people set about to take care of the tasks Rising Bear had mentioned earlier.

Before joining other men to gather wood and erect burial scaffolds, Wind Dancer walked to his tepee to check on his wife and the hawk, and was followed by his sister. "How is he?" he asked upon entry to his lodge.

Chumani looked up. "I have removed the arrow, but part of his wing is broken," she replied. "I seek to stop the bleeding and tend the cuts before I bind it tight in place until the bone heals. You fought a great battle, *mihigna,* and my heart soars with pride in your victory."

As Wind Dancer's gaze roved her for a sign of any harm, he murmured, "As does mine for your courage and skills in saving Grandfather." He was relieved the danger was past and she was safe, as he did not want to even imagine living without her. He was also glad the hawk survived.

"As does mine," Hanmani added. "I will help you tend Cetan before I go to help others in need if he will allow my touch and presence."

"He will do so if I command it, my sister, and I thank you for your good heart. Fetch the medicine pouch for me," Chumani requested.

"I will return later; I have sad tasks to do now," Wind Dancer said. "I will bring Cetan a rabbit or squirrel to eat since he cannot hunt his prey."

Chumani smiled at her husband, their gazes melding warmly for a time before he left the tepee. She took the pouch from Hanmani and pulled out many small leather-bound items. She looked at the treatments for cuts and bleeding and easing pain: spider's web, unripe puffballs, fern, yarrow, white pine, pond lily, wort, Horsetail rush, wild tobacco. She decided which ones to use on the large bird and began her work. After the bleeding was halted and the cuts were smeared with medicine, she used two sticks and thin strips of leather to secure the break in position and hold it there. Not once did Cetan attempt to peck or claw her, and he remained still and quiet and watchful. She noted that he also allowed Hanmani's touch as the girl assisted with the splint. "He likes and trusts you," Chumani told the girl. "When Waci Tate returns with his food, if you will feed and water him, he will become familiar with your touch before we ride from camp then you can tend him for me while I am gone. Will you do that good deed, my sister?"

"Yes, my sister, and I will be honored and happy to do so. Do not worry, Dewdrops, for no harm will come to him under my guard," Hanmani vowed as she smiled and stroked the hawk's chest as she chatted to him.

Chumani's heart filled with joy and relief when Cetan ducked his head under the girl's hand and nuzzled her palm with its crest, a sign of trust and affection and acceptance. "It is good, for you have become his friend and I will be calm in knowing he is well tended and protected."

Chumani secured one end of a strong tether to the hawk's leg and the other to a post driven into the ground. She told Hanmani it would be easier for the bird to remain still and calm inside the tepee without distractions and enticements from outside surroundings. She smiled again when the girl fetched water and placed the wooden bowl nearby. "Stay, Cetan, for we must go help others. Hanmani will return soon with your food."

Guards were posted around the village to make certain another raid by a third war party did not take place while they were occupied with grim tasks which required the remainder of that day to complete.

When the large group of Red Shields returned near midafternoon from their futile pursuit of the Apsaalooke, they were elated to discover the news of the awesome victory during their absence but were distressed by the losses their friends had suffered. Many praised Wind Dancer loudly and repeatedly for seeing through the Crows' trick to lure them from camp for a surprise attack and thanked the Strong Hearts for the defense of their tepees and families. They joined the others to repair damage to tepees, to tend the wounded, help construct scaffolds, assist with burials, and to hunt for those in need of fresh game who had lost their husbands on past suns.

By dusk, the *wiconte wicagnakapis* stood out on the verdant landscape against a darkening cobalt sky with seven bodies resting upon them—four females, two children, and an elderly man. Two of the women were wives and mothers, while the others were a girl of joining age and one of fifty whose mate had died during the past winter. Their deaths were mourned with sad songs, traditional chants, and cut marks on the legs and arms of adult family members. Even Mother Nature seemed to respond to the tragedy. The wind ceased to blow as if to honor those whose lives had been taken by fierce enemies. The sky's beautiful blue shade dulled as if in empathy and the sun hid behind a distant cloud as if unable to witness the somber sight. The birds were quiet and the animals remained concealed as if to prevent intruding on the people's sorrow.

After the burial ceremony was completed and all returned to camp, relatives and friends took in those tormented by grief and requiring help with children and husbands. The people ate in small and quiet groups before retiring, many to endure a restless night.

Chumani snuggled in Wind Dancer's embrace. Though they kissed and stroked each other, they did not make love, as sadness gripped their hearts. They drew comfort from each other and bonded more tightly from their sharing of such a terrible event. Too, their thoughts roamed into the past and they relived the tragic losses of their sons at the hands of the Crow warrior who had led the first attack to lure the others from camp so his companions could attack.

When Buffalo Hump had returned from chasing the first band, Chumani and Wind Dancer had made a shocking discovery. From Buffalo Humps description of the Crow leader's face design, they knew he was the same Crow warrior who had murdered their children. Each wished they had been with the war chief so the pursuit could have continued until their enemy had been overtaken and killed to avenge their sons' deaths. Yet, they somehow knew that their paths would cross again and vengeance would not be denied them, perhaps even be granted to them as a reward for their parts in the sacred quest, which was to begin in a few more moons. Each also knew another great event was to take place on the next sun.

The Red Shield Band of the Oglala Lakotas gathered in the center of their winter encampment as they awaited the start of the Sacred Bow ritual, as it was believed to yield powerful medicine for war and for peace. The people's hearts and minds were filled with mixed feelings on that day, for many had experienced terrible losses and others, great victories over their enemies. Despite the anguish of those with slain family members or close friends, all knew that each person's existence traveled in a circle as with the Sacred Hoop of Life, and death was a part of it. The fallen ones' spirits now dwelled with Wakantanka and that fact was soothing.

The elite Sacred Medicine Bow society's meeting lodge had been set up in the midst of the camp early that morning, with a sweat lodge erected beside it. The three other Bow Carriers—War Eagle, Raven, and Broken Arrow—participated in the event to show Swift Otter's skills were equal to theirs and he possessed the prowess to join their high rank. Following purification of the four men who were clad only in plain breechclouts and moccasins in the *initipi* and words spoken in private in the members' meeting lodge, the ceremony began with a prayer sent forth by Nahemana to the Great Spirit and other powerful forces of Nature—wind, lightning, thunder, hail, snake, and bear—to ask for guidance and assistance.

Four posts, which represented the four directions of the wind and Medicine Wheel, were already in place in opposing positions and were decorated with sacred symbols. The runners' bodies were painted red, the color of Mother Earth where the buffalo—the main provider of their survival—wallowed. Other Medicine Bow colors and designs were added. Yellow lines to depict lightning snaked across their faces, and their cheeks bore blue hailstones. A yellow quarter-moon was painted upon their bare chests.

Other sky-blue lines drawn on arms and legs evoked the
powers of the four winds. The four runners faced the west,
their expressions serious, their moods reverent. After the
signal was given, Swift Otter displayed his great stamina
and determination, easily matching the pace of the other
three participants, necessary competition to prove his
worth. Since it was not a contest between several hopefuls,
no token was collected at each post to determine the win-
ner. Each man simply touched the post in passing. All
reached Nahemana at almost the same time. More tests
quickly followed to prove weapons skills, prowess, endurance, and intelligence.

As Wind Dancer observed, he recalled the sun he had
performed the ritual with success; he had served that rank
well until he relinquished his medicine bow to become a
Shirt Wearer and Strong Heart. Great love and pride filled
his heart for his brother, as War Eagle—now seventeen—
had proven himself worthy of that and a warrior's rank at
a young age last summer. He knew that if anything happened to him and his father, War Eagle would make a
good chief and leader.

As Chumani watched the activities, she imagined her
husband participating. She knew he had collected all four
tokens and returned to his grandfather's side before the
next contestant even reached the third post. Her heart
pounded with love and desire for him, and it was difficult
to keep focused on the stirring event before her.

After the demands were met, everyone observed as Swift
Otter strung his new bow, one which was longer and heav-
ier than a regular weapon and exposed a lance point on
the top end. It now would be the man's duty to help bring
about peace for his band and to fight fiercely for it in
times of war. He was presented with a hanger, a staff for
supporting the sacred bow when not in use, as it must not
lie upon the ground or be propped against anything which
might drain or taint its special powers.

With Badger's replacement chosen, the Sacred Bow
foursome was once again complete. The other members—

four club bearers and four staff carriers—joined their society brothers in a ceremonial dance and chant. Afterward, the four participants re-entered the *initipi* for a final purification rite, during which their bodies were washed clean of paints and were rubbed with sweet and sage grasses in symbolic gesture to the land which fed the buffalo.

That night, the band met once more in the center of their camp to seek total unity and harmony as one body of people before they faced their coming challenges. The wife of Badger joined to a warrior who had lost his mate and tepee during the Crow attack, forming a new family with their children. Ceremonial dances were performed and recent coups were chanted, including those of Wind Dancer, Chumani, and Cetan. Prayers were said for lost loved ones and for guidance and protection during their impending annual hunt and during certain confrontations with enemies, Indian and White. Food was supplied by most families to be shared and eaten with others. The people were reminded that the sacred quest companions would leave on their first journey on the next sun as soon as Zitkala and Red Feather returned from the White Shield camp.

In their tepee, after Chumani tended Cetan and sealed their entrance flap, she turned to Wind Dancer to question him about a serious matter.

Chapter Eleven

Chumani tried to swallow the lump in her throat. For two days she had struggled to ignore her trepidation and failed to do so. She licked her dry lips and asked her husband, "What will happen if Zitkala and Red Feather do not return?"

Wind Dancer did not grasp her grave concern, as his thoughts traveled in another direction. He wanted to take advantage of the Brule woman's absence to make slow and passionate love to his wife while they had privacy before their journey. "We will wait for them."

Chumani went to sit beside him on the sleeping mat. She noticed how he eyed her and perceived his romantic mood, but she needed answers. "I do not wish to think of such anguish striking at us, but I meant, what if Crow scouts were watching our camp three suns past, saw them leave, followed, and . . . attacked them?" she asked, unable to say the word *killed,* as it knifed her emotions. "What if they never return to us? Will we delay our first task, go anyway with only War Eagle, or choose others to ride with us?"

Wind Dancer grimaced at the terrible thought of losing his best friend, and Chumani, hers. "I am certain they did not confront our enemies and will return to us." His voice held strong conviction. "The Great Spirit would not allow them to be harmed, as He has need of them."

Chumani smiled. "You are right, *mihigna,* and it was foolish of me to worry about them. I must have faith in Wakantanka. My fears came from enduring our enemy's attack and because the trickster has not struck at us again and I worry the evil one will do so soon."

"Do not be afraid, *mitawin,* for I will protect you from harm, as will the Great Spirit." His heart rate increased steadily as he gazed at her and saw her smile and relax. He noted the lovely curve of her chin and jawline, the flawless surface of her skin, and those brown eyes which drew him into them like dark pools of shiny water. He could not resist her magic, and hoped she found him just as alluring. She possessed so many good traits and ways that he could not name them all, but he was aware and appreciative of each one.

Chumani watched Wind Dancer as he studied her. She found his fascination with her arousing and flattering. She felt a rush of heat to her cheeks, as if a fire were suddenly kindled within her body. Her spirit soared with eagerness and delight. His gaze held a compelling power and gleam of tenderness which captivated her. She knew what he wanted and what she wanted were one and the same.

Chumani's hand reached out to graze his angular jaw-line, for she could not deny the heady impulse to touch him, to feel the stirring sensation of his flesh against hers. He had removed his shirt earlier and she let her fingers drift down his neck and across his hairless chest, as she admired the muscular hardness of his torso. Her gaze halted on his Sun Dance scars, as did her fingertips before she traced the marks which exposed his great courage and stamina and sacrifice to the Great Spirit.

Wind Dancer was enchanted and titillated by her bold exploration. She did not have to tell him she wanted him tonight, for everything about her proclaimed her rising desire. His blood pulsed in excitement and pleasure; his loins blazed in response. Surely if he could awaken her passions to such a great height, he could capture her love. He drew her closer for a deep and meaning-filled kiss.

Soon, they both were eager to surrender fully to what seemed so inevitable and right.

Parting only long enough to yank off their garments and moccasins, they sank to the buffalo mat locked in each other's arms, their lips melded in a hot kiss. They tried to work slowly, but their cravings were too urgent to be denied for very long. They united their bodies and aimed for love's sweet target. They attained and savored it with great elation.

Afterward, they snuggled, kissed, and stroked each other until they drifted off to sleep peacefully for the remainder of the night.

Chumani tried to keep herself busy and distracted as she awaited her best friend's return. She was pleased with how Hanmani tended and calmed Cetan, and how her hawk responded to the girl's gentle touch and soothing voice. She loved and trusted her two-winged companion, for they had been together for many circles of the seasons. It would pain her deeply if anything ever happened to him, though she suspected he would one day take a mate and leave her for his rightful existence as a soarer of the sky and dweller of the forests and mountains. Thanks to Hanmani, she would not worry about his care and safety while they were gone.

At midday, a shout went up from the children that Red Feather was returning, and Chumani's gaze rushed toward that direction. When she sighted Zitkala riding beside him, joy and relief flooded her. She did not wait for them to reach her; she almost raced to join and greet them. "You are back!" she cried. "It is good for my eyes to see you again."

Zitkala laughed at her friend's animated expression and teased, "Only three moons have passed since you did so, and it would be longer if we had not ridden fast, as the wind blows during the cold season."

"There was much danger and trouble after your departure. I feared our enemies had trailed and attacked you, though my husband said no."

Red Feather's smile vanished as he asked, "What peril struck?"

Quickly, Chumani related the gist of the grim incident during his absence and finished, "Wind Dancer tends our horses in the canyon and will return soon; he will tell you more. We are to leave after you rest and eat."

"I will seek him out to talk. We will come to his tepee soon."

After Red Feather took their horses to drink and graze for a while, Chumani and Zitkala went to the tepee to talk and prepare themselves.

In a near whisper and with a merry grin on her face, Chumani said, "I saw how you two were looking at each other. Tell me everything. Was your journey good? Has he entrapped your heart?"

"We shared many special words and kisses, but we did not unite our bodies on the sleeping mat. It was hard to resist the temptation to explore and enjoy such feelings, but we do not know each other well enough to surrender to them so soon." She paused before asking, "What is it like to do so with one you love and crave?"

Chumani knew her friend's words and mood were serious, so she made no jests. "It is the most wonderful experience you can have, Zitkala. It is as if all else fades away for a time and all you hear, see, feel, smell, and taste is your loved one. Love is powerful magic, my friend, it enslaves you."

"That is how it is with Wind Dancer but was not with Dull Star," her friend reminded her.

"That is true, for I did not love or desire my first mate; I did not even care for him as a friend or band member. His pride was too large, and his thoughts were as twisted as a hair braid. He was not gentle or kind. I was viewed and treated as a possession, a lowly one, despite my rank as our chief's daughter and his wife. Wind Dancer matches him in no way."

"That is good, Dewdrops, and it is the same with Red Feather. He is good and kind and gentle, but a great warrior and skilled hunter. There is no man in our camp to match him in all ways and deeds. He is the first man to flame my body, to cause my heart to beat fast, to make my mind roam as in a beautiful dream. He does not find my looks and manner repulsive. He does not view me as being foolish and manly. He praises my skills and encourages me to use them. He makes me realize I am a woman. He brings forth the feminine instincts buried deep within me. Is it wrong to yearn for him and such things so quickly?"

Chumani hugged her friend and smiled in joy. "No, Zitkala. Do you not remember how I desired Wind Dancer from the first time I saw him? I did not understand such a hunger and I fought it in a fierce battle. I did not win, and I am happy I lost that conflict. I am sure he desires and enjoys me on the sleeping mat. He accepts me as a wife, friend, and companion. But I yearn for more, Zitkala; I hunger for his love. Only by sharing love can our relationship grow strong, be happy and enduring."

"Have you told him of such feelings and thoughts?"

"I wait for them to fill my husband's heart and mind before I speak."

"How will you know if or when they do if he rides that same path of resistance?" Zitkala asked.

"He is brave, so he will tell me."

"He will do so, for he cannot resist your magic and challenge. I hope it will be the same for me and Red Feather. If he turned away from me after awakening such feelings, it would freeze my heart as water in winter."

"He is good and honorable, Zitkala, so he will not lead you down a cruel trail. I trust my husband, and he said his friend's interest is real and strong."

* * *

The entire band gathered in the center of camp to watch the five riders leave to carry out their first task. The small group listened as the shaman, with his wife, Little Turtle, beside him, prayed to ask for protection and guidance from the Great Spirit for what loomed before them.

As family, relatives, friends, and society members spoke with the men, Chumani glanced around at the Red Shields, many of whom had helped prepare the Crow garments and moccasins and had provided some of the enemy possessions to be left behind as implicating items. Her gaze paused on a stoic-faced Wastemna who stood with her parents. She smiled at the woman, but Wastemna did not respond in kind. What astonished and intrigued Chumani was the look on Wastemna's mother's face. She wondered if she were mistaken or if she had truly seen a brief expression of hatred and hostility toward her. If so, why? She realized this was not the time to ponder such a matter, so she dismissed both females from her mind. She looked at Hanmani with Cetan perched on the girl's shoulder and sent them a smile. She did the same with her husband's parents and grandparents. Then it was time to leave.

Wind Dancer, Chumani, War Eagle, Red Feather, and Zitkala guided their mounts out of camp, and soon left it far behind as they galloped over rolling grassland with scattered trees and bushes. They headed eastward toward the area where Whites had settled near several trading posts along the great river. Soon their clever trickery would begin, and all hoped it would provoke distrust and trouble between the *Wasicun* and Apsaalooke to distract those enemies from attacking the Red and White Shields.

For two and a half days and using a swift pace over fairly easy terrain, the small band traveled near the lengthy Sahiyela River, along whose banks were situated trading posts, trapping sites, many white settlers, and, further south, Fort Pierre, and upon whose swift and deep waters steamboats plied their trade.

They sneaked toward the first homestead under the cover of near darkness beneath a rising half-moon. They were clad in garments with Crow designs and colors just in case they were sighted, though their plan was to try to get in and out without being seen. They did not want to risk being wounded or slain by "firesticks" while they pulled their sly trick of stealing horses and then leaving them near a Crow camp.

When they reached the corral, the five talked softly, and gently stroked the nervous horses into a quiet calm. In a short time, they had the creatures tethered and led from the corral and another from a small barn. They walked them to where their mounts awaited and left quietly after discarding a broken Crow wristlet at the corral. That, along with the marked arrow and the distinctive moccasin tracks of each tribe, would cause the Apsaalooke to be blamed for the theft. They hoped the Whites would summon the Bluecoats to follow the horses' trail to where they would be found picketed near one of the Crow villages.

They repeated their actions at two more sites, adding the new animals to the enlarging herd hidden nearby, though all they left at those scenes were identifiable Crow moccasin prints, as their tribal footwear mounded on the outside and sank inward on the inside. They were happy to complete so much of their initial ploy without exposing themselves or confronting any perils. Yet, they knew their good fortune would not last, as some of the tasks looming before them were more daring and dangerous.

At the last location, a lengthy distance from the other three, they faced their first challenge. A white man was standing near the wooden fence, smoking a short pipe and gazing at the stars. The group discussed whether to skip that place or get rid of the man, who might impede their mission.

"Do not slay him, *mihigna,*" Chumani whispered, "for he may have a wife and little ones who need him. Strike his head, bind his body to a post, and silence him with a cloth from his shirt. Perhaps knowing he faces danger will provoke him to take his family and leave Indian lands to keep them safe from us."

Wind Dancer smiled and caressed her cheek. "Your words are wise and kind, and your heart is good, *mitawin*. It will be as you speak, for there is no need to slay him on this moon."

Chumani and the others watched in suspense as her husband sneaked up behind the man and gave him a blow to the head which rendered him unconscious. Then horror flooded her as she saw a large dog leave the woods, where it no doubt had been off roaming or hunting, and race toward that spot to defend its fallen master. She heard its fierce growls indicating readiness to attack. Yet, with lightning speed and awesome skill, War Eagle fired a nocked Crow arrow and ended that threat. She was certain the one yelp the creature sent forth was not heard inside the wooden dwelling, where only a faint glow of light showed at a square opening. She exhaled in relief, aware for the first time of holding her breath, so long that she felt lightheaded for a moment. She smiled faintly at Zitkala when her friend gently squeezed her hand in comfort, and she nodded her gratitude. She glanced at the quiet house once more and joined the others.

The white man was bound and gagged as she had suggested. A small pouch filled with tobacco seeds and beaded with a Crow design was dropped near his disabled body. The knot which held it suspended from a belt was untied to make it appear it had come loose and fallen off during the action. The Apsaalooke viewed those seeds as big medicine and they played a large part in their sacred rituals. They believed the Creator gave tobacco seeds to a past leader named No Vitals to plant and harvest each growing season and that as long as they performed that ceremony and possessed sacred seeds, their people would survive and prosper, just as the Cheyenne believed the same of their Four Sacred Arrows from Sweet Medicine's prophecy.

* * *

They did not halt to sleep that night, only to take short rests and to change mounts, having brought along two each to prevent overtiring the animals. While they had the landscape to themselves, they rode swiftly toward their next destination. The area was familiar to them, so they knew which locations to skirt to avoid making contact with other bands and terrain perils such as prairie-dog villages and sudden ravines. They also knew where they would have to be extra careful and even hide during daylight to prevent being exposed by hunters or pre-season buffalo scouts. They did not worry about encountering white trappers, as few worked along the banks of the Sahiyela which flowed too deeply into "hostile land," and most who labored along its beginning course and other rivers had left them to sell their winter catches. Yet, they had come to a decision that if a meeting occurred, the intruder must die by Crow arrows so he could not expose their true identities and purpose.

The next morning, they separated so Wind Dancer could ride ahead, War Eagle travel to their left, and Red Feather to their right to watch for an unexpected approach of others, ally or foe. As the men scouted for their party, Chumani and Zitkala guided the stolen herd toward their target. The women did not talk or stay close together, as they could not risk being distracted and must maintain control of the animals. Many creatures and birds were sighted on ground awash with the colors of numerous wildflowers, but they did not halt to hunt or cook meals.

During the day, the men returned at prearranged times to rest, eat, and change mounts. They ate food brought with them: bread, dried fruits and nuts, pemmican, and jerky. There was no want for fresh water, as streams and rivers traversed the area. Talk was sparse, as concentration was crucial. They realized that being caught with stolen animals would provoke a bitter conflict with Lakotas instead of the Crow. Each continually prayed for guidance, protection, and secrecy of their deed.

That night, they stopped only long enough to sleep for a short time before they pressed northwestward over rolling grassland and low hills. Even if they were already being pursued by Whites or soldiers, they had a huge lead and either group would camp for the night.

On the fourth moon after raiding the homesteads, their vigilance heightened as they entered enemy territory. From past scouting trips, Wind Dancer knew he wanted to leave the horses in a long and deep ravine where grass and water were located and ropes could be stretched from side to side to hold them captive. There, the animals would not be sighted by a casual rider from another tribe and taken before they could serve their intended purpose. He reasoned that if the Crow found the herd, they would seize it and take it to their village.

After the men completed that task while the women stood guard, two of the animals were kept for use in duping the Crow later. Their shod hooves would be covered by rabbit skins to hide their metal tracks during departure as soon as another precaution was taken. The five rode in the deep stream for a long distance before leaving the water and securing pelts over the stolen horses' iron moccasins. At last, the most dangerous parts of their first journey were over and they could head for home and rest.

During the next four days, the Red Shield party traveled in elated spirits. They laughed and talked, while they maintained their alert, and always kept a guard posted at night as the other four slept in shifts assigned by Wind Dancer. They spoke about the current adventure, past conflicts and battles, their families, impending episodes, and about their friendships and events they had shared since early childhood.

* * *

On their last night on the trail, they camped amidst dense trees and at a rambling river northwestward of their winter village, a location too far to reach that day, though a near full moon would light their path.

Back within Lakota territory, they could relax their alert slightly, so the women built a fire and roasted several rabbits the men had slain. Again, the group talked and laughed together about many things as they ate.

Afterward, Chumani went behind some bushes to excuse herself prior to joining Wind Dancer on their sleeping mat and was slightly distracted by thoughts of being in his embrace for the first time in many days. Then she sensed movement from the corner of her eyes. She came to instant alert as she looked in that direction, her hand going to the handle of the sheathed knife at her waist. She reasoned it was probably a nocturnal animal, but it could be an enemy trying to sneak up on them. She kept still as her gaze searched the shadows beyond her. Then she sighted her target, bathed in moonlight, as it appeared and halted beside a sacred cottonwood.

At first she thought it was a wolf but changed her mind. Yet, it did not look like any dog she had ever seen. Its eyes were tawny and seemed to glow, perhaps from the moon's reflection upon them. His fur was thick and long and had a silverish gleam, again perhaps a trick of the moon's light. As he returned her stare, she sensed an awesome power exuding from him. She was enthralled by the beast. He seemed to fill her with sensations of peace and joy. Was he, she wondered, spirit or real? Was he trying to communicate with her? If so, why?

Chumani continued to watch the beautiful creature until it nodded its head twice and backed into the shadows, to vanish among them. She looked and listened, but no further sign of him was evident. She rejoined the others and told them about the strange event as she sat down on her mat.

"Perhaps he came from the mating of a she-wolf with

a white man's dog who escaped their wooden tepee," Wind Dancer ventured, "for they have brought many unknown kinds with them to our lands."

"That is true," Red Feather concurred, "for I have seen them at the trading post. It is good he did not attack you."

"I sensed no danger from him. It was like . . . a mystical experience. His eyes and pelt seemed to glow like magic," she repeated earlier words.

"Perhaps he is a spirit and he comes to help us with the sacred quest," War Eagle said. "A strange beast traveling with us would frighten the Crow into fleeing from us." He grinned and added, "Perhaps you are so weary you fell asleep while standing and dreamed he was there."

"You tease me, my second brother," Chumani playfully scolded him as she glanced at a quiet Zitkala whose gaze was locked on Red Feather.

"I do, my second sister, but I mean no harm," he said with a chuckle.

"As I will mean no harm when I tell every young woman in camp, she has caught War Eagle's eye and they all pursue you with great hunger. You will be the one to grow weary from their chases and seek a place to hide."

War Eagle sent her a feigned grimace and chuckled again. "You would not play such a mean trick on me, for we are family now. But when the moon comes when I must take a mate, I will choose one like you."

Chumani smiled at her husband's younger brother. "Your words are kind and your tongue is smooth, so I will be good to you."

"Your words calm me so I can sleep this moon," War Eagle responded.

Wind Dancer was amused by their exchange of words. He was glad his wife and brother had become friends, as had his sister and wife. He told the others, "It is time for us to sleep, for the new sun brings much to do."

The Red Shield band encircled the five riders at the edge of camp, as their approach had been sighted and news of their return had spread fast amongst them. All listened as the stirring tale of their adventure was related by Wind Dancer in colorful detail. The group's courage, cunning, and skills were praised highly by the warriors, and the women concurred with nods and murmurs of *"Han,"* which meant *yes, that is right.*

Chief Rising Bear, Winona, Hanmani, Nahemana, and Little Turtle were especially relieved and overjoyed to see their loved ones return unharmed. He commended the party on their great achievement and prowess. Afterward, he said, "We must let them eat and rest, as they have traveled far and fast and must be weary."

"Come, my children," a happy Winona invited, "I have food prepared. Hanmani, fetch fresh water for us to drink."

Red Feather's parents smiled at him, and did the same to Zitkala at his side, who was asked to join them for the evening meal.

Zitkala was tempted to accept so she could spend time with her love, but she thought it best before his people to politely decline and to eat with the others. She thanked them for their offer and said she would join them on another day. Yet, she could not help but wonder if they had asked because Red Feather had revealed an interest in her to them.

As they reached the area where Wind Dancer's and Rising Bear's tepees were located, Chumani stared at the empty space to one side of theirs. "Where is the lodge of Buffalo Hump" she asked. "Was there trouble while we were gone? Was it destroyed? Were he and his family harmed?"

"Come inside," the chief almost whispered, "and we will tell you."

Chumani, Wind Dancer, War Eagle, and Zitkala followed Rising Bear into his dwelling where he disclosed shocking news.

"Hanmani and her friend Macha were doing their private task in the bushes in the forest when Wastemna and her mother approached, and spoke of doing a terrible deed. They planned to give Cetan bad meat to slay him and to do bad things to Dewdrops and Zitkala when they returned. They also spoke of many bad deeds they had carried out on past suns. They want to drive Dewdrops from our camp and my son's tepee. Evil stole their minds and hearts, for they desired for Wastemna to join to my son and their plan was defeated. If she could not have him, she would seek Red Feather as a mate. They were angry that his eye was also captured by a Brule woman. Hanmani returned to camp and told me all. I summoned the council and they were exposed before it. We voted to banish them from our camp and land. Buffalo Hump accepted our words and the truth of his family's evil. He loves them and could not endure losing them, and could not remain here to live in shame alone. He took them to join another band far away from our territory. Blue Owl was chosen to take his place as war chief. You can be happy now, Dewdrops, for no more mischief and evil will strike at you, my second daughter."

Chumani smiled at Rising Bear. "That is good, my second father, and I thank you for your kindness and help in that matter." Now she understood the strange look the older woman had given her before their departure; it truly had been one of hatred and hostility. At last she could relax, for the tricksters had been exposed and banished, though it saddened her to be the unbidden reason for the loss of their war chief and friend. She hoped the other Red Shields would not resent her.

"If the snake had bitten Winona before Dewdrops took its life, my beloved mate would be lost to me," Rising Bear added. "I thank the Great Spirit for sending you to us, Dewdrops, and I thank you for saving her life and that of her father during the Crow attack. It is good to have you live among us."

Chumani smiled again and nodded appreciation, her throat too constricted by deep emotion to respond with words. When Hanmani returned, she warmly conveyed her gratitude for solving that mystery and for tending and protecting Cetan so well.

"We are good friends, and his wing heals swiftly, but he cannot take to the sky until it is strong again. I am happy Wastemna and her mother will no longer trouble your spirit and tepee."

"As am I," Wind Dancer concurred with his sister. He was sorry he had ever experienced even a tiny suspicion that his wife had been to blame for the past mischief; he would never doubt her and her place in his destiny again. "We believed Wastemna was causing the mischief, but we could not accuse the daughter of our war chief and friend before others until she exposed herself. We did not suspect her mother worked with her."

"It is wise you waited for Wakantanka to reveal their evil to others, but our people would have believed your words to be true," Rising Bear told him.

"Do our people object to Red Feather's interest in Zitkala?" Wind Dancer asked for the Brule women's benefit.

Rising Bear glanced at the woman in question and smiled. "We did not tell them those words, for Red Feather has not revealed them and it was not our place to do so while he was gone. But I am sure his parents and our people will be happy for him to take a mate during the coming season. It will be good to be twice bonded to our allies, the White Shields."

Zitkala smiled and thanked the chief for his kind remarks. She had not expected her relationship with Red Feather to be exposed before they had grown closer and made a decision about a future together. She could not help but worry about the effect of that news upon him, as his "interest" might not be that serious yet, or ever.

Afterward, Winona and Hanmani served the food and water; and all sat on buffalo hides and rush mats to eat and talk together. Once more, the tale of their adventure was related and discussed, as was their next journey.

It was after dark when they parted company. Wind Dancer, Chumani and Zitkala went to his tepee to sleep.

Cetan rested nearby on a temporary perch, happy to have his longtime companion returned. It was as if he understood that another, a man, now shared her life and affections. Even so, he grasped she still loved and needed him. Yet, an instinct deep within him yearned for a mate of his own and soon he must seek and find one.

The following morning, Chumani went to the *cansakawakeya* to spend the next few days beading and quilling during her woman's flow. While she was there, Hanmani would tend her hawk, and Zitkala would cook and do chores for Wind Dancer and bring her food and water.

As she settled herself in the secluded willow shelter, she wished there had been time and privacy to discuss Red Feather with her best friend. She could not help but hope and pray they two would join and Zitkala remain there. She did not want to imagine how it would hurt her friend if that relationship failed to become more than friendship, as she was certain Zitkala was in love with Wiyaka Lute and wanted to become his wife and mother of his children.

Children . . . The appearance of her blood flow told Chumani she was not with child, though she had mated many times with her husband. She decided it was not the season for her to bear a son or daughter and the Great Spirit prevented that condition to keep her a part of the sacred quest. She now looked forward to becoming a mother again, especially since the baby would be fathered by Wind Dancer, a man she loved deeply. Just thinking of him caused her to quiver with renewed passion and her heart to sing with joy. She was so fortunate the Great Spirit had chosen them for each other and crossed their paths, that total trust and acceptance existed between and within them.

As she worked in solitude, she thought about the challenging and dangerous adventures which loomed before them. Within a few moons, their party of five would be leaving again to carry out their next daring and cunning task against the Bird Warriors. Afterward, they would head for the Plains with the Red Shields where their two bands would camp and hunt buffalo together, and where she would be reunited with her family and people for a short time. From that site, they would head for the trading post at Fort Pierre and hopefully dupe the Whites living there. To prepare herself for that perilous encounter and trickery, she practiced the Crow and English languages.

She was all too cognizant that if their cunning ploys succeeded, the Crow and Whites would be too busy battling each other to give them trouble during their annual buffalo hunt and ensuing move to their winter camp. But if they failed and were exposed, the Bird Warriors, white settlers, and soldiers would wreak vengeance upon them with a fury.

At dusk on the third sun later, Chumani carried out the customary departure ritual of bathing and donning clean garments. When she arrived at her tepee, she found Zitkala sitting and eating with Wind Dancer and Red Feather, savoring a deer stew and bread made from tradecorn.

The three greeted her with delight, and, after putting away her sewing, she joined them to eat and talk.

As they chatted, Chumani noted how radiant and happy Zitkala was. She noticed the smiling woman was wearing a fringed dress with lovely beading and a decorative ornament in her dark hair, which hung loose tonight around her shoulders. She realized Zitkala no longer wore a wide and tight band around her ample breasts to flatten them to conceal her femininity. Instead, her friend seemed to be trying to heighten feminine attributes, and she was succeeding. Her face seemed slightly fuller and softer, her hands were no longer rough, and white edges grew from the tips of her normally short or ragged nails. Even Zitkala's hair seemed thicker, shinier, and more flattering to her face. It was undeniable that no one could mistake Zitkala for a man.

Chumani was thrilled by those discoveries, elated for

her best friend, and not surprised by their powerful effect upon Red Feather, who could not seem to keep his glowing gaze off the other woman. She closed her eyes for a moment and thanked Wakantanka for that gift and blessing.

That next morning, Nahemana came to their tepee to relate the alarming dream he had experienced during the previous night: "I saw the Old Woman Who Quills At The Edge Of The World; she was alone. Her dog companion was gone, stolen, slain, or left of his own free will. That is a bad sign, *micinksi* and Dewdrops, for if he is dead or fails to return to her side to unravel her day's quilling, our world as we know it will soon end."

"Do not worry, Grandfather," Wind Dancer attempted to assure the old man, "for it was only a dream, not a sacred vision to warn us of danger. Perhaps you dreamed of a dog because I told you of the strange creature Dewdrops saw in the forest during our return."

"It was a sign from the Great Spirit, *micinksi*, for the moon was full and holds much magic when her face is bright. I fear for your safety."

"Do not be afraid or doubtful, Grandfather, for Wakantanka guides and protects us. Perhaps He sends the Spirit Dog as a helper to us during our tasks, for Cetan is injured and cannot go with us as planned."

Nahemana smiled. "Perhaps that is true. Perhaps I misread the message. Perhaps that is why he appeared to Dewdrops. Perhaps an evil spirit showed me her camp while he was gone to raise fears and doubts. I will seek another vision at the sacred mountain to give us answers."

Four suns later at dusk, Wind Dancer, Chumani, War Eagle, Red Feather, and Zitkala lay pressed to the ground and concealed by tall grass as they spied on a small band of Crow warriors at the edge of their territory. They had left their horses secreted in a dense treeline and wriggled their way closer to the scene where seven men sat around a campfire, talking and laughing and wearing warpaint upon their faces, a sign of their evil intent.

As one turned to retrieve something from behind him, Wind Dancer and Chumani inhaled in astonishment at the same time then looked at each other in shock. Here at last was the enemy who had led the lethal raids against their two camps two winters past, the raids which had taken the lives of their mates, sons, and others. At long last, their target was within reach.

Wind Dancer's gaze narrowed as he studied the Crow warrior whose face was painted half black and half red and displayed black coyote tracks traveling atop the lighter shade. He clenched his jaw. Hatred and a hunger for revenge consumed him. "We must attack and slay them. Their leader belongs to me. He is a dead man."

"They are seven and we are five, my brother," War Eagle reasoned in a whisper. "They camp in the open, so we cannot sneak up on them. Their weapons are within reach. It is foolish to challenge such forces who are prepared to retaliate swiftly. We must wait for them to sleep."

"No, my brother; we must attack while my blood is hot for battle. If we wait, others may come and their number would be too great to challenge. We can defeat seven. I will not allow him to escape my knife again. Prepare yourselves, for we attack soon."

Chapter
Twelve

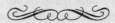

"Speak to him, Dewdrops, for this peril is great," War Eagle urged.

"I cannot, for he thinks and acts as I do," she responded.

"Your hearts are too filled with bitterness to have clear minds." War Eagle argued. "Do you not think it is strange they camp in the open? Perhaps others hide in the trees and below the ravine beyond them and they set a trap for us. Is that not the way of the Crow leader who brings fire to your heart?"

"That is true, my brother, but they do not know we are nearby. Do you think they set a snare with hopes we will ride upon them and fall into it?" Wind Dancer reasoned. "No, they camp outside the cover of the forest because their pride is too large, and they believe we are far away preparing to leave for the Plains."

"Our bows are with our horses, my brother. We must fetch them and send arrows into their camp and bodies before we rush out upon them. If others hide nearby, our action will lure them into the open and it will give us time to escape if their number is too large for us to battle."

Wind Dancer considered his brother's words. They had

left their bows behind because crawling on one's belly was easier without bringing them along. They had intended to scout the enemy camp, return for their mounts, and attack on horseback. "If we return to our horses, our presence will be seen. The wind no longer blows strong and moves the grasses to conceal us. We must fall upon them with our knives and take them by surprise."

"Perhaps it is us who will be surprised, my brother." War Eagle did not want to point out that two members of their party were women. He had been told tales of their great prowess, but were they skilled and strong enough to fight trained warriors in hand-to-hand combat? Too, he could not understand why his older brother would risk endangering his mate's life. And should not Red Feather want to protect Zitkala? Yet, it would be rude and wrong to ask such questions, as it could sound as if he was implying revenge was more important than his wife's life. He had to trust his brother and do what he was told, for that was their way.

As Wind Dancer looked over at War Eagle, Chumani's gaze widened as her eyes caught a strange sight. "Be still and look there," she told them.

As the two men's gazes followed the nod of her head, all five in their group saw a huge dog whose thick fur and large eyes were so pale a gray that they shone like silver in the brilliant rays of reflective sunlight. He had seemed to appear as if by magic, as if Mother Earth had spewed him forth from her fertile body. Though he made no sound, the swift and agile animal raced forward, snatched the Crow leader's quiver of arrows that was laying behind him, and rushed with lightning speed into the dense forest near their hiding place. They heard the astonished man shout at the animal, saw him leap to his feet and run after the sneaky and daring thief.

"It is the Spirit Dog I saw in the forest many moons past," Chumani whispered in awe. "He has come to help us defeat our enemies and we must follow his head. He has summoned our target away from his friends."

"Stay here while I trail and slay him," Wind Dancer commanded. "Do not attack the others until I return and give the signal."

Since he was their leader, the other four knew his orders must be obeyed. They remained low to the earth, still and silent, while Wind Dancer wriggled backward toward the trees.

Chumani noted a strong breeze had returned to vigorously sway the tall grass and wildflowers, cleverly masking her husband's retreat. Surely, she concluded, the Creator and the forces of nature and the elements were on their side today. Even so, she closed her eyes and prayed for her beloved's safety. She heard the other six foes laugh and call out to their friend, amused by the incident, and revealing his name as Chaheechopes, meaning "Four Wolves." She glanced at Zitkala, who sent her a smile of encouragement and then she looked at Red Feather beside Zitkala, but his gaze was locked on their foes and a knife was clutched in one hand as if ready to respond to any threat. She noticed, too, that Red Feather's other hand was resting atop Zitkala's. A warm glow traveled over her body to see that display of affection. Her gaze returned to the six Apsaalooke who sat cross-legged around their campfire and she focused her full attention upon them, eager for her husband's safe return.

In the woods, Wind Dancer sneaked up behind the man and sneered, "What prize do you seek on Oglala hunting grounds, *suska*?" As the Crow whirled to face him, he taunted, "Why do you not shout for your friends to come and save you from a warrior who stands high above you in skills?"

"I need no help to slay one lowly Oglala boy. Your eyes trick you; I am not slow or worthless. Send forth your death chant, for soon you will walk the Ghost Trail with others of your kind."

"I know your face paint," Wind Dancer hissed. "You are the coward who preys upon camps with women, children, and old ones while warriors are away hunting. Do you fear to enter them when we are there to battle against you?"

"I seek to kill all Lakotas, for Lakotas attacked my camp and took the lives of my family. If boys are slain, they cannot become men. If women are slain, they cannot bring forth more sons to follow their fathers in battle. If old ones are slain, it steals the joy and spirit of their families."

"It was not the Red Shields or the White Shields who killed your family, for we do not attack the innocents. We are true warriors; we fight only men, as it was meant to be."

"You lie, son of Rising Bear."

Wind Dancer stared at the man. "You know me?"

"I know the faces of all enemies who will gain me large coups. I will take your scalp and possessions to my camp to show others I took your life."

"Then come and do so, Crow dog, if you have the courage and prowess."

A fierce fight ensued as the two men struggled. They used knives, fists, feet, and hurled bodies to thwart the opponent's efforts. They seemed equally matched in ability, stamina, and strength. The conflict went on and on until their energy was drained, sweat beaded on their faces and torsos, and dust clung to their hair and garments.

But soon the Crow was taken off guard when the silver dog grabbed at one legging and snatched back on it, pulling him off balance. He stumbled backward and struck the ground, knocking the air from his lungs and preventing a yell of help when his rival leapt upon his fallen body, raised his armed hand, and buried a blade within his heart.

Wind Dancer stared down at his dead foe. He extracted his knife and looked all around, but the strange dog was gone. Then he heard another Crow shouting for his friend as a second Bird Warrior headed his way.

Wind Dancer hurriedly and quietly dragged the body into the bushes and concealed himself. As soon as he saw his new target and made sure the man was alone, he charged at the Crow from behind, simultaneously clamping a hand over his mouth to silence him and burying the knife in the center of his foe's back. The Crow reflexively arched toward him and tried to scream, then went limp in his captor's grasp.

Wind Dancer realized two were gone, leaving five in both groups now. He started to retrieve their bows and quivers, but decided that would take too long, as their horses were a good distance away in hiding; and the other five Crow might be getting suspicious. He took a brief time to search for the first Crow's quiver, but could not find it. He made his way back to the others and related his two clashes. "I think the dog belongs to the Old Woman Who Quills," Wind Dancer concluded. "When Grandfather saw him missing from her side and camp, it was because he was being sent to help us slay our enemies and make peace with our pasts. He vanished as the mist after the sun rises; he has returned to her side and our world is safe. Now our sons have been avenged, *mitawin,* and they can rest in happiness."

"It is good, *mihigna,* and my heart thanks you for that deed."

"Look," Zitkala whispered, "they go to seek their missing friends."

The hidden group peered through waving stalks of grass and dancing wildflowers and saw the five Crow heading toward the forest with weapons clutched in their hands. They heard one call out the names of the two who had vanished earlier. It was obvious they were on full alert for trouble, but Wind Dancer told his four companions he had concealed the bodies in thick bushes and brushed away all signs on the ground of their struggles.

"We will slip into the trees and await their approach. When they walk between us, we will leap upon them and defeat them," Wind Dancer began, then added other cunning details for their impending assault.

"Your plan is good, my brother," said War Eagle.

The two men exchanged smiles of affection and mutual respect before their band made a covert entry into the forest. They secreted themselves amidst the ample vegetation which grew on both sides of a well-worn animal path; they hoped their enemies would follow this path as the first two had done. Wind Dancer hoped to allow them to catch a glimpse of him to provoke them into chasing him into a trap. They waited in rising suspense as they heard one man call out again for his missing friends and heard his companions make speculations as to whether their disappearances were the result of trouble or if a joke was being played on them; and they seemed to lean toward the latter explanation.

Soon, the Apsaalooke approached their position; and they curled their bodies into tight balls near the earth and in the thickest parts of the greenery surrounding them. When their foes slowly moved between them on the narrow trail, Wind Dancer simultaneously let out a war whoop—the attack signal—and lunged from his hiding place, his outstretched arms seizing two startled Bird Warriors around their throats and his momentum carrying all three into the opposite bushes where Chumani was concealed.

Without delay, his companions sprang into action. Chumani jumped atop one fallen warrior, the smallest of the Crow party, though she was certain his strength and probably his skills were superior to hers. Zitkala shot out her feet to entangle and trip a third, Red Feather leapt upon and locked on to a fourth's back, and War Eagle charged the fifth astonished man. While they had the advantage of surprise, Chumani sliced across the right-hand fingers of her target to weaken his grasp, which compelled him to drop his weapon. Zitkala bounded upon her quarry's back and buried her knife in the writhing man's shoulder, though she had wanted to send the blade into his heart. As Red Feather rode his captive, who bucked like a wild horse, he sliced at the man's face and neck, scoring many cuts and infuriating him. War Eagle slammed his lowered shoulder into his opponent's abdomen and stunned him; and Wind Dancer thrashed in the bushes and vegetation as he attempted to overpower the largest and strongest enemy amongst all of them.

The clashes were fierce and swift. At one point, Chumani's opponent pinned her to the ground and attempted to choke her. Wind Dancer, who was straddling his opponent in close proximity, kicked out forcefully with one foot and knocked the scowling Crow from his wife's imprisoned body. Chumani took advantage of the moment and grabbed a handful of dirt and flung it into the man's face; it filled his nose and eyes, causing him to lose sight of her and to interfere with his breathing. As he wiped at his watery eyes, snorted, and coughed, Chumani rammed her head into his stomach, and followed that blow with one from her knife. As the man stumbled into Red Feather, he slashed outward with his blade, running it across an exposed throat and ended the Crow's life; then he concentrated on his desperate target.

Chumani hurried to assist Zitkala with her struggle, the two women slashing him in vulnerable spots until he was too weak to resist. One final cut with Zitkala's weapon ended their conflict.

Wind Dancer observed his brother's fight. Though he wanted to help complete it before War Eagle was wounded or slain, it was not their way to intrude on another's encounter; so he would take over only if his brother became impaired. Too, he was aware of War Eagle's elite prowess, and of an expertise which was large for a man of so few seasons of battle experience. He risked a distracting glance at his best friend, to find that Red Feather was the victor. He already knew his wife and Zitkala had been successful with their battles, and had witnessed his beloved's trickery. He recalled when his eyes had been blinded by dirt during the grizzly attack, and was proud of her for using that sly tactic.

The others gathered beside him to witness War Eagle's contest. It was clear the youngest member of their band was not playing with his opponent—they were simply very well-matched. Even so, the son of Chief Rising Bear soon defeated the last enemy and after receiving only one minor cut on his left forearm and a small nick on his right shoulder. As for the others and himself, they had received only a few cuts, nicks, scrapes, and bruises; and none were serious.

Wind Dancer glanced at each fallen body and smiled. "We have won a great victory this day, my friends and loved ones," he said. "No longer will Chaheechopes and his band scout and raid our camps and slay our people. We must carry their bodies to their campfire and place the blame for this deed upon *wasicun* settlers or Bluecoats and their half-breed scouts. We will take their possessions and horses as war prizes to be used later when we pull our trick at Fort Pierre. We will use the *wasicun's* horses we kept from our last raid to make iron-shoe marks around the Bird Warriors' campfire and we will leave the short firestick and piece of cloth from the white man's world so they will be blamed when these bodies are found by Chaheechopes' people or allies. Come, we must prepare the way to fool them, tend our injuries, and ride for home. This is a glorious day for us as companions."

The others smiled and nodded agreement, then set to work to carry out Wind Dancer's orders.

When they'd reached a safe location in Lakota territory and made camp for the night, Wind Dancer and Chumani left their companions sitting around a fire and headed over a low hill to take advantage of their last chance at privacy for a while. Though they had told the others they were taking a walk, their intent was no doubt clear. Yet, they did not care if their pretense failed to dupe anyone, as their need for each other was too great. A half-moon lighted their way as they strolled onward, and stars twinkled overhead. They had reached the season when days were warm and nights were mild. Night-blooming flowers added an extra fragrance to the air upon which the scents of day-flowers and grasses wafted in freedom. The almost ever-present wind was blowing, but the rise in terrain sheltered them on its far side from the strongest gusts.

At a secluded distance away from the others, they halted and sat down on the thick grass. For a time, they simply savored each other's company and the Creator's scenery. Soon they sank to their backs and began to talk in soft voices.

As he turned his head and looked into her luminous eyes, Wind Dancer murmured an admission he had yearned to make since they met, "You are a cunning thief, *mitawin*, for you have stolen my heart."

Chumani smiled and warmed, for his expression and tone revealed he was serious. "As you have stolen mine, *mihigna*. You fill me with love and desire for you. I am happy and honored to be your wife."

Wind Dancer rolled to his side and propped himself with an elbow. "As I am proud and happy to be your husband," he said, caressing her cheek and stroking her hair. "I was lost in you from the day your morning mist settled upon me in the Brave Heart forest. I was a man, a warrior, a hunter, and a future chief, but I was not whole and my life-circle was not complete until you entered it and filled the one remaining hole within me and my existence. I love and need you as I have no other."

Chumani lifted a hand so her fingers could trace his full and enticing lips as she disclosed, "Long before we met in the forest, you filled my mind with a craving for you after my eyes sighted you during our intertribal meeting. I could not get closer, for women do not approach men when they talk and game, but your magic reached out to me across that great distance. After our encounter in the forest, it grew as swift and high as the grass on the Plains. I believed our lives would never blend, so I tried to ignore and forget you, but you refused to leave my thoughts and dreams. After you came to my camp and claimed me, I was afraid to believe I could win your love and allegiance. My spirit soars to learn I have won a great and glorious victory. I, too, love and need you as I have no other, for you also make me whole."

"Do we dare to risk a union here where our minds will be distracted?"

Chumani could tell that he was jesting. "We lie beneath the Great Spirit's dwelling and upon Mother Earth's body, so They will protect us from all harm," she said. "I am yours, *mihigna*, take me."

Wind Dancer responded instantly to her words and seductive mood. His dark eyes roamed her lovely face, radiant in the moon's glow, as he murmured, "As I am yours, *mitawin*, so take me."

He sighed happily when she wriggled closer and snuggled against him. He had day and night dreamed of sharing special moments like this with her, and at last they had become realities. He wondered if the heartbeats he felt upon his chest were hers, his, or both of theirs. He shoved aside worries of her safety and survival during their awesome challenges, knowing he must trust Wakantanka to guard her life for him. All he wanted now was to concentrate on his wife, and their love for each other.

Chumani, too, could think of nothing except loving him. Perhaps they were risking peril by being away from the others, armed only with knives, but she was willing to take that chance. She could not seem to get enough of him—his touch, his scent, his words of passion. When he kissed her, she felt she was complete. As their mouths feasted in abundant delight, her questing hand wandered over his dark and sleek torso, her fingertips admiring his virile physique. He gave her joy, hope, and pleasure. He charged her with energy, as if renewing her very soul. He brought peace to her once-troubled spirit, and assuaged the anguish over her son's loss and caused her to long for another child. Because of him, she was excited and satisfied to be a woman and wife. He was perfection, and he belonged to her of his own free will. It would have amazed her to know those same thoughts and feelings filled him.

Hungering to caress each other's naked flesh, they

quickly shed their garments and moccasins and sank to the lush blanket of green as they embraced, stroked, and kissed. Their hands, lips, and tongues roamed each other in freedom and enthusiasm. All of their senses seemed heightened. They noticed how moonlight played over sun-kissed bodies and ebony hair and created sensual shadows on each other. They felt the ticklings of grass blades and wildflower stems and blossoms, and inhaled their pleasing scents. They felt the cooling night air gently settling upon them. They heard nocturnal birds calling to their mates, and they heard each other's pounding heartbeats.

Wind Dancer nibbled at her earlobe, neck, and bare shoulders, his playful tongue journeying from end to end along her collarbone, teasing the dip at the center of her throat, and pausing at each pulse point to test his potent and mounting effect upon her. She was powerful magic; she was irresistible allure; and she belonged to and with him. His caresses and kisses grew bolder as his passions burned brighter and higher. His hand drifted over her breasts, fondling and firming them. His lips followed that blissful trail and lingered there for a while as his hand walked a slow path down her flat stomach and past her hips to enter the center of her womanhood. He felt a heat like a smoldering fire radiating from her and yearned to tantalize her to an even loftier peak of suspense.

Chumani writhed as he worked magic upon her suscepti-ble body. She was taut with anticipation, as hot as a stone in a fire before the purification ritual. Every spot on her seemed to beckon him closer and onward. She loved and wanted him with every part of her being. She was so alive in his arms, and he was more important to her than her own survival. Not long ago, she had feared losing herself in him; now, that was all she wanted to do.

Soon, Wind Dancer thrust within the dewy core of her desire, and she welcomed his loving invasion, capturing his lower body with her legs and encircling his neck with her hands. No matter how many times they joined in this manner, it was never the same and was always better than any time before. "You are my heart and destiny, Dewdrops; I love you."

"You are my heart and destiny, *mihigna,* and I love you. Like your name, we will dance upon the wind this night and find great happiness."

As if by a mutual and unspoken signal, they set a steady pattern and matching pace as their soaring spirits chanted their own songs of love and enchantment. Every kiss, every caress, every word spoken was a reaffirming promise of the commitment between them. Their bodies moved together in an enthralling dance of love and bonding.

Unable to resist the urgent flood of fervent passion which swept her away in its swirling current, Chumani lost herself in its wild and wondrous course. Soon she reached a blissful crest and yielded herself to sweet triumph as she cascaded over its towering edge. Hearing her cry of pleasure, Wind Dancer let go of the weakened reins of his restraint and joined her in a burst of glorious splendor. As he gazed into her rich brown eyes during the last few moments of his climax, they seemed to gleam with contentment, great love, and intense elation—the same feelings that abounded in him.

For a short while, they cuddled together and whispered words of endearment and satisfaction.

Later, Chumani used the bladder bag she had brought with her to rinse away the pleasant aroma of their bonding and dried herself with a cloth she had secreted beneath her fringed top. Wind Dancer did the same. They pulled on their garments and moccasins, kissed and embraced, and returned to their campfire which was now burning low.

They decided their friends were either asleep or were successful in pretending to be so. They exchanged smiles when they noticed their buffalo mat had been spread out for them, and they reclined upon it. With a thin blanket covering their nestled bodies, they eased into peaceful slumber.

* * *

As the returning party entered their camp, the shaman and others came to greet them. All five stared at the elderly man with white hair and weathered skin as Nahemana disclosed astonishing news to them.

"After you rode from camp many suns past, I went into the sacred hills and ate the peyote so the Creator could speak to me. Wakantanka gave me a vision of powerful medicine which calmed my troubled mind. He showed me the Old Woman's dog companion sitting at her feet as she quilled the Life-Hide. Soon he looked toward a forest and raced that way, making no sound as he traveled. When he returned, he carried a Crow quiver with many arrows. He sat down at her feet again and chewed upon it until it was destroyed, as their threat to us will be destroyed with his help."

Wind Dancer exchanged looks of amazement with his companions. "We left camp to seek a Crow scouting or raiding party to defeat and blame their slayings on the *wasicun*," he explained. "But the Creator rewarded us by crossing our paths with Four Wolves, the enemy who led the attacks against us two winters past and since the last full moon, and the attack on the White Shield camp which claimed the life of Dewdrops' son. He and his band are dead."

Though it was not their custom to interrupt another while speaking and he had not waited to see if the chief's oldest son was finished, an anxious Raven asked, "Why do the Strong Hearts and Sacred Bow Carriers not attack our enemies in the open where we can strike many coups against them and show we do not fear them and are great warriors? Why does a small band pull sneak attacks we cannot share with our friends and allies?"

"The Strong Hearts and Sacred Bow Carriers are needed here, Raven, to guard our camp and people," Wind Dancer clarified, "for the Crow are sly and lack the honor and courage to fight us on even ground. The plan we use was given to me in my sacred vision and was placed in the thoughts of Dewdrops by the Creator," Wind Dancer reminded him and those gathered around him. "It is meant to evoke hatred, mistrust, and war between Whites and Crow. Their peoples are abundant, and the Bluecoats have mighty weapons. Do not forget the soldiers have a big firestick which swiftly sends forth many hard balls and tears into a warrior's body and slays him. We cannot remove enlodged balls and have no medicines to treat such strange wounds. If we allow them to make truce and come at us as one large force, we will be destroyed."

"My grandson speaks with truth and wisdom," Nahemana told Raven, as he had witnessed the destructive force of the howitzer when it was fired long ago at Fort Pierre.

"Tell us of your challenge and victory," Blue Owl coaxed.

Wind Dancer looked at the war chief and said, "As in Grandfather's powerful vision, a Spirit Dog helped us defeat the Crow band." While his family and people observed and listened in awe, he related the details of that victorious episode. Then he revealed, "We could not find the arrow quiver of Four Wolves which the Spirit Dog snatched and vanished with into the forest; he took it to the Old Woman Who Quills as Grandfather was shown by He-Who-Created-And-Knows-All-Things."

That night, the Red Shields celebrated a glorious victory over the Crow party that had attacked them twice in a vicious and despicable manner. Following a feast and the second retelling of the great deed, Wind Dancer walked around a huge campfire in a large clearing beyond the scattered tepees as he held aloft Chaheechopes's war shield, bow, and scalplock for all to view. As he did so, the Strong Hearts performed their society dance and they chanted his and Red Feather's coups to honor their fellow members.

Afterward, the Sacred Bow Carriers did the same for War Eagle as he displayed the war prizes he had collected. Then both societies chanted the recent coups of Chumani and Zitkala, who sat on either side of Rising Bear in places of great esteem. The chief wore a broad smile of pleasure and pride for his three loved ones, his son's best friend, and their Brule companion. As the two women were being praised for their courage and skills, Winona reached over and gave Chumani's hand a gentle squeeze, and smiled in affection, respect, and gratitude.

Chumani returned the gesture, then looked at Cetan who was perched on a thick leather strip on Hanmani's shoulder and appeared at ease there with his bandaged wing. She watched his head move from side to side as if he was following the animated talk between the girl and her best friend, Macha. She glanced down at the strip secured around her left forearm where she had sustained a minor injury during the recent clash. She had been tended to by Hanmani and Dawn who wanted to practice their medicine skills. The others in the visionquest party also had been tended again, by Winona and others who found great pleasure in doing those good deeds.

Chumani was glad when the activities ended and it was time to return to their tepee. She was both exhilarated and weary, for she had not gotten much sleep last night. Even so, she was not regretful, as she had spent the night blissfully in her husband's arms, laying in the grass and making love. Just recalling it warmed her body and spirit. She could hardly wait for Zitkala and Red Feather to experience such joy, and her two friends appeared to grow closer every sun and moon.

Once she was in her tepee, sleep failed to come. Too many thoughts filled her mind. Soon she would be reunited with her family and people when the two bands would jointly hunt the buffalo as was their summer custom and that elated her. The entire band would move to the vast grasslands where small groups of men and women would leave to spend many suns away from the others as the warriors hunted that game which was vital to their survival and the females skinned and gutted the massive animals where they fell. Young braves would transport the meat and hides back to camp on travois to be divided and prepared by each family.

She knew it was a lengthy and arduous task; and every family was expected to do its share of the work. In the large encampment, wooden racks would be constructed for hanging strips of meat while they dried and became *papa saka*. Other portions of meat would be packed in parfleches to be consumed as was. The remaining sections would be sun-and-air dried and pounded almost to powder, mixed with berries and hot fat, allowed to cool, then formed into rolls of *wakapapi wasna*. The latter was the main source of their nourishment in the winter, as it would not spoil for many circles of the seasons if made properly.

She had performed those chores many times in past seasons and knew them well. Though she had hunted smaller game to help feed her parents and others, she had never gone after buffalo because her father, brother, and male members of her band had believed that was too dangerous for a woman; and she was told her help was needed more by the females with their labors. Being an obedient daughter and tribe member, she had honored her father's command.

Her father's command . . . The thought came unbidden that another urgent request of his had compelled her into joining Dull Star. Yet, she reasoned, if she had not united with that repulsive man, she might have chosen another mate later and been unavailable when she met Wind Dancer. Perhaps it had been Wakantanka's plan. If she had not walked a sad trail long ago, she might not be walking this wonderful one now, for it had placed her in the right setting to find true love. That thought quieted her roaming thoughts so she could drift off to sleep.

For many suns, men hunted small and large game for their families and for those in need to use during the impending journey to the Plains. That was done as a safety precaution to protect the band while it was at its most vulnerable, for they would not need to halt along the way to hunt unless it became absolutely necessary. They scouted for any signs of an enemy approach, and posted guards around the area at all times. While in camp, they sharpened and repaired existing weapons and made new ones for those which had worn out. They worked on numerous arrows for the big hunt and for defense in the event of an enemy attack. They braided leather bridles and harnesses for their horses and conveyances. To ease their restless spirits—as most were eager to depart— and to relax after chores, they played games with each other and with young boys.

The women gathered berries, roots, and plants to complete their meals. They sewed extra parfleches for carrying food and for the imminent storage of the *papa saka* and *wakapapi wasna,* and made replacements for old water bags. Hides and pelts from the men's daily hunts were either staked to the ground or stretched on wooden frames to cure for later tanning. Torn garments and moccasins were repaired; unusable ones were replaced; and new ones were made for growing feet. The best poles from their winter tepees were chosen and marked to become part of their drag-alongs. Other poles would be piled near the rocks to be burned as firewood next winter, as nothing of the Creator's should go to waste.

The sun following the *Wi Yaspapi,* the fullness of the New Moon whose black face could not be seen at night, the departure signal was given by Winona for Rising Bear. Winona revealed that it was time to strike camp and begin their journey by taking down her tepee. Rising Bear knew the White Shields were timing their departure farther south to arrive on schedule at the site they had selected on the Plains.

The camp quickly bustled with activity as tasks were done with speed, eagerness, and efficiency. The numerous lodges were dismantled, belongings were packed on conveyances, weapons and horses were readied, water was fetched, children were given final instructions, babies were secured in their cradleboards, the elderly were assisted with rides, and the travel plan was repeated for everyone's benefit.

The Shirt-Wearers, including Wind Dancer, took their places as leaders of the event; they were the ones who set the daily schedule, chose the route and nightly campsites, and resolved any problems. The Strong Hearts—including Red Feather—and Sacred Bow Carriers—including War Eagle—rode to their assigned spots to act as guards along the way.

After everything and everyone was prepared, Rising Bear, poised at the head of a lengthy column, waved his hand in the air to indicate it was time to go; and the long line followed his lead.

As Chumani rode beside Zitkala—their mounts pulling travois loaded with their belongings, supplies and tepee— she looked at her best friend and asked, "I wonder what joys, rewards, and sufferings await us on the grasslands."

"I do not know, Dewdrops, but we will have answers soon."

Chapter
Thirteen

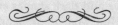

A vast expanse of rolling landscape stretched out before the band of Red Shields on the move. At first, their pace was leisurely to get the people's stamina and muscles in condition for traveling. Soon the sacred Paha Sapa would be left far behind, along with its cooler air and dense forest. Eventually, most trees they would encounter would be lining river and stream banks.

As each day passed without trouble, the people's excitement and anticipation increased, as the summer buffalo hunt was a vital part of their existence. The farther they traveled, the warmer the weather and the flatter and more repetitious the landscape became. Soon only solitary low hills would appear in certain spots and there would be nothing to shade them from a blazing sun except tepees.

A variety of intermingled grasses covered the terrain in lush abundance; some flourished in singular stalks and others in snug bunches or separate patches. Sunflowers, segolily, pasqueflower, mariposa, goldenrod, beeplant and other blossoms were plentiful. Plants with edible leaves, stems, roots, or bulbs thrived here and there. Also growing along the route were many varieties of berries and weeping willows for making flour. Some of those fruits, plants, and berries were ready for gathering and others would be ripe during the next full moon and the two following it. Herbs for seasoning foods or tenderizing meats cropped up in certain locations.

Scattered groups of antelope and deer, and an occasional coyote were seen. Small herds of buffalo roved the area, their massive and dark shapes easily sighted even at a long distance. But what their people sought were the large herds which spread over the green surface farther than the eye could see and roamed eastward of their current position. They had hunted before their departure, so the animals were left in peace to graze. Later, when a need for fresh meat arose, the group would halt for the men to hunt and the women to gather plants and berries.

Cetan was allowed to take flight and hunt for a while each day, as his injury had healed. Otherwise, he perched upon Chumani's travois and also observed the scenery in passing.

The sky was clear and blue, but storms could strike swiftly and violently during early summer. Once in the center of the Plains where nothing obstructed the view, an impending storm could be seen a long way off as it moved toward them, though some jumped upon them with little warning. Rains could be heavy and perilous, but were needed to quench Mother Earth's great thirst during the growing season. Lengthy and vivid rainbows often followed that awesome event, their colors, according to legends, stolen from flowers on the Ghost Trail.

As they journeyed forth, days appeared longer because there was little to nothing to block out the sun's light in any direction. The distance, between destinations was deceptive, the journey was always longer than it appeared; so knowledge of the territory was imperative, as was knowing when and where to halt to camp for safety and fresh water, a responsibility which fell into the hands of the Shirt Wearers.

* * *

One evening at dusk after a long day on the move, Wind Dancer and Chumani took a stroll after their meal. They did not go far away, just walked enough to give them a short time of privacy to enjoy each other's company.

As Wind Dancer gazed across the open terrain, he was reminded of one of the biggest differences between the Whites and Indians: the land and its creatures belonged to the Great Spirit and were to be used by man, not owned or abused or destroyed by him. He looked at his wife. "You must teach me more of the white man's tongue, *mitawin*. It is good and wise to know the words and ways of our enemies so we can defeat them. I know a little English, and a few words in French and Spanish, for trappers and traders with those tongues have passed through our lands and my people accepted them before they realized the great perils in doing so."

"While we camp on the grasslands, I will teach you all I know of their tongue," Chumani promised, then asked her husband, "Have you ever made friends or blood brothers with a *wasicun*?"

"No, I have been close in body only to White-eyes when I went with others to trade at Fort Pierre in past seasons. I no longer do so, for it encourages them to remain in our territory and for more to come. I try to get others to avoid them, but that is a choice each man must make for himself."

He lowered his gaze for a moment, then looked at her and divulged, "Long ago, a white woman lived in our camp, in my father's lodge. She was a gift to him from a Cheyenne ally for helping his band defeat Pawnee, who craved their hunting grounds. He did not wish to have a white slave, but it is not our way to refuse a gift from another chief. She was called Omaste, for her hair was the color of the sun. When my mother was captured by other Pawnee and taken far away twenty summers past and was believed lost to us forever, Omaste took care of me, for I was but four winters old. She was good and kind and accepted her life with us. One dark moon when my father's hunger and sadness for Mother were so great, he allowed Omaste to comfort him. She gave birth to a baby before the next summer. Father named him Cloud Chaser, for the wind blew so hard and fast that the sun and clouds above his birthing spot raced swiftly across the sky as if being chased by a spirit. She died when I was fourteen winters old. She was buried as with her kind, her body placed within Mother Earth."

Chumani was shocked to learn that a great and proud leader like Rising Bear had placed his seeds within the body of a white woman and created a child with her, but she masked her reaction to avoid hurting her beloved. "What happened to her son, your half-white brother?"

"Cloud Chaser vanished as the morning dew when I was fifteen. Father believes he was found and stolen by whites, for the trail of their wagons was nearby. He and his band followed the deep cuts across the face of Mother Earth for many suns, but they could not catch up to the cloud-covered wagons and rescue him. He was forced to return to camp and to accept that sacrifice. Omaste died of winter-in-the-chest six full moons before my brother was lost to us. It is good she was not here during that time, for it would have broken her spirit to lose her child."

"It must have saddened your mother's heart to share her mate with another woman, one who was not even Lakota. I could not share you."

"She did not have to share him," Wind Dancer explained. "Father mated to Omaste only one time and it was while he believed my mother was dead. After she escaped the Pawnee far beyond our lands and returned to us after two circles of the seasons, his heart was filled with joy, and only she lived within it and within his embrace. Omaste remained in our tepee and helped with chores until she died, for my mother understood and accepted what happened while she was gone. After Omaste left us, my mother raised her son as if Cloud Chaser were her own. She grieved over his loss, for he was more Indian than white in looks and spirit, and he carried my father's blood and seed."

"Perhaps the Great Spirit will return your second brother to your family one sun."

"I do not believe that will happen. If Cloud Chaser still lived and our ways still burned in his heart and mind, he would have returned to us by this moon, for he has reached nineteen summers and could find his way home."

"There is an unknown reason why Wakantanka sent him away and there is another for why he will be returned, or for why he will not be allowed to return. We do not grasp the thinking of the Great Mystery until such things are revealed to us."

"That is true, *mitawin*. Those were hard times for our family, so we do not speak of them. But that is how I know a little English; Omaste taught me as a game, as we taught her our tongue."

Chumani realized he wanted to cease talking about that painful and perhaps embarrassing episode. It had occurred long ago and during a hard time for Rising Bear. She had no doubt that the chief loved Winona and would not turn to another woman as long as his wife lived. Although her husband had another brother and a sister by his parents, it was obvious from his expression and tone that he loved and missed Cloud Chaser. "I will teach you more English," she promised gently.

"That is good, *mitawin*." He caressed her cheek as he said, "I do not see and touch you enough while we travel and this short time alone fills me with joy, but we must return to camp and sleep."

"My heart and body yearn for you in those same ways, my beloved husband. Do not forget, after we reach our new location, Zitkala will return to the lodge of her parents and we will be alone in our tepee once more." She saw Wind Dancer's smile broaden and his gaze gleam with anticipation and desire, the same feelings which flooded her.

"How can it be I come to love and want you more each sun and moon when you already fill me with such emotions? How does more water go into a bag which already overflows with it? Yet, I know that is true."

"I do not understand such a mystery, but I also know it is true. I never grow weary of seeing your face, of hearing your voice and laughter, of smelling your familiar scent, of feeling your touch and tasting your lips, of mating with you. They are as food to me and I must have them to survive. I thank the Great Spirit each morning and night for sending you to me."

Wind Dancer was consumed by happiness at her words. His Life-Circle was complete and wonderful with her sharing it. "I do the same, *mitawin*, for He has rewarded us greatly. My love and desire for you are larger than the sacred mountain, and I would challenge any force which tried to steal you from me."

"As I would challenge any force which took you away from me, even if it claimed my life to save yours," she vowed as a strange and powerful chill swept over her and caused her to shudder.

"You are cold?" he asked, and rubbed her bare arms with his hands.

Chumani sighed deeply to shake off that eerie feeling. "We must return now," she said, "for it grows dark and cool and there is little moon to light our path to camp. We must not linger here and risk an injury by returning in near blackness."

"Come, *mitawin*, a blanket and fire await you."

"All I need for warmth is your arms and body, *mihigna*."

"And you will have them," he said as he guided her toward the others.

At last, before the radiant sun was overhead, they reached their first temporary encampment on the lush buffalo gapland near the Sahiyela River which branched off into streams and creeks along its winding course as it headed southwestward. Trees, bushes, and other vegetation lined its bank, including the sacred cottonwood. Everyone knew the badlands area—*Makosica*—was located in a long stretch running east and south of them.

The Red Shield women went to work setting up their tepees, and Chumani was delighted to have Zitkala's assistance. While females were busy with that task, young girls and grandmothers watched babies and toddlers or played with small children. Boys too young to help their fathers romped together under the watchful gazes of grandfathers.

Winona and Hanmani erected their highly decorated tepee in the spot assigned to the chief, its entrance facing the rising sun as was their custom. On either side of it was Wind Dancer's as the future chief, leader of the Shirt Wearers and Strong Hearts, and the Visionquest Man; and Nahemana's, as their shaman. Across from it was Blue Owl's, their war chief. The dwellings of other Big Bellys—Nacas, past leaders and great warriors who no longer went on the warpath and hunting trail and now formed the head council—completed that inner ring. A large area was left unobstructed amidst its core for an eventual campfire where meetings, dances, and rituals would be held. From that large hoop which established the center of camp, the people's lodges were situated in ever-widening circles by rank of honor in the band. Ample space for seasonal work and movement of travois was left between every tepee and each row. Afterward, the women unloaded their family's possessions, gathered scrub wood, fetched fresh water, built fires beneath three-legged stands, and put food—mainly stews—on to cook.

While women performed their chores, the men carried out theirs. Horses were watered and grazed before being tethered beside their lodges. *Huyamnis* were set up at the entrances and weapons were placed upon them to soak up powers from the sun and earth, ready to be retrieved in a hurry if needed. They went to the river where trees and large bushes grew to gather and cut sturdy limbs with which they would construct drying racks for the game they would soon pursue and slay. They returned and erected many frames on their sites, tall enough to be out of the reach of wild animals and small children. Afterward, most sat on rush mats to whittle sharp pegs for staking out buffalo hides they would send or bring home. As they did so, some talked with friends working nearby and taught sons how to do male tasks. Others left the area to scout for signs of enemies and to locate the nearest herd's position; amongst those small groups were Wind Dancer, War Eagle, and Red Feather.

It was late afternoon when the White Shield band was sighted in the distance as it approached. News quickly spread of their imminent arrival.

An excited Chumani and Zitkala checked the fire and simmering food to be sure it was safe to leave them unattended for a brief span. Hanmani said she would watch the flames and kettle and Cetan for Chumani, as the hawk sat on his T-shaped perch nearby. The Brule women leapt upon their horses and galloped to greet their families and friends. They passed and waved to men who rode ahead to select their campsite. They slowed their pace as they neared the lengthy column to prevent stirring up excess dust. Chumani trodded alongside Tall Elk for a short time to speak with her father, while Zitkala proceeded to find her parents and do the same. The men who had been riding with the chief dropped back slightly to give them privacy.

"Much has happened, Father, and I will reveal it to you later. It is good to see you again, and I am happy you reached us in safety."

"It stirs my heart to look upon you again, my daughter, and to see a glow of joy lives in your eyes and upon your face. It pleases me you have accepted your new life and await the Great Spirit's workings in it."

Chumani smiled and related in a low voice for his ears alone, "Yes, Father, I am happy and I do well with the Red Shields. They are good and kind people, and they have accepted me into their band with love, pride, and generosity. I thank you for urging me to cast away my fears and doubts to honor Wakantanka's message to our shaman and His vision to Nahemana."

"It was hard to do so, my child," Tall Elk admitted in a near whisper, "as it was wrong when I asked you to join to Dull Star, for that union brought us much suffering and you, much unhappiness."

"It is not so with Wind Dancer; I am happy as his wife."

"I can see it has become a union of love and desire," he said in relief. "When you say his name or speak of him, your expression is as radiant as the sun, your eyes sparkle as the stars, and your voice softens as tranquil water flowing gently around rocks in a stream."

"That is true, Father."

"Is it the same for the son of Rising Bear?" he had to ask.

"Yes, Father, for he has told me so many times. Now I am eager to see Mother, so I will tell you other things while we work later. You will eat at our tepee, for I have prepared enough food for you to share with us."

Tall Elk knew her last words were not spoken as a command but as an invitation, which he accepted. After she left his side, he took a deep breath of invigorating air. At last he was convinced he had done the right thing for his daughter and his people, though his shaman had tried many times to persuade him of that fact. As if that thought mutely summoned Sees-Through-Mist, the white-haired man rejoined him, and they exchanged knowing looks. "All is good with her, my friend," Tall Elk related.

"That is the will of the Creator; she has found her true destiny."

Chumani waved to her older brother as Fire Walker traveled near their mother and his wife. After they greeted each other and shared a few more words, he left to ride and speak with their father near their journey's end.

Chumani positioned herself between the two women's mounts in the space required to prevent entangling their drag-alongs. With conveyances being pulled by women behind them and their leaders riding beyond them, it allowed them to speak in privacy. Chumani responded to Falling Rain's questions—almost the same ones her father had asked—in identical manner

"My heart sings at our reunion, my daughter, for I have missed you. I have prayed each morning and night for your new life to be a good one."

"Wakantanka answered our prayers, Mother, for they matched."

"And it was His will, my beloved daughter, for He did the chosing for you and Waci Tate, and He is never wrong or cruel."

"That is true, Mother, though we often do not grasp His purpose and yearn to disobey when His words are difficult to follow."

"That is why we must have faith in Him. Yet, it is also hard for me and your father to watch you head into danger in the duty set before you."

"When do you begin the vision-ride, Dewdrops?" Rainbow Girl asked.

"I will reveal all to you while we eat at my tepee this night," Chumani said, "for I will feed my family."

Rainbow Girl leaned closer to Chumani. "It is strange, but Zitkala looks more female on this sun. I saw her when she rode past us. She wears a woman's garment and her breasts are unbound. Her hair is not braided as a man's and she has a feathered rosette in it."

"She and the Great Spirit have worked big magic with her appearance and manner," Chumani explained. "Tell no one and say nothing to her, but an Oglala warrior has stolen her heart and eye—Red Feather, the best friend of my husband. He feels the same way about her, but they have told no one except me and Wind Dancer, for they still test these unfamiliar yearnings. Love softened her and brought forth her female side. Too, the Great Spirit has need of her to be a woman during our next challenge. I will speak of that task later. The child within you has grown larger since our parting," Chumani remarked as Rainbow

Girl stroked a slightly protruding abdomen and smiled dreamily.

"Yes, and he begins to stir a little. It is a strange but wonderful feeling, as if something tickles me inside. I am eager to see his face and hold him in my arms. He will come before the snows return to our land."

Chumani laughed and jested, "What if it is a girl and she kicks you for calling her a boy? Does my brother only desire a son?"

"We do not care if I bring forth a boy or a girl, for it is our child and we will love it. Yet, the shaman said a dream told him it is a son who will follow Fire Walker as chief. His sacred dreams have never been wrong in the past, and one was about your new life."

Chumani nodded in happy assent. "We will talk more while we work and eat together, for we approach your campsite and must get busy. I will go tend my food and fire; then I will help you set up your lodges before darkness comes."

The White Shield village was erected next to, but separate from their Oglala ally and in same circular pattern with the chief at its center. The work was carried out with swiftness and efficiency. Those who finished their chores first assisted those who had not done so.

While Hanmani continued to watch her fire and kettle, Chumani helped her mother and Rainbow Girl while Zitkala did the same with her mother in the second ring of dwellings. Before they completed their many preparations, the Red Shield riders returned to camp, and Wind Dancer joined Tall Elk and Fire Walker to give them a helping hand with theirs. Red Feather sought out Zitkala to assist her father with his work, and asked them to eat with his family when mealtime came; and they accepted.

A short time later, Sees-Through-Mist took a break from his chores and conversed with them for a while.

* * *

Before dusk arrived, hundreds of colorful and plain conical abodes stood tall against the darkening skyline. Campfires burned brightly where foods were being cooked. Men met in groups to talk. Children played. Women tended babies and put them down to sleep.

Everyone in Chumani's group halted what they were doing to go eat and visit in hers and Wind Dancer's tepee, for the Plains wind was gusting fast and would chill their food quickly.

As they ate, they spoke of recent events in the old White Shield camp and when Rainbow Girl's pregnancy was mentioned, a proud and joyful smile appeared on the handsome face of Fire Walker. Afterward, Wind Dancer and Chumani related news of the Crow attack on their camp and Cetan's injury, the rattlesnake incident in Winona's tepee—leaving out the reason the deadly viper was there—and their battle with the awesome grizzly.

"Your courage and skills are large, my daughter," Tall Elk said. "They bring pride and happiness to my heart. I give thanks to the Great Spirit for protecting you during such perilous times. I also give thanks to Him for choosing you a husband with mountain-size prowess and high rank."

Wind Dancer smiled. "Your words and feelings please and honor me, Tall Elk. I also give the Creator thanks for guiding me to Dewdrops, for no better wife could be found. There is more to tell you, for our sacred task began many moons past."

Wind Dancer explained their intention of "planting the war lance between the *wasicun* and Apsaalooke to turn their eyes and weapons away from our peoples and on each other. Its sharp point has been buried in the ground," he reminded them. "Now, we water it to make it grow fast and large." He related detailed accounts of the daring raids on white homesteads, how those stolen horses were left near an enemy camp and Crow possessions were discarded there to make the Bird People appear to blame. He disclosed Chumani's mystical encounter in the forest with the Spirit Dog and their defeat of the Crow leader who attacked both camps, a glorious victory made possible by the cunning help of the companion of the Old-Woman-Who-Quills. He told them about his grandfather's vision during their absence concerning the Spirit Dog, and about the ensuing camp celebration where the two Brule women's coups were chanted along with those of himself, his brother, and his best friend.

As he spoke, Chumani observed her family. She was thrilled by their approving nods and smiles, and flattered by their looks of amazement in her direction for her parts in those dangerous deeds. They appeared proud to be family to the Sacred Vision Woman.

Last, Wind Dancer divulged their impending task at Fort Pierre trading post. He did not have to tell his wife's family it would be risky, as that was apparent from what he and his vision party planned to do there. "It is your turn to speak, Tall Elk. Then your family can do so."

For a while, Wind Dancer and Chumani were praised and questioned by her family, who fully agreed with their plan. Fire Walker offered to go with them on any journey where he was needed, but it was obvious, despite his desire to be a part of such glorious episodes, he wanted and felt he should remain nearby to hunt for his family and to protect his pregnant wife.

Tall Elk rose. "We must go, for darkness will soon blanket the land and the moon is not yet full to light the way to our lodge," he said. "There is much work to do on the new sun and this has been a long and busy one. Our hearts have been warmed by your generosity and our spirits have been stirred by your words and deeds. We would fear for our daughter's safety and survival if she was not protected by Waci Tate and Wakantanka."

"Your words please and honor us, Tall Elk," Wind Dancer replied.

To all of her family members, Chumani said, "It is good to be reunited." To her mother and brother's wife, she added, "We will do our chores together after the sun rises."

After the four Brules departed shortly before they would have needed a blazing torch to see their way to their abodes, Chumani made sure her cook fire was out. Then she sealed the entrance flap and spread out the buffalo mat. She stripped off her garments and moccasins, grinned seductively at her beloved husband and said, "It is time for sleep, *mihigna.*"

Wind Dancer chuckled at her jest. He discarded his garments fast and lay down, his arousal jutting forth when freed from his breechclout. He pulled her into his embrace and whispered, "No, *mitawin*, it is time for this," and kissed her, seeking her sweet essence. His tongue danced with hers as he drew her closer and closer, wanting no space between them. His lips brushed over her face, then he nuzzled his neck and face against hers, thrilling to the contact between them and the sheer joy of touching her and sharing such wonderful intimacy again.

Chumani responded eagerly. Her hands traveled his body, giving and taking pleasure from the sensations she aroused. "I love you, *mihigna,*" she murmured.

"You are as food and water to my starving spirit. You are as the air I need to breathe to stay alive. I would cease to be if you were lost to me. Our Life-Circles must forever remain enjoined. I want to see our child growing within you. I want you beside me each moon, and nearby on every sun. You are a large part of me, *micante,* and I would perish without you."

"It is the same with me, my beloved. I am sad when we are apart, and overjoyed when we are together. I hunger to be at your side no matter where you are. Before our births, we were destined for each other."

They explored each other in the velvet darkness, gradually fueling the embers of their passion until the blaze nearly consumed them. When they could wait no longer, they joined their bodies and thrilled to the sensation of being truly one. Soon, they lay sated and content, rested in each other's embrace.

"I love you, *micante,* with every part of my body," Wind Dancer whispered.

Chumani's spirit soared high as he called her "my heart" again. "I love you, *mihigna,* and will belong to you forever, as you will to me."

As early-morning sunlight splashed across the windy Plains, the Red and White Shields gathered beyond their tepees for the ritual to begin the first of many hunts during the summer season. Men who had been chosen to carry out the initial task—including Wind Dancer, War Eagle, Red Feather, and Rising Bear—sat upon their buffalo horses and awaited the signal. The men who had been selected to remain behind to act as protectors and leaders—including Tall Elk, Fire Walker, and Blue Owl—gazed at the mounted riders with an emotion close to envy in their hearts for what loomed before the others. The women who had been assigned to go with them on their quest—including Winona and Hanmani—waited nearby with their travois, ready to follow the hunters to all of the slain creatures to prepare their meat and hides for hauling back to camp.

Chumani's gaze settled on her husband who sat straight and proud on his swift and sure-footed horse who had been specially trained to race with the massive and unpredictable beasts. Wind Dancer, like the others, wore only a breechclout and moccasins. A bow encircled his torso and a quiver filled with arrows with his markings rested upon his broad back. His knife sheath was suspended from the belt which banded his waist and secured his only garment to his stalwart body. His ebony hair was braided to prevent it from blowing into his eyes and obstructing his vision for even a moment at such a time when peril could strike without warning. He wore no adornments—no wristlets, armbands, hair feathers, or medallions; nor did his mount. A small and light water bag also hung from his belt. Today, he hunted for those in need, for those women who had lost mates and not yet replaced them and for families with men and women too old or disabled to do that part of the task themselves. Later, she would go with him to seek their winter needs.

Nahemana and Sees-Through-Mist stood together before the large crowd. Both were clad in ceremonial regalia: buffalo cap headdresses and flowing buffalo robes with colorful adornments of dangling rawhide strips with beads and various feathers and many attached weasel tails. Hairbone breastplates rested upon chests which had lost much of their strength. Their remaining garments were decorated with beads, hackle feathers, and enemy hairlocks. White hair whipping around their age-furrowed faces and their stooped shoulders gleamed like silver in the morning light. Both were loved and respected by their people, and esteemed by their allies. Each shaman lifted a painted buffalo skull with wrinkled hands and held it high as they sent forth prayers to Wakantanka in voices strengthened by the stirring occasion.

Nahemana spoke first as he earnestly evoked, "Great Spirit, Creator of all things, Provider of our needs, Protector of our lands and people, we stand before You this sun and ask You to give us much success on our many hunts. Grant our warriors the skills to find and slay enough buffalo to feed, clothe, and shelter Your people during the cold season. Guard our hunters and women as they work upon the grasslands; return them to us alive and unharmed and loaded with our means of survival. Ask Mother Earth to share her bounty with us as our women seek other needs upon her face. Hear and see us, Great One, as we send our message to you."

Sees-Through-Mist fervently requested, "Great Mystery, Knower and Seer of all things, see and hear our prayer to You. We give You honor, thanks, and loyalty for all You give and bring to us. Share Your creature's skills with our hunters. Give them keen eyes like the eagle's, the strength and courage of the grizzly, the cunning of the wolf and fox, the swiftness and stamina of the deer. Make them as one with their horses. Send their arrows on a true flight. Grant us these needs, Great Spirit, and we will honor You in song, dance, and offerings when our task is finished."

Afterward, eight men beat on a large drum as the two shamans danced around their buffalo skulls which had been placed atop hides where a bunch of dried sweetgrass and herbs, four eagle feathers, grizzly claws, deer antlers, and the tails of a wolf and fox lay. When the drumming and dancing halted, ceremonial arrows with sacred markings were pointed in the direction in which the scouts had located an enormous herd. Both elderly men shouted, "It is time to ride, for the buffalo await your coming!"

With the signal given, the mounted riders whooped and yelled and galloped off to seek their prey. The women left shortly behind them.

As the shamen spoke for the last time, Wind Dancer glanced at his wife, then nodded and smiled as a farewell message. His heart warmed when she returned those gestures. Though he would be gone for only a few days, he knew he would miss her. Yet, he carried her image in his head and the remembrance of last night to give him comfort during their separation.

Wind Dancer was confident in his prowess and in his horse's skills. He raced like the wind from which had come his name, speeding across open grassland with low hills here and there. As he topped the final one, his gaze took in a sight that always filled him with awe: an enormous herd of immense creatures extended far beyond his sight, as if a dark blanket had been spread across the green surface and it slowly wafted in the wind. The huge animals either moved along in leisure as they grazed or they lay or rolled in wallows they had made. Females tended their calves and kept them close by; they would not be slain so the herd could survive to feed them in seasons to come. Some of the males still wore partial ragged winter coats, but most had rubbed them off not long ago. He knew rutting season would not begin until after the next one or two full moons. When that season came, the humpbacked, bearded beasts would bellow challenges to both rivals and intruding men, and they would be dangerous in that state. For now, Wind Dancer decided, hunting should be easy and safe.

After everyone arrived and stood poised on the hilltop, the charge began as they plunged headlong down the gentle incline and galloped toward the furry fringes. It took a while for the buffaloes to realize what was happening, especially those farther away from the attack scene. As if news was passed along by their grunts and stirrings, the herd began to move onward, their pace increasing as the full reality of their peril sank in; and the hunters pursued them with vigor. They would slay as many as the women could skin and butcher today, rest for the night, and begin the task again at sunrise. They would continue that routine for several days, then retrace their path to camp, where another group would head out to do the same.

Back in the encampment, Chumani, her mother, Zitkala, and Rainbow Girl went about their chores as they awaited the return of travois loaded with meat and hides to prepare, as the first ones should arrive before late afternoon. As soon as they were unloaded, the young braves would guide them back to the hunters and butchers for another haul.

The women checked drying racks, put stews on to simmer for future times when they were too busy to cook, gathered firewood, fetched water, and collected berries and plants which grew nearby. River rushes were cut to make sitting mats and herbs were plucked, bound, and hung up to dry to be used in foods and medicines.

Chumani knew why her husband and the rest of the vision companions went on this first hunt; they could not leave for Fort Pierre Trading Post until her woman's flow had come and gone in a few suns. She knew Wind Dancer would be reluctant to allow her to accompany him on the next adventure if she were carrying their child. She and other women erected a hut near the river, using the shade of cottonwoods to keep the willow *cansakawakeya* interior cooler than on the sunny Plains.

As she worked, Chumani daydreamed of her husband, of the past suns with him since their joining, and of their passionate night together. She loved and desired him completely, and would be tormented if she lost him. Again that strange and alarming chill swept over her body, as if she were being sent a grim message which she could not grasp.

For the past three suns, Chumani had labored with the other women who had been left in camp during the first hunt. When her blood flow revealed itself on the morning of the fifth sun since their arrival, she hurried to the willow hut in a contradictory state of joy and sadness. She yearned for their baby, but she also yearned to remain a part of the sacred vision tasks. At least she was not responsible for choosing which path to follow; that was in the hands of the Great Spirit and Mother Nature, and They had spoken.

During her second day of confinement, Chumani heard a commotion which indicated the first group had returned to camp from their hunt. She peered between spaces in the willow branches, straining her eyes and ears for a sight and sound of her beloved. When she spied him and knew he was back safe and unharmed, she smiled and thanked Wakantanka.

At sunrise following the afternoon of her departure from the willow hut and carrying out her purification custom, Wind Dancer, Chumani, and the others in their vision party mounted their horses to leave for Fort Pierre as their people began the second buffalo hunt. Riding quickly, they would reach the trading post in a few suns and would confront one of their greatest and most perilous challenges.

Chapter
Fourteen

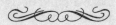

For days, they traveled near the bank of the Sica River where trees and scrubs and other vegetation would provide quick concealment if needed, as its waters flowed straight to their destination. They also had a full moon which would enable them to see a possible threat approaching at a long distance. The daytime sky was vivid blue; early-summer air, temperate; the sun, radiant; and the wind steady. At night, the air was cooler but pleasant, and no campfire, which might reveal their presence, was needed for warmth. Nor was one required for cooking, for they had brought plentiful supplies which were ready to eat.

Crossing relatively flat terrain for most of the way, the ride was easy, the pace swift. Their spirits heightened and anticipation mounted daily. Often they rode through gaps in buffalo herds and were careful not to overly disturb the animals and provoke them into a race across the Plains which would trample anything and anyone caught in their thunderous path. They sighted numerous antelope and deer, some scattering in panic and some ignoring them as the riders passed near them. They also saw many other creatures foraging on the lush landscape or seeking live prey. Birds, small and large, darted by or hunted overhead.

Wildflowers bloomed in colorful profusion, and insects feasted greedily upon them.

Although the journey seemed a safe and serene one, each knew that trouble could strike at any given time, from enemy or powerful nature. They did not talk during the day as staying highly alert was necessary. They knew they must be ready to make a rapid decision to fight or make a hasty retreat if the odds were too great to challenge. When they did share words at night in camp, they could not plan their impending task, as they did not know what loomed before them until Chumani and Zitkala completed their scouting inside the post. Each was aware anyone— or everyone—in their party could be slain in battle or captured and held as prisoners to be "executed" by the Whites or soldiers. Yet, even at the risk of their lives, this deed must be done for their people to survive and for their hunting and sacred grounds to be retained.

As they neared their destination, the plateau grasslands gave way to low, rolling hills which eventually became higher and broader ones. Ravines and gulches became more frequent sights where the face of Mother Earth had been eaten away by heavy rains and melting snow. Trees and scrubs dotted the lumpy region and flourished in abundance along the two rivers and their offshoots. They left the watery course they had followed for days and made their way to the last group of hills overlooking the post. There the men could use the landscape for concealment as they waited the women's return. They dismounted and climbed the grassy rise before them. Hugging the ground with their stomachs and hidden by thick vegetation, they checked out the setting while Wind Dancer and Red Feather enlightened the women about it.

Chumani and Zitkala observed that their target sat in a near flat valley surrounded by high dirt-and-grass ridges partly bordered by two rivers. On three of its sides were scattered or clustered tepees, some with Indian families around them and others with hairy-faced trappers and their "squaws" and "half-breed" children. Since most of the abodes had unpainted surfaces and most of the Indians wore plain garments, it was impossible to guess to what tribe they belonged. Yet, some were clearly Pawnee, Cheyenne, Dakota, and Lakota. Even so, none of them should recognize the two Brule females who would pretend to be Cheyenne instead of Apsaalooke.

Wind Dancer pointed out a steamboat which was heading southward on the wide and muddy river, and two keelboats which were floating on the water but secured at that location. White men labored on or near those crafts, loading some items and unloading others. A worn trail for hauling goods to and from the post was bustling with movement. It was apparent from the size and sturdiness of the settlement, the many activities in progress, and number of people there that the Whites did not intend to ever leave Lakota lands unless they were forced out.

Wind Dancer disclosed that Fort Pierre was one of the largest and most crucial trading and supply posts for fur trappers, settlers, and travelers along the river's lengthy course. He told them that many men whom Whites considered important had visited there, and almost everyone who entered the territory made it one of their stops. Two large doors—facing east as did Indian tepees—could be shut and barred like when trouble arose, and were closed at night for protecting people and goods. There was a second opening in the wooden wall for stock to use, and it also stood open at that time.

Chumani thought the post was shaped like an enormous parfleche, and she easily viewed its interior from their advantageous position. It was enclosed by tall and strong cottonwood logs, and she resented the enemy's use of sacred trees to encroach upon their lands. It had structures built against or near its inner sides, all with pointed tops like tepees, though their smoke and fresh air flaps were vastly different. From two overhanging blockhouses at the front and back corners, an awesome view of the river and Plains had to be visible. They contained slits—as did the walls—for firing weapons at enemies. She knew the three branches of the Dakota Nation—collectively Sioux to them—fit into that group.

Three red, white, and blue cloths which her husband told her the *wasicun* called American flags waved constantly above the main structure and atop the blockhouses. She noted the wooden lodges were high and had many openings for obtaining light and air; from the English she had learned, she knew they were doors and windows. There were fences and sheds for visitors' mounts and for the post's animals to be kept at night, though most appeared to be grazing outside the wooden pickets at that time of day, under the watchful eyes of armed guards. She saw men—two Whites and one Indian, probably a scout—returning from morning hunts with fresh game; she watched them unload the already gutted animals and head out to slay more. She saw others stacking firewood, fetching barrels of fresh water, cleaning out animal enclosures, repairing some of the dwellings, and doing other chores she did not recognize. She even observed some Indian women washing the intruders' garments and hanging them out to dry on racks she felt should be built on the grasslands and holding buffalo meat. She did not understand why some Indians would prefer to dwell around and work for Whites instead of living proud and free upon the grasslands and in the forests. As she witnessed two Pawnee staggering out the main entrance, stumbling toward a cluster of tepees, and collapsing upon buffalo mats beside them, she hoped and prayed the enemy's "firewater" would never become appealing and enslaving to her loved ones. She sighted numerous mounds of dirt and knew it was a burial ground, and recalled the many deaths caused by the enemy's strange illness not long ago.

Wind Dancer halted Chumani's observations, telling her that many of the nearby settlers wanted the post to become a military site for soldiers to protect them from "hostiles" and from bad whites who preyed upon them, but the owners refused to sell out to the Bluecoats. He said there were about twenty-five men who worked and lived within the lofty enclosure. Added to that number were trappers and other traders who stopped in to make exchanges, visit, rest, and resupply, travelers passing through the area, newly arrived settlers, men seeking work or begging for handouts after a bad hunting and trapping season inland, and Indians come to bargain.

"It has been many seasons since I have been there, *mitawin*, so many changes may have happened," he told Chumani after finishing his description of the post. "Use the eyes of the hawk and cunning of the fox while entrapped with them. Do and say nothing to challenge them. The sun rests over our heads. Return before it rides halfway between this spot and Mother Earth or we will come for you."

"We will be careful, *mihigna*," she promised and smiled at him. "We must go now so we will have plenty of time to learn their secrets before you and Red Feather are attacked by fear for our safety," she said in an almost teasing tone.

"We will worry even if you work fast or slow," Wind Dancer's best friend replied. He looked at Zitkala and said, "Return to me this day."

The older Brule woman smiled and nodded, a slight blush coloring her cheeks after his bold and tender words before the others. "If we are slow in returning, Red Feather, do not rush to rescue us until you are certain we are in danger. To do so will prevent the great task we must do later."

"We will watch and wait and not be foolish," Wind Dancer told them.

War Eagle added his words of encouragement and hopes for much success.

At last, Chumani and Zitkala left their loved ones to ride to the post on the pretense of trading furs, pelts, and hides for goods offered there. Many of their people had donated the animal skins for this purpose and they were the best available in their territory and should be worth much if the Whites did not try to trick them. Even so, they could not argue against such deceit, as it would call attention to them.

They rode at a slow pace toward the front gates, each holding the tether of a second horse in one hand, both bearing a pile of furry skins. A blanket and half of a buffalo hide was between them and their mounts for comfort during their supposedly long journey. A large deerskin pouch of trail supplies and a water bag with their ends tied to a rawhide rope were suspended on either side of their animal's body to make it appear they had camped along the lengthy way to the post. The only weapons they carried were common knives in sheaths at their waists. Their fringed garments and moccasins bore no tribal markings, but their hairbone chokers and beaded belts and parfleches—gifts to some of the Red Shields from Cheyenne allies in the past—bore that tribe's colors and designs to imply membership to it. They did not talk as they remained alert for trouble and made observations.

Chumani found it insulting to see an eagle—the noble warrior of the sky—painted on the flat wood over the main entryway of the post, along with colorful and well-drawn pictures of Indians and *wasicuns* talking and trading with each other. Perhaps it was to tell Indians the purpose of the post and to extend a welcome, or to make a clever show of feigned friendship to them. The women dismounted and walked to the opening where a bearded man halted them, a long firestick in his grasp and another shorter weapon in a waist sheath. She saw how he eyed them thoroughly and glanced at their possessions before speaking to them.

"You women come to make trade?" he asked.

Chumani—who was to do the communicating—kept her expression impassive as she used intertribal sign language to tell him she was Cheyenne, as if she could not understand or speak English. The man watched her rub the back of her left hand with the fingertips of her right one for *Indian,* then use the index finger cutting action to imply she was *Cheyenne*. Next she gave the gesture for *trade*. She motioned to the pack animals, then made the hand signals for *kettle, beads, cloth, mirror*.

"Cheyenne, huh? Shaiyena?"

"Heehee," she responded, nodding her head to match her yes.

"I don't know Shaiyena, but I'm pretty good with sign talk." He made the motions for not speaking Cheyenne but he knew a little sign language.

To permit them to eavesdrop without notice, Chumani made it appear as if she only understood his hand-talk as he welcomed them and motioned for them to follow him.

As Chumani and Zitkala trailed his lead, they heard men talking about the places inside with names like *carpenter's shop, smithy, tinner, saddler, trading-house, living quarters, kitchen,* and *storage rooms*. They halted near a large wooden one when he gestured for them to *stop* and *wait* there.

Chumani watched as he approached the door and called out to a man inside, "You're gonna love these Cheyenne beauties, Bert; they got some choice pieces for trade if all of 'em match those I see on top. Don't speak no English, but they can sign good and speak Cheyenne."

A second white man joined them and welcomed them in sign language, to which Chumani responded. She watched him walk to the loaded horses and lift some of the skins as he examined the furs, pelts, and buffalo hides.

"You're right, Zeb; these seem like prime pieces. Let's take 'em inside and I'll give 'em a good lookover. Tell 'em to follow me and we'll make a good trade, then help me get this load to the counter."

Zeb chuckled. "You ortta be able to steal these goods easy. I bet they ain't very bright in the head, but I wouldn't mind gettin' under their skirts and doin' a little pokin' around. How about you?"

Bert scowled at him. "Don't talk too loud; we got Injuns inside who understand our words. They might get offended if they hear such jawing."

Chumani and Zitkala watched Zeb sign for them to

follow him inside after he and Bert collected part of the skins. They entered the trading-house where whiskey and tobacco were being given to Indian males before bargaining began. The other men present—Whites and Indians—only glanced up at them briefly. Bert signaled for the women to look around while Zeb hauled in the rest of the load and Bert examined their offerings on a long counter to decide their value. As soon as he finished helping Bert, Zeb returned to his guard duty at the gate.

Chumani and Zitkala studied the many shelves and barrels and crates which almost filled the large room from floor to ceiling and held an assortment of goods. A display of Indian weapons, beadwork, and headdresses was suspended from pegs on one wall. She wondered if they had been gifts, exchanged by owners for weapons and whiskey, or were traded by enemies who had stolen them in raids or won them during battles. She was resentful that one item was a Black War Bonnet Society shield, as its markings were considered powerful and important medicine symbols, and had belonged to a Lakota somewhere.

As they looked around, the white men they passed acted as if they either were not there or could not understand English, talking about them freely and often crudely to themselves or their friends. It suited the women fine to have them duped, as they gathered useful and interesting information from their enemies' words and careless behavior.

Bert finally joined them and pointed out his offerings: Among them were guns, knives, hatchets, traps, coffee, sugar, flour, salt, needles, cloth, thread, kettles, utensils, tincups, mirrors, beads, trinkets, ready-made shirts and pants, belts, ropes, cans of food, matches, lanterns, axes, shovels, canteens, shoes, white man's undergarments, blankets, and many more items. He laughed at their reactions as he related the uses of the unknown ones and gave them tastes of sugar and salt. He showed them how easy sewing would be with the needles and thread. He chuckled when he saw their amazement to "big magic" matches kept in a small metal box. He held up mirrors for them to view themselves, and handed each a comb to try.

When another man summoned him to ask a question, Bert left them to look around some more while they made their choices and placed them on the counter beside the skins they were trading as he had instructed through signing.

Chumani and Zitkala placed the last two selections atop the others, all except one item to be gifts to those who had donated the furs, pelts, and hides. Chumani looked at Bert as if to tell him they were ready to deal and watched him study the piles and take a deep breath. He hand-signed for her to *wait*, then looked at the other men present.

"Any of you speak Cheyenne? I can use some help over here. What about you, Henry? Don't you work along that section of the Missouri?"

Chumani watched a scraggly-haired man come forth and she tensed, hoping he wouldn't expose their identities.

"I spent some time with 'em during two winters, with Lone Wolf's band," Henry told Bert, "I know a little of their tongue. Whatcha need?"

"Thanks, Henry. These two don't speak any English, and using that sign language would take a long spell. Tell 'em these things have to be brought from a long way off and cost plenty to get 'em here. Tell 'em they can have everything if they'll add those two packhorses to their payment."

Chumani watched the trapper look through the hides. He wore high-top moccasins and had a beard almost to his waist. A foul stench emanated from him.

Henry evaluated the skins slowly. "These are top quality pelts and hides, Bert, and tanned good, best job I've seen; no cuts anywhere," he concluded. "They're well-worth the items these women chose without adding them two horses. That's a raw deal. All you're gonna do by cheating them is make them mad and mistrustful. If you want them to come back and send their friends to you, it's best to deal straight with them."

"Just tell them what I said. I got men itching to buy horses to replace some stolen by Crow recently. I'll give you a bottle of whiskey and pouch of tobacco for your help." Bert eyed the reluctant man. "Ah, hell, you drive a hard bargain, Henry. I'll throw in two traps and some coffee and salt. You can take 'em now, or I'll credit them to you to pick up later this year."

Chumani covertly observed the rough-looking man near her and realized he did not want them to be cheated, but was being given an enticing offer to aid the bargaining in Bert's favor. She was strangely disappointed when he dishonored himself.

"It ain't right, Bert, but I'll do it if you throw in some flour and jerky. I had me a bad season last winter and I didn't earn enough on my pelts and furs to stake myself for next season. We got a deal?"

"You're a tough barterer, my friend, but I agree."

After Henry repeated Bert's words in Cheyenne, Chumani looked at the pile of furs, at the trade goods, and pretended to think for a while. She replied to Henry in Cheyenne, "I will trade one horse, the large brown one; the small spotted one is not mine to trade and is needed for carrying our goods. What goods must I not take for the trade to be a fair one?"

Henry related her answer to Bert, who removed one of the kettles, a knife, and two blankets. "Give her the blankets and it's a deal," Henry said. "Even giving me my stuff, you're making at least twice what's fair."

"Like I said, Henry," Bert scoffed, "you're a hard man to barter with, but I'll do it. They can tie up their stuff in their blankets and haul it away."

Chumani watched Henry as he told her he had asked the man to be generous and allow her to keep the blankets and Bert had agreed. He bragged about the quality of the furs and her skills with tanning them. He admitted they were worth more, but that was the best deal Bert would offer and advised her to take it. He smiled and looked relieved when she agreed and smiled again when she thanked him in Cheyenne, *"Ne-aese."*

After the trade was completed, Bert summoned a worker to haul the skins to a store-house while he took the brown horse to the post stable. Henry offered to help the women tie up their goods in their new blankets and load the bundles on the spotted horse.

As he did so, Henry asked their names, *"Ne-toneseve-he?"*

Chumani pointed to herself and said, *"Na-tsesevehe He-eheeno."* She motioned to Zitkala and alleged her name was *Hestoekeheso.*

"Tosa a ne-hesta-he?" he asked where they came from.

Chumani hoped her apprehension was concealed as he questioned them in a friendly manner and she tried to come up with responses which would not arouse his suspicions. She told him they came from far beyond the *Mo ohta-vo honaaeva,* the Black Hills.

When Henry asked who their leader was, Chumani said, "Sharp Lance," a Cheyenne who lived and hunted in that area, according to what Wind Dancer had told her. Again, she hoped she appeared calm and he had never met that man and could not ask her things about him which she could not verify.

Henry related he had spent part of two winters with Lone Wolf's band along the *E ometaa e,* what the white man called Little Missouri River.

Chumani remarked in Cheyenne, "He is the brother of Fights-Hard; we have traded with his people. We thank you for helping us speak to the trader and load our horses. Now we must leave, for it is a long ride home." Panic raced through her as Henry voiced another question, and she wondered if he suspected anything about them.

"Why did you two women come so far alone to Fort Pierre when Fort Laramie was closer to you?"

"There are many Bluecoats there and they frighten us," Chumani said, looking him straight in the eye. "Others told us the traders here would give us more for our furs and hides." If he noticed she did not respond to the part of his question about traveling alone, it did not show to her.

"Those are good and smart reasons. Ride safe, Blackbird and Fawn."

"We thank you and ride for our camp. Come, Fawn, we go."

They saw Zeb grin and nod to them as they passed him at the gate. They saw his sky-colored gaze sweep over the size of their bundles, and he grinned again as if aware of and amused by Bert's trickery. As they headed toward the rolling hills, both sensed the man's lustful gaze on their backs. They yearned to gallop off and escape it, but knew that was unwise.

As soon as they were out of his hearing range, Chumani scoffed, "He is an evil man, and I would like to shoot an arrow into his breechclout shaft."

Zitkala laughed. "It would burst into flames, for the fire in his breechclout was large and hot for you. The one with long hair on his face was not all bad; some of his words and feelings were good," she added in a serious tone. "But fear leapt within me when he asked you so many questions."

"As it did with me, my friend, but I believe we guided him down the wrong path and he did not learn the truth about us."

"I was no help, Dewdrops, for you tricked him, tricked all of them, with your cunning words and your sly face. If I did not know you spoke false, I would be misled as they were. My pride and love are large for you."

"You honor me, my friend, and I thank you. But I could not have come here alone; only with you at my side did I feel brave and cunning."

"We have ridden, hunted, and fought together many times on past suns, but this glorious deed stirs my heart and soars my spirit more than any other occasions for we traveled into the white wolf's deepest den, defeated him there, and left unharmed. Our companions will be pleased by our victory."

Chumani watched Zitkala's gaze fly as an arrow to where the men awaited them, and she teased her best friend in affection. "Your eyes soften and your cheeks glow as with the sky when the sun goes to sleep. Your love and desire for Red Feather grow larger each sun and moon, do they not?"

Zitkala touched her flushed cheeks. "That is so, Dewdrops, but those feelings are still strange to me. How can I be sure he truly loves and desires me as I do him?"

"His eyes, voice, and body will reveal what lives in his heart. Gaze into his eyes as he speaks, listen to the sound of his voice when he speaks, watch how his body stands or moves when he talks to you. If only friendship and desire live within him, it will be revealed in those places. That is how I knew Wind Dancer spoke the truth to me. It is not wrong or weak for you to be wary and to walk this new path slowly."

"Your words are wise, Dewdrops, and I will follow them."

As they neared the men's location, they ceased their private talk. When they were out of the post's sight behind a lofty hill, they dismounted.

Wind Dancer embraced his wife, closed his eyes, and thanked the Great Spirit for returning her to him. He leaned away from her with hands resting on either side of her waist, smiled, and said, "Now my breath can come easy; my heart slow its swift pace."

"As can mine, *mihigna*," Chumani replied as her gaze swept over him. She was warmed and elated as his look of concern waxed to relief and joy. The expression in his dark eyes, the tone of his voice, and the gentle touch of his hands told her he loved her as much as any spoken words could reveal.

Red Feather smiled and echoed that sentiment, "As can mine to have Dewdrops and Zitkala returned to us. We have not rested in ease since your departure and our eyes have not left the post. I am proud and happy you carried out your daring task successfully. With so many White-eyes there, a rescue would have been hard and dangerous, but we would have attempted one as soon as darkness blanketed the land.''

Zitkala smiled at Red Feather, for his gaze was on her as he spoke and it seemed as if he sneaked a special message to her between his words. Her heart swelled with intense and powerful emotions.

"Tell us of your deed," War Eagle coaxed as he watched the couples exchange smiles and looks of shared love and desire, though Red Feather and Zitkala tried to conceal theirs from their observers and each other.

"We will sit and talk after the horses are tended," Wind Dancer told his younger brother as he glanced at the dark, threatening sky. "They must be unloaded and given water so they can graze while we speak."

During the women's return ride, huge white clouds had formed in all directions and drifted overhead, their snowy surfaces attacked by ever-darkening gray splotches. Often, the sun would vanish behind them for long periods, providing temporary shade from its glowing heat.

As more time passed, the Plains wind began to gust more forcefully and the early-summer air cooled slightly. All prayed the weather would hold steady until after they carried out their daring plan.

After those tasks were completed and the five sat in a circle on the grass in cross-legged positions, the two Brule women related the episode in detail.

"It is good the Whites blame the Crow for our raids on their dwellings, and soon the Crow will blame the Whites for raids upon theirs."

"That is true, my brother," Wind Dancer said, "but it did not provoke them to attack the Crow camp as we hoped."

"They did not do so, for there were too many Bird Warriors for that number of *wasicun* to challenge," Chumani reminded the men. "The men talking inside the post said they did not send for Bluecoats, for the Crow and the stolen horses would be gone before the soldiers could reach their camp. But the families along the great river banded together and placed guards around their wooden tepees, and many kinds of creatures. Some I have not seen before," she added, referring to the chickens, cows, and pigs. "It is the same with those at the trading post, they take their animals inside while the moon rides the night sky."

"We will make it too risky for the Whites to live and hunt in our lands, and too dangerous for our Crow enemies to attack us," War Eagle proposed.

The other four nodded agreement.

As they awaited the needed cover of night, they lay on their stomachs atop the hill in tall grass and observed the trading post. At one point, Bert walked to the gate with another man and spoke with Zeb. Chumani identified them as the trader who had cheated them and the guard who had lusted for them, but she did not recognize the third man, who held two sets of horses' reins in his grasp.

They watched as Bert talked to Zeb, as he pointed in the direction of the women's recent departure. Zeb shook his head as he motioned to the ominous sky surrounding them and seemed to argue against the other man's orders. Finally, Bert nodded and left the gate, as did the third man with the saddled horses, and Zeb returned to his guard duty, glancing skyward again.

Chumani frowned and surmised, "The evil trader seeks to send them after us to steal our horses and trade goods. Our three horses will bring him much ... 'mon-ney,' he said, so he wants them to sell."

"And he can trade your goods to another Indian for more furs and hides," Wind Dancer explained. "They will wait until the storm passes before they ride after you, for they know you will travel slow and must halt when it strikes. If they can find our tracks after Mother Earth refreshes her face with much water, we will welcome them into our camp and arms," he scoffed.

"It will be a good and victorious fight and we will punish

them for their evil,'' War Eagle ventured, and the other men smiled and nodded.

As they went over every angle and possible obstacle to their impending raid and talked about other important things the women had overheard, the storm's violent threat heightened. Soon, they knew, they must decide whether or not to carry out their already difficult challenge if the storm struck with great fury, which it did within a short time.

Chapter
Fifteen

❧

As rain poured upon them, lightning flashed across the darkened sky in dazzling displays, and thunder followed in loud and lengthy peals which often shook the ground. A fierce wind pummeled stalks of grass and wildflower stems and tore loose thick green blades and colorful blossoms. Its powerful force yanked at their soaked garments and braided black hair. Streams of clear liquid flowed down their faces, arms, and legs, dripping swiftly from their leggings to the already saturated surface. The sun, early rising stars, and recent full moon were concealed by the deep gray covering overhead. Only frequent bright charges and the last remains of daylight allowed them to see each other, and the heavy deluge obliterated a clear view of the post and their targets.

They reasoned that the awesome storm would keep all Whites and the Indians who camped nearby inside their dwellings either until it passed or until morning. They had watched the post's grazing animals being gathered and herded into the lofty enclosure. They had seen both gates being closed and assumed they were barred afterward for protection. They saw extensive and prolonged lightning bolts separate into several branches which split into smaller limbs. Thunder rumbled almost continuously, reminding them of war drums beating.

At last, Wind Dancer crowded them together to give his orders. "We must go while they are held captive by the storm," he said. "We will take my horse to carry our raid goods, for he is well trained and obeys me in all times. Dewdrops, you will stay here and guard the others or the fury of the sky spirits might frighten them away. We cannot stake them to Mother Earth, for her face is too soft from rain to grip them tightly enough. If we fail to return before the moon sleeps, go to our camp and tell our people all that happened here. Do not try to rescue us if we are taken captive or avenge us if we are slain, for it is certain death to do so."

A surprised Chumani asked, "Why must I be the one to stay?"

Wind Dancer grasped her slick hands in his. "I do not choose you to remain here because I love you and fear for your safety or doubt your skills. You are the Vision Woman, so you must live to continue our sacred quest if I cannot do so. If both of the vision leaders are lost, our people may lose hope and will not know how to walk our path to victory. And our horses need comfort and protection. Zitkala is larger and stronger and must help us with our task, as are Red Feather and War Eagle. My words are hard to accept, *mitawin*, but they are wise and true."

"That is so, *mihigna*. I will obey," she said as her gaze locked on his.

Wind Dancer smiled, pleased by her quick compliance. "Do not worry, *micante*, for we will return soon and leave this evil place together."

"That is so, *mihigna*." Chumani turned to the small group. "Be careful," she said to them and each nodded to her. She wanted to embrace her husband and best friend, but reasoned that might appear as if she doubted their chance of survival. Yet, as she watched the four vanish into an impenetrable deluge, she was all too cognizant of the grim possibility she may have seen them for a last time.

* * *

At a prechosen site on the bank, Wind Dancer and Red Feather—clad in breechclouts and barefooted—slipped into the swift and muddy Mnisose to swim toward two keelboats which were tied up at the post's landing. Enormous strength and stamina were required to battle the river's awesome currents and intense concentration needed to evade branches and logs that were bobbing furiously on or just below its choppy surface. It was even more perilous when they hastily ducked beneath the water whenever lightning illuminated the area to prevent being seen by an enemy, a few times almost ascending in the perilous path of a large limb.

Much earlier, they had seen twelve keelmen—six per boat—hurriedly setting up tents to escape the storm's impending fury, that encampment situated a short distance away on higher and harder ground. With the aid of a dazzling lightning display, they had sighted two men on the front boat who were crouched beneath a canvas shelter. They had suspected guards might be left aboard, so they had approached their first goal with great caution.

After reaching it, the two Oglala warriors heaved slick and chilled bodies over its side where eight men sometimes sat on benches to row the boat downstream and a sighter stood at all times to watch for hazards. Wind Dancer and Red Feather concealed themselves behind a large oblong wooden structure in its center, certain their movements went unnoticed on a steadily undulating boat. They exchanged hand signals as they made an assault plan. Using the plankways where four men walked back and forth on each side as they poled the craft upriver, Wind Dancer sneaked along the right one and Red Feather crept along the left, the storage area separating them.

They struck simultaneously and caught the white men by surprise, rendering them unconscious before they could shout for help or defend themselves. Wind Dancer and Red Feather only bound and gagged their helpless prey, as there was no honor in or coup to be earned from killing men who did not linger in their land. They made their way to the second boat, but there were no men standing guard there; they thought that was strange since the load to be sold upriver at other trading posts was said to be valuable, if the two women had overheard two keelmen's talk correctly. They assumed no one was in the wooden room because there were no windows and its three doors were locked from the outside. The men considered it fortunate that the entryways were located on the structure's side away from the riverbank, as it would obscure their presence and actions from enemy eyes.

Wind Dancer waited until the thunder quieted before he sent forth a series of bird calls to summon War Eagle and Zitkala to join them. Then the four of them gathered on the far side of the keelboat. Wind Dancer took the Crow hatchet from War Eagle to chop away the storage room's three locks, timing each thud to be muffled by thunder which growled like an angry grizzly. They opened the doors and looked inside. When lightning flashed to illuminate the area, they found stacks of oblong crates, large barrels and small kegs, so many that no space had been left for the keelmen to sleep aboard out of the rain.

Wind Dancer used the hatchet to pry off a crate top. He lifted out a long weapon and said, "They are filled with firesticks as Dewdrops and Zitkala learned at the post. We must push the *wasicun's* weapons into the river. The water spirits will destroy them so they cannot be used to attack us and our allies or be used to slay the Creator's buffalo and other creatures."

Wind Dancer told them they could not use a torch or lantern, as the glow of either might be sighted from the rivermen's camp. More important, gunpowder was dangerous and deadly. He reminded them that black powder fed the long and short firesticks, the swift spitting howitzer, and the powerful cannon.

The four set to work easing unsealed heavy crates of arms and opened barrels of gunpowder into the greedy currents which either gobbled them up immediately or

sent them floating along until they filled with water and
sank. Although the storm's violent attack on the area continued, they did not shove the load overboard recklessly
and risk creating noisy splashes or scrapes against the boat's
surface. They moved gingerly on the slick deck, relieved
their moccasins gripped it sufficiently to prevent accidents.
As they labored, all they could do was pray that the lightning would not strike them, which could be fatal. Rain
gushed over them and dripped from their garments. They
yearned for dry clothes and footwear, a warm blanket, a
cozy tepee and fire, and a hot drink made from refreshing
herbs gathered on the Plains. Their muscles ached from
their constant exertions, yet they knew what they were
doing was important, so they refused to halt until they
either finished or were forced to flee the scene.

After they emptied one keelboat, they rushed to the
second to do the same. As so much time had passed during
their previous task, Wind Dancer assigned Zitkala to watch
for any approaching threat. Without her, it required longer
for them to dump that load; and they were aware of the
gradually vanishing night and slowly subsiding storm, along
with the fact they were afoot and had a long way to retreat
across ground with little to conceal them and the horse.
They saved one small keg of gunpowder, a few weapons,
and some of the supplies to use during future raids on the
Crow.

While War Eagle, Zitkala, and Red Feather hauled those
items to the lone packhorse and secured them in place,
Wind Dancer lingered to plant possessions they had taken
from Four Wolves and his small band in places where the
traders would find them and hold the Apsaalooke to blame
for this daring and destructive deed. Chaheechopes's bow
and another's quiver—since Four Wolves's *wanju* had not
been recovered from the Spirit Dog's cunning theft—were
placed near the still-unconscious guards as if those weapons had been forgotten or left behind in a rush to escape.
He placed the Crow hatchet atop the other boat's center
structure, then hurried to join his companions behind

dense scrub brush. With their bold deed completed, they knew that all they had to do was get away without encountering trouble.

Chumani waited in mounting dread and suspense. She knew the raid would take a long time, but she thought they should have returned by now. The weather had worsened after their departure, though it appeared to be improving as the night slipped away. She worried they had gotten captured or been injured, and struggled against the thought of a worse fate. She had heard many booming sounds but was certain it was only thunder, not the noise of the *wasicun's* weapon. She was sure they could find their way to and from the locations even blindfolded, so they could not have gotten lost. Yet, they had gone afoot and near weaponless. She knew she could not bear it if anything dire had happened to her beloved husband and her best friend, and she would grieve over the losses of War Eagle and Red Feather. How could she, Chumani fretted, carry on with daily life and with the visionquest without them? Surely the Great Spirit would not demand such horrible sacrifices from them, from her, in order to obtain peace and survival for their people.

More time passed, and her tension grew. The violent lightning and crashing thunder decreased, and gradually the rain slowed its pounding force and ominous clouds dispersed. A half-moon peeked from behind them, yet its light was not enough for her to locate her loved ones at the river.

She knew she could not stay where she was to greet the morning sun and what it brought with it. Besides the discovery of her companions' daring deed and the ensuing uproar over it and search of the surrounding area for those responsible, Bert was sure to send his men after her for the horses and trade goods. She had to confront and accept the bitter truth: if they were alive and unharmed, they would have returned by now. With the moon in occasional view, she could not lie and say she did not know it had reached the location in the sky where her husband had told her to leave; and she had promised to obey him.

With clothes and hair soaked and her spirits low, Chumani descended the almost slippery hillside after scanning the area one last time. She gathered their possessions and loaded them. She had never imagined she would be making the return ride alone. She told herself she must not lose faith and hope; she must believe they would catch up with her soon, even though she had their horses and weapons. She mounted, grasped the other four horses' tethers, and headed toward the Sica River to follow its bank toward their summer camp.

As she journeyed over the rolling landscape, the gentle rain halted. The storm was gone, and would not conceal her departure tracks. The wind still blew forcefully, but the air warmed steadily. The sky cleared and brightened as dawn approached from her rear; now she would be visible from a distance until she reached concealing trees. Yet, she knew she was leaving a trail even a small boy could follow. She kept her weapons ready to use, as she was certain they would be needed when the post trader's men eventually pursued her.

Every few minutes, Chumani glanced over her shoulder to see if Zeb and the other man were galloping up behind her, and sighed in relief each time the terrain was clear of attackers. Then, without warning and close upon relief, came the dreaded; she sighted two riders—white men— galloping in her direction. She urged her horse onward at a swifter pace and pulled on the other four's tethers to coax them closer and faster. If she could make it to a section of trees and scrubs not far away and dismount before they reached her, she knew she had a better chance to defend herself. She almost did not care if they stole the packhorse and trade goods, but she did not want them to take the horses and weapons of War Eagle, Zitkala, and Red Feather, and especially not the possessions of Wind Dancer.

Chumani glanced over her shoulder again and realized

the men were gaining on her fast. As her destination drew nearer, she was certain she could reach it before they closed the gap between them. As soon as the horses' thongs were secured and her husband's weapons were protected, she would give the two enemies a surprise they would never forget, for they would not expect an attack or ever imagine her to be so skilled with a bow and arrows.

She rode into the trees to use them as shields for herself and the winded animals. She bounded from her horse and tied all leashes to sturdy bushes. She grabbed her bow and quiver and darted behind a cottonwood where she jabbed the sharp tips of several arrows into the rain-softened ground, readying them for hasty retrieval. She made a daring plan of attack as she nocked the first chokecherry shaft. She knew she had to shoot fast and accurately once she showed herself and before they could take aim and fire their weapons. At least there were only two of them. She heard them approach and halt several tepees' length from her. She stayed still and quiet and listened to their offensive words.

"Come on out, woman, 'cause you cain't git away from us!"

Zeb laughed. "You're wasting your breath, Harry, 'cause she don't speak no English. Keep alert, man, 'cause she might try to jump us. I don't plan on getting bit, scratched, or stuck with no rusty knife today."

"You said she was a real looker, Zeb, so I'd like a piece of her afore we slit her throat. You know we can't leave her alive to go a tattling to her people about us stealing her horses and goods. You said there wuz two of 'em, so where's the other one? And where did she git more horses?"

"Probably stole them near the post. I guess the other one's riding ahead for some reason. You can't ever tell with them dumb Injuns. I guess we got to dismount and look for her. Just keep your eyes and ears open."

Chumani took a deep breath and invoked the Great Spirit's help. She leapt from behind the large cottonwood, prepared to fire at the one named Harry. She was releasing the arrow just as Wind Dancer and Red Feather jumped the two white men from tree limbs above them, sending forth war whoops as they did so. With sharp reflexes, she jerked the bow toward the left and altered its path before it could wound or slay her beloved husband. As her widened gaze watched the hand-to-hand battles, she thanked Wakantanka for allowing her to save Wind Dancer's life. Taken by surprise and pitted against warriors with superior prowess, the white men were slain quickly.

Wind Dancer's dark gaze left his conquered foe's body and focused on his wife. He smiled at her. "Your skills grow larger each sun, *mitawin,* and your courage and wits are great. We were forced to wait until they walked beneath us," he explained. "We did not reveal our presence to you, for your reaction may have exposed us."

"Why did you slay them?" she asked as he walked toward her.

"They saw our faces and horses and would remember them. We did not let you fire your arrows at them, for we have no Crow ones to put in their places. We will hang them by their feet from the trees with their throats cut, as is the way of our enemies who will be blamed for this deed."

Chumani spoke into his chest after he reached her and held her close. "My arrow almost struck you."

"It could not do so," he said, "for your skills are large and the Great Spirit protects us. It warms my heart to look upon your face again and to touch you. It is good you obeyed my words to leave before the sun appeared. We found great victory during the storm, and will reveal all things to you while we travel to our camp."

As if his words awakened her from a daze, she asked in a rush, "How did you reach this place first and hide in the trees? What happened at the river? Why did you not return to me? Where are Zitkala and War Eagle and your horse?"

Wind Dancer chuckled as questions spilled from her

lips like gushing water over a rock fall following a heavy rain, but he quelled his reaction, realizing how worried she had been. "The storm was traveling away and sunrise was approaching fast and it was near your leaving time when we finished our deed, so it was too late to return to where you waited for us," he explained. "We knew which path you would ride, so we ran as fleeing deer along the riverbank to reach this place before you did. War Eagle and Zitkala go on ahead for a short distance; they are unharmed. From the last hill, we saw you coming and saw the White-eyes tracking you even before you sighted them. I knew how and where you would confront them, so we hurried here and our companions rode onward to conceal themselves and our raid goods. We must prepare these enemies to trick their people and leave this place fast. Others will come soon to search for them and to search for the Crow who attacked the boats."

Chumani smiled. "You know me as I know myself and the Great Spirit knows me. It is good we have lived and ridden together for many suns and moons and we have no secrets between us. I am filled with joy to see your face and feel your touch again. I will water the horses and gather my arrows while you and Red Feather do your task."

Unmindful of their friend's presence, they embraced and kissed, then exchanged another loving smile.

Red Feather handed her the arrow he had pulled from a tree nearby while the couple shared a short but special time together, the kind of moment he longed to share with Zitkala.

"Thank you, my friend, and it is good to see your face again."

"As it is good to see yours, Dewdrops. Your skills are large and many, and so are those of your best friend. The man who captures Zitkala's love and becomes her mate will find great happiness and victory in his Life-Circle."

"That is true, Red Feather, and I hope he is a good friend to me and my husband, for it will give us great joy to have her live in our camp."

The warrior grinned at her and Wind Dancer before he replied, "My joy will match yours only if I am that good friend and she shares my tepee. But that is the only path she is slow and fears to walk."

"Then you must share with her the courage and desire to take the first step along that wonderful journey."

"If I hold out my hand to her, Dewdrops, will she take it?"

"All I can say to you, Red Feather, is to do so; for until she learns of your feelings, there is no choice to be made."

By the time they halted to camp at dusk, Chumani's head was filled with revelations about the successful episode last night. They had told War Eagle and Zitkala about the confrontation with Zeb and Harry, and how they had laid a false trail toward Crow territory to mislead the Whites who came looking for the two missing men and the boat raiders.

As the women excused themselves in bushes a short distance away, Chumani told Zitkala about her unexpected exchange of words with Red Feather. "Did I speak too soon and too bold, my friend?" she asked.

"No, Dewdrops, for I have great love and desire for him. I will wait and watch for him to approach me with such words. I do not wish to think and hope until he speaks of his feelings and I know they are true."

"It is good if you join with him, for it will keep us close in the seasons to come. There is much I wish we could say now," she said with a sigh, "but we must return to camp. We are tired and have a long ride on the new sun."

Later, as they lay on their sleeping mats, Wind Dancer knew they were safe while concealed from view in the ravine; he also knew his horse would awaken him if anyone approached their location. He cuddled Chumani close to him and savored the contact with her. He was all too aware either or both of them could have been slain during this perilous journey. He was glad the Great Spirit had guided him to her before the white men reached her, though he did not doubt her ability to protect herself. He nibbled at her ear and whispered, "I needed you at the river to warm me after my swim in its cold water."

"We will both need the use of cold water from melting snow soon if you continue to enflame us when we cannot join," she whispered in return. She felt his body move as he struggled to suppress the amusement which filled it. "Do not laugh, *mihigna*, for it is true; a fierce blaze burns at me now, and you might awaken the others."

"If we were alone or in our tepee, I would put out your fire after I caused it to flame higher and hotter, for my love and need for you are large."

"As mine are for you, but we are not alone or in our lodge. If you do not halt your gentle attack upon me, I will be too restless to sleep."

Wind Dancer sensed how aroused she was, and knew her words were serious. "As will I, *micante*, so I will lie still and quiet."

"Only until we reach our lodge; then, you must tempt me again."

"I will do so, *mitawin*," he promised.

As they camped for the last night during their journey, Red Feather asked Zitkala to take a walk with him. They strolled a short distance away from the others along the bank of the Sahiyela River. The air was balmy and felt good on their flesh; the constant breeze, gentle and invigorating; the sky, clear of dark clouds and splattered with glittering stars. Mingled scents of wildflowers and grasses teased at their noses. The sounds of crickets, frogs, and nocturnal birds filled their ears. It was as if nature had created a romantic and enticing setting just for them.

Red Feather stopped near a gently swaying willow and looked at her. "When you entered the white man's post and I feared you would be slain or captured and lost to me forever, I knew my love and desire for you were great," he revealed. "I want you to become a part of my Life-

Circle. I yearn for you to join to me, Zitkala, when we return to our camp."

A surge of contradictory emotions and thoughts assailed her. She had expected this to happen, yet his words surprised her. She believed him, yet, how could a virile and handsome male like Red Feather love and desire her and want her to be his wife and to live with him forever? Why was she both sad and elated? Trusting, yet, doubtful? Why was she so afraid to reach out to him? So afraid she was dreaming and would awaken soon?

"Speak, Zitkala, so I will know what lives in your heart and head."

Needing to be convinced a true bond was possible, she reasoned, "It is too soon after our first meeting to become mates, Red Feather. We must learn more about each other and test our feelings as we test ourselves upon the battleground and on the hunt. We must be sure that more than desire lives in our bodies and joy in our spirits as vision companions. Our bond must come from love to be strong and to last for our remaining suns."

Red Feather captured her hands as he vowed, "My love is strong and true, Zitkala. The Creator crossed our paths for this purpose, as He did with Wind Dancer and Dewdrops. Join to me soon." When she lowered her gaze, he asked, "Do you not love and desire me as I do you? Do my eyes see and my heart hope for what is not there within you?"

"My love and desire for you are large, Red Feather, but my fear is large as well. I have never been close to a man in the past, so the swiftness of our feelings frightens me and makes me wary. I could not bear it if we joined and you learned your heart and mind had misled you. Wait until the buffalo season is over; if you feel the same on that moon as you do on this one, I will join to you and forever be your mate."

"I will wait until your fears and doubts are gone. But," he added with a grin, "I will pursue you every sun and moon until that time comes."

Zitkala smiled. "That is good, Red Feather, for you stir my heart and body as no man ever has."

"And you fill me with all things as no other woman ever has. From the first time I gazed upon you and heard your voice, I was lost to your pull."

"As I was lost to yours, Red Feather, when I first entered your camp and saw your face and heard you speak."

"We are matched in all ways. I will be a good husband to you, and I will never seek to change you, for I love you as you are."

"Speak those last words again," she coaxed as her heart pounded in joy, her spirit soared, and all doubts fled her mind.

"I love you, Zitkala," he murmured before he kissed her, and was thrilled by the passionate way she responded to him.

After the five reached their encampment, they were greeted by their people who were not away hunting and butchering buffalo on the Plains. Everyone halted their chores and gathered around to hear the revelations of their glorious tales. A celebration was held that night where eating, singing, and dancing were shared by all; and the five's coups were chanted as they were honored for their new deeds. Those who had donated furs, pelts, and hides for the women to use during their post visit were given the trade goods. Their parents and relatives beamed in pride and joy. Their friends and society members were elated. Their shamans sent forth prayers of gratitude for their victories and safe return.

For a short while, Wind Dancer and Red Feather left to conceal the gunpowder, weapons, and matches in a safe location in the event they had surprise visitors, especially Bluecoats or Crow.

Wind Dancer and Chumani had yearned for privacy and rapturous contact for many days, and at last they had it. She sealed their tepee flap and they eagerly stripped off their garments. He embraced her and she savored the feeling of his warm flesh against her own. When he kissed her, she nearly purred with satisfaction, and the sound of her pleasure made him smile. As they kissed and stroked each other, they learned ever more about nurturing the passion that was always present in their joinings. Chumani hoped it would always be so.

Shafts of moonlight played over her face from the ventilation opening above them and revealed her beautiful features for him to enjoy. She was awesome magic, and he was a willing captive to her spell, as she was to his. When she arched against him, her hands clutched at his shoulders, and she moaned in bliss, he surrendered to his own release.

They kissed and caressed even after their journey was completed; then they cuddled with her back pressed against the front of his body. Soon, they drifted off to sleep, sated and serene.

Shortly after dawn, Wind Dancer, Red Feather, and War Eagle joined the next group's hunt for buffalo to help with that seasonal task before they left to carry out another raid on either the Crow or Whites. Chumani and Zitkala went along with the women's party to skin and butcher the slain creatures, taking their travois with them for young braves to use for hauling those parts back to camp to their families and others who would begin the meat-drying and tanning processes. As customary, the men left first and the women trailed behind them, watching and waiting and chatting until their arduous work began. Both groups were filled with exhilaration and suspense, as the hunt was such an important part of their lives—the main source of their shelter, clothing, food, and items for daily use.

As the women topped a hill, Chumani saw the vast herd stretched out before them as if it went on forever, the lush grass obscured in many places by dense clusters of dark bodies. Although the animals appeared slow in mind and speed, she knew they were smart and swift and agile. She saw the hunters, including her loved ones and friends, plunge into the midst of the outer fringes and fire their arrows at close range, aiming for spots where the creatures were most vulnerable. The warriors felled many buffaloes quickly and mercifully in a short time, their horses working in deft unison with their owners, though they would not slay more than they could use. Some of the animals scattered; others continued grazing as if no threat existed, and some lay in wallows undisturbed by action, especially old males.

Chumani and the other women spread out and began work on the huge carcasses, after seeking and finding the first one with her husband's marked arrows embedded in its body. Using sharp knives, she and Zitkala skinned the animal—its hide to supply many needs—and gutted it. They carved out the selected hunks of meat and placed them on the hide. They collected the horns, hooves, and certain bones to use for cups, spoons, knives, and glue. The tongue, liver, and tail were removed. The stomach and bladder were cut out to become water bags. The task was a long, and a bloody one. They saw air and land scavengers looming overhead and lurking at a short distance to await their turns at the kill, which would complete the buffalo's circle-of-life and purpose for creation.

They secured the large bundle with sturdy thongs, signaled a brave with an empty travois it was ready for removal, and headed toward their next target after helping him load it and watching his departure for camp.

As they labored on their second beast, Chumani heard the awesome sounds of the *wasicuns'* firesticks and saw a large band of Crow warriors charging toward the left side of the giant herd. Her gaze widened in horror as she realized an attack was imminent. The grazing buffaloes halted their feast; those in wallows bounded to their feet swiftly; the males gathered around the females and calves; and the cows nudged their babies closer to them. The leading bulls assumed stances of intimidation to warn off the encroachers. Soon they realized they were being challenged to a fight.

Chumani saw the massive heads of the male buffaloes jerk upward and thrash about, as prelude to their bellows of rage. Some pawed the ground in warning. Their skinny tails shot upward and arched over at the fuzzy tips before straightening. Then the enormous and infuriated animals began to run, their hooves striking the earth in a thunderous noise. At most times, the beasts would rush past anyone—or anything—in its path without inflicting harm. But when they were provoked to such panic and crowded close together, they would trample any intruder. Antelope and scavenging coyotes fled toward safety, as did birds, insects, and rabbits. Prairie dogs scurried into their burrows, their barks masked by pounding hooves. Chumani's frantic gaze searched for her husband and saw him racing toward the commotion. She realized he was challenging their foes to cease their provocation. She wanted to keep her eyes on him, but knew the best thing she and Zitkala could do was crouch behind the carcass they had been working on. They would hope and pray the stampeding herd heading for them evaded them.

As the Oglala and Brule hunters sought to turn the herd from where the women worked, they tried to avoid the beasts' sharp horns and head rammings. They knew that the rumbling force would continue to race over hills and flat areas in a direct line with their joint encampment.

Wind Dancer saw Raven's horse trip and fall, then lie still, no doubt with a broken neck. With several Crow bearing down on the vulnerable warrior, one of their four Sacred Bow Carriers, he had no choice except to attempt a rescue. His code of honor as a warrior and a friend and his ranks of Shirt Wearer and Strong Heart member demanded he do so. He galloped toward the man who now stood facing his oncoming threat, a hunting bow and a few remaining arrows his only weapons, as his Sacred Bow was used only during warfare and rituals and was safe in camp.

As Wind Dancer almost reached the downed man, he shouted for Raven to be ready to leap up behind him, a rescue action all Oglala warriors practiced frequently. He held his bow and tether in one hand and extended the other for his friend to seize in a hurry so Raven could swing up behind him and they could flee their enemies fast. He was stunned when the Crow attackers fired many arrows and slew his beloved buffalo horse. The dead animal toppled to the ground and sent Wind Dancer tumbling into the tall and thick grass, knocking the air from his lungs and the bow from his grasp. Before he could recover, he was shocked again when—by order of their leader— three Birdmen took the life of Raven in a cowardly manner.

As he leapt to his feet and struggled to breathe, Wind Dancer found himself encircled by Apsaalooke wearing warpaint and fierce glares. He knew it was foolish to grab for the knife in his sheath, as two foes had arrows pointing at him and would send their tips into his hand, he could not risk a disabling injury to it. He straightened himself to his full height and assumed a spread-legged stance of defiance and confidence. His chest was extended to reveal his scorn and courage, as did his expression. His ebony hair whipped about in the wind and his dark gaze locked on the band's grinning leader as he awaited his own death.

Chapter
Sixteen

Wind Dancer was not afraid to die; he would do so with honor and courage. He would complete his Life-Circle with a generous sacrifice, even though Raven was dead. He firmly believed that if his journey upon the face of Mother Earth ended this day, it would be the will of Wakan-tanka and there would be a purpose for his death which only the Great Mystery knew. The only regrets he had were leaving his family and people to battle their enemies without his aid and being taken from the arms of his beloved wife who would grieve terribly over his loss and be compelled to achieve the sacred visionquest alone or with other companions. He dared not let his attention stray by glancing toward the hill behind him, but he was sure Chumani was watching this grim event, as he sensed her powerful gaze and could almost hear her words of love and encouragement inside his head as a soft whisper. The thunderous noise of countless hooves told him the stampede was still in progress, and he knew his wife and others were in the path of those enraged buffaloes while he was unable to rescue her and help the other hunters turn the massive herd away from their camp. Surrounded by twelve foes who were armed and on horseback while he was afoot and near weaponless, all he could do now was pray for the panicked animals to calm soon, slow down, and change direction.

"You do not beg for your life, first son of Rising Bear?"

Wind Dancer did not show his surprise when the leader revealed he knew his identity or spoke in the Oglala tongue. He stared at the man in contempt as he replied in his enemy's language, "That is not our way, Crow dog, though it is yours when you face a superior force. Do the Apsaalooke have so few coups and crave them so badly they attack others without any show of honor? What coup lies in slaying a disabled and entrapped man, as you did to my friend? What coup lies in slaying one of the Great Spirit's creatures, as you did to my horse? Did you stain your face with such evil and cowardice to prevent Wind Dancer and Raven from fleeing you to battle you on another sun?" He knew from the man's narrowed gaze and lift of his shoulders that he had provoked him to anger. He knew his best chance for survival was in working on the leader's excessive pride.

"The one who lies dead was of no value to us, but the next chief of the Red Shields will feel the pains of our hatred and revenge. You will die as slowly as the porcupine crawls. You will suffer and bleed as no other captive ever has. We will find great joy and victory in slaying Waci Tate."

"The son of Rising Bear does not die quickly or easily, Crow dog."

"I hope your words are true, but die you will, and long after you crave to walk the Ghost Trail to end your sufferings and shame of defeat to me."

"I challenge you to fight me to my death or to my freedom. Dismount and we will learn who is the better warrior. I die or I go free."

"I do not accept your challenge to fight here," the Crow leader sneered, "for many others must watch and enjoy that event."

Confident he could win a fight, Wind Dancer tried to trick his truculent foe by ridiculing him. "Does your heart pound with such fear and are your skills so few that you do not wish to face me man to man?" he asked. "Do you need the help or encouragement of others to defeat only one opponent? Is it not also the Apsaalooke way to allow a brave warrior to earn his freedom?"

"Not when that captive is a large enemy of my people. I will show great strength and wits in not battling you at this place and time. I will show great generosity in allowing my people to see you die."

"Will you battle me one-to-one in your camp," Wind Dancer taunted, "or will you need the help of others when you confront me?"

"Sroka needs help from no friend or spirit to defeat a weakling Sioux."

Wind Dancer glared at the pugnacious man whose face was painted red and bore solid black circles to signify blood and death. He had recognized Sroka, but had behaved as if the malevolent warrior was not important enough to be recalled or feared by him. Their bands had clashed during past raids and fought during tribal battles. He surmised the Crow had named him a "Sioux," a white man's word for the threefold Dakota Nation, as friend and foe were aware it was an insult. "Crow dog, you walk and sniff behind the *wasicun* so much to beg for his truce like a bone that you speak as he does. Have you forgotten your people's name for us, *Da-kkoo-tee?*"

"I have forgotten nothing, *Waci Tate,* who is now my prisoner."

"Why do you attack while we hunt the buffalo?" Wind Dancer asked to glean helpful information. "This is not the season to fight."

"If your people have no food or shelter or garments for winter, they will starve and freeze and die. There will be fewer *Da-kkoo-tee* to battle in the coming seasons, and soon this land will be ours as it was long ago."

"If you sacrifice your suns and moons attacking us during the hot season and do not use them preparing for winter, your people will die. That is foolish, Sroka, and it is not the Indian way."

"No more talk. Mount behind Pariskatoopa and give him your knife. We ride for our camp and your death. Do you fear to face it?"

Wind Dancer grinned. "I do not fear death, for it is a sacred part of every man's Life-Circle. I am eager to fight you." He decided it was best to cooperate at that point, for it would call away at least twelve enemies from the band still harassing his people and it would keep him alive to plot and carry out an escape. He relinquished his weapon, swung up behind Two Crows as indicated, and said, "I am ready."

"Alaxiia Bilee, gather their weapons and take the medicine bundle and a scalplock of the fallen one to hang in my lodge. Soon I will show all I have won the weapons and life of Waci Tate of the Oglalas."

As Fire-in-Heart obeyed Sroka's orders, the leader told his other men to ride on either side and behind Wind Dancer and to wound him with lance cuts if he tried to escape or to slow them down. He signaled for the rest of his band to abandon their strike on the hunting party and to follow them.

As they galloped away, Wind Dancer took a breath of relief to know the enemy threat was over and the herd was quieting down. He realized they would be long gone before a band of his warriors could arm themselves, mount up, and pursue them. Yet, surely his father, despite his anguish, would not allow an attack on a large and powerful Crow camp to attempt to rescue him. Surely they would leave any escape plan up to him.

Her spirits low and her heart pounding in dread as she lay atop a knoll to avoid being sighted, Chumani watched her beloved husband being carried away from her by a malicious foe, no doubt to face torture and death. The large Crow party had broken off their attack and those enemies now raced after the smaller band after being summoned by Sroka, whose face pattern she also recognized. The charging herd had been averted and now moved off in the distance, and their hunters were returning. They and the women who had taken cover behind a hill with Zitkala were safe. With the buffalo heading in the opposite direction, the camp was safe, and by now might have been alerted to their peril by one of the young braves with travois duty. Everyone was out of danger except the man who was her life, her true love. Yet, as long as he was alive, there was a slim chance of him escaping or being rescued.

Red Feather, War Eagle, and Fire Walker joined her at the base of the high knoll after she stood and signaled to them. "Why do you smile on such a dark sun?" she asked as the mounted men gazed at her.

War Eagle, like his companions, looked at her in confusion. "We have saved our camp from the buffalo and our hunting party from the Crow. We are all unharmed."

"But you have lost a brother and a good friend, Wanbli."

The three warriors looked over their shoulders, but all they viewed were the bodies of buffaloes in various stages of butchering and a few abandoned travois where they had been hunting and the women working earlier. They did not sight Wind Dancer among the men who were checking on the women for injuries and calming them.

"Follow me up the hill," Chumani almost commanded them and headed to the top in a hurry. On its peak, she motioned toward the grim scene beyond it where the slain Raven and two dead horses lay upon the grass, multiple arrows protruding from their bodies.

Red Feather, his heart thudding in trepidation and his gaze wide, spoke before the others could. "Where is my friend, my spirit brother?" he asked as Zitkala joined them and also stared at the solemn sight.

Chumani related the grim tale and saw the men's shocked reaction to Wind Dancer's entrapment and the mention of Sroka's name. "I remained here and watched," she continued, "for I had no bow and arrows to use. I could not run to help him, for there were twelve warriors in Sroka's party. I could not hear their words, but they spoke for a time, then took him away.'' She related how Raven and her husband's horse had been slain without just cause, as if from sheer evil. She revealed the theft of their possessions and the taking of a scalplock from Raven. ''Sroka knows the face and rank of Waci Tate and wishes to walk my beloved amongst his people in bonds before he tortures and slays him for all there to see. Raven's body must be recovered and placed on a scaffold. We must prepare ourselves to go after my husband, but we cannot go as a large band, for that is what they will expect us to do. All must stay and guard our camp except for the five of us; we will save him and bring him back to his people.''

''How can we do so, my sister, when he will be held in the center of their village, and he and their camp will be guarded against our approach?''

Chumani looked at Fire Walker, her heart full of anguish and her mind with worry. ''The Great Spirit has put a plan within my head, and I will share it with all of you later. If you must stay in camp to protect your wife, unborn child, and our parents, that will not show weakness on your part. You are the future chief of the White Shields, my beloved brother, and must live to become their leader.''

''We have many skilled warriors amongst our two bands who can protect our loved ones and people,'' Fire Walker said firmly. ''I must help save the life of the future chief of the Red Shields who is our ally and friend, and my sister's mate. We will be victorious, for it is not his time to walk the Ghost Trail, as he is the Vision Man; and the task given to you and him has not been completed.''

''That is true, my brother, and it is why I know we must do this deed.''

They heard riders approaching and looked in that direction to sight a large band of their warriors with Rising Bear at their lead. They went to join him and related the bad news of his son's capture and Raven's vile slaying.

Chumani wasted no time in disclosing a daring rescue plan to the Red Shield chief, who listened, considered it, and nodded agreement. She perceived how tormented the older man was with the grim events. "Do not worry, my second father," she said gently, "for we will save him."

"I will pray for the Great Spirit to guide and protect you, my second daughter. I trust your skills and wits, for Wakantanka chose you as the Vision Woman and my son's mate. You have proven yourself worthy of both ranks. But if it is the will of our Creator for my son to join Him and the risks are too great to challenge, do not endanger your life."

"I will be wise and careful, and I thank you for your good words."

Everyone returned to camp and the distressing episodes were related again. The warriors yearned to ride after the Crow and challenge them, but realized, from the advice of the shaman chief and council, that would leave their camp unprotected and probably provoke Wind Dancer's slaying. Plans were made for guarding the camp and hunting party while seasonal work was being done. The body of Raven was prepared and placed upon a burial scaffold constructed by his fellow Sacred Bow Carriers, which also meant another man must be chosen to take his place, as had occurred with Badger not long ago. The two fallen horses were honored and left for nature to claim.

Supplies needed by Chumani's rescue party were gathered and loaded on their mounts. She had War Eagle put a tether on Wind Dancer's war horse to take with them for her husband to ride during their escape, as that animal was the smartest, bravest, fastest, and most nimble and loyal one he owned. On a recently tanned deerhide, she placed an old and stained dress which for some reason she had not discarded or torn apart to use for other purposes. She added plain and long past useful moccasins from a friend who, strangely enough, also had not gotten rid of them. Chumani told the woman it was the mystical workings of the Great Spirit. The same was true for the frayed Crow blanket another friend gave to her for tossing over her head and shoulders under which she would stoop to aid her pretense. She secured a small pouch which contained white ash from a past fire and pale dirt used to mix with grease to make white paint which Hanmani had gathered for her to whiten her dark hair, along with the crushed wooden embers to smudge her face and arms and hands to help conceal their youthfulness. She laid a gnarled walking stick with a smoothed branch grip atop that pile. With all the props, she could disguise herself as an old woman and pass with no questions asked to reach her beloved. She tied the bundle and went to load it on her horse.

Tall Elk and Falling Rain arrived as she completed her preparations. She looked at her worried parents, smiled, and embraced them.

Tall Elk said in an emotion-constricted voice, "Ride with eagle eyes, the deer's speed, and the fox's cunning, my brave and generous daughter, for we must not lose you in this way. Take this; you know how to use it."

Chumani accepted the fieldglass which she considered great magic, as it would help her spy on the enemy camp from far away. She knew it was a gift from a French trapper many winters past for saving his life, one of the few *wasicun* who had visited their camp and been called a friend. She remembered how her father had made a clever game of teaching her and Fire Walker how to use and not fear the eye-glass. She hugged him. "Your heart is good, my father, and I thank you."

"Your love for your husband is large, my daughter," Magaju said, "but you must not endanger your life to save his unless a safe path is opened to you."

Chumani nodded. "I will do only what I must, Mother. Watch over Rainbow Girl while my brother rides with us. This separation will be frightening for her with their child growing inside her. Do not allow her to work too hard to distract herself from worries. We will both return soon."

"We will pray for our children to return to us unharmed and alive."

Once more, Chumani exchanged hugs with her parents.

The others in her party joined her and she told her parents, "We must ride fast while the sun gives us light, for the dark moon will offer none after the sun sleeps."

Sees-Through-Mist stepped forward and said a prayer for the group's safety and success. He smiled at Chumani and added, "Many challenges and joys await you and your husband; you will both survive to meet them, for help will come in strange forms and ways."

"I do not understand your last words, Wise One."

The elderly shaman smiled again. "They will be clear soon."

Chumani glanced at all those who gathered around to bid them farewell and good luck. She took a deep breath and said to her companions, "We must ride, my friends; my love awaits our help." She had meant to say her *husband,* but she did not correct herself. She saw almost all of those around her smile knowingly. She looked at her hawk and summoned him. "Come, Cetan, for you travel and work with us this time."

"We must halt here, Dewdrops, where there is water for our horses and trees to conceal us," Red Feather urged. "Soon the sun sleeps and we can no longer see their tracks, for the moon wears a black face this night. We must rest and begin our task again when the sun returns to show us the way. Do not forget, they are less than a half-sun's ride ahead of us, and could be camped nearby. We cannot risk encountering their lookouts in the shadows. If we are sighted or attacked, all hope of saving Wind Dancer is lost to us."

Chumani could not dispute Red Feather's words, but she hated to stop the journey toward her husband. She could imagine the vile treatment he was enduring, if he still lived; and she prayed and must believe he did. Since he had not been slain with Raven and they had not come across his . . . body, that had to mean Sroka intended to take him to their camp. If only they knew where Sroka's band was heading, other than in the direction from which the winter winds came, they would know if they had a short or long ride looming before them, and they could plan their impending actions better if they knew the camp's surrounding terrain. She nodded in agreement with Red Feather and dismounted as Cetan left her shoulder and perched in a tree. She tended the two horses, nibbled on food which Zitkala forced into her hands, drank water from the Sahiyela River, then lay down upon her buffalo mat. She was glad no one tried to give her words of comfort, as her mind and heart were in no mood to hear them. She could not bear the thoughts of never seeing her beloved husband again, never kissing and touching him again, never hearing his voice again, never having him lie beside her and hold her in his arms . . . never to make love to her again. She closed her eyes as if that action would shut out such torment, but it did not appease her anguish.

Sleep eluded her for a long time, and then came only in short spurts. Each time she awakened, she prayed more fervently than ever to be able to reach him in time and to be given a way to save him.

Nearby, the others also sent forth prayers for Wind Dancer's survival.

Zitkala knew how she would feel if Red Feather were taken captive. She, too, would risk anything to save him, even her own life. She turned her head in his direction but could not see him in the darkness, as it was too dangerous to have a fire. Yet, even lacking moonlight, she felt safe, as Cetan and the horses would alert them if anyone approached their location. As if Red Feather sensed her questing gaze, she felt his hand touch hers; and she gave it to him, just as she would give herself completely to him after the buffalo season. She would tell him that again, along with how much she loved him, when the sun rose. He gave her hand a gentle squeeze, and she returned the gesture and smiled in happiness. After that comforting contact, she drifted off to sleep.

* * *

Wind Dancer entered the Apsaalooke camp still riding doubleback with Two Crows and amidst great excitement from its people, as several warriors had ridden ahead with news of his capture. They had traveled hard and fast and used all daylight for the past *two* suns. They had crossed *two* large rivers and reached the camp, which was situated on Rabbit Creek, at dusk. Once more he was aware of how the number *two* invaded his life.

Some of the women rushed forward to reveal their hatred and contempt of all Oglalas by either jabbing him with sticks or clawing and pinching him with their fingernails or by spitting upon his bare legs and moccasined feet, as he was clad only in a breechclout and leather footwear. Some of the male youths darted forth to show their courage by striking him on the legs or hips with open palms or balled fists. Others yelled insults and a few tossed rocks at him. Sroka did nothing to halt such abuses, as was his right to do; in fact, the leader foe appeared to enjoy such vicious behavior. Despite his harsh treatment and the stinging pains, the son of Rising Bear sat tall and proud, his expression impassive, before his bitter enemies. He knew this was only the beginning of the torture in store for him.

Pariskatoopa threw his leg over his horse's head and leapt to the ground. He seized Wind Dancer by the left arm and yanked him down, the action almost causing him to stumble and fall. He straightened himself and locked his gaze on Sroka as the man related the blood-stirring event. He heard people mumbling words and sounds of praise and amazement; and he, too, was astonished by his first capture. He was bound to a large post in the center of camp with his ankles secured snugly to it and his arms stretched behind him so tightly he wondered if they would be pulled loose from his shoulders. He knew bruises and welts were rising on his body, just as he felt blood oozing from cuts and scrapes to slowly roll down his sweaty flesh.

He was glad his cherished wife and people could not see him like this, and he prayed to Wakantanka to allow him to flee or to die with honor intact.

Wind Dancer listened as Sroka told his people they could touch and inflict small harms to him but that he must not be wounded badly or slain; and must not be given food or water or medicine. "Does Sroka need to weaken me before he can defeat me?" he scoffed. The man turned and glared at him, then grinned and refuted his taunt.

"You were not denied food and water during our journey."

Wind Dancer recalled how a few scraps of dried meat were tossed on the ground near him as if he were a dog, and how water was poured into his open mouth from a height above him which caused most of it to be lost in splashes over his face and neck. Yet, he had eaten and drank to retain his strength for escape. He stared at Sroka as the man taunted him again.

"Surely a few strikes will not weaken a man who is claimed to be a strong and brave warrior. Do the Red Shields not train to go without food and water for many suns and moons to show their strength and endurance?"

"That is true, Sroka, but we do not weaken foes before we fight them. If an opponent is not at his best, how can such a victory be a true one?"

"I will allow my people to have fun with you for two suns; then you will be tended, fed, and watered to regain your strength to battle me upon the rising of the third sun."

Wind Dancer realized his ploy to avoid anything that would drain him of power which he needed for escape had failed. He heard Sroka reveal his decision to his tribe, who cheered for him new coups and his generosity. Sroka also ordered guards to be posted around the village in the event the Red Shields attempted a rescue. Yet, Sroka added that he was doubtful the Red Shields were so foolish, as they could not leave their camp so vulnerable by sending enough warriors to challenge them. Even if it cost him his life, Wind Dancer hoped his father prevented such an action, as this band was strong and well armed and on the alert, and there was no way anyone could reach his position to free him before both were slain by countless arrows.

As many men, women, and children closed in on him, Wind Dancer braced himself for what was to come and to last for *two*—that number again—days. He told himself if he could endure the formidable Sun Dance Ritual, he could withstand anything. Yet, there was a good reason for that sacred ceremony and its rigors when there were none for this malicious occurrence. He lifted his gaze skyward and called the image of Chumani to mind to distract him from his ordeal. He envisioned them in their tepee, talking, laughing, and making love.

When they halted to camp at a side branch of Canpa Creek where numerous wild-cherry trees grew amidst cottonwoods and willows and other types, Chumani was besieged by mounting tension and dread. They had traveled over rolling grassland and crossed many streams and creeks which were mainly offshoots of the Sahiyela River. They had entered an area of infrequent buttes, grassy hills, low knolls, and odd formations. Yet, the landscape was mostly flat for great stretches. They had seen many buffalo, deer, antelope, coyote, and other creatures. The sky had remained a pale blue; the summer air, hot and dry; and the Plains wind, constant and strong. They had not halted until daylight was almost gone, and she knew there would be no moon showing again tonight.

"We ride too slow, Zitkala," she fretted.

"We ride fast, Dewdrops," Zitkala gently corrected her. "It seems slow, for you fear for your love's survival and are eager to reach him."

"The Crow ride faster and harder, for their hooves cut deeply into the face of Mother Earth; they leave us behind more and more each sun. If the moon's face was not hidden, we could ride longer and overtake them."

"No, Dewdrops, for we and our horses need rest. We

must not reach our enemies too weary to fight and escape them. Do not fear, for our shaman told us he will live to finish the visionquest. Do not forget Wakantanka watches over and protects him and gave him a sacred task."

"Your words are wise and true, Zitkala, and I am shamed for having such weakness and doubts. Even so, those feelings sneak into my body and trouble my spirit. I will try harder to resist and destroy them."

At dawn, a bloodied and battered Wind Dancer was aroused from a light doze by women who kicked or spat upon him as they walked past his place of confinement to begin their morning tasks. He knew those were only the first of countless strikes and insults he would receive during this day and the ensuing one. He had tried for most of the night to loosen his bonds, but they were too tight and secure to do so. He was thirsty and hungry, and the hot sun would soon blaze down upon him. Winged insects now feasted upon his numerous oozing wounds. A few ants crawled over his feet and up his legs, biting him on occasion.

He looked upward and saw dark vultures circling overhead as if they had caught the scent of impending death. It was a certainty the Crow would not wrap his body in a buffalo hide, secure it with thongs, and place it atop a burial scaffold; it would no doubt be discarded outside the camp for scavenger birds such as these and creatures to feast upon until only bones—or nothing—was left. That was not how he wanted to leave the face of Mother Earth, and could not believe the Great Spirit would allow such an evil to beset him.

He was convinced that even if he won his fight with Sroka, another Crow warrior would take his place, and another and another until he was exhausted and lost to one of them. He had to face the reality of his fate: he could not escape, he could not be rescued, and death surely loomed before him in one or more hand-to-hand battles.

Although he had been ensnared while performing his duty and a generous deed for a helpless friend, he felt shamed by his capture; he felt soiled by the touches of his enemies; he felt—though he struggled to resist it—abandoned by the Great Spirit, and he prayed for that wicked thought to leave his mind. He wanted to believe a *wicohan tanka*, a miracle, would occur and release him, but perhaps it was the season for his death. The sacred vision had revealed he was to ride against their enemies—the Crow and the Whites—to plant the war lance between them to obtain a respite for hunting. He had done so, and was perhaps not meant to complete the quest for a truce between them. After the passings of two more moons, he would know the truth and must accept it.

Late that afternoon, Chumani, Zitkala, Red Feather, War Eagle, and Fire Walker lay on their stomachs atop a distant hill and amidst thick grass. Cetan and their horses awaited them at its base, ready to be mounted if a quick escape was necessary.

Chumani spied on the large village with the powerful fieldglass, careful not to allow the sun to reflect upon its lens. She told the others what she observed: the center of camp could not be seen due to the off-set positions of the tepees in numerous circles, but the village was ringed with armed lookouts who were spaced about five lodge lengths apart. There were rolling hills and ravines closer to the village on two opposing sides, but men occasionally rode to them to check for encroachers. "There is no way beneath the sun's light for me to sneak to their camp to enter it," she concluded aloud. "I would be sighted long before I reached it. We must change our plan. I will leave now and take cover there," she said, motioning to the chosen location. "I will sneak into camp after dark, free Wind Dancer, and hide nearby until you show yourselves at dawn and lure the enemy in your direction."

"They will be certain to look in all trees and ravines for you after he is found missing. There is no moonlight to guide you there, my sister. Even if you count the steps needed, you could walk into a guard in the darkness or their dogs will bark warnings of your intrusion."

"That is a risk I must take, my brother. Once I reach the camp, their fires will show me the way to my husband. If he is being guarded, I will sneak up on that Crow and slay him. The scents of ashes and smoke upon my garments and flesh will take away my unfamiliar smell that their dogs and horses might perceive. I will cut and cover us with grass until it is safe to retreat. Cetan will go with me and he will take flight to signal you to begin your task to draw them away from our position."

"How will we know where you hide, Dewdrops, to lure them away from you?" War Eagle asked.

"Watch for Cetan, for he will fly from it. But if he comes to Zitkala with a feather tied to his leg before that time, do not carry out your part of the plan; it will mean you must ride for our camp fast."

"What of you, my sister?" Fire Walker asked in dread.

"The feather signal will mean you must not endanger yourselves as my beloved lives no more and I am safe and away, or he cannot be reached to free him, or I have been captured and cannot be rescued."

"We cannot leave you as their captive!" Fire Walker argued.

"If I am taken, my brother, you must not risk your life to come for me. It is foolish to give more lives to our enemies. You must survive to lead our people, to see the face of your unborn child, to help these companions carry out the rest of the sacred task. If Waci Tate and Chumani die in this place and on this moon, it is the will of Wakantanka and must be accepted."

"Dewdrops speaks wisely, Fire Walker, and we must follow her words," Red Feather told her worried brother.

War Eagle and Zitkala nodded agreement, their expressions saddened by unbidden thoughts of perhaps losing two good friends tonight.

"It must be this way, my brother; do not resist the truth."

Fire Walker nodded resignation. He embraced his sister, perhaps for the last time, his gaze misty with love.

The four watched her ride away to skirt the distant hills, take cover where she had indicated, and prepare herself with the cunning disguise. They saw Wind Dancer's horse trailing behind her, Cetan perched on her shoulder, and all prayed for her safety and success.

Wind Dancer felt weak and dizzy, more from a lack of water after sweating so heavily beneath the fiery sun, than from a lack of food or the many blows he had endured during the day. He was relieved night had come with a cooling breeze and his tormentors had taken to their lodges until morning. Secured in a standing position and his bonds tight, his body ached and felt numb in some places from restricted blood flow. He leaned his head against the large post and closed his eyes, causing his head to feel as if it were spinning in a whirlwind. His mouth and throat were dry. He knew his body was sagging, but did not have the strength to straighten himself; and the way in which his legs were bound refused to allow him to sit or even squat.

Something caused him to open his eyes and he saw the nearest fire had gone out and the guard beside it was asleep, two lapses which would earn him great punishment if discovered. With night upon the land and no moon to brighten it, he could barely see beyond the tepee-encircled center where other small fires burned. It seemed unusually quiet; no sounds of crickets, frogs, or nocturnal birds reached his ears, and all enemy horses were silent. Was he the one who was asleep and dreaming? he wondered.

He strained to see an old woman who now stood before him, as he had not heard her approach. A blanket was tossed over her head, shielding her face from his view. Her scent was unfamiliar, but since the camp dogs were quiet, it must be known to them. He was astonished when she held a buffalo horn cup to his lips and gave him water that tasted strange; then she used a buffalo bladder bag to pour water over his flesh. Oddly, his injuries seemed to gain comfort and his body to gain strength from it. He wondered why an elderly Crow female would help him and why she did not speak to him. Perhaps he was truly dreaming. Yet, it did not seem as if he were asleep. He felt as if he were growing stronger and he wondered what had been in the water he had drunk and which flowed over him. His hands and legs were freed then, and he was surprised his knees did not buckle on him. She grasped his hand and pulled on him to follow her, which he did without asking questions.

She guided him past numerous tepees, some with fires nearby. He was amazed that no horse or dog exposed their presence. She led him into the darkness beyond the last circle of lodges and into the stream nearby. They walked for a while, then he felt the bank nudge his ankle. He stepped from the stream and felt his renewed strength vanish, forcing him to sit down. He extended his arms but could not locate the woman. Or perhaps it was a *Bate,* a feminine Crow male who dressed and lived as a woman, a rank which was accepted and even revered by the Apsaalooke.

"Where are you? Who are you? Why did you help me?" he asked in Crow, then in Lakota, and received no response. A strange weariness crept over him and his body sank to the grass. His eyes closed and reality vanished into a beautiful and peaceful dream about his wife.

Chumani kept pressing onward toward the dim fires in the Crow camp, taking careful steps to avoid obstacles and counting them so she would know how many to take when retracing her path to their horses. She prayed her disguise would trick anyone she encountered and her masked scent would fool the camp animals into allowing her to pass unchallenged. Cetan had been left with the horses, the signal feather secured to one leg in the event she did not return before dawn, as he would instinctively take flight then. Even if the hawk did not go to Zitkala without being ordered to do so, the feather on his leg could be sighted through the magic eye-glass she had left with them.

As she moved along, Chumani told herself this situation had been the cause of her recent strange feelings, those chilling sensations. Just as she neared the fringe of the camp, a large dog blocked her path seeming to come from the night air itself. She lowered her head and gazed in haste to show she was not a threat, a sign of submission to animals, and tried to go around him. Yet, every time she sidestepped, so did he, as if he refused to allow her to enter the perilous area. She looked up and her gaze widened in astonishment: it was the same creature she had seen in the forest and who had helped them defeat Chaheechopes and his band!

Her mind filled with questions. How and why had he traveled so far from those two sightings? How could she see him when there was no moon and the nearest fire was a good distance away? Surely his glowing eyes and shiny fur did not give off enough light to reveal his presence to her, but she could not deny reality. He moved toward her, and she retreated a few steps. He halted, nodded his massive head, and wagged his tail.

When he moved toward her again, Chumani—her heart pounding and her body trembling, held her ground. When he reached her, he licked her hand, closing his jaws around it gently and tugged her in the opposite direction. She gathered he wanted her to follow him, but away from camp, away from her beloved? Why? Was he a spirit helper sent from Wakantanka to save her life? Was it too late to save her husband and would her life be endangered if she walked onward? Or was he a disguised evil spirit trying to lure her away from rescuing her love and perhaps lure her into a trap? Should she go with him or yank free and continue her quest? If she did the latter, would he attack her or send forth a warning to the Crow or allow her to proceed?

Chapter Seventeen

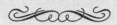

Chumani yielded to her instincts, which were to trust the dog who had helped them in the past, for she believed he was a mystical being sent from the Great Spirit. Even if he were real, surely Wakantanka was using and controlling him and his actions. As signs of friendship and compliance, she stepped closer to him and stroked his head. He released a gentle grip on her other hand, turned, and flopped his tail against it. She deduced he wanted her to clutch it, so she did. They withdrew from the enemy camp and soon were blanketed by blackness. She could not see the creature or where they were going, so she held on to her link to him. She walked until he halted and turned her way, so she released his tail. He grasped her hand with his mouth again and pulled her toward the ground. As she obeyed, her other hand and knees made contact with a prone body. She reached for the face and fingered each feature as she had done many times in total darkness with Waci Tate; within seconds she knew it was her cherished husband who lay there. She leaned over and listened to his chest, rejoicing when she detected steady breathing and heartbeats. She trailed her hands over his entire body and discovered many cuts and abrasions, but she could not tend them without a medicine bundle. She gingerly pressed her lips to his parched ones.

"He is weak and hurt, but he lives and is free. Thank you, Great Spirit, for returning him to me. And thank you, my friend," she whispered to the dog as she stroked its head and back.

She lowered her mouth to his ear and murmured, "Can you hear me, *mihigna*? It is Dewdrops. You will be safe soon and I will heal you."

A soft moan escaped his throat and he roused slightly for a moment—though not long enough to speak—before he was motionless and silent again. She sighed in relief, wondering at the same time how she could get him to their horses in his disabled condition. The path of retreat she had made in her head was of no use from this unknown location. Enemy campfires were still within viewing range, but she could not discern any symbols upon those tepees to use as markers to determine her origin point, and the landscape beyond them was obscured by darkness. Then, she heard hoof-steps and felt someone place tethers in her hand. Their surroundings must have lightened a little, for she could now see an old woman and the dog. "You come to help us escape?" she asked.

Chumani saw the blanket-covered head nod before the woman bent over to help her get Wind Dancer on his mount's back. It was a struggle, but he managed to stir enough to assist them, as if the woman's touch gave him a short surge of fortitude. She heard the soft chatter of a beak and saw Cetan perched on a tree they were near. He made no attempt to attack either the strange woman or the dog. She leapt upon her horse's back, but the old woman took the tethers of both animals and guided them away from the stream, her companion loping beside her as if he possessed a wolf's blood and traits. Soon, that familiar ebony shade of a moonless night closed in on them again, but not before she saw Wind Dancer slumped over against his horse's neck.

Chumani perceived a detail that oddly had gone unnoticed earlier: the wind's course, that told her they were withdrawing in the same direction from which she had come. Somehow the woman knew that, as she had gone there to gather their horses! She glanced over her shoulder and saw the dim glows of campfires as the distance between them grew wider and wider. She sat in quiet awe as they were led to safety, amazed her helpers could travel through near darkness.

After a while, the horses were halted. She called to the old woman in whispers, but received no response. Using the wind's direction, she looked to their rear. No campfires were in sight. She reasoned the hill she had chosen and used earlier was between them, so she dismounted and helped Wind Dancer to the ground. She found the bladder bag and forced water into his mouth and held him nestled to her chest as if he were a child and let him get needed sleep. There was nothing else she could do until morning when the sun would guide her retreat.

She reasoned the mysterious pair were gone, without the woman having spoken to her a single time. She held her beloved close and guarded him for the remainder of the night, thanking Wakantanka many times for saving their lives and for sending the Old Woman and her dog to help them. She kissed Wind Dancer's forehead several times, but resisted the urge to hug him, as she did not know the extent of his injuries and could hurt him. He was in her arms again and still a part of her Life-Circle and was getting healing sleep, which was all that mattered at the present. Reaching home and tending him were important things to be considered later.

At the first sign of dawn's approach, Chumani was astonished when she saw her love's bow, quiver, and knife in the grass nearby; she was elated that Sroka would not have them as coup prizes and her husband would not feel shame in losing them to an enemy. She lay her beloved on the ground and removed one of his marked arrows. She held it out to her hawk and said, "Take it, Cetan, and find

Zitkala." She watched him leave his tree perch, swoop down, close his talons around the slender shaft, and take flight, to soar high overhead and locate his target. Chumani had no doubt he would succeed, for she had trained him to pass messages and weapons back and forth between her and Zitkala during hunts and battles. They had practiced that skill many times and he had never failed her. Yet, she prayed Cetan would reach her companions before they risked their lives to lure the Crow from their camp. Surely they would comprehend that the arrow which had Wind Dancer's markings upon it meant they were both alive and free and a decoy ruse was unnecessary.

She could not wait around to see the results of her action; it was mandatory to get Wind Dancer farther away before the Crow awakened and found him missing and began a search for him. She pressed the water bag to his lips and coaxed him to drink. His eyes opened and he gazed at her, then darted to their surroundings.

"You saved me from Sroka and his band," he murmured in a scratchy voice as he noted her disguise and tried to sit up to caress her dirty cheek.

As she assisted him, Chumani corrected in a hurry, "Dewdrops did not free you, *mihigna;* it was the Old Woman Who Quills and her spirit dog. I came to rescue you, but they did so before I reached the enemy camp and guided me to your side. We remained here while you slept, for I had no moon to guide us. Our companions hide nearby and will join us soon along the way. We will speak of such things and I will tend your wounds later. We must ride before the Crow come looking for us; we are still close to their camp and the sun is rising. Can you climb upon your horse with my help?" she asked.

"My strength comes and goes, but it is with me now. The strange water she gave me to drink and poured over my body returns it for a while, then seems to take it away again to force me to rest and sleep."

"Then it is powerful and good medicine and must be obeyed."

After he was mounted, Chumani asked, "How will I load your weapons, *mihigna,* as it is forbidden for a woman to touch them. Our spirit helpers rescued them from Sroka's grasp; they lie there upon the ground."

Wind Dancer looked at his belongings. "Give them to me, *mitawin,* for your ranks as a warrior and vision companion make you worthy to touch them without staining them and weakening their powers. After we return to our camp, they must be purified of an enemy's touch." *As my body must be,* he told himself, as he did not want to worry her with that when she had other matters to concentrate upon at that time and place.

Chumani passed the weapons to him and waited for him to suspend the bow and quiver around his torso and slide the knife into his sheath, which, strangely, Sroka had not removed. She leapt upon her horse and said with a smile, "I am ready; we must leave this place where evil now dwells."

As the Crow camp stirred to life at dawn, Sroka left his tepee and made a shocking discovery. He rushed to the guard and kicked Apite twice to awaken him. "Where is my captive?" he shouted as more of his people spilled forth from their lodges and observed the event.

The startled man looked at the empty post and things piled and painted there. Crane's gaze widened in fear and he replied, "I do not know. A strange feeling stole my eyes and body. It is the work of a *Baleilaaxxawiia.*"

"No evil spirit did this thing! You failed in your duty and speak falsely to conceal your weakness. Your weapons will be broken; you will be beaten; your tepee will be cut to pieces; your possessions will be taken and given to others worthy of them. You have shamed yourself and must be punished."

"I speak the truth. Do you not see the signs left there?" Crane refuted as he pointed to them. "An evil spirit came for him or Old Man Coyote desired to take his life. Or the Little People sneaked him away. Do you not see the marks of the Sun, coyote, and Thunderbird painted upon the post? Do you not see Sun Dance people laying there? Who could enter our tepees and take them while their owners slept except Little People or a Spirit?"

Everyone looked at the solid yellow circle and at black coyote and buffalo tracks and an ebony Thunderbird symbol painted on the wood's surface. The Sun was viewed as their Supreme Being and called Old Man and Old Man Coyote. The Thunderbird was honored and prayed to for rain to give them a good tobacco-growing season. They saw the Sun Dance dolls of many warriors piled around it; the *Ashkisshilissuua Baakaatkisshe* were believed to possess great power. They were made by divine guidance through a sacred vision and were always protected at the first sign of trouble. The dolls were passed down from father to son and so on for countless seasons, and were easily recognizable by most tribal members. They saw withered tobacco plants and burned seeds scattered about the sturdy stake. The Creator had given the first sacred seeds to a past leader, No-Vitals. It was believed that as long as they planted, harvested, and retained seeds from those original ones, their people would live and prosper, though its tobacco was never smoked.

"How could Crane do such things while he was held captive by a strange sleep?" Apite reasoned. "The Little People entered our camp and—"

Although it was rude and rare to interrupt another while speaking, Sroka did so, "The *Daaskookaate Bilaxpaake* did not leave their small lodges in the crevices of Medicine Rock to do this wicked deed; they live to give our warriors strength and to make our aims true to their targets. They would not free an enemy to return with his people to attack us!"

Frightened by the weird incident, Crane said, "We must leave to find a safe hunting and raiding ground. This place holds *zawiia baawaalushkua.*"

"The only bad magic here lives within you, coward and

liar! I should slay you with my bare hands for such weakness and trickery!"

"Ikye!" the chief shouted for attention as he lifted his hand for silence. He felt he had allowed the bitter quarrel to continue for too long between the confused guard and their tribe's greatest warrior. "Akbaatatdia, He Who Made Everything, has sent us a message, Sroka. Old Man Coyote tells us to halt our raids on our enemies and to hunt the buffalo who provides our needs. He has freed Waci Tate or allowed him to escape so He can turn our eyes where they should be gazing. The summer season has traveled too far for us to ride to the land where water gushes and boils from the face of Mother Earth to hunt there. We must prepare for the winter season here in *Da-kkoo-tee* territory. When that task is finished, we must return to our land and not enter this one again. What do you say, my people?"

Shouts of *"E!"* and *"Eeh!"* were sent forth, relating the tribe's agreement with that decision.

Only Sroka scowled in rage. He stiffened himself in sullen silence, as arguing with them would be useless at this time. But soon they would be willing and eager to ride the warpath against the Red Shields and all *Da-kkoo-tee*, ready to take back this vast territory which had belonged to their ancestors long ago; he would make certain of it. He was convinced the men who rode in his band concurred with him, but they would not speak against their chief's and people's wishes at this time. There were sly ways they could provoke the Red Shields to attack them, and his tribe would be forced to defend itself.

Unnoticed by the Crow, an old woman and a wolfish dog observed the scene from a hilltop not far away. Her shoulders were slumped, her hair was a grayish white, and her sun-darkened skin was wrinkled. Yet, she was strong, and wise, her mind and gaze, clear and sharp. The survival of her Dakota people was her reason for living. She wore the only garment she possessed, and carried no weapon or supplies. She teased the thick ruff on her companion's neck and scratched its ears in love and respect. She smiled as he looked up into her serene face and licked her hand in response. "We must go, my friend," she murmured to the loving creature. "Our task here is done and we have much work to do in our camp."

Shortly after Chumani and Wind Dancer reached the campsite, the others arrived and dismounted with haste. War Eagle hurried forward and embraced him, and Red Feather did the same.

"It is good to look upon your face again, my brother."

"It is good to look upon yours, War Eagle. I am happy you returned from the Crow's reach in safety," Wind Dancer told the four people. "It stirs my heart to know you would risk all to save me."

"How did you do such a large deed, Dewdrops?" Zitkala asked. "When Cetan brought your husband's arrow to us, we feared to trust our eyes."

As if speaking his name summoned him, the hawk swooped down and landed on a branch nearby and sent them a shrill greeting. Chumani smiled and praised him, and the bird extended his chest and lifted his head in pride. "I did not free him from our enemies," she began her astonishing revelations. The others stared at her in amazement, then asked questions and made comments after she finished the stirring tale.

"Surely the Great Spirit watches over us, guides us, and protects us."

"That is true, Zitkala. Now, my husband will tell you of Sroka's attack and what he saw and heard and endured in the Crow camp."

Wind Dancer related those incidents and sufferings, increasing his friends' awe. "I do not know if they were flesh, blood, and bone or if they are spirit helpers. She did not speak, but her touch was real. She gave me powerful medicine in water to drink and poured it over my body; it gave me the strength to flee the camp and to travel here."

"Your body says Sroka's tribe was cruel to you, *mitakola.*"

"That is so, Red Feather, but it will heal. Dewdrops tended me with her medicine bundle when we stopped to rest. I was to be slain on this sun, but I live and ride free with the help of my wife, brother, two friends, Wakantanka, and the old woman and her dog. I will prove myself worthy of such good deeds and love."

"You have done so many times on past suns, my brother. I strive on each new one to be a great warrior and wise leader as you are."

Wind Dancer smiled at War Eagle and nodded his gratitude for those words. "We have not seen Crow following us, but we must put more distance between us; there is much sunlight left for us to do so."

"It is strange, *mitakola,* but the Crow do not come after us, not even a small band," Red Feather disclosed. "After the hawk flew your arrow to us, we watched their camp for a time with Dewdrops' magic eye to be certain we grasped its message. Their scouts were summoned and they break camp to leave that place. We do not know why, but they do so in a hurry, as if evil spirits or a powerful force drives them away from it."

"Perhaps the old woman and her dog did bad magic there and frightened them. Surely they are good spirits sent by Wakantanka to help us."

"What is the magic eye you possess, *mitawin?*" Wind Dancer asked instead of remarking on Chumani's previous speculations.

"Your wife will show you, my brother," War Eagle said, and retrieved it from his bundle.

Chumani told him where and when she had gotten the fieldglass and from whom her father had received it. "This *wasicun* gift is good, for it helped us to watch their camp. That is why Wakantanka sent the hairy-face to us long ago, to prepare us for this sun."

Wind Dancer nodded. "The Creator knows all things and has prepared us in many ways on past suns to meet our challenges." He looked at his brother. "Soon you must leave us, War Eagle, and ride swiftly to our camp," he said. "You must tell my Strong Heart brothers to prepare the sacred cottonwood pole. I must submit myself to the Sun Dance after I return."

"No, *mihigna,* you cannot do so! It is too soon to face such great danger while you are injured and still weak. You will not survive it."

Wind Dancer caressed her flushed cheek. "Until I purify myself in the sweat lodge and surrender to the Sun Dance Ritual, I am unworthy of my duty as a Shirt Wearer and of my ranks as a Strong Heart and future chief and Vision-quest rider, and I am unworthy to touch you again."

Chumani struggled to quell her anxiety and to soften her tone. "That is not true, my beloved mate. There is no loss of face and honor in being captured while trying to save a friend's life and for yielding to a foe to halt an attack upon your people."

"That is true," he admitted, but added, "I have been touched by the enemy and am stained in body and spirit. I must cleanse myself of their evil and I must give thanks to the Creator for saving my life. I must prove to myself and others I am strong and brave enough to lead them. If the Great Spirit was ready for me to join Him this season, I would walk with Him this sun. He did not call me to Him, for He has many tasks here for me to do."

Chumani exchanged gazes with him for a short time as they spoke without using words. With misty eyes and a troubled heart, she nodded he was right and acquiesced to his intention, as it was their way.

Chumani sat on a rush mat and tried to quell her fears and doubts. She stared straight ahead as her husband came forward to be prepared for his perilous challenge, as defeat or death was a grim possibility; and she knew he preferred the latter of those dark choices. Although she was in a large gathering of their people and was positioned between his parents and hers, she felt alone. Since their return to camp one and a half suns ago, Wind Dancer had refused to even kiss, until he felt worthy to do so again. She had needed that comfort badly, but understood his motive and had to respect his decision. He had allowed her to tend his injuries and they were healing more rapidly than she had imagined. She wondered if that was a result of the old woman's medicine. Even so, he was still weak from the abuse his body had taken from the Crow.

He had purified his body and readied his spirit in the sweat lodge at dawn, which had drained him of more energy. Now he lay on the ground awaiting the next step of the ritual. Usually it required four days, but custom had been put aside to make it shorter. There had been no ceremonial dancers with painted bodies to perform the preliminary Buffalo Dance. No warrior had been chosen to select a cottonwood tree to be sacrificed, and no women had chopped it down and debarked it: those tasks were done by members of the Strong Heart Society who also painted and carved the sacred symbols upon its smooth surface and who would take turns dancing around it and blowing eagle-bone whistles during the entire ritual to show honor to their leader and to give him encouragement. No other man would participate in any of the many levels—no dancing and chanting until one could no longer stand and speak, and no offerings of tiny bits of flesh to be removed and placed at the pole's base. Only Wind Dancer would perform the rite and at the highest level of difficulty and danger, the final feat of self-sacrifice and endurance. Once he began, there was no turning back until he either pulled free or yielded defeat or died trying; and Chumani knew it would be the first or last of those three choices. She recalled what Sees-Through-Mist had told her at sunrise: "Do not worry, Dewdrops, for he will survive this great challenge." She prayed that was true, yet, could not help but fear the worst.

Nahemana leaned over the prone warrior, smiled, and cut two slices on the left side of Wind Dancer's chest, then did the same on the right with a ceremonial knife. Blood seeped forth and rolled toward his armpits. The shaman forced the sharp talon of an eagle's claw through the sensitive underflesh. He pulled upward with the bird's leg to lift the pierced section so he could pass a long thong through one opening and out the other. He repeated that procedure on the other side. He gestured for his grandson to rise, and the thongs were secured to a rawhide rope attached to the cottonwood pole. Nahemana noted with great pride and love that Wind Dancer never winced or flinched, only kept his expression impassive, his tongue silent, and his body motionless. He placed a peyote button in the participant's mouth, though Wind Dancer would not chew it until later in the ceremony. Before stepping away, the shaman fluttered an eagle feather over his entire body as he chanted a prayer to invoke the attention and help of their Creator and the forces of Mother Nature.

Wind Dancer summoned his courage, sent forth a prayer of his own to ask for survival and victory, and began to dance around the pole as he blew on his eagle-bone whistle. Often, he would pause to lean backward to force the thongs to pull on his chest confinements. The more times he did that, the more pain he experienced. Blood now ran down his stomach and soaked the waist area of his breechclout, his only garment. His secured flesh became raw and swollen, and sharp twinges radiated through his entire torso, up his neck, and pounded agony inside his head.

Soon, it hurt him even to breathe; and to blow on his whistle, part of the ritual, became even more difficult. His throat was dry, as were his lips. It was difficult to lift his now heavy feet to take another and another step on legs that trembled. His arms, hanging by his sides, felt as if some unseen and strong force pulled them toward the ground, and his fingers were going numb. Yet, he must continue until he pulled free, as failure was not an acceptable alternative.

Chumani observed the arduous ritual in rising apprehension and empathy. His suffering knifed at her heart and mind. Yet, great pride and deep love and respect filled her at his awesome displays of courage, prowess, and dedication to their Creator and their beliefs. He had known what he must endure, as he had submitted to the Sun Dance long ago and bore the scars of that ordeal. As Chumani watched the solemn event, she prayed for a speedy end to it.

At last, one side was released from its torture, and the jagged ends of Wind Dancer's torn flesh protruded from a bloody and gaping wound. He was given encouragement and a burst of energy from that first victory. He used a trotting dance step to approach the pole to touch it with his open hands to elicit power from it, and to retreat to the full length of his remaining tie to the revered cottonwood. Each time, he flung himself backward to put a straining force on the thong, but it refused to tear loose. The sun blazed down on him, causing salty sweat to pour from his body and to sting his ritual wounds and those he had received in the enemy camp. He knew his flesh exposed many bruises, pricks, and cuts. Yet, the sweat lodge and the moisture flowing from him now would cleanse him of all impurities.

Wind Dancer chewed and swallowed the peyote button with difficulty, for his throat had grown more parched with each minute. As soon as he felt its first stimulating effect, he jerked backward with his remaining strength, pulled the rawhide rope taut, and pitted all of his weight against the stubborn thong. He clenched his teeth and continued his leaning and yanking actions as he blew rapidly on the whistle. Sweat dripped from his body and blood flowed from the resistant spot.

I beg you, Great Spirit, the almost frantic Chumani prayed, *accept his great sacrifice and release him from more suffering.* She sent forth another prayer of gratitude as a divine response came rapidly as the bond suddenly gave way and released him.

Wind Dancer almost fell to the ground, but managed to prevent it. He let the whistle drop from his mouth, as it was suspended around his neck. He lifted his hands and said, "It is done, Great Spirit, and I thank you for my survival and victory."

Chumani did not leap up to assist him as she yearned to do, but watched him as he walked to the Strong Hearts' meeting lodge to be tended by its members and their shaman, as custom dictated. At last, the perilous feat was accomplished. He was alive. He was freed of any shame and weakness. He had proven his value to his people and to himself. Now he could return to normal life and recover fully. Now he would consider himself worthy to touch her, and she could hardly wait for that special moment to arrive.

As Wind Dancer remained in the other tepee to rest and complete the vision-inducing portion of the peyote, Chumani lay upon their buffalo mat alone, missing him and recalling the events of the last few suns. They had reached camp without confronting any trouble from Sroka's people, other enemies, or nature's forces. They learned that Raven had been replaced during their absence as a Sacred Bow Carrier by Talks Little. Upon their arrival at camp, Raven's brother had gifted Wind Dancer with a buffalo horse to replace the one slain during her husband's attempted rescue of Raven. Later that day, Wind Dancer's weapons had been purified of the enemy's touch by smoking them over a low fire made of special herbs and grasses and sacred tokens. Their people were awed by details of the stampede and the strange appearance of the old woman and the dog, and the assistance they had given. Their bands were jubilant to hear that Sroka's people were last seen loading up to move, and everyone hoped their destination was far away.

During a short council meeting, it was voted that retaliation against Sroka would take place later if the Crow remained in Dakota territory, as they must prepare for winter before heading into battle.

After a feast the previous night, they were honored with coup chanting. It was evident their people loved, respected, and were grateful to them. And their parents, friends, and the men's societies were filled with pride and elation with their deeds and safe returns. Rainbow Girl had been so overjoyed to have her husband back alive and unharmed that she could not keep her eyes off him and quickly coaxed him away to privacy.

Chumani wished she had privacy with Wind Dancer tonight, but that was not to be. Worse, they were breaking camp at first light to move to their next hunting site, as they must follow wherever the largest buffalo herds roamed. Chumani closed her eyes and ordered herself to go to sleep, for there was much work ahead for her.

They traveled for several days past small groupings of buffalo and halted when their leaders sighted an extensive herd and with a river nearby to provide fresh water. The men began carrying out their chores, and some were assigned as guards around the large camp, others sent to scout the surrounding area for signs of enemies. The women went to work setting up their tepees and drying racks while young girls fetched water and collected buffalo chips and scrubwood for fires, and the elders tended their grandchildren for busy parents. Soon meals were being cooked, and the willow hut to seclude themselves during their blood flows had been erected.

The willow hut was completed shortly after Chumani's flow began and she went there in a near dejected spirit. She was happy she was not with child at this busy and hazardous time, but she had looked forward with great eagerness to a passionate night alone with her husband. It had been eighteen moons since they had last united their bodies, and hers was starved for his intimate touch.

During their journey to this campsite, Wind Dancer had ridden close to her for most of the time, as he was still recovering from recent events. He had been in a good mood every sun and moon, and grew stronger with the passing of each. His injuries, except for those received from the ritual, were healed, and those sacred cuts were doing fine with her tending. She had enjoyed his conversation and light touches, but she yearned for more, something that sleeping in the open amidst a crowd did not allow. *Soon,* she told herself, as three days of separation was all she required.

As other females joined her in the *cansakawakeya,* Chumani received news of the happenings beyond her confinement. As planned, they were situated closer to the enormous herd than usual so the hunters, butcherers, and travois riders could be protected during their tasks, along with those working near their lodges. A hunting party did not have to camp on the grassland for days before changing places with the next one; it could return at dusk and leave again the next dawn, as the men were careful to hunt on the herd's fringes and to prevent spooking the beasts into moving away.

The women in camp had busied themselves drying meats to prepare in several ways, washing garments at the river, collecting plants and berries and soils for making dyes and paints, and doing other daily chores.

Some groups of women gathered sources of other foods, medicines, and flavorings from along the banks of the river and nearby streams and on the bountiful Plains.

So far, no trouble had struck at their bands, and Chumani was relieved. Yet, she felt helpless and excluded and tensed by this natural part of a female's Life-Circle, as there was much she wanted to be doing, much of which included being with her beloved husband. She scolded herself for some of those bad thoughts and feelings, but they continued to creep into her mind.

A full moon seemed to pour liquid light through the top ventilation flap which was spread open to its widest angle for fresh air, as the entry flap was sealed. Its glowing stream washed over two naked bodies positioned beneath it as Wind Dancer and Chumani finally cuddled together after their lengthy separation. At last, twenty-one moons of denial would end, and they were filled with joy and excitement.

Wind Dancer was thrilled to be holding her again. Even passing one sun without her in his arms or sight was a great sacrifice. He lay with his left hip touching the buffalo mat and his right leg nestled intimately between hers. For a while, all he did was admire her beauty. Thoughts of her had helped him endure both the Crow brutalities and the demands of the recent ritual. He could never love or possess her enough to sate himself.

Chumani used the sole of her left foot to stroke the hard muscles on his calf, delighting in the feel of his flesh. As his hands roamed her body and fondled her breasts and his mouth teased a meandering path across her face and neck, her fingers wandered over his strong back and shoulders. She was careful to avoid the injured areas on his chest where a snug leather band was secured to hold the jagged flesh in place while it healed. Her lips pressed kisses to his temple and hair as his head moved constantly to give her various pleasures. She could not suppress happy giggles as his tongue playfully flicked her nipples, then he nibbled at her earlobe.

Wind Dancer paused to murmur, "It is good to hear your laughter again, *micante;* its sweet sound touches and pleases me as the songs of the Creator's birds." His questing mouth closed over hers and he welcomed her ardent response.

"I love you, *micante.* You fill me with more joy and peace each sun than I believed was possible when I joined to you, and that was as high as a mountain and as wide as the Plains. You are as much a part of me as my body and spirit, and they cannot survive without you to feed their needs. I thank the Great Spirit every sunrise for giving you to me."

"As I thank Him for giving you to me. When I saw Sroka and his band encircle you, I feared you would be lost to me. I sent many prayers to the Great Spirit to save you and return you to me. When you were taken to his camp, my fear grew larger and it was hard to have faith in our Creator. I did not wish to exist without you in my arms and life. My heart leapt with joy when the Spirit Dog guided me to you. I thanked Wakantanka and asked forgiveness for my doubts of Him and His powers. Then, I was forced to watch you challenge the Sun Dance and face death again. I must not lose you, *mihigna,* for you make my existence each sun and moon worthwhile.''

"You will never lose me, *mitawin,* for we are bound as one forever, matched and joined by the Great Spirit, and blessed by Him."

Their mouths met in a kiss of deep commitment and endless love, as they united their bodies and sought sweet ecstasy. They murmured words of endearment as they traveled passion's wild and wonderful trail.

As they lay snuggled afterward, Wind Dancer remembered he had not told her about his vision following the ritual before they broke camp. He had wanted to wait until they had privacy, but decided this was not the time to share that bad news and risk spoiling this special moment.

Many suns passed as the Oglala and Brule bands carried out their daily and seasonal tasks, and many moons were filled with passionate encounters for Wind Dancer and Chumani. He continued to delay his revelation about his vision, as he did not want to raise fears and unhappiness until it became necessary. Both shamans, chiefs, and the Strong Hearts knew of the sacred message to him, but, they, too, did not want to alarm their families and people during this time of peace and hard work.

At last, they were compelled to relocate their camp again to follow the buffalo's movements. Then their tasks began anew.

Three suns after they relocated, scouts returned at midday to relate bad news to Chief Rising Bear, who summoned both councils and their warriors. Chumani, as the Vision Woman, was allowed to sit in on the grave meeting, but

was not permitted to smoke the ceremonial pipe as it was
passed from man to man until all had shared the breath
of Wakantanka.

Nahemana stood to speak to the large gathering. "It is
as my grandson saw in his vision after his Sun Dance ritual;
Sroka and his people have not left our lands and must be
driven out by force. Our scouts sighted their camp one
sun's ride from this place. We must carry out the message
given to Waci Tate. Speak, *micinksi,* and all will listen and
obey."

Chumani watched her husband in confusion and dismay; she could not understand why he had not confided
such important things to her. She listened in rising
astonishment to what he had kept from her so long.

Wind Dancer rose. "When I was taken captive by Sroka,
he revealed his plan to defeat us," he said. "He wanted
to destroy all we possessed and prevent us from gathering
food and other needs for the coming winter so we would
freeze and starve and the Crow could steal our land. We
will use his evil trick against him and destroy theirs. We
must halt their threat to our people; we must attack his
camp."

"How can we protect our camp while we attack his?"
Blue Owl asked.

"Twenty Strong Hearts will be chosen from each band
to carry out this deed while all other warriors remain here
to defend our camp. The Strong Hearts will pull stones
from a pouch; those with marks will join my war party, as
will Red Feather, War Eagle, and Fire Walker."

Chumani realized neither her nor Zitkala's name had
been included. She wondered why, but thought it best not
to ask during the meeting.

"How can only forty warriors and four leaders attack
such a large and powerful enemy?"

Wind Dancer looked at their war chief. "We will set fire
to his camp. We will burn their lodges and the provisions
they need to survive winter."

"Grass is dry in this season; fire will spread across the Plains."

"No. Blue Owl, the Great Spirit will not allow his creatures to be harmed or the face of Mother Nature to be destroyed, only our enemies. That is what I was shown in my vision."

"How will you make such a large and powerful fire?" Blue Owl continued to ask the questions which filled the others' minds.

"This is the plan shown to me in my vision," Wind Dancer said, and related it, causing many gazes to widen and many heads to nod in awe and agreement. "We will choose the war party now and ride out as soon as we gather our supplies. We will attack the Crow camp on the next moon."

Chumani was consumed by dread. Was there still a chance she could lose her beloved husband this season? Could his daring and dangerous plan succeed? How so when the Apsaalooke tribe was many and powerful? And why could she not go with him this time?

Chapter
Eighteen

After they reached their tepee, Chumani asked, "Why did you not tell me about your vision? Why am I to be left here?"

Wind Dancer caressed her cheek. "After I found victory in the ritual, much happiness lived in your heart and life; I did not want to take them from you for a while," he began his answer. "I did not want worries of Sroka to dwell in your mind each sun and moon when they could change nothing looming ahead at a distance I did not know. It was the same for our people; they had much work to do and joy filled their hearts; we did not want to distract them from their tasks and bring them sadness and fear. I knew the Great Spirit would give us a warning when danger approached; that is why we sent scouts to search the area each sun."

By "we," Chumani knew he referred to their shamen, chiefs, and his Strong Hearts Society. Upon discovery of this secret, as the Vision Woman, she had been surprised that Sees-Through-Mist had not confided in her. She had been dismayed her father had not revealed such information to her and hurt and disappointed Wind Dancer had withheld the truth. Yet, her husband's motives were wise and kind ones, so she quashed those unjust feelings against him and the others. She listened and smiled as he continued.

"You must prepare to ride, *micante,* for you and Cetan go with us. Bring the magic eye with you. You will remain at a safe distance from their camp and watch for my signal. When you see it, you must tell Cetan to take flight. When the Strong Hearts see the hawk, that is the sign for them to fire the grass they have scattered around the fringe of Sroka's camp. The blaze will trap our enemies within its circle and will eat into their camp."

"Why does Zitkala not ride with us?" Chumani asked.

"Her presence as a woman would distract the men, for they have not ridden with her and viewed her great prowess. Red Feather, too, would be distracted from his duty in protecting her from the attention of the others; and he must live."

"How will my husband and the Strong Hearts fight so many warriors after they strike against your party?"

"If we remain hidden to their eyes, they will believe an evil spirit attacks them in this new camp as one did in their old one; it should frighten them from our lands forever. The grass is dry and will burn fast; a ring of fire will stop them from leaving their camp to find us. Its flames will eat at many lodges, winter foods, possessions, and weapons. They will not be strong enough without those things to attack us again."

"It is a sly plan, *mihigna,* "Chumani said with admiration. "It will be a great coup for you and your war party. It will avenge the deaths of Raven and your horses and your abuse."

"We do not take captives to live in our camp. When Omaste was given to my father long ago, she was treated well. For those who take captives from the Whites or other tribes, it is wrong to treat them with cruelty."

"That is good and wise, and it is the same for the White Shields. Now we must ready ourselves, for soon the others will await our leaving."

Zitkala approached their tepee and called out for permission to enter, though the flap was thrown aside. "Is there help you need, Dewdrops?"

Wind Dancer summoned the Brule woman into their lodge and smiled at her. "Dewdrops will tell you what you desire to know after I am gone." He told his wife what he needed for his mission so she could pack those things while he went with Red Feather and War Eagle to fetch items stolen from the keelboat and homesteads which were hidden nearby.

As she worked, Chumani related Wind Dancer's concerns to her best friend. "I know staying behind troubles your spirit, Zitkala, but his words are wise. If you have not peered into the river or the trader's looking glass, you do not know how you have changed. No eyes could gaze upon you now and mistake you for a man; you have become much of a woman."

Zitkala, clad in a doeskin dress and wearing a feathered and beaded thong in her flowing hair, could not resist smiling upon hearing that news. She had checked her appearance several times recently on the water's surface and in a "mirror." She had been afraid to trust her eyes to speak the truth she saw there, but Chumani had just confirmed her hope and her best friend would never deceive her, even for a good reason.

"How could the Strong Hearts without wives think of their tasks when you filled their gazes?" Chumani half jested. "How could Red Feather do his perilous deeds when he feared another might attempt to steal your eye and heart from him?"

Exhilarated, Zitkala embraced Chumani. "It is the work of the Great Spirit and Mother Nature, for I have done little to make myself different. They have blessed me with this change, for Red Feather can now join a female who does not look or behave as a man."

"You have revealed your love and desire to him, and he feels the same way about you. I eagerly await your joining when we reach our winter camp. I along with many others, will help you sew and erect your new tepee, as is our custom. It will be their show of thanks to you for all you have done.''

Before Zitkala could respond, Wind Dancer and Red Feather returned and said they must leave shortly. Chumani suggested their best friends share a short privacy while she and her husband loaded their horses, to which both men agreed.

Soon the war party rode away as their people stood watching their departure. Many guards were posted around the encampment, and scouts took their places beyond to watch for trouble and to send forth a warning— a flaming arrow shot skyward—if necessary. The others returned to their tasks of hunting and preparing buffalo and doing daily chores.

Chumani, with Cetan sitting nearby, observed the furtive action beyond her concealed position. Dusk was rapidly departing. Beneath a moonless and ominous sky, it was becoming difficult to see her companions as they carried out their daring tasks; if not for the powerful fieldglass, she could not sight them at all. They were clad only in breechclouts and moccasins, allowing them to move silently. Their dark hair was covered with wide strips from deerhides, its shade blending with the color of the grass during this time of the summer season.

She had watched her small party scatter a thick layer of dried grass around the fringe of the enemy camp and make piles of it to the rears of their tepees in the last ring. They had even tossed bunches between those lodges to prevent allowing any escape path. The men had poured lantern oil, contained in water bags and stolen from the *wasicun,* atop the yellowed grass and splashed it upon the backs of those same outer tepees. Each of the men had two matches and rough rock, the magic sticks she had gotten from the evil trader at Pierre. She hated to think about children and women being harmed, but they, too, were vicious enemies who had been brutal to her husband.

Her party was doing to Sroka and his people what they had planned to do to hers.

She knew why their presence had gone unnoticed: Besides the cunning stealth and cloaks they used, the distant guards had been located with the spy-glass and slain, a brewing storm had summoned all hunters and butcherers back to camp, and the Crow were gathered in the center area to feast, sing, and dance around a large fire. She could hear the pounding beats of their drums, muffled vocables, and rare shout of exuberance. Their enemies were so intent upon their activities that they failed to grasp their peril. As her party crawled on their bellies toward their target, she sighted the Old Woman's companion leading the camp dogs away, so those animals were not there to bark warnings.

Chumani could not help but recall the last time they had seen Sroka was also on a night of the Black Moon. Yet, she was confident the plan would succeed, as the timing with nature and the spirits was perfect. She saw Wind Dancer, a tepee concealing him from their enemies' view, lift and wave his arms just as the remaining daylight was almost gone. "It is time for you to help us, Cetan. Fly, my friend, fly," she coaxed, and the hawk obeyed.

With the signal given and received, Chumani saw sparks in the increasing shadows, and soon a glowing barrier encircled the camp. Flames wriggled up tepee surfaces as if they were dazzling snakes following the paths and feasting on the lantern oil. She saw the spaces between their lodges join the other flames' work. It was as if daylight had returned to the setting. The drumming halted. Screams and yells erupted from the entrapped people in the center clearing. Some Crow grabbed blankets and hides to beat at the flames, others tossed water from bags upon them. Horses sent forth frantic whinnies, and some broke free of their tethers; those animals raced between the lodges seeking an escape path, some leaping over the flames, and some trampling possessions and supplies.

Shortly after Cetan and her companions rejoined Chumani, the storm broke overhead and a deluge of rain began. The greedy flames were doused; the horses and Crow were spared, though some were injured. The grassland was saved from destruction. The enemy camp was heavily damaged.

As the combined Red and White Shield party lay on the hillside and watched the event unfold, they talked in excited and awed tones about the accuracy of Wind Dancer's vision and their great victory. They were being drenched by the rain, but that did not matter to them. Sounds of constant thunder had replaced those of the enemy's drums. The wind's pace had increased. Evening air had cooled. Radiant charges danced across the dark sky and allowed glimpses of their wounded target. They saw no band attempting to mount and seek out an attacker; their foes appeared too busy trying to save their remaining possessions, and were perhaps confused and misled by the cause of the fire. They did not care if the Crow believed they had been assailed by evil spirits or violent nature; they had been weakened badly, and that was the aim.

While they had use of the lightning's recurrent flashes to guide them during the moonless night, they left to head back to their people. They would travel for as long as nature's torches allowed them to see the terrain ahead, then camp until sunrise to complete their journey. War Eagle and three men without wives stayed behind to observe the Crow to see if they left and where they traveled if they did so.

Chumani had given her husband's brother the "magic eye" so he could do his task from a safe distance away. She was certain the Crow would have neither the time nor means to retaliate, and would be compelled to seek a safe area where they could prepare themselves again for winter. For a while, she hoped, they should be safe, if no other enemy decided to attack them.

The following night in their tepee, Chumani lay snuggled against her husband's virile body with her head resting at the crook of his arm. She smiled to herself as she recalled their heartwarming welcome after a glorious victory over Sroka and his tribe. "Our deeds give our families and people great joy and pride, *mihigna*," Chumani said happily. "Our alliance is a good one."

"That is true, *mitawin*. Soon our task here will be finished and we must leave to make our winter camp in the sacred Paha Sapa. The hot season has begun its journey away from our land; the face of Mother Earth is changing. Grass grows from green and yellow to brown. Berries, plants, and flowers will be gone shortly, and the buffalo will roam to its wintering grounds. We have much meat and hides; the cold season which travels slowly toward us will not harm us as our enemies planned. Perhaps while we are sealed in our tepee when it snows, a child will be given to us."

"Surely that is true, *mihigna*, for our sacred task will be over before cold winds blow over our land. And you do try many times to plant your seeds within me," she added as she laughed and tickled his ribs.

Wind Dancer squirmed and chuckled as he captured her playful hand. "There is much joy and pleasure in doing that work." He kissed her fingers.

"It is . . . 'work' to arouse and sate us, my love?" she teased him as she pulled her forefinger free of his grasp and traced his lips with it.

"My tongue spoke too swiftly as you clouded my mind with your magic. It is large and powerful, Dewdrops, and I cannot resist its force."

"There is no need to do so, my love, and I eagerly yield to yours."

"We are well matched, *micante*," he murmured against her palm before pressing kisses to her warm flesh.

Chumani quivered with delight. "That is true, *mihigna*. Why do you not begin your task, for there is much . . . 'work' to do before we sleep? You are a skilled hunter, provider, and protector; you must seek your prey, feed this great hunger within me, and defend me against the pain of denial."

In one sweeping motion, Wind Dancer rolled his cherished wife to her back and lay half atop her. "My hunt will begin here," he murmured as his mouth met hers. . . .

On the eighth sun following the fiery attack on Sroka's camp, War Eagle and the Strong Hearts returned at a swift gallop. They dismounted with haste, handing their tethers to young boys with a quick request the animals be tended, and rushed to the Red Shield chief's tepee. The shout which had gone up at their rapid approach had summoned Rising Bear to greet them, as it had others. A crowd gathered to listen and observe.

"We rode as the wind after they camped, but the journey to their new location was reached slowly," War Eagle divulged. "It is not good news, my father and people. They gather with many Crow bands beyond Rabbit Creek where large rocks were spit forth from Mother Earth and many trees grow."

"That is only two suns fast ride from our sacred Bear Mountain!"

"That is true, Blue Owl. We believe they meet to trade with other bands. We do not know if they will talk alliance and war against Oglalas. But there is good news for my brother and Raven's spirit; the one called Sroka was attacked and slain by his warriors, for they believed he called down evil spirits upon them; they do not know we attacked them."

"How did you learn such things, my son?" Rising Bear asked.

"Each moon, one of us sneaked to their camp and listened to them. I was watching when Sroka angered his band by calling them weaklings for running away and not attacking our people and others to replace their losses. When he would not hold his tongue and said he would attack the enemy alone, many of his people shot fatal arrows into his body."

"That is good, my son, for Raven's spirit can now rest and my first son has been avenged by the Hand of Wakan-tanka working in a mysterious way, for surely He enflamed Crow hearts against their greatest warrior."

"We must make a plan of defense, Father," Wind Dancer suggested, "for we do not know if the Apsaalooke will join forces and attack us."

"It has been made long ago, *micinksi,* by the Creator," Nahemana said.

As soon as the Red Shield shaman explained his meaning, Sees-Through-Mist, with a look of astonishment on his weathered face, disclosed he had seen the same event unfold in a dream long ago and had told it to Chief Tall Elk and to Chumani before she joined to Waci Tate.

Wind Dancer turned to his wife beside him, his gaze inquisitive.

Her own gaze wide with amazement, she nodded. "It is true, *mihigna;* our shaman spoke such words to me after an owl messenger came to him in a dream during a full moon. Our Wise One said he was told to make and give me a white garment and moccasins from the sacred buffalo. He said I would wear them two times during the coming season and both would be big medicine and I would help save our people from our enemies. He said they were left unbeaded so the enemy could not read our tribal markings and doubt my words. Sees-Through-Mist said the Great Spirit had been working in my life since birth and had trained me for such challenges. He said I would take another mate and together we would ride away and do great deeds. He said he saw me standing in our camp wearing the white garment during my joining ceremony and he saw me again standing on a high hill with Cetan upon my shoulder. Not many suns passed before you came and we were joined. He did not know where the hill was located or what I would do there, but that was revealed to Nahemana in his vision."

"The dream and vision are powerful medicine and must be obeyed," Rising Bear remarked in awe.

Both shamen nodded, as did most of those standing
around them. While they talked, another rider—a
stranger—galloped into camp with one of their scouts.
Markings on his garments and weapons indicated he was
an Oglala Lakota. The two men dismounted and joined
the intrigued group.

Rising Bear asked who he was, *"Nituwe hwo?"*

"Waun He Topa, Mahpia Luta kola."

Chief Rising Bear of the Red Shields greeted Four
Horns, friend of Red Cloud, an Oglala Teton chief of great
fame, influence, and power, *"Hau, He Topa.* Why does
Mahpia Luta send you to us?"

"The Great White Chief far away has asked the *ateyapi*
Broken Hand and his friend Mitchell to parlay for peace
between the White-eyes and Indians and between warring
tribes of all Indians."

Rising Bear knew the one called Broken Hand was
Thomas Fitzpatrick, the Indian Agent for the High Plains
for the last five circles of the seasons, a white man who
had been a fur trader and a guide for Whites long ago.
He also knew the other man was named David Mitchell;
he was called the Superintendent. It had been explained
to him that Broken Hand was like a combined Shirt Wearer
who resolved troubles between Whites and Indians and
between tribes and a Pipe Owner who spoke for peace.
Mitchell was compared to a Big Belly who gave Broken
Hand his orders to be carried out. He listened as Four
Horns continued his revelations.

"The Great White Chief says he will give all Indians
cows and steers and many other goods to replace our losses
from the white man's passings across our hunting grounds
and for the game and grass they take while doing so and
the animals the hunters take to feed the Bluecoats and
others if we allow the snow-covered travois to cross our
lands without attacking them. Treaty talk will begin at Fort
Laramie in seventeen suns from the one above us." He
pointed skyward. "Many Dakotas and Cheyenne now pitch
camps near the Bluecoats lodges. The *wasicun* leaders send

word to all tribes, ally and enemy, through the traders and trappers at fur posts in all territories. Red Cloud sent me to you, for he has great respect for Rising Bear and Tall Elk and their people. Our shaman told him your people and the White Shields do many things to help all Dakotas battle the *wasicun* and *Apsaalooke*, though word of your deeds has not been sent to us. He waits to learn of such bold and brave coups when you gather with us at Fort Laramie."

Rising Bear was amazed such a vision had been given to the Teton shaman. He knew that Fort Laramie to their southwest was called a "way station," land-marker, and fur trading post by the Whites. Two summers past, the Bluecoats had taken over the fort and made it even larger and more powerful, for many braves attacked the wagontrains which encroached on their lands, a path which had become known to Whites as the Oregon Trail. As more Whites came to stay or passed through and more Indians camped around the post, hatreds and hostilities had increased. He had been told that the emigrants were heading for "free land" offered by the Great White Chief in places called Oregon and California and some men sought the yellow rock in the latter location.

"Why would we want to make peace with the *wasicun* and our enemies when they encroach on our lands and attack us?" Rising Bear reasoned. "Long ago, the numbers of traders, trappers, settlers, and travelers were few; now, more stay or cross our lands than number whole tribes. The settlers come while the grass is green; their animals graze upon it and their wagons cut deeply into the face of Mother Earth and they kill or chase away the buffalo and other game. We traded with those at Fort Pierre and Fort Laramie long ago, but we halted such foolishness. They cheated us, offered us whiskey to dull our wits, gave us terrible sicknesses, take our women as 'squaws', and cause many braves to become weak and to seek all goods from them and to do their tasks. Many live around the posts and forts and become lazy; they forget the old ways or do not practice them. We must not become dependent on the *wasicun* for survival even in hard times, for it will give them great power over us.''

After most of the men concurred, Four Horns replied, "Red Cloud also says more Whites and Bluecoats will come each season with their powerful weapons and hunters to feed them. Our buffalo herds grow smaller and roam farther away with each increase. The White chief offers us much meat and many goods if we allow settlers to cross our lands in safety; such things will be needed if we are to remain strong to fight them one season, as war between us is sure to come as the White-eyes's greed grows larger than the grasslands and swifter than its spring blanket.''

"To listen and sign their paper is only a trick?" Rising Bear asked.

"That is true, for the white man will not hold to his treaty with us in the dark moons to come. We will take their gifts and make our signs on their paper, but we will not trust them to keep their word and we will remain ready to battle them when tricked and challenged.''

"What of our worst enemies, the Crow, Arapaho, and Pawnee?" Rising Bear asked.

"The Pawnee, Comanche, and Kiowa will not come to talk, vote, and sign," Four Horns began his explanation. "The Arapaho, Shoshone, Gros Ventre, Assiniboin, and many tribes and bands of the Cheyenne and Dakota say they will do so if the words of the Great White Chief and Broken Hand are wise and fair and many goods are given in exchange for a truce. The Crow meet to talk and vote among themselves to decide if they will go. If they do not and join forces with the Pawnee against other tribes and Whites, trouble will come fast. It is good the Arapaho do not think the same way as their ally the Pawnee. Broken Hand also wishes to split ally from foe and halt our many wars by marking our lands into separate territories; any who invade the other's will be punished.''

"Even if we do not agree and sign, Father, we must go to Fort Laramie to listen and observe.''

Rising Bear looked at his oldest son and took a deep breath. "What do you say, my people? Do we send a party to Fort Laramie to trick our enemies?" The chief glanced around as he saw all heads nod in agreement. "It is settled, *He Topa;* we will ride to the parlay to listen and talk."

Four Horns said he must leave to rejoin Red Cloud's band which was en route to the Big Council, and he would tell his chief that the Red Shields and the White Shields would meet with them at Fort Laramie.

After the Teton warrior was gone, Wind Dancer said they must carry out the plan of the vision and dream and scare the Crow into going to the parlay, as it would halt the battles between them for a while. A reprieve would give their people time to journey to the Black Hills, set up their winter camps, and finish their late hot season tasks there. As they did so, the five original visionquest companions could travel to where the Crow held their powwow and make sure they were forced into heading for Fort Laramie.

As Chumani rode to their destination, she noticed the changing landscape. There were numerous huge and odd rock formations, boulders of assorted size, scattered buttes, higher and more frequent hills, many trees—cedar, spruce, pine, and hardwoods—scrubs, and rougher terrain. The grass offered many colors during that season: green, yellow, brown, and red. Porcupines, deer, antelope, coyote, vultures, and other creatures and birds were abundant in the area. They knew another section of vast grassland loomed beyond the rocks and forest. But their goal rested between those two contradictory landscapes.

As they approached the enormous Crow village where many tribes were gathered to talk and trade, Chumani was aware her blood flow had not begun when she had expected. Perhaps, she reasoned, it was delayed by the Great Spirit and Mother Nature so she could complete her work, or perhaps she was with child. She would tell no one of that latter possibility. If she related it to Zitkala, her best friend might worry and tell others out of concern for her, so for the first time, she kept a secret from the other woman. If she revealed it to her husband, Wind Dancer would probably refuse to allow her to perform her perilous task; and she and Cetan were the only ones who could carry it out.

Soon, they reached the area which War Eagle and his companions had reported as the Crow encampment. Using the fieldglass and a high boulder, they selected their action site, a furtive approach route to it, and finalized their daring plan.

After everything was prepared, Chumani—dressed to appear as Bishee Chia Biakalishte, their name for Pte Skawin, White Buffalo Maiden—lay on a high brownish gray rock overlooking the Crow village, atop a blanket to avoid soiling the unbeaded white garment. Scattered or clustered atop the low formation and around its wide base were many trees and bushes. Cetan had been dusted with finely ground powder from white and yellow soil and soft rocks to make him appear as a ghostly spirit. Upon her word, the hawk swooped down over the camp and dropped several large cottonwood leaves bound with long blades of grass into the center fire. As soon as the flames ate through the leaves containing stolen gunpowder, a loud and smoky explosion ensued, startling the people there and telling Chumani to leap to her feet. She heard many shrieks and shouts. She saw many women grab children and flee into tepees, and saw warriors retrieve their weapons and look about for the cause of the commotion.

Red Feather, concealed from their sight to her rear by a downward slope on the high setting, tossed black powder into a small fire he had built there, but did so from a safe distance and closed his eyes against damage, skills he had learned from numerous games of toss-the-hoop. That second loud noise and puff of smoke drew the Crow's attention to her. They watched the odd-colored hawk fly to her and perch upon her shoulder; a thick leather strip to prevent his sharp talons from piercing her delicate skin was concealed beneath her snow-white garment.

Chumani saw many armed Crow head in her direction from a distance of about ten tall tree lengths away. She shouted in their language, *"Ikye!"* to seize their attention. She held up her right hand and yelled for them to halt. That was the signal for Wind Dancer, concealed in thick bushes and by a grass-covered hide below her lofty location, to strike a match from the metal box to set fire to the semicircle of gunpowder he had spread around the gray base of the rock. From the center of that black trail, he sent sparkling and hissing snakes darting in both directions until the two reached their destinations where a large pile of gunpowder exploded.

The warriors jerked their bodies at those sounds and were halted by their chiefs and shamen. All eyes gazed at her in either awe or suspicion.

"Ahkuxpatchiahche, Apsaalooke!" she yelled to the astonished Crow. "Do not approach or attack me or I will destroy you as I destroyed the Dakota brave who tried to do so when I took the Sacred Pipe and Seven Sacred Ceremonies to his people as their Creator commanded. This sun, I have been sent by Akbaatatdia to bring you a message."

Red Feather, who had crawled upward on his belly and hidden behind a dense cluster of fragrant spruce, called upon his talent with a game he often used with children to amuse them. In the Crow tongue and throwing his disguised voice outward, he made it appear as if his words were coming from Cetan who clacked his beak and fluttered his large wings at Chumani's command. Red Feather said in a loud and strange voice, "I was sent by Dakaake Suua to command you to listen to her words and obey them. If you do not, I will return to Dakaake Suua and tell the Thunderbird Spirit not to send any rain in coming seasons to grow your sacred tobacco plants and to grow the grass your horses need. Do not come near her, for she is big medicine and is protected by the Creator."

Chumani observed the Crow's amazement and fear as the hawk spoke, jerked his feathered head about, his round eyes watching them intently. Without moving her lips, as Red Feather had taught her, she whispered for Cetan to cease his clacking and movements, and he settled himself again.

The most powerful chief who was in charge of the pow-wow, took two steps forward and shouted, "What message do you bring from the Creator? Speak Old Man Coyote's words. We will listen and obey."

Chumani had practiced this event many times, but she spoke slowly and carefully so she would not make a mistake and use a Lakota word or sign. "Go to the Big Council at Fort Laramie and make truce with the Whites, Dakotas, and other enemy tribes," she instructed. "Leave these lands forever or more evil will visit you, just as it was sent to Sroka's tribe when it invaded Lakota lands to attack its people when it should have been hunting and preparing for winter in their own territory. It is foolish and lazy to raid others for what should be earned with your own hands, wits, and skills. Go to the parlay and sign the white man's paper for truce. Then return to your lands where the stones are yellow and the ground boils and spews forth water and to the land where powder marks the banks of its large river; there, the Creator and his forces will protect you and provide for you, my people."

She took a quick breath and gave more force to her voice. "If you do not obey this message, Mother Earth will not grow your sacred tobacco within her belly; any seeds you plant in her will wither and die," she warned. "The Little People will not give your arrows strength or true aims, and your enemies will slay you. The Thunderbird will turn his eyes from you and deny you the rain you need. If you do not believe such things will happen as punishments, ask the tribe of Sroka which was twice attacked by such forces in warning to them. When the son of Rising Bear of the Oglala Red Shields was snared by Sroka, whom all know his name and coups, Akbaatatdia sent His spirit-helpers to free their captive, for he turned the eyes and wits and hands of Sroka's people from their seasonal tasks. Old Man Coyote filled their hearts with such hatred and anger against Sroka that they slew their greatest warrior with many arrows. Are my words not true, Sroka's tribe?"

Chumani watched as that chief stepped forward and nodded, shocking the others present. "Hear me, all Apsaalooke, for you will not be warned again. I will send my helper to Akbaatatdia with your answer," she said as she stroked Cetan's chest. "What will you do, my people?"

A vote was taken and a reply given to her. She smiled and nodded, then told Cetan to take flight. All eyes followed his path and their bodies turned away from her as if to see where their Creator dwelled. That distracting tactic allowed her the time and chance to seemingly vanish as she hurriedly sneaked down the rock's decline with her grinning companion. With haste, she, Red Feather, and Wind Dancer crept to another site, using the series of large formations to conceal their presence and passings, along with the rabbit furs secured over their feet in the event someone climbed and checked the site.

The three joined Zitkala and War Eagle at their horses. They mounted and walked for a long distance behind high hills and around rocky upheavals until they knew neither they nor their dust could be sighted by the enemy. Soon Cetan gave a shrill cry from overhead as he caught up with them. Then they galloped toward the Paha Sapa and their people.

Following a glorious night of fiery passion in their tepee, which had been erected during their absence by the women of their families and with help from other friends, Chumani stood with Zitkala at the edge of their camp to watch Wind Dancer and Red Feather ride away.

Chumani wished her husband had been left in charge

of his people, since his father and brother were going, but
War Chief Blue Owl was to have that important duty. Red
Feather and many other warriors had gone with them, as
had her father and many of the White Shields, though her
brother had been left in charge of his band's protection,
an action which greatly pleased his wife. She was elated
that the White Shields were camped nearby for the winter;
that would allow her to visit her family and friends often,
to help Rainbow Girl when her baby was born, and to
assure her of their safety. Yet, she was apprehensive about
her loved ones' journey to Fort Laramie, perhaps to face
great perils. With so many enemies—Indian and White—
gathered there, conflicts were inevitable.

Chapter
Nineteen

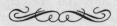

Wind Dancer's party reached the sprawling valley near Fort
Laramie where an immense throng of Indians—allies and
adversaries—were camped; and more were arriving in
large masses each day. Riding between his father and
grandfather, with War Eagle and Red Feather behind
them, he could not help but wonder if the Bluecoats and
settlers were apprehensive with so many heavily armed and
highly trained warriors close by. Yet, the fort was well-
manned and the soldiers possessed awesome guns and
cannons for protection. They had ridden fast to get there
before the talks began, and had succeeded by one day.

Vast grasslands, coloring themselves for the fall season,
stretched in several directions. The visually impenetrable
Platte and the clear and winding Laramie rivers were
nearby, as was lofty Laramie Peak which was used as a
landmark by both cultures. Westward, foothills swept up
into the Laramie Mountains which flowed onward into the
massive Rocky Mountains. A profusion of trees and bushes
grew along the riverbanks and in dense clusters here and
there where water was close to ground surface. An extensive prairie dog village dotted the landscape not far away
with many furry creatures poised atop their burrows as if

to observe the action while remaining ready to dive into safety or race out to quickly forage for food. Old Fort John, with its whitewashed adobe enclosure, sat on a low bluff overlooking the river. Beyond it were the assorted structures of the newest section of the military post. A few of them had flat tops, but most had high pitched roofs with one or more chimneys and the majority had extended windows. The white man's flag on a tall pole—according to the wind—either waved gently or popped wildly on their Parade Ground. Close by were the conical dwellings of Indians who lived off the white man's handouts.

Rising Bear, in his full ceremonial garb, now led the way as they rode onward to an already trampled meadow where an enormous encampment was situated. The gatherings of lodges were separated only by short distances for diverse tribes. They located the site of Red Cloud and his Tetons and dismounted.

Wind Dancer sighted the Peace-Maker's camp of many tents, which was protected by an abundance of Bluecoats. Soon talks would begin, and he could only imagine what extreme changes they would wrought.

At the fort, Thomas Fitzpatrick was dismayed, as the promised goods to be used in exchange for the chiefs' signatures on a treaty document had not arrived and word was they would be several weeks late. He knew if he didn't think up a cunning ploy, the Indians would return to their lands and the chance for initiating another council and peace were rare. For now, all he could do was hope the wagons hurried and he could persuade the Indians to stay until they came and an agreement could be made.

As Wind Dancer's group visited with Red Cloud, soldiers from Mitchell came around to tell them, as they had the others, that this location would soon be barren of grass needed by Fort Laramie's stock and for thousands of Indian horses in the coming days and they should find a site where there was sufficient grass to graze their animals.

The Bluecoats said that Superintendent Mitchell and Indian Agent Fitzpatrick wanted the chiefs to talk amongst themselves and make a suggestion since the area was familiar to them. They were told that Mitchell had ordered them to turn loose many head of cattle from the fort's herd so their braves could capture, slaughter, and cook them, as most were present without their families, and meat would be easy for the men to roast over open fires.

Wind Dancer guessed the white leaders were stalling for some reason, and they assumed a full belly would calm the restless warriors. He and his people would not chase the cattle, for they had brought food with them. He almost laughed in amusement when he overheard a brave speculate about the cattle being tainted and the gift being a trick to sicken them. Wind Dancer doubted the white men would be that foolish amidst a throng of Indians they surely did not want provoked against them. He was grateful for the Peace-Maker's decision not to offer the Indians whiskey. Perhaps the fort sutler had been ordered not to sell any "firewater" to the "redskins." If whiskey entered the uneasy setting, trouble would surely erupt with a myraid of disparate tribes in such close proximity.

Despite that caution, trouble was sparked the next day when Washakie and his Shoshones, escorted by soldiers and accompanied by the mountain man Jim Bridger, arrived just as Mitchell was preparing to speak. A Dakota warrior tried to attack Washakie in retribution for a past misdeed. One of the men acting as an interpreter halted the Dakota's charge before a fight could break out and spread hostility to those men's companions.

Wind Dancer watched how Mitchell, Broken Hand Fitzpatrick, and the soldiers handled the potentially perilous situation, and was impressed. His insightful mind reasoned that not all white men were evil and scornful, but their numbers were all too few. The site of their new location, the first matter, was discussed and settled quickly. It pleased him, as it took them farther away from the fort, its detachments, and its dreadful weapons.

The assembly of Indians and Whites moved eastward to Horse Creek, an offshoot of the Platte River. Many Bluecoats traveled with them, most riding on the group's fringes as they watched for trouble and stayed ready to handle it swiftly. One of the wives of a white officer rode with them, no doubt to prove to the Indians they were trusted not to attack the Whites.

Wind Dancer thought of his beloved wife and wished she were there with him to witness this unpredictable event. He missed her terribly and, having been an equal part of the visionquest, she deserved to be there to see their efforts come to fruition. Yet, the Crow village they had hopefully tricked recently had not arrived, and their absence worried him. Even so, the Red and White Shields were camped close to each other at the edge of the Paha Sapa and their warriors were to remain on constant alert for danger, so she and their bands should be safe during his absence. He and Chumani had ridden a long and perilous path together and now that a truce loomed ahead with their enemies, he must not lose her for any reason.

A huge campsite was erected at Horse Creek on Friday. After Mitchell sent word around that it was a White custom to rest over the weekend, it was announced the peace talks would begin on Monday morning, September the eighth, at nine o'clock. The signal to gather would be the ceremonial firing of their cannon.

Again, Wind Dancer had the feeling the Peace-Maker was stalling for time. He prayed it was not to give time for more soldiers and powerful weapons to arrive and they had not been lured into a trap. He was aware of how much death and destruction could be carried out with cannons, howitzers, and black powder thundersticks.

"Father, we must stay on alert for trickery," Wind Dancer disclosed before voicing his previous thoughts. "I do not trust most of the Whites and Bluecoats, though

Broken Hand seems honorable. We must stay ready to defend ourselves and to escape if a threat appears."

"That is wise, my son, and you must reveal such words to Red Cloud."

"I will do so before I eat and sleep, but I am sure his thoughts and feelings match mine. Use eagle eyes and sharp ears while I am gone."

During what the white man called the "weekend," various tribes and bands—excluding Wind Dancer's—entertained the Peace-Maker and his party with processions of their warriors in their finest garments and headdresses. Certain dances were performed in colorful costumes, accompanied by loud drumming. Songs were sung, vocables were murmured, and coups were chanted. Foods cooked by some of the warriors' wives and other female members of their families were offered to the observers, though most only pretended to eat or taste the unfamilar or—to them—unsavory gifts.

To thank the participants for their diversions and offerings, Mitchell passed out items from his own supplies: coffee, sugar, salt, tobacco, flour, and a few blankets he had brought with him.

Wind Dancer observed as the Whites met in a shady setting on Sunday morning to sing, pray, and listen to their shaman's words as the gray-haired man read from a large and worn black-covered book in his hands. It jogged his memory to travel to seasons long past when Omaste performed those same actions, and when Sunshine tried to teach Cloud Chaser to do the same, though his half-white brother rebelled against a custom which conflicted with the Indian beliefs taught by their father and people. He could not help but wonder if Cloud Chaser was still alive somewhere and if he could ever return to them. If so, how would a man with mixed bloods be greeted and treated by their people and by other tribes, especially if this attempt at peace between the two so dissimilar cultures failed?

* * *

Monday morning, the cannon was fired to signal the opening of the treaty talk. Many Indians were surprised and angered when the officer's wife sat with the White leaders, as their women were never permitted to sit in council, and some viewed it as a bad sign. Even so, neither her husband, nor Mitchell, nor Fitzpatrick, nor the highest ranking military officer present sent her away.

As the ceremonial Peace Pipe was being smoked, the Crow, Gros Ventre, and Assiniboni arrived in a large and noisy party, swelling the count of Indians to over ten thousand. Another White shaman rode with them—Father DeSmet, a Catholic missionary and Culbertson of the American Fur Company which had once owned Fort John and Laramie.

Yet, it was the Apsaalooke which swarmed down on the previously serene setting like buzzing insects as they whooped, shook feathered lances overhead, and made their highly decorated horses prance or paw the air. They, too, were clad in their finest array and had adorned themselves with wooden or trade combs and dangles in their hair, extra feathers on their bonnets, rings on their fingers, numerous layers of neck beads, and glass trade beads in various colors sewn on their possessions. Many wore seashells or suspended thongs with beads in their ears. Some had their hair chopped off at different lengths near their faces; others displayed topknots secured by decorative thongs and oddly placed feathers.

Wind Dancer sighed a deep breath of relief; for once, he was happy to see Crow faces, and he recognized many of them from the camp they had tricked and others from past conflicts.

At the first meeting, Mitchell said the multi-band Indians had to select one man as a head chief to meet, speak, and sign for their tribal bond at the second talk in two days.

Wind Dancer was amazed that friend and foe alike agreed to that unfair demand; all but the Dakotas. Their

Nation was one of the largest and most powerful with three distinct branches growing from the Dakota trunk, with thirteen smaller tribal branches thrusting outward, and with many twiglike bands extending from those thirteen limbs. How could one man, he and others asked, speak and vote for numerous bands when many were diverse and secluded from others? How could a woodland or plant-growing tribe speak for what was best and just for a Plains tribe; or the other way around? How could a stranger represent them as head chief, particularly in such an important matter? How could that man know which points they would agree to and which they would reject? How could he know if they considered the goods offered as sufficient recompense for the white man's unknown requests? Yet, Mitchell stuck to his strange requirement.

As chiefs talked with their bands concerning the offensive matter, Wind Dancer spoke privately with his father. "Cast your vote for Brave Bear as the white leaders and many others desire, for he has no power or influence over our people," he urged. "When the time comes and the truce is strained and they say we break our word, we can tell them your name is not signed upon their paper, so we have not broken our word. If they say you helped choose Brave Bear, you can say you spoke against their desire for a head chief but they would not continue the treaty talk until you agreed, and you did so because you wanted peace between us and all enemies."

"That is good, my son, and I will follow your wise words."

Soon the Brule Brave Bear was selected by a majority vote, a warrior who did not think and feel he was best in all ways to be the head chief of all Dakotas, to speak and sign a treaty which would affect all of them in similar and in different ways. Yet, Mitchell was satisfied.

The second talk began on Wednesday morning, September tenth, with the head chiefs in control of the Indians' fates, and with their peoples crowded behind them to listen to the provisions of the treaty.

Ateyapi Broken Hand Fitzpatrick praised them for allowing his people to live in or to cross their lands. He admitted they had come and done so without permission, and apologized.

Wind Dancer decided that Thomas Fitzpatrick, a tall man with gray hair, was trustworthy, brave, and strong in body and spirit. It seemed to him as if Broken Hand sought what was fair for both sides, a matter which existed only because his people had encroached on their lands. Yet, since the Whites had come and would remain until or unless driven out by force, Broken Hand wanted them to live in peace with each other; he wanted the Indians to cease their hostilities which often encompassed the Whites in the area of their dispute. He spoke of the Indians' past and future losses and said they would receive reparations for them. He said food and other needs would be given out to all tribes once every circle of the seasons.

Certain numbers, amounts, and words meant little to Wind Dancer: "$50,000" worth of cattle, "staples," and other goods "annually" for "fifty years." Yet, he was certain that was a lot of meat and goods and would be passed out for a very long time. Long enough, he feared, for many Indians to become too dependent upon the Whites, a conclusion which seemed to be accurate when an interpreter put the offer in revealing terms. He was concerned when the *ateyapi* spoke of Whites teaching them and their children the *wasicun* ways and tongue, and teaching them how to "farm" the land. They were not growers of seeds and plants as some tribes and bands were, he mentally scoffed; they were hunters, mainly of the buffalo! Yet, as Broken Hand pointed out, how long could the buffalo feed them when herds were hunted by Indians and Whites, and more and more each season? Forever, Wind Dancer's mind scoffed again, if only slain by Indians for food, garments, shelter, and other needs; as the Indian always left alive enough bulls for breeding and enough cows for bearing offspring who would repeat that sacred Circle-of-Life! It was the *wasicun* who hunted only for hides and left meat to rot or feed scavengers, or persuaded greedy and foolish braves to do so in exchange for whiskey and trade goods! Still, things were shifting so drastically that perhaps there was no way to stop the deadly changes.

When disputes arose over territorial boundaries, Father DeSmet, Jim Bridger, *ateyapi* Broken Hand, and others parleyed together and came up with suggestive lines of segregation for enemy tribes. The dispute between Crow and Dakota over hunting grounds was given much consideration and it was decided that each nation would have an area where they would live and hunt, but when the buffalo roamed from their territory, they could follow and hunt as long as they did not attack others in that location.

Wind Dancer was especially interested in that part of the meeting since he had been captured and tortured on Dakota lands by an encroaching Crow band. Now that an agreement had been reached, any Crow who raided or killed in another's territory during the hunting season would be punished both by the Bluecoats and other Indians.

Wind Dancer wished he could read the white man's markings on the papers, as he suspected more was recorded there than was revealed; just as he feared the head chiefs did not understand many words and terms and their repercussions. How, he reasoned, could they live in peace forever—Indian with White, and foe with foe— when neither the Whites nor their enemies of many generations would keep their promises? If his half-white brother had not been stolen from them long ago, Cloud Chaser could expose the words, as Sunshine had taught him to "read" them.

Wind Dancer recalled that painful period in his life when his mother had been stolen from them. Winona had escaped captivity and returned home after the passings of two circles of seasons with the enemy when all believed her dead. That had been twenty winters past. It was during that lonely time for his father that Chief Rising Bear had taken the captive white woman to his sleeping mat to appease his torment, and Omaste had born their half-Lakota son before he vanished at ten winters old. Following his mother's return, she had given birth to War Eagle and Hanmani, and Sunshine had died. It was as if both people with white blood flowing in them had been sent away so his father would not have to confront his moment of weakness anymore. It was strange, he reasoned, how the Great Mystery worked His way at times.

Wind Dancer wondered why his lost brother had visited his mind so many times recently. Were these thoughts, he wondered, connected also with the Great Mystery? He could not forget what Nahemana had told him only one moon ago: "The past is not wrapped in a blanket or buffalo hide and does not rest on a death scaffold. It hides in clouds and will be seen before many more seasons pass. This I saw in a dream when last we slept."

"What does the dream mean, Grandfather?" he had asked.

Nahemana had shaken his head and said, "I have not been shown."

Despite many difficulties, the head chiefs finally signed the Treaty of the Long Meadows on Wednesday, September seventeenth. A great celebration ensued. Indians held more processions in their full regalia and displayed many warrior skills. They sang, danced, drummed, and feasted joyously. Soldiers fired the cannon several times, did many multiple gun salutes, sang their songs, and gave demonstrations of their skills with sabres, rifles, and horsemanship.

"Do we leave for camp now, Father?" War Eagle asked.

"No, my second son, we must await the gifts or the Peace-Makers and other tribes will think we do not honor the agreement. The *ateyapi* says the loaded wagons will arrive in three suns; then we will leave."

"That is a wise plan, Father," Wind Dancer praised him. "I am glad you were not chosen as a head chief to make such difficult choices and to be held responsible for the paper they signed. I would not want you to travel far away to the white man's Big Council Lodge. Broken Hand takes eleven of the signers with him when he carries the treaty paper to the Great White Chief in the place called Washington."

"That is true, *micinksi*," said Nahemana, "But when they return, we must visit with them to learn of the *wasicun's* ways, numbers, and powers."

Wind Dancer smiled. "You are also wise, Grandfather, and it will be as you say: we will seek the *wasicun's* secrets to learn more about them. We must be prepared for the sun when a great war comes between us."

After the combined Red and White Shields party returned to their winter camp, the gifts given to them by the Peace-Makers were passed out amongst their people and a report was given on the council and treaty.

Wind Dancer and Red Feather were joyously greeted by their loves. As the two couples shared a cozy evening meal, they talked about many things, including the mate Cetan had found during the men's absence and the joining of Zitkala and Red Feather in two suns.

As they lay together on their sleeping mat, Wind Dancer murmured, "We have much to give thanks for to the Great Spirit, *micante*. Our people have truce, peace, food, shelter, and safety for now. Our visionquest is over and our victory was large. We have been joined for the passings of five full moons and have done much together. We have been blessed with each other and with the child you carry which will begin its Life-Circle on or near the moon we were joined in the last rebirth season. My heart and mind are filled with love and eagerness to see it born."

"A warrior and hunter's spirit no longer dwells within me, *mihigna;* all I yearn to be is your wife and the mother of our children. Wakantanka matched us better than twin fawns and we will remain together forever. Our dark suns in the past no longer trouble us."

Wind Dancer gazed deeply into Chumani's dark brown

eyes and saw there her great love and desire for him. He smiled as his fingers reached out to stroke her soft cheek. "I love and need you with all I am and with all I will ever be, *micante.*"

Chumani smiled in return as she gazed into his shiny eyes whose gaze reflected the same emotions which flowed within her. "As I love and need you in those same ways, *mihigna.*" She leaned over and melded their mouths and caressed his bare chest as she savored and heightened their passion for each other.

Soon they were lost in the wonder of their emotions and united their bodies to seal their bond again. Each took and gave exquisite pleasure and continued to kiss and embrace afterward as contentment blanketed them.

Chumani looked at her beloved. The wild wind which had blown across their lives and Lakota lands was now a gentle breeze, and the only wind which affected her was the smiling and dancing one nearby.

Not far away, a gray-haired Dakota woman stood between her faithful dog companion and a female sacred white buffalo. She stroked the heads of both as she smiled and her eyes seemingly twinkled with joy as if she knew what was transpiring in the lover's tepee. "It is time to go, my friends," she said. "Our work here is done for three circles of the seasons and we are needed elsewhere." She looked overhead and gazed at wispy white clouds approaching the moon's glowing face. Then she spoke to one only she could see. "Chase her quickly and bravely, or she and all you desire will escape your reach forever."

Author's Note:

This is the first saga in my new four-book "Lakota Skies" series, about the children of Chief Rising Bear and Winona. Each saga will feature the chosen mate, romance, and adventures of one of their children as the main characters, with the rest of the family playing minor roles as they did in this story. I hope you enjoyed reading about Wind Dancer and Dewdrops and learning about the Lakota People and other tribes. I also hope you will look for *Lakota Dawn*, *Lakota Flower*, and *Lakota Nights* in Kensington hardcovers and Zebra paperbacks.

If you would like to receive a current Janelle Taylor newsletter, bookmark, and descriptive flyer of other books available with pictures of their covers, send a self-addressed stamped envelope (long size best) to:

Janelle Taylor Newsletter #33
P. O. Box 211646
Martinez, Georgia 30917-1646

Reading is fun and educational, so do it often!

Best Wishes from

Janelle Taylor

Here is an excerpt from the next book in Janelle Taylor's marvelous LAKOTA series, LAKOTA DAWN, available now in hardcover from Kensington Publishing Corp. Look for it in a bookstore near you or order directly from the publisher by calling (toll free) 888-345-BOOK. Read on to sample the adventure awaiting the second son of Chief Rising Bear, the long-lost Cloud Chaser, and the lovely Dawn . . .

LAKOTA DAWN
By Janelle Taylor

Chapter
One

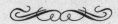

Chase Martin took a deep breath and slowly released it. He kept his rifle sheathed and his handgun holstered to indicate he was no threat to the approaching Red Shield warriors as he guided his horse from concealing trees. He was not surprised that the party's leader spotted him immediately and alerted his followers to a stranger's presence. Chase reined in and lifted his hands to signify he only wanted to parley with them. He wasn't afraid to die for a just cause, but his heart still pounded in suspense and blood sped through his veins in anticipation of what he would learn. He watched the warriors race forward and encircle him. He said to the young man who sat astride a mottled mount before him, "I've come to speak with Chief Rising Bear. Will you take me to his camp and tepee?"

As Chase saw the leader's keen gaze search the trees behind him, he added, "I've come alone to see your chief. This is no trick or challenge. Do you speak English and understand me?"

The warrior nodded, still on alert. "Why you seek my father?" he asked.

Chase eyed the speaker with great interest as he said, "My words are for the ears of Rising Bear alone. I come in peace, War Eagle."

"How you know my name, *wasicun?*"

Chase knew he appeared to be at least part Indian, even if War Eagle had called him a white man, and in a near insulting tone. Considering the past and growing hostilities between the two races, he was lucky he hadn't been slain on sight. "At Fort Pierre, I was told Rising Bear has two sons: Wind Dancer and War Eagle. You are Rising Bear's second son?"

"It true. Why you ask men at trading post about my family? You Bluecoat come to scout our camp for attack?"

"No, War Eagle, I'm not a soldier or an enemy. I come from far away and had to ask questions at Pierre so I could find Rising Bear and his camp. You must take me to him, for the words within me are powerful medicine." *If they don't heal me, I don't know what will . . .*

"What big medicine words you bring to my father?"

"I must speak them to Rising Bear; only he can tell them to others if he so chooses." Chase observed as War Eagle scrutinized him intently and considered his bold request. He listened as the leader spoke with his hunting party, pleased that he understood the Oglala tongue he had not heard for many years.

War Eagle felt there was something oddly familiar about the intruder, but he could not determine what it might be. From somewhere deep within him, a voice—perhaps the Great Spirit's—advised him to take the evasive man to his father. "Give weapons to Swift Otter."

Without protest or delay, Chase surrendered his rifle, pistol, and knife to the warrior, who edged close to his mount and confiscated them.

"Come. I take you to my father. If you speak false words or seek to harm him, *wasicun*, you die by my hand before this sun sleeps."

"Trust me, War Eagle, for I speak the truth."

"I trust no white man, for truth does not live in their

hearts or come from their mouths; they prove this on each rising sun. Come. We go."

Chase knew it was futile and a waste of valuable time to argue with War Eagle, so he remained silent. He rode behind the leader, with the other warriors positioned on either side of him and to his rear. *So far, so good,* he told himself.

They journeyed over the edge of the Great Plains where tight bunches and singular stalks of various grasses swayed in a constant wind, and traveled into foothills of fragrant pine and cedar and fully leafed hardwoods. Along the way, they encountered straggling buffaloes who were not members of the vast herds which spread across the rolling grassland like enormous dark blankets and unknowingly awaited the Indians' impending annual summer hunt. They also sighted small groups of antelope, several coyote, a few turkey, and many deer. Amidst flower-filled meadows with winding streams and creeks, they spooked grouse, other birds, and burrow-dwelling creatures. Beyond their current position were canyons and higher elevation of ebony or gray granite boulders, towering needles, spiky spires, and picturesque cliffs. Those rugged mountains with their jagged peaks and lofty pinnacles comprised the Black Hills, the sacred Paha Sapa.

From childhood recall and the maps he'd studied, Chase knew they were between Swift and Bear Gulch creeks, and north of a site called Cave of the Winds, where powerful spirits allegedly dwelled. He realized he would soon reach the Red Shield camp to face Rising Bear and others. A multitude of contradictory feelings and thoughts filled him: tension and serenity, eagerness and dread, trust and doubt. The moment of truth would be at hand soon.

At long last, the village was in view. Numerous buffalo-hide tepees with lodgepoles jutting upward were situated on the relatively flat surface of a canyon floor, which was sheltered against the harsh winter forces by evergreen-tree-covered hills and large, dark rock formations. Most featured what he knew were colorful paintings of their warrior's skills and exploits. There was no circular pattern to the arrangement, as was the custom on the Great Plains for self-defense in the open. In the spaces between them, Chase saw racks with pelts and hides being dried and stretched for tanning. He saw campfires enclosed by rocks. Kettles were suspended above the fire from three-pronged stands over them and smoke and vapors rose from the simmering meals. Some horses were picketed near conical abodes, and others were grazing and drinking at the nearby river. Weapons were proudly displayed on trilegged stands as they soaked up the powers of the earth and sun. Women were busy with daily chores. Older children played on the camp fringe; younger ones and infants were tended near their homes by their grandparents or sisters. Men talked and worked on their tasks, mainly preparations for the impending annual buffalo hunt. It was all so familiar and yet alien to Chase. For a moment, he wondered if he had been wrong to come there, if he should have left the past dead and buried. Yet, even if he had made a grave mistake, it was too late to change his mind now.

Chase noted that many people halted their chores and headed toward them—whispering and pointing—as the riders entered the busy area and dismounted near their chief's tepee, their curious or narrowed gazes focused on him, a white man who arrived unbound. Several young boys took the horses away to be tended, including his own. He waited in silence as Wind Dancer and Rising Bear scrutinized him with keen dark eyes before looking quizzically at War Eagle for an explanation. The leader hurriedly related the news of Chase's "capture" and persistence in speaking with the chief.

Wind Dancer gave the man another quick study and had a strange feeling they had met before. He asked in English, which he had learned from his wife during the last few years, "Who are you and why do you come to see my father?"

So, like War Eagle, you don't recognize me, either. I guess the same is true for our father and everyone else here. "I want to

speak with Rising Bear alone; my words are not for the
ears of others unless he so chooses." Chase waited and
listened as Wind Dancer translated those words into
Lakota, and the older man responded to his eldest son.

"My father says you can speak your words before his
family and people," Wind Dancer said. "But who are you?
Why do you come to our camp?"

Chase had yearned to be remembered and for this initial
meeting to take place in private. His hurt and displeasure
sent forth a response in a near-surly tone as he frowned,
"Does Mato Kikta not recognize the face and voice of
Yutokeca Mahpiya, son of Rising Bear and Margaret Phil-
lips, the white woman he called Omaste, Sunshine, for her
golden hair? Is my father not happy I have found my way
home after being stolen from him twelve summers past?
Has he forgotten his own flesh and blood?"

A shocked Wind Dancer glared at the scowling stranger
and almost gritted out the angry charge, "You lie, *wasicun!*
My brother is dead. You are foolish to come here and
claim to be him. What evil trick is this?"

Chase leveled his gaze on the man whose height
matched his own of six feet. "Do I look dead, Wind Dancer,
my brother who is five winters older than I am? Do you
not remember Cloud Chaser who followed in your shadow
on most suns after he learned to walk? It isn't a trick or a
lie. I have proof: the clothes and possessions I was wearing
when I vanished long ago, they're in the saddlebag on my
horse. In my medicine bundle is the feather you gave me
from the first bird you killed with an arrow. Also there is
the sacred red stone my father gave to me following my
first vision and the golden lock of my mother's hair, and
I wear the locket which holds her parents' image. If I'm not
Cloud Chaser, how would I have and know such things?"

Wind Dancer eyed the stranger with astonishment. He
and Cloud Chaser had been separated by evil forces when
Wind Dancer was fifteen winters old and his half-brother
was ten, and Cloud Chaser had been presumed dead or
lost to them forever. Was this man speaking the truth? Was

that what evoked such eerie feelings within him? If this was Cloud Chaser, he had changed from the almost black-haired and -eyed boy who had looked Indian to a man who appeared mostly *wasicun* with his medium brown eyes and hair with lighter streaks. His features were larger and different, but the passing of time could account for those changes. As a curious Rising Bear nudged his arm and questioned his reaction, Wind Dancer's muddled thoughts cleared. He translated the shocking words to his father, whose widened gaze jerked toward and stared at the stranger who oddly tugged at his emotions.

Two Feathers snarled in the Lakota tongue, "It is a trick! Cloud Chaser walks the Ghost Trail, not the face of Mother Earth! This man is a white man who has come to spy on us for our enemy! We must slay him where he stands. I will do the deed for our chief," he offered as he withdrew a weapon.

Wind Dancer told his irate first cousin in their language, "Hold your tongue and sheathe your knife, Two Feathers, and allow him to speak." In English, he asked, "Who are you, *wasicun*, and why do you come here?"

Chase ignored his hostile cousin as he avowed, "I told you such news should be revealed in private to my father. Our long-awaited reunion was not for the eyes and ears of others." When Rising Bear failed to smile, embrace, and welcome him home, disappointment and bitterness shot through Chase and provoked angry words, still in English. "Tell me, Father, would you have tried to find and recover me if I weren't half white or if I had been one of your other three children? Does it bring you shame and sadness to have me return and remind you of past dark days?"

Of necessity, Wind Dancer translated those words to their father.

"Do not speak such bad words and show such bad feelings to our chief or your tongue will be taken!" Two Feathers shouted in a threatening tone.

Chase disregarded his cousin whose Lakota words he

had understood. "If my father will not answer the questions which trouble my heart, then you tell me, my brother, how long and how hard did he search for me when I was stolen by the Whites? Why didn't he follow the cloud-covered wagons? They move slowly and he is a great warrior, so he could have easily overtaken them and rescued me. Was he glad to have me gone?"

"He and others searched many suns and moons, but Cloud Chaser could not be found," Wind Dancer rebuffed. "He followed the wagons but did not see him among the Whites, so it was foolish to attack them and call forth a war with the Bluecoats. He found Crow tracks near his last moccasin prints; he followed our enemy and recovered his pony, but all Crow were slain in that battle and there were no signs of him in their camp. He did not know where he was or what happened to him. If you are Cloud Chaser, why did you wait so long to return to us? Why do you return in this season?"

"I was wounded by the enemy," Chase began his explanation, "and thrown from my pony; my leg was broken. White settlers found me, tended me, and took me with them to a place far away called Oregon and named me Chase Martin. I was told my people were attacked and killed and that I must remain with them to recover and be safe. And I did not know the long path home. Before my white father died, he revealed the truth to me, but begged me to forgive him and to stay with the woman who raised me as her son to help her on the farm and to protect her. After her death, I returned here."

"Why did those who took you speak such lies?" Wind Dancer asked.

"Because they wanted a son badly and couldn't have children. They also believed I was a white captive being held and reared by the Indians. They said nobody came searching for me or claimed me, so they kept me."

After Wind Dancer translated those words for their father, Two Feathers snarled, "The Oglala blood he carried at birth has been slain by his many seasons with the

Whites; he is more *wasicun* than Red Shield. He must be slain or sent away or he will cause much trouble for us."

Chase glared at his cousin and refuted, "The blood of Rising Bear lives strongest within me; that is why I have returned to him and the Oglalas."

"You speak our tongue?" Two Feathers asked in astonishment.

Chase replied again in Lakota, "I speak the tongue of my father and our people. I have forgotten little about my life here long ago." He realized he had to settle down or he would be sent riding before he gleaned the truth. "Give me time, Father, and I will earn your love, respect, and acceptance; but you must also earn mine and my forgiveness. I will—"

"You speak foolish and dangerous, half-breed!" Two Feathers shouted. "How do we know you are Cloud Chaser and not a *wasicun* who uses his thoughts and possessions to trick us?"

"I have not forgotten what I was taught as a child, but you have done so. You forget it is not the Oglala way to walk upon the words of another, son of my father's sister. Do you still hold a wicked grudge against me for the many times I beat you in foot races and in arrow practice? After so many years, do you still hate me and wish me dead?"

"Do you come to cause trouble and to shame our chief? Do you—"

"Be silent, Two Feathers, and let him speak what lives in his heart and head," Wind Dancer interrupted his angry cousin. "Do you wish to speak in our tongue to my father or will I reveal your words to him?" he asked Chase.

"It has been a long time since the Lakota tongue has lived in my mouth, but I will speak it." He turned to the chief. "What of the Four Sacred Virtues, Father? You must show Courage and Generosity by allowing me to return and to prove myself. Where is the Wisdom in rejecting or slaying me? Where is your Fortitude, your strength of mind and body at this difficult and painful event? Are we not taught to be fiercely loyal to our family and people? I did not leave them by choice; I was stolen from both by the enemy. You did not refuse to take back your wife when she returned from our enemy's captivity, so why do you retreat from one who carries your blood and came from your man seeds? What Red Shield or Lakota law have I broken that says I must be banished? Give me until the first snow falls from the sky to prove I am more Lakota than White. If I fail to do so, you can slay me or order me to leave and I will obey; you have my word of honor as a man and as your son by blood."

Nahemana stepped forward. "Three summers past when we gathered near Fort Laramie for the Treaty of the Long Meadows," he said, "I had a dream and revealed it to Wind Dancer. The sacred dream said: 'The past is not wrapped in a blanket or buffalo hide and does not rest on a death scaffold. It hides in clouds and will be seen before many more seasons pass.' That message has come to be: Cloud Chaser is alive and has returned."

Chase remembered the shaman, father of Rising Bear's wife, and grandfather to Wind Dancer, War Eagle, and Hanmani—his half-brothers and half-sister. It was evident from everyone's expression and reaction that the elderly white-haired man with much weathered skin and stooped shoulders was loved and respected and was believed to know and speak great wisdom.

Nahemana continued. "The moon your adopted white mother died, an Indian maiden appeared to you in a dream and said it was time for you to return to this land and your father's people. Is that not true?"

Chase was amazed by that news. "How did you know about my dream?"

"The Great Spirit put that thought inside my head, for He knows and sees all things," Nahemana replied. "He has a purpose for calling you back to this land, but He has not revealed it to me."

Wind Dancer knew his grandfather's revelation about his dream long ago was true. Yet, even if this man was Cloud Chaser, the motive for his return might not be a good one. Perhaps evil forces were at work in Chase's life and heart, powers which could endanger his loved ones. Wind Dancer decided that until he was certain his half-brother was no threat to their father and people, this long-lost man must be watched closely.

"You must prove yourself worthy to rejoin our band, if that is the Great Spirit's will," Nahemana told Chase. "You must prove when the time comes, for surely it will do so during this hot season, you are more Oglala than White and you will side with us in all things and ways against our enemies, those who carry the same White blood as did your mother and the people who reared you far away. Can you turn your face from the Whites forever? Can you raise your weapons against them when they attack us?"

"I will do whatever I must, Wise One," Chase vowed to the shaman.

"Let him prove himself at the Sun Dance pole," Two Feathers scoffed.

"I will surrender myself to the Sun Dance to prove myself worthy to be a Red Shield and to give thanks to Wakantanka for bringing me home, but I will do so when the time is right, not by your challenge, my cousin."

"Are you afraid to—"

Rising Bear lifted his hand. "Enough, Two Feathers. Our shaman has spoken and so it will be until the Great Spirit tells him otherwise or our laws are broken." He said to Chase and his other two sons, "Come to my tepee; there are many words to speak between us."

As the four men headed for the chief's dwelling, Chase glanced to his left. His gaze widened and he missed a step as he stared at a young maiden not far away. If he didn't know she was real, he would swear it was the female spirit who had appeared to him in his beckoning dream months ago! She was the most beautiful and tempting woman he had ever seen. He saw her lower her gaze and turn to speak with a younger girl beside her, and he refocused his strayed attention on his retreating father and brothers. Even so, he experienced a strange and powerful pull toward her and knew he must discover her identity. As he glanced toward Two Feathers, he saw the warrior's sullen gaze flicker from him to the maiden and back to him. Judging from the scowl on Two Feathers' face, Chase concluded the other man was going to cause trouble for him as he had in the past, but he would ponder that problem later. For now, other matters were more important. He was eager to see how his father and brothers treated him in private, for they had shown no affection, joy, and acceptance in public, to his dismay.

As the crowd dispersed to return to their chores, the two young women walked into the forest to speak beyond the hearing of others.

Hanmani, cherished daughter of Rising Bear, told her best friend Macha, "I was only four winters old when he vanished, so I am not sure I remember him. After living so long as the half-white man he is, why would he want to return to a land filled with conflict and hatred between the two bloods he carries? How will he bring himself to side with one against the other? If he is not loyal to his mother's and adoptive parents' side, how can we trust him to be loyal to ours? Dawn, what do you think of him and his coming?"

Macha vividly remembered the boy called Cloud Chaser, though she had been only six when he disappeared. Even at that young age, she had loved him and used many pretenses to be around him. Now he was back, a grown man, a handsome and virile one with great courage, strength, intelligence, and boldness. "Perhaps the Great Spirit has summoned him here to help bring peace between our two peoples."

Hanmani shook her head. "Father and others say there can be no peace with the Whites who seek to destroy us and steal our lands. Already they have misused and broken the Long Meadows Treaty with us and other tribes. If a treaty born only three summers past has withered and died, what and who can give it new life, and how long will the second one last? It cannot be, my best friend, for our peoples and desires are too different."

"If there can be no peace as our leaders say, perhaps there can be a better truce, for the Whites are here to stay, Hanmani. Even if all enemies who live or travel through our lands are slain, more will come, as will a bitter war if we attack them. Do not forget what we have learned: they have many powerful weapons and their numbers are larger than the buffalo herds which cover the grasslands. If we do not find an honorable way to live with them or a means to utterly defeat them, we, along with the buffalo, will vanish, and we will not be able to return as Cloud Chaser did. Perhaps the Great Spirit allowed his capture so he could learn the white man's ways, then return to teach them to us, or to help us use those ways against our enemy."

That speculation intrigued and excited Hanmani. She smiled and asked, "Do you really think so, my friend?"

Macha thought for a short span, then sighed and shrugged. She could not outright lie to her best friend, but she was not ready to expose her deepest feelings on the matter. "I do not know why he has come, but surely the Great Spirit will soon reveal it to our shaman."

"If he seeks to trick us, he will be slain by Wind Dancer or War Eagle."

"Could they truly slay their own brother?"

"If he is a threat to us, they will do what they must. I am sure they will watch him as keen-eyed hawks until they know he can be trusted. We must gather our firewood so we can hurry back to see what happens."

As they worked, Macha struggled to quell her fear at that possibility, and her elation and suspense at his sudden return. It was as if she had been dreaming and waiting for Cloud Chaser to reappear since the day he had vanished. Why, she did not know, as any kind of relationship with him was impossible. She had noticed Two Feathers' study of them when they had glanced at each other. The warrior had begun to crave her as his wife. Yet, she could think of little which would be more saddening or repulsive than mating with Hanmani's cousin. Macha sighed. She felt trapped in a powerful whirlwind that was blowing her in two directions at once: one toward the bond to her people and one toward the man who caused her body to warm and tingle, her heart to pound, and her mind to race with forbidden thoughts and desires.

As she did her daily task, several questions plagued Macha. What if his *wasicun* blood and years with the Whites had changed Cloud Chaser from the boy she remembered? What if his reason for returning was not a good one? What if he called down the wrath of their enemies upon them? Even if he had not become more White than Indian, what if he could not bring himself to choose sides when that awesome moment arrived? If he could not convince the others he was being truthful and sincere, would he be slain or simply sent away? She, too, must watch him for answers.

When their woodslings were filled and they headed back toward camp, Macha somehow knew that her parents, especially her father, would tell her to come home whenever Cloud Chaser visited his family and to avoid him completely. Could she—would she—obey that impending command? She could not decide how she would react if Cloud Chaser approached her, especially in private, or surmise how she was going to handle the imminent and repugnant joining offer from Two Feathers.

Help me, Great Spirit, for my heart and mind are caught in traps and I do not know how to free myself.

DEAD LINE

Something slammed into Caroline from behind. The phone flew from her hand and she landed facedown on the ground beneath the curtain. A weight came down hard on her back. Caroline tried to scream, but the plastic curtain stopped her mouth and nose. Terror crashed over her as a pair of hard hands grabbed her neck. She tried to roll away, push up, fight back, but the slick curtain and the slippery clay prevented her. The hands let go of her neck, grabbed the curtain, pulled it tighter. Caroline couldn't breathe. She clawed and bit as her chest grew heavy. Her lungs begged for air, screamed for it. Her heart pounded hard in her head. Black spots danced in her vision.

And then the curtain was gone. So was the weight from her back. Caroline sucked in huge breaths of cold, wet air as she pulled away from her assailant. Mud plastered her skin and clothes. She tried to get to her knees, slipped on the clay, tried again, managed it. She flung a wild glance around her but saw no one in the dark and rain.

Get to your feet try to run go for help god who is it where is he where is

A pair of feet stepped onto the clay in front of her. Caroline looked up. Something swung down at her, and she had time for one, short scream. . . .

IDENTITY

Steven Piziks

Based on the motion picture written by Michael Cooney

POCKET STAR BOOKS

New York   London   Toronto   Sydney   Singapore

This book is a work of fiction. Names, characters, places and incidents are products of the author's imagination or are used fictitiously. Any resemblance to actual events or locales or persons, living or dead, is entirely coincidental.

An *Original* Publication of POCKET BOOKS

 A Pocket Star Book published by
POCKET BOOKS, a division of Simon & Schuster, Inc.
1230 Avenue of the Americas, New York, NY 10020

ISBN: 0-7434-7653-0

First Pocket Books printing April 2003

10 9 8 7 6 5 4 3 2 1

POCKET STAR BOOKS and colophon are registered
trademarks of Simon & Schuster, Inc.

For information regarding special discounts for bulk purchases,
please contact Simon & Schuster Special Sales at 1-800-456-6798 or
business@simonandschuster.com

Printed in the U.S.A.

ACKNOWLEDGMENTS

Thanks to my agent, Lucienne Diver, for handling various and sundry arrangements that help me write. And thanks to Brian d'Arcy James for various and sundry bits of information that helped me write this book.

1

Greg Kerrick closes his eyes, takes a deep breath, and says, "Gary home" into his cell phone. The receiver pressed to his ear feels hard and unyielding, and Kerrick's fingers are cold. The courthouse lobby is deserted, as might be expected at half past midnight. White marble walls and polished tile floors reflect every sound. In the darkness beyond the revolving door, rain falls in cold sheets, unusual in Nevada. Flash flood warnings are probably jamming the airwaves by now. Judge Taylor, Kerrick muses, is going to be in a double shit mood when he gets here.

The line rings once, then twice. Pain shoots through the fingers on Kerrick's other hand. He looks down to see what the hell is wrong and realizes he is clutching his briefcase so tightly his fingers are cramping up. Kerrick forces himself to loosen his grip.

The third ring is interrupted by a click, a series of thumps, and silence.

"Uh, Gary?" Kerrick hazards. "You awake?"

"Am I awake?" mumbles the man on the other end. A slight echo tells Kerrick he is on speaker phone. "Yeah. Greg? What the hell—?"

Kerrick plunges forward. "There's gonna be a midnight hearing in the Rivers case. The defense found some notebooks misfiled in evidence. They're diaries. Greenfruit argued to the State supremes that we suppressed the stupid things."

A sharp click comes over the line and Gary Bywater's voice snaps into loud clarity. No more speaker phone. Kerrick braces himself. "What the *hell* are you talking about?" Bywater shouts.

"They punted it to Judge Taylor an hour ago," Kerrick says, keeping his voice neutral. "They told him if he wanted Rivers' execution to go forward, he'd have to hold an evidenciary hearing tonight. I'm guessing Taylor will show up in fifteen, twenty minutes."

"This is not happening," Bywater snarls. "No goddammed, shit-assed, *fuck-faced* way is this happening."

A car screeches up to the curb out front, and the part of Kerrick's mind that isn't dealing with an unhappy, half-past-midnight boss realizes it is an

unmarked cop car. A broad, stocky man springs out clutching several folders to his chest in a pathetic attempt to shield them from the rain. He sprints for the revolving door.

"No one's here yet," Kerrick says, hoping this small plus will calm Bywater down. "No cameras or reporters. It all happened under the radar. The transport left Ely State Prison only an hour ago, so there hasn't been time for—"

"What do you mean 'left Ely'?" Bywater interrupts. "*What* transport?"

The man with the folders shoves impatiently through the revolving door like a pissed-off kid riding a merry-go-round, and Kerrick recognizes Detective Drew Valrole. Valrole rushes past Kerrick with a hasty nod, leaving a trail of water on the tile floor as he heads for the elevator.

"The diaries gave them an opening, Gary," Kerrick says into the phone. "Defense is arguing insanity again. They said they need Rivers present, so they pumped him up with drugs and put him in a—"

"This is fucking unheard of!" Bywater bellows. "The night before his *execution?*"

"It's outrageous," Kerrick agrees.

"Fucking right it is. Rivers is supposed to be on his way to Carson City for an early appointment with the medical goddammed examiner. How the *hell*

could you let this happen, Greg? Jesus *fucking* Christ. You drop the ball more often than a Chicago Cubs shortstop."

Kerrick's fingers tighten on his briefcase again. It always works this way. An unexpected complication arises in a case and somehow it ends up being Greg Kerrick's fault. "Gary, there was nothing I could—"

"They can't chauffeur a blue-watch prisoner around the desert in the middle of a fucking *hurricane*. They're out of their goddam *minds!*"

"I couldn't stop it, Gary," Kerrick says, unable to keep the pleading note from his voice and hating himself for it. "I tried to call you, but—"

"Just fix it. You hear me? Fucking *fix it!*" Bywater booms. "Friday morning if I don't read that cocksucker's obituary, you can write your own!"

Another loud click as Bywater slams down the phone.

2

Paris Nevada carefully lit the birthday candles, humming "For He's a Jolly Good Fellow" under her breath. When the entire circle was burning merrily, she tossed the lighter aside, ran her fingers through her dark-blond hair, and put a sexy pout on her face. She wore only a pink negligee and zebra-striped shoes. The thin six-inch spikes on the heels were hard enough to punch through linoleum. It had taken Paris most of a day to learn how to walk in them. She leaned over the hotel bed in a passable imitation of Marilyn Monroe.

"Happy birthday to you, happy birthday to you," she sang. Her breath stirred the candle flames. "Happy birthday, Mr. Vanderschmitz. Happy birthday to you."

On the bed, Mr. Vanderschmitz tried to squirm, but the leather cuffs that fastened his wrists and

ankles to the bedposts afforded only a small range of movement. A piece of duct tape covered his mouth. The birthday candles were stuck to his enormous belly, and he groaned every time a drop of hot wax landed on his skin. Reddi-wip covered the rest of his enormous torso and a fair amount of it coated his chest. Paris figured he had a hard-on in there somewhere, but between the whipped cream and the body fat, it was hard to tell.

"Do you want me to blow?" Paris asked in a low, breathy voice.

Mr. Vanderschmitz grunted pleadingly, and another drop of wax made him wince. The actual birthday cake—chocolate—sat on the nearby nightstand. Paris carefully blew out a single candle and stole a glance at the bedside clock. Twenty minutes left. She could probably stretch this out to another hour and make Mr. Vanderschmitz pay for the extra time. God knew she could use the money. But no— you don't become one of the better-priced call girls in Las Vegas by fleecing clients. If your clients don't trust you, you lose business.

Not that Paris intended to stay in business much longer.

The urge to get out, run, flee crashed over her again, and it took every bit of self-control Paris had to stay in the room. She blew out the rest of the can-

dles one by one, then sashayed to the head of the bed, where she loosened one of Mr. Vanderschmitz's cuffs so he could work a hand free. She swiped a blob of Reddi-wip off his chest, let him watch her lick it clean, then snagged her lighter and high-heeled it into the front room of the Luxor Hotel suite. She shut the door and immediately kicked off the stupid zebra spikes. They and the cigarette lighter went carelessly into a suitcase that lay open on the sofa.

Creaking and rustling noises emerged from the bedroom. God, she wanted out of here. Her last client ever, and it felt longer than her very first. To distract herself, Paris pulled on a long Luxor Hotel bathrobe, arranged her hair into a small bun, and tried to shut the suitcase. She had to sit on it before the latches caught. Beside the suitcase on the sofa lay a duffle bag along with a red leather jacket, matching shoulder purse, blue jeans, a white T-shirt, and perfectly normal underwear. Her getaway outfit. Thelma and Louise, her movie heroes, would have been proud.

Paris checked the clock again. Fifteen minutes left. Fifteen long minutes. She went to the window and stared down at the Vegas strip. It was six o'clock, and dusk was falling. Traffic rushed up the street, and spotlights stabbed into the sky like harsh fingers.

Casino lights glittered and gleamed and danced like a herd of Christmas trees on cocaine. Pretty soon Paris would never have to see it again. No more desert, no more lights, no more shows, no more guys with weird-ass fantasies. Hell, Paris wasn't even thirty yet—plenty of time to start over in a new place. It was going to be scary as hell, and a hell of a lot of fun. And unlike most of the "working" girls Paris knew, she had a plan. Paris knew where she was going, what she was doing, and how she was going to do it. First stop—Florida. Her new Mecca.

Ten minutes left. If Mr. Vanderschmitz kept to schedule—and he always did—he was using the whipped cream for something besides its intended purpose, and he was about to reach the peak of his performance. Her cue. Maybe she should just leave. Mr. Vanderschmitz couldn't stop her. But no—he had paid for the hour, and Paris owed it to him. She could last a few more minutes. Paris put a stern, matronly look on her face and burst into the bedroom.

"What do you think you're doing, young man?" she barked.

Mr. Vanderschmitz jumped guiltily and whipped his pudgy hand away from his Reddi-wiped groin. His other hand and his ankles were still cuffed. The duct tape stayed firmly in place as well.

"What a filthy thing you are," Paris continued. "My God, you've ruined both our birthdays!" With that, she picked up the little cake from the nightstand, squashed it into his chest above the half-melted candles, and stormed out of the room. Mr. Vanderschmitz gave a mighty groan of release as Paris slammed the door.

Exultation swept over her. Free! At last she was free!

Paris dropped the robe, yanked on her clothes, snatched up her bags, and fled. The roll of bills she had collected from Mr. Vanderschmitz an hour ago made a comforting bulge in her pocket as she took the elevator down to the lobby. A few moments later, she was in the parking garage and climbing into an aging Trans Am. Jackie, Paris's roommate, called it an "aftermarket convertible" because Paris's ex-boyfriend had removed the roof with a chainsaw six months ago in a post-breakup hissy-fit. For that little trick, he'd gone to jail, though this didn't get Paris's roof back. In Las Vegas, having a roofless car didn't matter too much, but other parts of the country got actual rain. Florida, for example. Maybe she should wait around, try to arrange another car.

But then the overwhelming urge to leave took her again. She gave in without further thought, and peeled out of the parking garage, earning herself a

dirty look from the attendant. Less than an hour later, she was pointed out of town and driving fine. The evening desert wind streamed through her hair and blew the hasty bun to smithereens. She would drive until sunrise, she decided, and see what happened next. No schedules, no clients, no beeps on her cell phone. Freedom stretched in all directions around her, wide and flat as the desert itself beneath a moon that shone like a silver dollar. She let out a barbarian whoop of joy. Thelma and Louise lived! Better than Thelma and Louise, in fact—Paris wouldn't make the mistake of screwing a cute hitchhiker, even if he *did* look like Brad Pitt, and she certainly wouldn't drive *her* convertible off a cliff.

Paris drove for quite some time, until the lights of Las Vegas faded into nothing. She found a fleck of dried Reddi-wip on one knuckle and gnawed it clean. It occurred to her that she hadn't eaten this evening. Oh well—you couldn't think of everything. Eventually she'd pass an all-night truck stop or something. It was more likely that she'd pass a McDonald's first, but Paris refused to eat there anymore. After reading *Fast Food Nation*, she didn't much have the stomach for it. Unless it was an emergency, of course. Or if she had a serious craving for something quick and greasy with cheese. It was hard to maintain principles when faced with a growling

stomach and a hunger headache, something she had learned while giving her first blow job behind an alley dumpster. That fifty bucks had gotten her a bed at the Y for a couple days and some decent food. A week later, she'd lost her virginity to a guy in a business suit and paid her rent up for the rest of the month. No looking back after that. 'Course now she was looking forward.

"Forward, ho!" Paris shouted, and laughed at the unintentional pun.

She was still hungry, though. At one point she passed a neon sign that flashed "Golden Palm Motel" at her, but the diner portion of it was dark, so she kept driving, and it quickly vanished behind her. Not another neon sign in sight. Oh well.

Time to celebrate with a cigarette.

She fumbled one from the pack in her red jacket pocket, then patted her pockets. The Trans Am's lighter had long ago disappeared, so she had to use her own, but where the fuck was it? Purse? No. Glove compartment? No. Then she remembered tossing the thing into her suitcase.

The suitcase sat placidly on the rear seat next to her duffle bag. Without slowing down, Paris reached back and fumbled with the latches. They didn't budge. Cigarette firmly clamped between her lips, she continued to wrestle with them. Cool desert

wind rushed over her like a lover. The Trans swerved left, then right, but Paris refused to slow down or stop. That would be breaking the getaway rules. Thelma and Louise never slowed down, why should she? Besides, there wasn't anyone else on the road.

The car swerved again, and the right tires left the pavement. Paris slapped both hands back on the steering wheel until she regained control, then turned her attention back to the suitcase. She hadn't spun the combination lock, had she? It should still be set to 0510, her birthday. Paris risked a glance at it and saw it was set to 0511. Gritting her teeth, she reached back and located the fourth digit by touch. She flicked it once with a red fingernail, which set the car to swerving again. With a silent growl, she straightened out and shot the suitcase another glance. 0510. Perfect. She reached back and the first latch gave easily. At last things were going her way. Another touch released the second latch.

The suitcase exploded open. Clothes, caught on the wind, flew up and back, scattering behind the Trans like colorful tumbleweeds.

"Jesus shit!" Paris said.

One of the zebra-striped shoes leaped out and rolled end-over-end on the pavement until it came to a stop, heel sticking straight up as it if were giving someone the finger. The wind snatched away a cheap

feather boa, and it soared into the night sky like a fluffy flying snake.

"Fuck it," Paris said finally. Who cared if she lost a few call girl clothes? Her questing fingers found the errant lighter, and as she brought it to the cigarette, Paris realized that the moon was gone. So were the stars. What the hell?

She flicked the lighter to life, but before she could get the cigarette going, the flame vanished with a slight hiss. Paris glanced up just in time to get a fat raindrop in the eye.

"No," she said just as the sky opened up. Cold rain drenched her hair and dripped inside her collar. This was the fucking desert. They called it the desert because it never rained, right? So why the fucking downpour? Swearing, Paris tossed the cigarette away, flicked on the wipers and the radio, and snatched up a Burpee catalog from the passenger seat to hold over her head as a makeshift rain hat.

"Storm sweeping through eastern Nevada," said the radio. *"Several inches of rain are expected overnight, and flash flood warnings are in effect for the following counties."*

She twisted the off button and drove grimly onward. It wasn't supposed to work this way. It hadn't rained on Thelma and Louise, for God's sake. Why did it have to rain on—

Water erupted around her in all directions. The car slammed to a stop, and Paris found herself crushed against the steering wheel. She pulled back, trying to figure out what was going on. The car wasn't moving. It took her a moment to realize that the Trans Am was submerged in water halfway up to the hood. What had looked like wet pavement turned out to be a small lake. The road ahead of her was completely washed out. Praying the Trans wouldn't stall, Paris slammed into reverse and backed away until the car was clear of the flood. She swore again and tossed the useless Burpee catalog into the rain. No choice now but to head back the way she had come. So much for Thelma and Louise.

Angrily, she wrenched the Trans around and backed up, trying to execute a three-point turn. This time the collision slammed her backward into the seat springs. Sparks snapped, and a pair of heavy wires came down, barely missing the car. Paris looked up into the rain and realized she had hit a fucking telephone pole. It was leaning like a drunken sailor's dick. God only knew what her rear bumper looked like.

"Fuck!" she yelled.

Paris turned down the road and floored it. This was supposed to be her adventure, her freedom. Instead she was cold and wet and pissed off. Grimly

she kept driving. Eventually she'd outrun the storm and then she could stop long enough to figure out what to do. At least nothing could get worse.

Then the engine bucked and died.

Edward Dakota leaned forward in the driver's seat in a futile attempt to get away from The Nightmare in back. The limousine glided smoothly down the highway despite the unexpected rain, and the wipers were up to the task of keeping the windshield clear. If he concentrated on driving, maybe he could ignore The Nightmare. Ed grimaced. Fat chance of that. Because of The Nightmare, this assignment was ending more than a week early, and Ed was paid by the hour. He was already behind on his rent, and the collection letters from Visa had stopped being polite. The latest had been of the "we break thumbs" variety. Maybe he could pick up a few hours as a security guard somewhere, or maybe—

"Can't you go any faster?" The Nightmare demanded.

"I'm sorry, Miss Suzanne," Ed said in a neutral voice. "This car isn't very maneuverable, and it wouldn't be safe in this weather. Regulations."

"Look, buddy, I'm paying a butt-load of money to rent you and this hunk of junk, and I want it to go faster. What's so hard about that? Or are you just

congenitally stupid? I know—your family tree doesn't fork, right?"

Ed clamped his teeth together. "Sorry, ma'am," he replied firmly. "You can complain to my supervisor if you like."

"You think I won't, don't you?" she said. "You think I'll just shut up and forget about it like a good little girl, don't you? Well, I don't take shit from anyone, bud, including a low-life limo driver. Got that?"

Ed didn't answer, though he couldn't help flicking a glance at the rearview mirror. In the backseat sat The Nightmare. She was a fortyish woman with red-blond hair—probably dyed—and a memorably pretty face—probably lifted. Although Caroline Suzanne had acted in several movies, no one remembered any of them. The public—and Ed—always thought of her as Georgia Peters, the beautiful-but-spunky English teacher on the sitcom *School Dazed* in the early eighties. The show still ran in syndication. When Barney had called up with this assignment, Ed had thought it would be kind of fun. He would get to spend a couple weeks in Vegas driving around one of his favorite actresses from when he was a teenager. How cool was that? Unfortunately, the reality, as it so often did, turned out to be pretty sucky.

"I said, 'Got that?'" Caroline Suzanne said.

"Yes, ma'am," Ed replied, but he didn't speed up. Let her complain. Barney would make apologetic noises, tell her Ed would be disciplined, and then hang up the phone with a shrug. Barney only pretended to take shit from the Beverly Hills crowd.

With a put-upon sigh, Miss Suzanne took out her cell phone and punched in a number. She waited impatiently.

"Come on, Harry," she muttered. "Pick up. Pick up the phone."

Ed continued to drive.

The cell phone chittered like a nervous squirrel. Harry Vanderschmitz almost choked, then looked up, startled. His hands and mouth were full of chocolate cake and whipped cream. Who the hell was calling him now?

The phone rang again. It lay nestled in the pocket of his suit jacket, which was currently hanging over a chair across the room. Harry looked down at his cake-filled hands and at the leather cuffs that still locked his ankles to the bedposts.

"Shit," he said, then shrugged and went back to eating. No use wasting perfectly good cake.

"Jesus," Miss Suzanne muttered. "Answer your phone, you fuck."

17

Ed pulled at his tie and glanced into the mirror again. He had curling black hair, dark eyes, and a handsome face with a pointed chin. The Nightmare, phone still in her ear, stared out the tinted passenger window, as if daring something else to go wrong today. A moment later, she apparently got a voice mail prompt.

"Harry, it's me," she said. "We need to talk. I walked off the set. I'm in the hired car and I'm going home early. I know they're going to call you and tell you I'm in breech, but clearly they didn't read my deal. They had me in a room with no tub and sealed windows at a Ramada Inn on the same floor as the fucking A.D.! You tell *me* who's in breech. I'm on my cell right now, but I'm going to try you on your—"

The phone gave a shrill warning tone, then quickly died.

"What the hell?" Miss Suzanne said, and checked the phone display. "Dead? I just charged this thing. God dammit! Hey, I think I have a spare battery up there. Hello? Hey, you!"

Ed suddenly realized The Nightmare was talking to him again. "Excuse me?" he said.

"I think I put a spare battery in the side pocket of my Vuitton. Beside you."

My Vuitton. Ed hated it when people said things

like that, as if saying the designer's name instead of calling it a bag changed the whole thing into a mystic talisman worthy of awe and the occasional reverent prayer. Ed glanced at the seat next to him. Nearly a dozen black leather bags occupied the front passenger seat and floor because Miss Suzanne didn't want her precious luggage to "rattle around in a filthy trunk." All the bags bore a gold "VL" logo.

"Any idea which—?" he began.

"In the duffle. Just look!" she ordered. "It's right on top. Inside pocket on the left."

What was he, an octopus? Outside it continued to rain. Reluctantly, Ed managed to unzip the duffle bag and open the top. It was hard to watch the road and rifle through the bag. Makeup case, sponge bag—did women still use those things?—powder, hairbrush.

"I'm sorry, Miss Suzanne, but I don't see anything. Not even the pocket."

The Nightmare leaned forward impatiently. "You're not looking! Under the flap. There!"

Ed glanced down again with a suppressed sigh but still didn't see it. He looked back at the road.

"Jesus!" he yelped.

"Watch out!" shouted Caroline Suzanne.

* * *

"Four times twelve is. Forty-eight," droned the mechanical voice. "You are correct! Now do. Five times six." Pause. "Five times six is. Thirty. You are correct!"

"Tim, I can't hear the radio," said George York without taking his eyes off the road.

Alice York turned in her seat. Timothy, age ten, was ensconced in the back of the minivan amid a pile of toys and books. At the moment, he was playing with a talking math game.

"Timothy, honey," Alice said, "can you not do that right now? We're trying to hear about the storm."

George took a risk. He removed one hand from the steering wheel and turned up the radio. He managed to get his hand back into place with no perceptible loss of driving control. He gave himself a brief nod of congratulation.

"At the top of the news," said the radio, *"we have a freak storm sweeping through eastern Nevada. Several inches of rain are expected overnight, and flash flood warnings are in effect for the following counties: Clark, Lincoln, Nye, White Pine, Eureka, and Elko. The weather service is cautioning residents and drivers to watch for washed-out roads. In other news—"*

Alice turned the radio off. "Sure you don't want me to drive, George?"

George shook his head. He wore heavy, horn-

rimmed glasses and kept his hair slicked back. Alice, in contrast, was trim and attractive, with vivacious blue eyes and fantastic legs. George's brother was always teasing him that the president of the science club had somehow managed to marry the captain of the cheerleading squad.

"Let's stick to the plan," he said. "I'll get us to Anderson. You take over after we get something to eat. Seventy-six miles. That's an hour and"—he glanced at the speedometer, which lay precisely at fifty-five miles per hour—"twenty-two minutes at this speed."

Alice shrugged and went back to staring out the window at the rain. Tim had apparently found something else to occupy himself with, because he was silent as well. George was glad of it. It took precise, careful order to plan a family trip, and right now the rain was threatening to throw them off schedule. Mother wouldn't like it if they were late for their biannual visit. He could already hear her complaints.

"That's so like you, George," she would say, *"keeping an old lady waiting and worrying while you take the scenic route through the desert. Don't you have any thoughts for* my *feelings?"*

George decided he'd better come up with a backup plan in case they hit an unexpected obstacle,

like a flooded road. Maybe he should have Alice get out the road map and check alternate routes. No, she was no good at that kind of thing. He'd have to do it over dinner in Anderson. Maybe they could buy a second map and give it to Tim, let him work out alternate routes. He probably wouldn't come up with anything usable, but it would keep him occupied for another—

Something went *bam*, and the steering wheel jumped in George's grasp. The van went into a skid. Alice cried out, but George remained calm.

"Turn into the spin," he muttered to himself, and followed his own directions. "Apply the brake with short, firm pumps. Check mirrors."

And the van stopped. George flicked on the emergency flashers and turned in his seat. "Is everyone all right?"

Tim, still in the back seat, looked a little pale, but he flashed a thumbs-up. Alice had both hands on her chest and was breathing hard.

"I'm fine," she said. "Just a little shaken. Thank God for the seat belts."

George, who buckled his belt even in the car wash, tried to peer out the windshield into the night and rain. The driver's side of the van had a definite list to the left.

"I think one of the front tires went flat," he said,

taking a flashlight from its clip under the front seat. "I'll have to check it out."

"I'll help," Alice said, grabbing an umbrella. "Tim, sweetie, you stay in here where it's dry."

They got out of the car and were almost instantly drenched by the downpour. George hadn't figured on needing to keep a slicker within easy reach on a trip through the desert. He made a mental note for next time. No use in complaining about the rain; there was nothing for it, and the soaking served him right for not planning ahead.

The front left tire had indeed gone flat. George was already examining it with the flashlight by the time Alice scurried around the front of the van, holding the tiny, all-but-useless umbrella.

"What happened?" she asked. "We just replaced the tires last month."

In answer, George reached into the wheel arch, pulled something out, and shined the flashlight on it. Black and white stripes gleamed wetly in the beam.

"What is *that?*" Alice demanded.

"I think," George said dubiously, "it's a spike-heeled shoe." He handed it to her, then went to the back of the van for the jack and temp tire. Rain continued to stream over him, spattering his glasses and making it hard to see. His sister often urged him to try contact lenses, but some people devel-

oped eye problems from them, and he refused to take such a risk. If you didn't have your health, Mom always said, you had nothing. Easier to deal with glasses.

It took twenty cold, wet minutes to jack up the van, remove the flat tire, and replace it with the temp. Alice did the best she could to shield him with the umbrella, but she really wasn't much of a help. He considered telling her to go wait in the van, then decided against it. She obviously felt the need to contribute in some way, and it would hurt her feelings if he took that away. George York's Rules of Marriage Number Four: If it makes her happy and doesn't hurt anyone, keep your mouth shut.

The temp tire looked small and pathetic compared to the other three. George got up and wiped his hands on the handkerchief he dug out of one pocket. Few people carried handkerchiefs these days, but George always had one. He remembered reading *The Hobbit* when he was a kid and how Bilbo Baggins had been forced to leave his warm, comfortable hobbit hole without even a pocket handkerchief. The lack had bothered George all the way through the book.

"Why didn't we get a better spare?" Alice said. "And why didn't we just fly out to your mother's?"

"Do you know what an extra radial would cost?"

George said, picking up the jack and heading to the back of the van to put it away. "Let alone airplane tickets."

"There's no need to be defensive."

"The whole point is to save up money so we can put Timmy into the right school. That means we drive instead of flying and we get a temp tire instead of a spare."

To Alice's credit, she didn't mention that if they wanted to save money, they could also skip the hated biannual trip to see George's mother. Instead, she just sighed. "I think the rain is slacking off a little. Do you want a juice?"

"No, thank you." George meticulously stowed the jack in its proper place beneath the floor of the minivan. He replaced the floor cover and was working on restacking the luggage he had shoved aside before he noticed the tire iron lying on the road at his feet. George closed his eyes in irritation. Now he'd have to move all the luggage *again*, pull out the floor cover *again*, and put the tire iron back. Maybe he could, just this once, leave it out and put it back later.

"It's not done until it's done right," Mom admonished in his head, and George sighed. They were already going to be late. May as well put the tire iron away properly. He picked it up. At least the open

rear door made a crude awning, protecting him from the worst of the rain.

A rapping sound from the van's interior caught his attention. Tim was knocking on the side window. Alice, still outside with the umbrella, looked in at him. He smiled and pressed his hand to the glass. Alice pressed her hand over his and smiled back. Tim took his hand away and smiled. Alice took her hand away and smiled. George had to grin himself despite the cold and the rain. He and Alice had only been married for two years, but he felt like Tim had been his son from the beginning, and he liked watching him and Alice together.

Tim pulled at the corners of his mouth with his pinkies and stuck out his tongue. Alice mimicked the gesture. Tim shuffled on knees backward from the window and smiled. Alice took a step back from the window and smiled.

And then she was gone in a flash of light.

George blinked. The van window was dark and empty, as if Alice had simply disappeared. Something rushed past the minivan and there was a screech of tires. Timothy's eyes and mouth opened wide with terror, but no sound emerged from him. Still puzzled, George leaned around the minivan and looked at the road.

A limousine had screeched to a halt in the mid-

dle of the road. Alice's crumpled body lay beneath a speed limit sign. Terror gripped George. Still carrying the tire iron, he flew across the road to Alice's side. In the light of the limousine's headlights, he could see her neck had been laid open. Blood poured onto the gravel at the side of the road. George's heart wrenched and he found it hard to breathe.

"Alice!" he cried. "Oh my God!"

He turned to look at the limousine. It sat motionless and quiet, like a sleeping dragon. George ran to it and pounded on one of the dark windows.

"What have you done?" he screamed. "God, what have you *done?*"

Ed stared, frozen. The woman had stepped out of nowhere. He'd had no time to change course, no time to brake. She'd hit the grill of the limo, rolled up the hood, and bounced off the windshield like a life-sized rag doll. Now she lay in his headlights, broken and bleeding. Ed sat immobile, unable to take in what had just happened. The man—her husband?—continued to beat on Ed's window.

"Jesus fuck," The Nightmare whispered from the backseat.

Her voice broke Ed's stupor. The man left Ed's window and ran back to the woman. Ed fumbled at

the door to follow, but Caroline Suzanne leaned forward and dug her fingers into his shoulder.

"What are you doing, you idiot?" she hissed. "If you help them, you assume responsibility."

Ed pulled away from her. "I hit her. It *is* my responsibility."

"Don't say that," she ordered. "And don't tell them I'm in here. If they get a glimpse of someone famous, they'll smell blood and call the *Inquirer*. Or the *Times.*"

Ed ignored her and got out of the limo. Rain drenched him almost instantly. He darted across the road, his practiced eye taking in the scene at a glance. Road sign, accident victim bleeding on the ground, man—probable husband—kneeling next to her, minivan with temp tire at side of road. The man leaped to his feet as Ed approached. He was holding a tire iron. Ed tensed.

"What have you done?" the man shouted again. "What have you *done?*"

"Let me take a look. I'm trained in first aid," Ed said, keeping an eye on the tire iron, though the man seemed completely unaware he was holding it. Ed squatted cautiously next to the woman. Guilt shoved at him, ate into his stomach. It was his fault she was hurt. But he hadn't hit her on purpose. She had stepped right out in front of him. He'd had no

time to react. Still, the guilt weighed heavy. Maybe if he did something to help her, he wouldn't feel so bad.

Behind him, the man started muttering. "The driver of every motor vehicle who is in any manner involved in an accident originating from the operation of a vehicle . . ."

The wound in her neck looked nasty, but Ed got the impression it looked worse than it was. He checked her pulse and breathing. Both were fast and furious. Her skin was cold and clammy, but that could have been the rain.

"I think she's going into shock," Ed said. "We shouldn't move her until an ambulance arrives, but if we leave her here in the rain, she might get hypothermia." He looked up and was startled to notice a kid standing next to the van. The kid was staring at the woman. Oh, Jesus. The woman had to be the boy's mother. "Uh, you got a sweatshirt or a blanket in the van, mister? And something we can use for a bandage? A T-shirt would work."

". . . shall, within ten days after the accident, report the accident to the . . ."

"What's your name?" Ed interrupted.

The question roused the man. "George. I'm George York. That's my boy, Timothy. My wife's name is Alice. *Why didn't you see her?*"

"George," Ed said gently, "we need an ambulance. Right now. Do you have a cell phone?"

George looked dazed. "No . . . no. You can't have those things around children. Brain cancer . . . microwaves . . ."

"Okay." Ed got to his feet, a little confused by George York's behavior. On the other hand, he couldn't expect rationality from a man whose wife had just been hit by a limousine. Ed's limousine. He reached over and carefully took the tire iron from the other man's unresisting grip. It was cold and heavy. "George, you stay here. Crouch over Alice and keep her dry as best you can. I'll be right back."

Ed trotted over to the limousine. The engine was still purring, and the lights were still on. He touched the door handle just in time to hear the lock snap down. He yanked on the handle and glared at his reflection in the tinted window.

"Open the door, Miss Suzanne!" he yelled. "We need your phone!"

No response. Ed rapped smartly on the window. "I'm not kidding around, Miss Movie Star. That woman might be dying and we need your phone!"

Still no response. Without a word, Ed brought the tire iron around and smashed in the passenger window. Caroline Suzanne squeaked in fright as Ed reached into the car and snatched the phone from her.

"Jesus!" she yelped. "Just take the thing. It's dead, remember? I looked in the duffle bag. There's no battery. You happy, driver-boy?"

Ed Dakota flung the phone back into the limo. It bounced on the leather seats. "Unlock the door, Miss Suzanne," he said in a low, dangerous voice. "I'm adding ambulance driver to my chauffeur's license."

3

Vanna touched the little white rectangle, conjuring up a Q. Larry Washington raised his tequila bottle in salute to the tabletop TV, then splashed a shot into the glass on the desk in front of him. The contestant, a blond college frat boy, stared at the puzzle board and considered his options. Or maybe he was watching Vanna's ass.

"Buy a vowel," Larry said. He was a fortyish man with graying dark hair, a beaky nose, and large, square hands. Silver had crept into his goatee. "Come on, guy—you just caught a Q. A vowel is a gimme."

"*Buy a vowel, guess the puzzle, or spin,*" Pat Sajak urged, in case there was anyone left in America who didn't already know the rules of the game.

"Vowel, dammit," Larry said. "What are you waiting for?"

"*Uh . . .*" said the frat boy. Larry decided that if the

next word out of the kid's mouth was "dude," he would personally drive to Burbank and throttle him. *"I think I'd like to buy a vowel, Pat. Is there a 'U'?"*

"Yes!" Larry whooped, and slammed down the tequila shot. It burned deliciously on the way down. He gleefully wiped his mouth on the sleeve of his ill-fitting manager's shirt and refilled the glass in preparation for the next vowel. Was it stupid to get excited about a *Wheel of Fortune* drinking game? Probably. But the Golden Palm Motel was empty tonight, and with a freak storm going full blast out there, it was likely to remain that way.

Larry sighed and looked around the seedy lobby. The place had fifties mom-and-pop operation written all over it. Fake palm trees, rack of ancient tourist brochures, long, low desk across from the door, wheezy ice machine in the corner, connecting door to room number one. Someone had tried to update the place in the seventies by installing plywood paneling, but it had chipped and cracked over the decades. Larry should probably do something to spiffy the place up. It wasn't as if he had anything else to do—the motel was empty more often than not. He could at least dust the fake palm fronds and order new brochures from the Tourist Bureau.

"Is it 'Jack be nimble, Jack be quick'?" said the frat boy.

"You got it," Pat told him with a wide grin. The audience burst into applause. Larry slammed back another shot of tequila. Fuck the dust. It was raining and it was chilly out. TV drinking games were the way to go on a night like this. He'd do the other stuff later.

The door smashed open. Startled, Larry leaped to his feet. A man wearing heavy glasses burst into the lobby carrying a limp woman in his arms. Blood dripped from a crude bandage at her neck.

"She won't stop bleeding," the man said.

"Jesus," Larry said. "What happened?"

"It was an accident," the man moaned. "There was an accident. May we use your phone?"

Larry snatched up the receiver and punched the button for an outside line. No dial tone. He clicked the flash button several times, listened again. Nothing.

"I'm not getting a line," Larry said. "Shit. It happens sometimes when it rains, though last month some bozo hit the junction box on the telephone pole up the road a piece, and it was two days before—" He realized he was babbling and shut up just as a second man rushed into the lobby carrying a kid. Jesus, how many people had been hurt?

"The phone isn't working, Ed," the first man said to him. "What are we going to do?"

The guy named Ed set the kid down and Larry saw to his relief that the boy didn't seem to be hurt, though he stared at the injured woman with large, round eyes.

"Saint Jude's has twenty-four emergency," Ed said, crossing back toward the door. "Thirty miles east. You stay here, get her in a bed, and keep pressure on the wound. I'll come back with an ambulance." He left.

"My name's George York," the man told Larry in a daze. "We'll need nonsmoking. Alice hates cigarettes."

Outside in the rain, Ed Dakota began pulling bags from the front of the limo and stacking them on the curb. "It's a step down from the Ramada, Miss Suzanne, but it's gonna have to do."

"What are you doing?" Miss Suzanne demanded in a stunned voice. She was still inside the limo. "I am not staying *here*. Put my bags back this instant! Don't forget, driver-boy—you work for me!"

When Ed ignored her, she reached over the seat and grabbed his hand. "Look. I understand that bleeding woman has a medical condition. But so do I! My lung walls have . . . depleted scilia. If I stay here, I will asphyxiate. Do you want that on your hands as well?"

Ed wordlessly opened the passenger door, seized the actress by one wrist, and yanked her bodily from the limo. Her screech of surprise and rage was drowned out by a crack of thunder. Ed slammed the limo door, jumped into the front seat, and sped away in a snarl of wet rubber.

"I'm calling your goddamned supervisor!" Caroline Suzanne shrieked after him, but Ed was already on the road. Wind and rain roared into the back seat through the shattered passenger window. He ignored it and drove as fast as he dared.

The image of Alice York's body flying through the air kept smashing through his mind. She was lying there, bleeding, in a seedy motel room because of him. He leaned forward, as if that would make the limo go faster. The miles flashed by and rain pelted the windshield like it was trying to get in. Maybe he should—

Ed hit the brakes. Jesus, he was an idiot! Why had he left Alice behind? He should have put her into the limo and taken her to the hospital with him. He obviously wasn't thinking clearly. Maybe he was more like George than he thought. Should he go back and get her?

No, he decided. At this point he might as well keep going and bring paramedics back with him.

He punched the accelerator again and had just

gotten the limo back up to a decent speed when a figure leaped out from the side of the road. His heart lurched, and visions of another accident flashed through his brain as he hit the brakes yet again. The limousine started to slide. Ed fought with the wheel as the car fishtailed left, then right. Ed pumped the brakes and wrenched the steering wheel one more time. The figure, a woman with a suitcase and duffle bag, jumped back to the side of the road. At last, the limo halted. Ed swallowed hard and panted as the woman ran up to knock on the glass by Ed's ear. She was pretty, even though her hair was plastered to her head and she was soaked to the skin. Rain ran in small rivers down her red leather jacket. Ed rolled down the window.

"You want me in back or front?" she said without preamble.

"Front," Ed said without thinking.

The woman darted around to the passenger side, flung her bags into the back, and got in next to him. "Thanks for stopping, guy," she said. "I think the rain flooded my engine or something. The little bath my car took didn't help."

"No problem," Ed said vaguely, and started down the road again. Water continued to stream into the broken window in back and Ed wondered if he was going to have to pay water damages as well as reim-

burse Barney for the shattered glass. Jesus, this trip was getting worse and worse.

"My name's Paris," the woman said. "Paris Nevada. You're not a pervert or anything are you?"

"No. You?"

She laughed. "Touché. What happened to your window?"

"Accident. There's a woman at a hotel back there who needs an ambulance, but the phone's out. I'm going for help. My name's Ed Dakota."

"Oh." She paused. "You know . . . you're headed east. That's the direction *I* was going."

"The hospital's this way."

"It's *flooded* this way. It's a dead end."

Ed kept on driving.

"Did you hear what I just said?" Paris asked.

"Yes."

Paris rolled her eyes, but Ed ignored her. She might be wrong, have gotten herself turned around in the dark. The hospital was this way, and he needed to go this way. That's all there was to it.

Paris's eye fell on the little open compartment between the driver and the passenger seats of the limo. It contained several bottles of pills—Ed's—and a couple paperback books. She fished out one of the latter. Ed continued to drive.

"*Being and Nothingness* by Jean-Paul Sartre," Paris

said, and cracked the book open to a well-worn page. *"Everything which exists is born for no reason, carries on through weakness, and dies by accident. What the hell is that?"*

"My life," Ed said.

The little copy machine hummed and exuded a green glow. When the light faded, Larry nimbly opened the top and plucked the driver's license from the glass. He went back to the manager's desk, squinting down at it.

"Caroline Suzanne," he said, and looked up at her. "Hey, didn't you used to be that actress?"

Caroline shot him a withering look for a moment before her features relaxed into a small, forced smile. "Yes."

"Wow," Larry said, awed. "I don't think we've ever had a movie star stay here. I remember watching you when I was a teenager."

"Thanks ever so," Caroline said in a clipped voice that made Larry think of a bear trap slamming shut. Had he said something wrong? To cover his confusion, he snagged a key from the board on the wall behind him. A small tag hung from a short chain. The tag said "8." The good motels these days had keycards and electronic locks, but the Golden Palm had given up trying to be a good motel before key-

cards had even been invented. Larry usually told guests who asked that the Palm was preserving a quaint throwback. Yeah, that was the ticket.

Caroline Suzanne didn't ask. Instead she produced a black wallet and extracted a fifty-dollar bill. The wallet had a gold "LV" stamped on it and looked impressively full. Larry found he couldn't take his eyes from it. How much did an eighties TV actress make, anyway?

"Is that a nice room?" Caroline said doubtfully. "Although I'm leaving soon, I'd still prefer a nice room." She plucked out a twenty and laid it next to the fifty. "Your nicest, if that's possible."

Larry tore his eyes away from the plump, inviting wallet. "Eight's pretty cozy," he said. "Cozy and nice."

"Very well. Could you have someone take my bags up for me? They're outside."

"Uh, I suppose I can bring them in," Larry said. "No charge."

"Thank you." She favored him with a real smile and suddenly Larry was fourteen years old again and wishing Miss Georgia Peters from *School Dazed* was his English teacher instead of bitchy old Mrs. Huff.

"Right this way, Ms. P—Ms. Suzanne," he said. "I'll get your bags and show you to your room."

It felt like some surreal dream. On a rainy night in

the desert, a bleeding woman showed up with her frantic husband, a big-eyed kid, a limo driver, and a famous actress. Any minute now a pink horse would ask him directions to Carnegie Hall.

Larry had already helped the Yorks settle into room four. George York had insisted on doing everything by the book, including handing over his and his wife's driver's licenses for copying despite the blood dripping from Alice's neck, something that weirded Larry out pretty bad. Now Larry was checking in a famous actress and taking her to her room. What was next? Some kind of seduction? Larry imagined himself setting Miss Suzanne's luggage on the floor and turning to see that she was already sliding out of her wet clothes. He would freeze in surprise as she sauntered up to him and put her arms around his neck.

"It's time for your tip," she would say breathily into his ear. Larry felt the beginnings of a hard-on.

"What are you waiting for?" demanded a strident voice. The daydream vanished and Larry was back in the motel office. Miss Suzanne had her hands on her hips. Flushing—had she noticed his crotch?—Larry fled outside.

Near the front door under the overhang that sheltered the unloading area, Larry found a small pile of black leather bags. The storm's intensity had increased, and a solid waterfall cascaded from the

eaves. The parking lot beyond looked like something from an episode of Jacque Cousteau, and the ancient neon sign that proclaimed this the Golden Palm Motel looked distorted from all the rain. The chill air killed Larry's wood, and he wondered uneasily if any of the rooms would flood.

Like most fifties motels, the Golden Palm made a U-shape around a flat parking lot. The office was at the bottom of the U, and the twelve rooms made up one arm of it. The other arm was a separate diner, closed. Behind the U lay a courtyard with a laundry room, a pool house, an empty swimming pool—no longer quite empty, thanks to the rain—and an old Airstream trailer where Larry lived.

A covered sidewalk ran in front of the rooms and the lobby, and the eaves of the building extended over the concrete so guests and workers—or Larry, anyway—could reach their rooms without being flash-fried by harsh Nevada sunlight, though at the moment it served as a shield from the rain. The door to each room opened directly onto the parking lot, and each room had a front window that allowed guests to keep an eye on their cars, if they were so inclined.

Larry gathered up the heavy bags with a slight grunt and turned to see if Caroline was behind him. She was.

"Right this way, ma'am," he said, and led the way to room eight. Rain drummed the tin eaves and thrashed at the parking lot. The backsplash soaked Larry's pant legs and shoes. What did desert animals do in storms like this?

They passed room four, the Yorks' room. The door was shut, and dim light showed through the closed curtains. Larry decided that on his way back, he'd look in on the hurt woman—what was her name? Amanda? Allie? Alice. And George and Tim. He also wondered if she was still bleeding. How long could a human bleed and not die? He had no idea.

The bags were heavy, and it was with relief that Larry reached room eight. When they arrived at the door, Ms. Suzanne hung back expectantly, and Larry realized she expected him to open it for her even though his hands were full. A spark of irritation flashed through him, but he pushed it aside. She was a movie star, and expected a different class of treatment. He set the bags down, fumbled for the key, and opened the room.

The room was done up in tired desert browns and faded yellows. A pair of sagging double beds were the main feature, accompanied by a tiny television on the low bureau. A sink stood just outside the bathroom, which boasted only a rust-stained shower and toilet. No tub. The bathroom had a

small window of pebbled glass. A smell of dust hung in the air.

"Here you are, ma'am," Larry said, setting the bags on a bed.

Caroline Suzanne looked around the room, obviously unimpressed. "Where do those go?" she asked, pointing to a set of doors that stood on the left and right walls.

"Those lead to the rooms on either side," Larry said. "Seven and nine. All the rooms are connected. But you can lock your side."

"Wonderful," she said dryly.

"Ice machine's in the lobby," he said. "Checkout time is noon, though we aren't exactly booked up, so we can probably squeeze you in if you want to stay a little longer."

"I don't think I will," said Caroline Suzanne.

In room four, George York continued to press the bloody towel against his wife's neck as she lay on the bed. His wet clothes clung coldly to his body, but he couldn't leave Alice. It was tempting to pull the towel away and examine the wound, but he had read a little on first aid, and knew that would be against the rules. He had also propped her up with pillows to elevate the site of injury.

"Maintain pressure until the bleeding stops," he

muttered. "When it does, bind the wound tightly with adhesive tape or a bandage. If none is available, use a piece of clean clothing."

A draft of chilly air caught his attention. Tim had opened the door and was staring out into the rain.

"Come in, Timothy," George said. "And close the door. We don't want Mommy to catch a chill."

"How's she doing?" came a new voice. Larry, the motel manager, was standing in the doorway. Tim stepped aside and stared at him.

"I don't know," George admitted. "I think she's still bleeding, but I'm not sure. I'm afraid to lift the bandage and look. Uh, do you suppose you could take over for a moment?"

"Sure," Larry said. He shut the door, took up George's position by the bed, and continued applying pressure to Alice's neck wound.

The Yorks' main luggage was still in the minivan several miles up the road, but George had somehow managed the presence of mind to snatch a couple of overnight bags after bundling Alice into the limousine. George caught up one of them and stepped into the bathroom, where he stripped off his sopping clothes and put on dry ones. It felt much better to be dry and warm. Then he called Tim into the bathroom. The boy had been standing in the rain as well, and was just as wet as George had been. George

helped him out of his wet clothes, dried him off, and put him in new ones. Tim didn't say a word throughout. George dug around in the overnight bag and came up with a pair of pill bottles. He swallowed one pill from each bottle, then extracted a childproof plastic bottle. A spoon was fastened to the side by a rubber band.

"Here, Tim. You need to take your medicine, too," he said. "Then we'll get a book for you to read while I take care of Mommy."

The limo front was drowning in two feet of water. Ed glared at it, then gave the rocker panel a splashing kick. Rain, the stupid fucking rain, bucketed down. "Goddamit! Shit!"

Paris leaned out the passenger window. "I told you."

Ed was about to respond when pure white light blinded him. He flung up a hand to shield his eyes and realized another car was coming up behind the limousine toward the flooded road. Quickly he sloshed to clear pavement and waved wild arms.

"Stop!" he shouted. "You can't get through! There's no way through!"

The car, an elderly Honda Civic, slowed to a halt. Ed squished over to the driver's window and rapped on it. "Hey! Hey in there!"

The window came halfway down. Inside the car Ed could see a young woman, probably early twenties. She had brown hair with blond streaks and a fresh, round face. Beside her sat a guy the same age. His seat was reclined, and he wore dark glasses. Grunge clothes. The woman gave him a jab in the ribs with one elbow. He muttered sleepily.

"I need help," Ed said.

"Lou," said the woman. "Wake *up*."

The man roused himself. "Wha—? Whass goin' on, Ginny?"

"I need a cell phone," Ed said urgently. "Do you have one?"

"Uh . . ." Ginny began.

"Who wants to know?" Lou interrupted, now fully awake.

"Look, there's been an accident and I need a phone. Now!"

Lou peered at Ed over the dark glasses. "Dude, *slow down*. First of all, we don't know who you are. Second of all, I don't see no accident, so—"

Suddenly furious, Ed leaned into the car straight over Ginny and grabbed Lou's collar. Ginny pressed back into her seat with a squeak.

"Jesus!" Lou gasped.

"Listen to me, *dude*," Ed snarled, "I am having a very fucked-up, very wet, very bad fucking day, and

if you or your girl have a phone in your possession—"

"All right! Okay!" Lou said. "We don't have one. Calm down, guy. Let go."

"Fuck." Ed pulled back out of the car and ran a hand over his dripping face. Then he turned his attention to the woman. She was staring up at him uncertainly. "Sorry. Ginny, right? Look, I was going for help after a car accident. A woman was hurt bad. Then we hit this flash flood thing. The limo stalled out and I can't get it started. I need you to give us a lift in the other direction. Can you help us out?"

"It's flooded back that way, too," Ginny said. "Worse than this."

Ed's heart sank. "Oh, Jesus. Are you sure?"

Paris appeared beside him in her open red jacket and white T-shirt. She was soaked, and Ed could see the outline of her breasts beneath the wet shirt. Her jeans clung to her hips, and Ed realized she was one of the sexiest women he had ever seen. She was carrying her bags.

"We're sure," Ginny said.

Lou leaned closer. His gaze drifted rather pointedly over Paris's body. "Only thing between there and here is a shit-bag motel."

"That's where I came from," Ed said.

"We're really up a creek here," Paris added. "And limos don't come equipped with a paddle. Please?"

Ginny looked up at Paris with suspicious eyes. Lou's eyes, on the other hand, were still aimed at Paris's chest. After a second, he tapped Ginny on the shoulder.

"Unlock the doors. Let 'em in."

Ginny turned toward him, her face hard.

"What?" Lou said. "It's pouring out there."

With poor grace, Ginny unlocked the doors. Paris headed for the rear passenger side while Ed dashed back to the limo. He snatched up his own overnight bag, stuffed his paperbacks inside, and sprinted back to the Civic. He climbed into the back and slammed the door as Paris was settling herself inside with her luggage. Lou looked over his head rest at her.

"Hey," he said.

"Hey," Paris said, putting several pounds of pointed disinterest into a single word.

"All set," Ed said. "Let's go." And Ginny put the car into reverse.

The ride back to the motel was silent. Ginny was obviously pissed off, and Lou was just as obviously unaware that anything was wrong. Ed wondered how long it would be before the fireworks began, and he hoped Ginny would wait until they reached the Golden Palm to go ballistic. Paris, for her part,

pulled her jacket closed and stared out into the rain.

When they arrived at the motel, Ed thanked Ginny for the ride and fled to the relative safety of the motel lobby without waiting for Paris. Larry was back at the desk watching TV.

"The phones still out?" Ed asked.

"Yeah." Larry gestured at the parking lot as Paris, Lou, and Ginny entered the lobby. "Where's your limo?"

"Stuck in the run-off two miles from here," Ed said. "The other way's fucked, too. Paris here was stranded. The kids Lou and Ginny gave us a lift. Seems to be a night for meeting new people."

"That one a hooker?" Larry asked with a nod at Paris. "She looks like a hooker."

"Look," Ed said, refusing to stray from the point, "is there another way out of the valley? Can I just cut through or go overland or something?"

Larry shook his head. "You wouldn't make it five hundred feet. Ground's all baked clay and the water's got no place to go. It's one giant lake right now. A four-by-four or a Humvee might have a chance, but that's it."

Ginny wandered over to the ancient brochure rack and idly plucked one from the display. It featured pictures of Native American relics and paint-

ings of a bloody battle. The brochure title read "The Shoshone Burial Ground." She glanced over at Lou, who was, in turn, watching Paris as the woman approached Larry's desk. Ginny's face darkened.

Oh boy, Ed thought. *Oh boy*. "How's Alice?" he asked aloud.

"Still breathing last I checked," Larry said. "I put them in number four."

"You have rooms?" Paris asked, leaning on the counter. Even that simple, lithe movement was sexy.

"I don't rent by the hour, honey," Larry told her.

Oh boy, Ed thought again.

"You're funny," Paris said sweetly. "Are you still serving food or has that pesky health department come by again?"

"Vending machines are outside around the corner," Larry said, talking in Ginny and Lou's direction. "Rooms are warm, dry, and thirty bucks in advance with a copy of your driver's license. Any takers?"

"Excuse me," Paris said, and stepped directly in front of Larry. "I was talking to you. I'd appreciate it if you looked at me."

"I like to look at normal people," Larry retorted.

"I take it you don't own a mirror, then."

"I'll go check on Alice," Ed said, and fled the lobby.

A few minutes later, Tim let him into room four.

George was sitting by his wife. Alice looked pale. Her eyes were closed, her breathing was labored. Tim took up a chair by the window and Ed ruffled the boy's hair as he passed. George had made a crude bandage with a towel and strips of what looked like T-shirt material so he didn't have to keep pressure on her wound.

"She won't wake up," he said. "Can we get her some help?"

"We're a little stuck here, George," Ed said reluctantly. "I don't think we can get out tonight. I'm sorry."

"She keeps shaking."

"She's probably in shock. Let me have a look."

George relinquished his spot and Ed gently peeled back the T-shirt dressing. Blood wept copiously from an ugly gash. Behind him, Tim gasped.

"Did your wife pack a sewing kit?" Ed asked.

"I do all the packing," George said, wringing his hands. "But I didn't pack one of those. It was stupid of me. Next time, I'll . . . I'll know . . ."

He trailed off and Ed knew he was thinking, *If there is a next time.*

Ginny Iana hurried up the walkway, room key in one hand, Shoshone Indian brochure in the other. Behind her, Lou struggled to keep up, hauling their

bags. The sound of the rain on the tin overhang was deafening.

"Hey, Gin," Lou called over the noise. "Slow down!"

Ginny plunged ahead, ignoring him. Lou gave a put-upon sigh and followed. Ahead of them, Paris was already unlocking her own room. Her tight, wet clothes accented a lush figure that probably attracted men like rotting meat attracted flies. Even soaking wet she looked sexier than Ginny did, and Lou was broadcasting this fact to anyone with half a brain. He probably thought she hadn't noticed him adjust his crotch. Twice.

Paris slipped inside her door as Ginny approached her and Lou's room, which was the next one down. Ginny unlocked it with a savage twist of the key and grudgingly held the door open for Lou.

"Six," he said, glancing at the rusty number tacked to the door. "At least we got a good number."

Ginny rolled her eyes and slammed the door the moment Lou cleared the threshold. The abrupt motion kicked the number loose, and the top pivoted down. The six swung back and forth for a few moments, then came to rest upside-down as a number nine.

In the room, Lou dumped the bags on the floor and the two of them glanced around. There was a full-sized bed and a lumpy-looking couch, along

with a sink, bathroom, dresser, TV, nightstand, doors to adjoining rooms.

"Which side do you want?" Lou asked.

"Both sides." Ginny nodded at the couch. "You're over there."

"What?"

"You don't get to stare at the hooker's tits all night and sleep with me."

"What?"

"You sound like a lightbulb, Lou. How many watts you got in you?"

"I wasn't staring at the hooker's tits," Lou protested, voice climbing. "Jesus, I wasn't staring at anything, let alone the hooker's tits."

Ginny stood firm. "I think you were."

"You're wrong," Lou shouted. "You think that just because—"

Footsteps. Lou fell silent, and a knock came at the door. Ginny opened it. Paris stood there.

"Three things," Paris said. "First, thank you so much for rescuing us in the rain. I really do appreciate it. Second, I'm next door in number seven, and these walls are real thin, so if you could keep the 'hooker' comments to a minimum, that would be great. And third, Lou—yes, you were. Good night."

And she left.

Lou looked to Ginny. She looked back, bland and expectant.

"Fuck," he said, and dropped his suitcase on the sofa.

Caroline Suzanne slammed down the dead phone receiver, then angrily shoved the front window open in an attempt to get some air moving through the room. The place smelled like a graveyard. Unfortunately, the open window afforded very little breeze. With a silent snarl, she whipped open the door to the connecting room—room nine—and opened that front window for good measure. That earned her a whole hint of a draft.

Caroline sniffed. It smelled marginally better in room nine, so she tossed her bags in and abandoned room eight altogether. She had, after all, forked out seventy bucks for this pisshole, more than twice the normal rate, and for that she deserved two rooms. Once in her new "suite," she rummaged through her things until she found her cell phone charger, plugged it in by the sink, and connected her phone to it. Then she lit a scented candle, one marked "Stress Relief." A delicate smell of lavender and rosemary filled the air.

The mirror was fly-specked. Caroline examined her face in it, stuck out her tongue, then rolled her

head, trying to calm down. It wasn't easy. She had spent the entire day being pushed around by pushy men. The limo driver. Harry, who was being pushy by ignoring her. Larry, who was being pushy by . . . by . . . well, he was pushy in some way, she was sure. All men were.

In Caroline's younger days, she'd been pushed around by men all the time, and she had accepted it as part of being a lady. Even landing the part in *School Dazed* had been the result of her (male) agent pushing her into the audition. And then she became the plaything of the male-dominated studio. Stand here, walk there, say that line, show this much cleavage, reveal that much leg. Smile, look thoughtful, bat your eyes. Now kiss the assistant principal character. Miss Georgia Peters's popularity had soared, but Caroline had no idea how popular she really was until she snuck into the men's restroom on a dare from a giggling extra. The echoing bathroom was empty. Caroline was looking around for something to swipe in order to prove she had been there when the door opened. Without thinking, Caroline dove into one of the stalls, shut the door, and squatted on the toilet seat so her pumps wouldn't give her presence and gender away. Two sets of footsteps sounded on the tile floor. Her heart beat like a frightened bird. If one of those men out there opened the stall

door, she was dead. Caroline had no idea what happened to a woman who got caught in the men's room, but she had a hazy image of a torn blouse and scornful laughter. Or something. Maybe she should just make a dash for it, hope she could get away before they recognized her.

She heard the sound of two zippers coming down, and suddenly her fear was replaced by curiosity. How did men behave in the bathroom? It must be weird to pee in front of someone else like that. Was it rude to look at the other guy's . . . parts? Maybe they held secret contests about whose was biggest. Or smallest. A wave of giggles swept over her, and she clapped a hand over her mouth.

"You interested in renewing Suzanne's contract for next season?"

The giggles died and Caroline froze. The voice belonged to Scott Dill, one of the directors for *School Dazed*. He liked to poke his head into her dressing room without knocking "just to let you know" that there had been a delay in the shooting schedule or that the air conditioning was back on or some stupid thing. He hadn't caught her undressed yet, but it wasn't for lack of trying. She had finally persuaded a stagehand to install a bolt on the inside of the door.

"Damn right I'm renewing. Hell, she's the best set of tits that ever bounced across a set, and popular as

a free hooker in a football locker room," came the reply. It was Will Consin, the show's producer. "Shit, she'll do whatever you tell her. Best part is, she doesn't even know what she's got, so she comes cheap. Paul Jackson gets half as much screen time and earns twice as much."

"Too bad Jackson's not a dumb blonde, too, though I hear he's a faggot." Scott sniffed hard, then hawked and spat into the urinal. "Fucking head cold."

A slow anger burned in Caroline's chest as the two men emptied their bladders into the urinals. So that was the way of it. Caroline was nothing but a set of cheap tits. She considered bursting out of the stall to confront both men. Wouldn't that be hilarious, watching them spin around with surprised looks on their faces and dribbling dicks in their hands. It would be a perfect metaphor. But she restrained herself. Knowledge was power, especially when other people didn't realize what you knew. Plus she had the feeling they'd find a way to fire her no matter how popular she was. Instead, Caroline crouched quietly on the toilet seat and waited for the men to leave.

The men finished and flushed. Scott sneezed hard. "Hold on—I have to blow my nose."

To Caroline's horror, footsteps approached the stall where she was hiding. If that door opened, it

would all be over. Caroline held her breath, praying he'd choose the next stall over. A jolt of fear slammed into her when Scott's fingers curled over the top of the stall door.

"We should get some lunch before the meeting," Will said. "How about Indian?"

Scott paused. Caroline silently braced herself with one hand and stretched the other toward the stall deadbolt. Her fingertips brushed the shiny chrome but couldn't get a purchase. She leaned forward a little more and managed to get a firmer hold.

"I can't handle curry," Scott said without moving his hand. "Japanese?"

"Sounds good."

With aching slowness, Caroline slid the bolt sideways. What if Scott noticed the vibration? Bit by bit the bolt inched home. Bit by bit it crept closer to locking. Abruptly Scott yanked on the door.

It stayed shut. The bolt had just caught.

"What the hell?" Scott said, and tried again. "Hey! Someone in there?"

Caroline bit her lip. Her arms were getting tired from bracing herself against the stall walls.

"It's probably just broken," Will said. "Hurry up, will you? I'm hungry."

Scott's fingers vanished, and Caroline heard the next stall over open. The scuffed tips of a pair of

white sneakers poked underneath the partition. Caroline's arms began to tremble. Scott pulled some toilet paper from the roll, blew his nose with a juicy snort, and left the stall. A few seconds later, she heard footsteps, followed by the sound of the bathroom door swinging shut.

Caroline waited a few more seconds just to be sure, then climbed off the toilet and bolted from the room. Outside in the hallway, the extra—a young woman named Melissa—snagged her arm.

"Are you okay?" she squeaked. "Like, I totally *died* when those guys walked in there. Did you, like, hide or something? What was it, like, like?"

"Informative," Caroline growled. "Come on—I need to find a phone."

Within the hour, Caroline had fired her agent and hired Paul Jackson's. Within the day, Scott Dill had noticed an abrupt change in her attitude on the set. Within the week, Caroline had a new contract, one with a salary that reflected her current popularity. Caroline had been surprised at how easy it was—and how wonderfully liberating. All she'd had to do was stop being a doormat.

Now, however, she was staring at her reflection in a seedy motel room after walking off another movie set where the director and producer had tried to shaft her. Again. Caroline fumed. You couldn't budge

an inch, not ever. The moment you did, you got a reputation as a pushover. Trouble was, Harry, her manager, didn't understand that.

She needed to work out what to say to him. All shows needed rehearsal, even private ones.

"It's not about money, Harry," she said to the mirror. "It's about respect. It's about work conditions." She paused, as if listening to a reply. "So you're calling me—your client—a liar? I don't know how to say this Harry, but . . . I'm going to have to find new management." Pause. "That's right." Pause. "Because I deserve more. Because I *am* more."

Oh, that was good. "Because I *am* more," she repeated.

A gust of wind blew through the window and extinguished the candle.

4

A disheveled man wanders uncertainly down a long, marble hallway toward a desk. He is a broad man, with a serious face, a goatee, and enormous brown eyes that make him look younger than he is. The desk is occupied by another man, one wearing a bailiff's uniform.

"Can I help you?" the bailiff asks.

"I'm sorry," the disheveled man says, "but I'm here for an emergency hearing in the Rivers case. I'm afraid I'm a bit late due to the weather, and I'm not sure where—that is, I understand it's in the judge's chambers, but I don't know—" He fumbles in his jacket pocket for his wallet and produces his ID. The bailiff examines it.

"It's in the conference room," the bailiff says, rising. "I'll take you. You're fine, by the way—the judge ain't even here yet."

The man follows the bailiff down the corridor, brushing raindrops from his topcoat. "Would you know if the prisoner transport has arrived yet?"

"Sorry, sir. I have no idea."

A few moments later, the bailiff ushers the disheveled man into a dark-paneled conference room lit by fluorescent lights and then withdraws. One long table runs down the center surrounded by wheeled chairs. A stenographer is quietly unfolding her kit in the corner by the rain-spattered window. At the table, three men in suits are engaged in a heated discussion. The disheveled man recognizes Assistant District Attorney Greg Kerrick and Police Detective Drew Valrole. The third man is Marty Greenfruit, defense lawyer. Several damp folders are scattered across the table in front of Detective Valrole.

"Diary or no diary," Valrole is saying, "Malcolm Rivers—your happy client—confessed to the murders. What difference would a set of damn journals make?"

"My happy client," Marty Greenfruit says evenly, "was screwed at the trial, and you both know it. He was denied an insanity plea in a clear attempt to railroad him into—"

"Let's call this supposed hearing what it is, Marty," Assistant D.A. Kerrick interrupts. "It's a Hail Mary."

"Listen, Counselor," Valrole puts in. "Let me tell you what *I* think is insanity. The fact you got this hearing, that's insanity. The fact that you got some specialist to poke around in Malcolm Rivers's head and give him meds, that's insanity. But the idea of that maniac riding around in a van out in that storm, out of communication—that's not insanity. That's just fucking frightening."

"Gentlemen, I can assure you—"

"No, Marty," Kerrick says, "I can assure *you* that at midnight tomorrow, an injection of potassium chloride is going to stop your client's heart, and I'm going to get the best night's sleep I've had in years."

"The families of his victims don't want him medicated, Counselor," Valrole chimes in. "They want that monster fucking *dead*."

"True," says the disheveled man, "but in our rush to satisfy them, we must remember to exterminate the rat, not burn down the house."

All three men turn slowly to look at him.

"Excuse me," Kerrick says, "but who the hell are you?"

"This," says Marty Greenfruit with a tight smile, "is Dr. Charles Mallick. Malcolm Rivers's psychiatrist."

Ed Dakota rummaged through the cabinets and drawers behind the lobby desk with swift efficiency.

Junk. Lots of junk. Old guest ledgers, carbon paper—geez, did they still make that stuff?—basic office supplies, ancient phone messages. But no sewing kits.

Ed straightened, tried to figure out where else to look. A framed picture sitting on a wall shelf caught his eye. An older man with a widow's peak was smiling and holding up an enormous carp on a hook. Ed wondered briefly who the man was. Larry's father, maybe?

Red and blue lights washed across the dimly lit lobby. Ed jerked his head around. A dark sedan pulled past the front windows into the parking lot, police blinkers flashing.

Larry, dressed in an ill-fitting rain slicker and armed with a waterproof flashlight, shined the light beam upward. It was difficult, tracing a phone line in the dark and rain. The wind whipped the wires around, making it hard to keep an eye on them, and cold rain kept washing into his face. But if the phone problem lay close to the motel, maybe he could fix it, get an ambulance down here. Or maybe call in one of those flight-for-life helicopters.

Eerie flashing lights blinked at the entrance to the parking lot. Larry spun around in time to see a police sedan heading his way. His hand jerked, and he almost dropped the flashlight.

"No . . ." he said.

The cop car parked near the lobby door, under the overhang.

Stay calm, Larry told himself. *Nothing to be worried about here, no sirree.* But he couldn't help shooting a glance at the dark diner across the parking lot.

In room six, Ginny finished putting her underwear in the bureau drawer. Lou was peering out the window. For want of anything else to do, Ginny picked up the faded Shoshone Indian brochure and leafed through it. "The Shoshone Burial Ground," it read, and Ginny imagined it as being read by Ian McKellan. Or maybe Patrick Stewart.

In 1865, the American government succumbed to pressure from cattle ranchers and forcibly moved over two hundred Shoshone Indians from their treaty lands to a desert reservation. Unfortunately, the new lands were barren, with no deep springs, wide rivers, or other permanent supplies of water. The first summer after the relocation, a drought struck the land. The meager supply of water dried up, and the Shoshone began to die. According to legend, the last Shoshone to perish was a shaman who declared, "The whites will never find peace on our lands."

In the end, only one Shoshone survived the ordeal. He buried his tribesmen, then disappeared from history.

A large yellow arrow pointed to a red star on a map, indicating the location of the place where the drought victims had been buried. Near as Ginny could tell, it was only a quarter mile away. An image of dry, desiccated voices begging for water flashed through her mind. Soft cries of children mingled with the weeping of their elders beneath a scorching hot sun. Ginny shuddered, set down the brochure, and went to the sink to splash cool water on her face. Abruptly, she straightened with a small gasp. Lou, still looking out the window, made a surprised sound.

"Cops," he reported. "Wonder what's up."

"Did you feel that?" Ginny asked him.

"Feel what?"

Ginny shuddered. "Cold."

Ed came out of the motel office in time to see Larry approach the cop car. Larry's flashlight beam was clearly unsteady. What was going on?

A man in a dark suit opened the door of the sedan so he could step out of it beneath the shelter of the eaves. He was tall and trim, with night-black hair and

startlingly pale blue eyes. Ed noticed a second man in the backseat.

"You the manager?" asked the first man. He was looking at Larry.

"Maybe," Larry said cautiously. He clutched the flashlight and looked ready to break and run. Ed wondered why he was so nervous. It might be nothing. Cops did make some people edgy, even people who were innocent of wrongdoing.

The man flashed a police ID badge. "Officer Samuel Rhodes, Corrections. I'm transporting a convict. The law grants you the right to decline us service, but the roads are flooded and I could use a room."

A muffled cackle emerged from the sedan. Ed barely made out a shadowy form in the backseat.

"Ring around the rosey. A pocket full of posies. Ashes, ashes," chanted a voice. "We all fall *down!*" More cackling. Uncertainty joined the nervousness on Larry's face.

"It's an emergency," Rhodes continued as if nothing had happened.

A thought occurred to Ed. "Hey, you got a radio in your car?"

"Who's this?" Rhodes asked Larry.

"His name's Ed Dakota," Larry said. "He's a limo driver. Had an accident."

"I got a lady in there who's pretty banged up," Ed said. "We could use an ambulance."

Without hesitation Rhodes reached into his car for the radio sending unit. He clicked the button. "Four-four-two requesting medical. Over."

Static from the radio.

"Four-four-two requesting medical," Rhodes repeated. "Over!"

More static. The rain smashed against the eaves like a waterfall on steroids. Rhodes tossed the mike aside.

"I haven't been able to raise anyone for the past hour," he admitted. "I was hoping the problem had cleared up. A heavy electrical storm like this will do that sometimes."

"You got a first aid kit?" Ed persisted. "She's losing blood."

Rhodes glanced at the trunk. "No, sorry. This ain't a patrol car. We don't carry shit like that."

Ed looked to Larry. Larry shook his head. "Don't have one," he said. "Never thought about it."

"How about a needle and thread?" Ed persisted. "It might save her life."

". . . maybe . . ." Larry said hesitantly.

"Maybe what?" Ed demanded. "Jesus, she might *die*. What's wrong with you?"

"Maybe . . . in the diner."

Ed immediately made a move in the diner's direction, but Larry snagged his arm.

"No, I'll get it. The building's locked," he said, then turned to Rhodes. "I'll be right back to get you a key. I'm gonna put you in room nine, okay?" And he hurried off.

Rhodes checked his watch. "Shit."

"What you got back there?" Ed asked, nodding his head toward the sedan.

"Prison transfer."

"Maybe when you get him situated, you can come to room four, take a look at the lady. I could use a second opinion. Your first aid is probably more up-to-date than mine, you being a cop and all."

"Uh, sure," Rhodes said, clearly less than enthusiastic.

Frustration clenched Ed's stomach. Every time he tried to do something to help poor Alice, something else got in the way. Two flooded roads. Dead telephones. A cell with no batteries. A radio that didn't work. A cop who didn't seem to care. And through it all, the goddamned, fucking rain. Ed was abruptly sick of being damp, sick of being stuck in a fleabag, sick of fucking *everything*.

"I'll see you in four," he said, barely keeping the snarl from his voice. "If you can spare some time

from the protecting and the serving, that is." He stomped away.

Samuel Rhodes watched Ed go. Who put a bug up his ass?

"Looks like you're fucked," said a voice from the sedan.

"Shut up."

Robert Maine leaned forward into the light shed by the office. A devious sneer twisted his mouth and a dark luminescence glowed in his panther eyes. Spiky blond hair, sharp chin, lithe build. He *looked* like a killer. "I'm sorry, Officer," he said in a distinctly feminine voice. "Was I speeding?" Then in a cop voice, "Four-four-two, requesting medical. We all fall *down!*"

Rhodes rounded on him, ice in his pale eyes. "Listen, psycho, you've had a very lucky day. Now shut your fucking mouth. When that guy gets back with our key, you are going to get out of this car, calm and compliant, and you are going to walk with me, calm and compliant. If you don't, you will be in shit deep enough to make a fertilizer manufacturer cream his jeans. In other words, you crazy fuck, one wrong move and I will *hurt* you. Understand?"

Robert Maine grinned with perfect white teeth. "Better watch how you talk to me, *Officer*. Given the

circumstances, I'd say you're the one who's in deep shit."

Larry knocked on room four. Ed admitted him, and Larry triumphantly held up a needle and a spool of black thread. "Found some," he said. "I remembered seeing it in the coat closet. Probably put there by a waitress in case her uniform snagged or something."

"You didn't run the diner?" Ed asked, accepting the implements.

Larry shook his head. "It closed before I took over the place and I haven't tried to re-open it. Not with just me here. I keep some food in the fridge, but that's about it."

Alice lay on the bed, quiet and pale. George held her hand. Tim sat in the corner pushing buttons on his math game, though it didn't speak.

"We need to sterilize this stuff," Ed said. "Is the diner stove working so we can boil some water? I should have asked earlier."

Larry's stomach clenched. "I might be able to get the stove going," he said reluctantly. "But it would take a while."

"I have a bottle of alcohol," George volunteered.

"That should do," Ed said, and Larry felt relief. Ed washed his hands thoroughly at the sink, then care-

fully removed the washcloth bandage from Alice's neck. It still oozed blood, and the cloth was soaked with scarlet. Ed's face had a tight look to it, like he was screwing up his courage and didn't want to ask for a drink.

"Either of you know anything about sewing?" he asked hopefully. Both Larry and George shook their heads. "Right. Hand me that plastic cup, then, George. And get me some more washcloths."

Ed poured enough alcohol into the cup to submerge the needle and a length of thread. He dropped them in, then poured more alcohol over Alice's neck. Larry winced in sympathetic pain, but Alice, still unconscious, didn't move. When the wound was cleaned to Ed's satisfaction, he fished the needle and thread from the cup and took a deep breath.

"Here goes, then." He set to work, carefully sliding the needle into Alice's skin and using the thread to draw the edges of the wound together. Twice he asked George to pour more alcohol over the area to remove the oozing blood. Larry watched in mingled fascination and disgust. At last, Ed tied off the final stitch in Alice's neck. Alice hadn't moved once. A row of neat X's marched across the side of her neck.

"I wish I had beige," Larry said. "That would've been better."

"It's fine," Ed said. "Thanks. Can you get her some clean sheets?"

"No problem," Larry said.

George stepped closer to inspect Ed's handiwork. "Where'd you learn to do that?"

"Pretty much in the spot where you're standing," Ed admitted. He accepted a clean washcloth from George, soaked it in the last of the alcohol, and used it as a bandage. It stayed white.

Ed sank into a chair and blew out a heavy sigh. Timothy was at the window, looking into the rain. Ed wet his lips. "Uh . . . it probably isn't my place to say, George, but he hasn't made a sound since the accident. Maybe he . . . you know . . ."

George shook his head. "Oh no. Timothy doesn't talk much. Not since two years ago, when his dad . . ." He made walking motions with his fingers. "Guy had temper problems. I'm Tim's stepfather."

"I better go grab those sheets and get the cop situated," Larry said, and exited without further comment into the watery night. Back at the office, he found Rhodes dragging Maine out of the sedan. Maine's hands were cuffed behind him, and although he didn't exactly hinder Rhodes's efforts, he didn't help, either. At last Rhodes hauled him clear of the car. Maine looked Larry up and down and licked his lips. Larry felt suddenly cold.

"Can he get away?" Larry asked.

"No," Rhodes replied shortly. "Can we get checked in, then?"

"Sure. I'll need a copy of your ID and thirty bucks."

Rhodes hauled Maine into the lobby. Larry followed. The muscles on Maine's back moved like quicksilver, and Larry had a sudden vision of the man slipping the cuffs and going berserk. When cop and convict reached the desk, Larry went around the other side, feeling a little better with a barrier in front of him, however meager.

"ID?" Larry asked.

"I left mine in my cell," Maine purred.

"Shut up," Rhodes said, and passed over his shield. Larry considered demanding a photo ID, then thought the better of it, made a copy of the badge, and returned it. Rhodes handed him thirty dollars. Larry stuffed it into the cash box and plucked key number nine from the board. Back at the desk, Rhodes was admiring the photo on the shelf.

"Big fish," he said.

"Sure is," Larry said, brandishing the key. "Let's go."

"To hell," Maine said.

"Shut up," said Rhodes.

The walk to room nine was the longest of Larry's life. The thunderous rain hid the sound of Maine's

footsteps, and Larry's neck prickled with cold fear. He knew Maine and Rhodes were behind him, but he couldn't hear them, and that made it worse. It was like that Greek story about that guy who went to the underworld to get his wife back. Hades had said he could have her as long as he walked all the way back home without looking behind to see if she was there. Except he couldn't hear her footsteps, so he spun around to make sure—and she disappeared forever. In this case, Larry was afraid if he spun around, Maine would *not* disappear.

"L-a-a-a-r-r-y," Maine said. "Your jacket doesn't fit so good. You want me to get some scissors and fix it for you, Larry?"

Larry swallowed a ball of bile but didn't look back.

"Larry . . . wary . . . bury . . . scary . . . *fairy*," Maine said. "Want to know what else rhymes with—ow!"

"I said, shut *up!*" barked Rhodes.

Number nine was just ahead. Larry had the key out and ready when he reached the door. With a quick twist, he opened the room.

A shriek cut straight through the rain noise. Larry jumped back and Caroline Suzanne scrambled off the bed clutching her bathrobe shut. A paperback book tumbled unheeded to the floor.

"Jesus Christ!" she yelled. "What the hell?"

Larry recovered himself. "Miss Suzanne? What are you doing in here? I put you in eight."

"That . . . that *box* you put me in doesn't deserve a number. And the phones don't work in . . ." She noticed Maine standing just outside the door and trailed off. "My God . . ."

Maine took her in like a morning cigarette. A long, slow smile slid across his face. He half-closed his eyes and whistled. "Nice tits, honey. Who did 'em?"

Caroline Suzanne leaped forward and slammed the door, barely missing Larry's toes. He sighed. "How about room ten?"

"Good idea," Rhodes said.

"She was pretty. I can show her a real fine time. Real fine."

"Shut up, Maine."

Larry led them down to room ten and unlocked it with his master key. "I'll bring your room key in a bit. Sorry the furniture's for shit."

"Yeah," Rhodes observed.

"If you need to cuff him to something, the toilet's bolted down good."

Maine glared at him. "Thanks so much for your assistance. Larry."

"You're welcome," Larry said automatically, then bit his tongue. Rhodes, for his part, hauled Maine toward the bathroom. Maine growled low in his

throat, but Rhodes took no notice. Larry followed, interested now despite himself.

Maine burst into song. "I got stripes, stripes around my shoulders."

The toilet was an old-fashioned one, with a visible pipe connecting the tank to the bowl. Rhodes shoved Maine down to the floor, released the cuffs, and whipped Maine's hands around the pipe. The cuffs were back in place before Maine could react.

"I got chains, chains around my feet," Maine sang. "And them chains, them chains, they're 'bout to drag me down."

Without changing expression, Rhodes smacked Maine's head against the toilet bowl.

"Ow!" Maine complained. "Bastard!"

Rhodes left the bathroom and slammed the door. He turned to Larry, but before he could speak, Maine started howling.

"You're meant to feed me every three hours, Officer! I know my rights!"

"Let's take a look at that lady," Rhodes said.

"I need to stop at the office and get her some clean sheets," Larry said.

"And nothing with fucking mayonnaise!" Maine yelled.

* * *

In room four, Samuel Rhodes helped Ed and Larry change the sheets. Then he examined Alice, checking her stitches, her breathing, and her pulse. Her husband, who introduced himself as George York, watched every move, as did the boy Timothy. Ed quickly explained the situation while Larry leaned against the door.

"Any luck with radio?" Ed asked as Rhodes finished.

Rhodes shook his head. "I'll try again in a minute. Good stitch job. Her pulse is shallow but steady. I'd say we should just keep her comfortable." He moved toward the door.

"Hey," Ed said, "maybe we should do shifts on the radio, try every few minutes. If that's all right."

"No," Rhodes said with a stiff smile. "It's not all right. I can manage." And he left before Ed could comment further.

Outside, rain, endless rain, continued to fall. The air carried a definite chill, and Rhodes pulled his suit jacket closer. His stomach rumbled. Hadn't he passed a set of vending machines on the way to the room? He backtracked and found a Pepsi machine beside a snack machine. A woman in a red leather jacket was kneeling in front of the latter, her arm stuck up inside it. Rhodes automatically took her in. Tight pants, nice ass. A moment later, she

seemed to sense he was there and she twisted around.

"You gonna bust me, Officer?" she asked.

He blinked. "Now how'd you do that?"

"Do what?"

"Know I'm a cop."

"New laces in old leather."

"What?"

"Your shoes, Officer O'Malley."

He automatically glanced down. The laces were almost new, the shoes obviously old. "Oh. Oh shit. Yeah."

The woman smiled and turned back to the machine. Rhodes edged closer.

"Cheetos for dinner?" he said. "That ain't right."

She shoved her arm another inch into the machine, but her questing fingers didn't touch anything. "You got a better idea?"

Sure do, he thought with a glance at her chest. "I worked mess in the service. Maybe that diner's open. I could whip something together. For both of us."

The woman pulled her arm from the machine and sighed. "You got change for two singles? This stupid machine doesn't take bills."

"I can make that."

The woman gave him a pair of ones. He dug a handful of change from his pocket and dropped

eight quarters one by one into her ivory palm. His eyes met hers and locked for a moment. She was sexy, in a confident, feminine way that Rhodes found enticing, even intoxicating.

"You got a name?" he asked, a husky note in his voice.

The woman turned back to the machine, shoved some quarters in, and pressed buttons. Treats fell. "Paris."

"Paris?" Rhodes smiled his most charming smile. "I've never been."

She scooped up the snacks and turned for the walkway. "You ain't going tonight, either." And then she was gone.

The Golden Palm Motel, lonely in the pouring rain. Thunder prowled the distance like a dragon and the mercury lights in the parking lot had to work at holding back the dark.

Room 4: George York watched his wife Alice with a fearful look on his face. Her breathing was steady but weak. Timothy was sound asleep, tucked in on the sofa. Ed stood in the connecting door to room three, watching.

"Please be strong, Alice," George said gently. "Please don't leave me. Don't leave Timothy. We need you, Alice."

Room 3: Ed Dakota closed the connecting door to room four. His overnight bag sat on the bed, and he opened it. He pulled out his books, and the dim light glinted off the metal barrel of a snub-nosed pistol beneath them. Ed ignored the gun and took out a blue plastic box, which he opened. Inside sat rows of smaller boxes, carefully arranged for each day of the week. He snatched Wednesday's dose and tossed it back with a glass of water from the sink. After a moment's consideration of the night so far, he tossed back Thursday's dose as well.

Office: Larry Washington sat at his desk and swept the drinking game paraphernalia into the trash. Glass crashed and clattered. He looked up and saw the photograph of the older man with a widow's peak and a big carp. In one swift motion, he snatched the picture from the shelf, dropped it into a file drawer, and slammed the drawer shut. Then he locked his green money box. Vanna White was conspicuously absent from the television.

Room 7: Paris Nevada dropped her vending machine bounty on the bed. After checking that no one could see through the drapes, she opened the wardrobe, revealing her suitcase and duffle bag on the cabinet floor. She checked in the storage pocket underneath her clothes and pulled out a large wad of cash. Thelma and Louise money, a healthy amount

of it. Satisfied everything was still there, she dropped her jacket over the case, shut the wardrobe, and crossed back to the bed and her junk food dinner. Her shadow followed on the worn carpet and slid unnoticed under the door to the next room.

Room 6: Ginny Iana, curled up on the sagging bed, looked at Lou, stretched out on the lumpy sofa. Paris Nevada's shadow slipped under the crack of the connecting door as she walked across her next-door room. Was Lou asleep? Or watching Paris's shadow and thinking about her lush, wet body?

"Lou?" Ginny said softly. "Lou, you awake?"

Lou didn't respond.

Room 10: Samuel Rhodes rinsed his face in the room sink, pushed back his night-black hair, and stared at his own eyes in the mirror. Smiled at himself. He was still damned good-looking. Okay, so the bitch had shot him down. Her loss.

"Why don't ya love me like you used to do?" Maine sang from the bathroom. "Why do ya treat me like a worn-out shoe?"

Rhodes's eyes darkened, but he remained silent. Time to get some air. Although he wasn't particularly cold, he reached for his jacket. There was a small, bloody puncture on the back of his shirt, one he didn't feel like explaining. Jacket safely in place, he opened the door to take in the wind and the rain.

Bathroom: Robert Maine sat on the cold linoleum floor. Empty bags of Cheetos lay scattered about him. It had been a challenge to eat them in handcuffs. Maine shifted position as he heard the door slam, then he pulled at the cuffs fastened around the toilet pipe. The pipe was just a little loose, and the handcuff chain made it rattle. Maine's lithe back muscles bunched and shifted. *Clink clink clink . . .*

Room 9: Caroline Suzanne's cell phone beeped, indicating it was charged again. With a weary sigh, she picked it up to dial, then noticed the display read "No Signal."

"For crying out loud," she groaned. "Roaming coverage, my ass."

She wandered around the room like a prospector with a Geiger counter, phone in front of her, trying to get a signal. Nothing. She opened the front door. The sound of the rain exploded into full volume and a burst of chill air washed over her. A single bar of signal strength flickered on the display and just as quickly vanished. Caroline stuck her arm further outside.

"Come on, little bar," she cooed at it. "There you go!"

The bar came back to life, stayed active for a full second, and disappeared again. Caroline chewed the inside of one cheek and stared at the cold rain, con-

sidering options. She didn't have a raincoat or a slicker, and the wastebaskets didn't have trash bags in them, even if they had been big enough. Her gray-eyed gaze wandered around the motel room and fell on the bathroom. A smile spread across her face.

Five minutes later, Caroline Suzanne stood outside in the deluge, a transparent shower curtain draped over her like the shroud of a latex ghost. The noise of the rain was deafening under the makeshift umbrella as Caroline followed her phone, trying to find a signal. The best she could do was one bar. She tried to look through the plastic curtain, but the torrent made it almost impossible to see. Her feet took her past the motel pool and out a gate as she stared down at the phone's signal indicator. It flickered a little more strongly.

"Oh yeah," she muttered. "Here we go."

Caroline kept going. Darkness closed in around her as she got further and further from the lights of the motel. Slippery clay made footing treacherous and dirtied Caroline's shoes. Rain poured ceaselessly over her in a cascade of noise and water. Part of the noise, however, sounded rhythmic—a regular, tapping, squishy noise. Footsteps? Caroline was about to turn around when the phone beeped. She looked down at it, took another two steps forward, and heard it beep again.

"Yes!" she said. It was amazing how such a small thing could make you feel triumphant. She hit speed dial. Her manager was number two, her agent was number one. She wondered if either of them knew it or would get the joke if they did.

Silence on the receiver, then a click and the welcome burr of a ring tone. Caroline's triumph faded, replaced by impatience. "Come on, Harry. Pick up!" A second ring tone, then a third.

Something slammed into her from behind. The phone flew from Caroline's hand and she landed facedown on the ground beneath the curtain. A weight came down hard on her back. Caroline tried to scream, but the plastic curtain stopped her mouth and nose. Terror crashed over her as a pair of hard hands grabbed her neck. Caroline tried to roll away, push up, fight back, but the slick curtain and the slippery clay prevented her. The plastic was as good as a net. The hands let go of her neck, grabbed the curtain, pulled it tighter. Caroline couldn't breathe. She clawed and bit as her chest grew heavy. Her lungs begged for air, screamed for it. Her heart pounded hard in her head. Black spots danced in her vision.

And then the curtain was gone. So was the weight from her back. Caroline sucked in huge breaths of cold, wet air as she rolled away from her assailant.

Mud plastered her skin and clothes. She tried to get to her knees, slipped on the clay, tried again, managed it. She flung a wild glance around her but saw no one in the dark and rain.

get to your feet try to run go for help god who is it where is he where is

A pair of feet stepped onto the clay in front of her. Caroline looked up. Something swung down at her, and she had time for one, short scream.

5

Ed Dakota bolted awake and glanced wildly around the room. A dark figure stood in the connecting room door. Ed's hand automatically snaked toward the gun in his overnight bag on the floor. He touched cold metal and started to yank the pistol into open air.

"Did you hear that?" said George York from the doorway.

Ed relaxed his hand and let the gun fall back into the bag. "A scream."

"Maybe we should check it out."

Ed, who slept in sweats, shoved his feet into his shoes and rushed for the door, not looking to see if George was behind him. Outside, water poured off the eaves, the gutters, the roofline, forming a translucent veil and collecting in black Rorschach puddles in the parking lot. Larry appeared at the other end of

the courtyard, holding a baseball bat. He looked over at Ed and sprinted toward him.

"You hear that?" he called as he ran.

"Yeah."

Ed crossed to room six and banged on the door. The loose number swung gently back and forth. "Ginny! Lou! You guys okay in there? We heard a scream. Hello?"

The door opened a crack, revealing a sleepy brown eye. "Wassgonon?" Lou asked.

"You all right?" Ed said.

"Yeah. Why?"

"Where's Ginny?"

"I'm here," came her voice from the darkness inside the room.

"Keep your door locked," Ed said, and moved down to number seven. He pounded hard as Larry came up behind him, still armed with the baseball bat. "Paris? You in there?"

No answer. Ed pounded again. "Paris!"

Still nothing. Ed turned to Larry. "You got your master?"

Larry pulled a jingling wad of keys from his pocket, selected one with shaking fingers, and opened the room. When he tried to push his way in, Ed held up a hand and stopped him. Cautiously, Ed peered inside. The lights were on, the room empty. A

faint sound came from the bathroom. Larry suddenly ran past Ed toward the bathroom door.

"Larry!" Ed hissed. "Wait!"

Larry flung the bathroom door open, baseball bat raised. Swearing, Ed scrambled to get behind him.

Paris stared up at the two men, speechless. She was sitting on the toilet, jeans around her ankles, a pair of headphones in her ears. Ed heard tinny music. Larry was too startled to move.

After a moment, Paris said, "I wanna hear beeping when you *back the fuck out of here.*"

Face flaming, Larry fled, still clutching his bat. Ed slammed the bathroom door, shouted, "Sorry-we-heard-a-scream," and followed him.

When Ed reached the safety of the eaves, Larry was already knocking on room number nine. Ed hustled over and his foot came down on something hard. He backed up a step to see what it was.

"Miss Suzanne?" Larry hollered over the rain.

No reply. Ed picked up a rounded piece of plastic from the sidewalk. It looked like a shower curtain ring. Another one lay on the cement further down the walkway. Ed showed it to Larry.

"What the hell is that doing out here?" Larry asked, then pounded on the door again, this time with the bat. "Miss Suzanne!"

Ed jerked his head at the door. "What are the odds

of two women with Walkmans sitting on the potty?"

Larry nodded and unlocked the room. Again, the place was deserted. Ed checked the bathroom. The shower curtain rod hung empty. No sign of Caroline Suzanne. Larry and Ed raced out of room nine and almost barreled into Rhodes, who jumped back just in time to avoid being trampled.

"What's going on?" Rhodes demanded.

"The actress I was driving—she's gone," Ed said. "I heard this . . . scream. Miss Suzanne's shower curtain is missing."

"Maybe she moved again," Rhodes said doubtfully.

"And took the shower curtain with her?" Ed said.

"Which rooms are empty?" Rhodes asked.

"One, two, five, and eleven," Larry said.

"I found this in front of the door," Ed said, holding up the curtain ring. "And there's another one over there. We should follow them."

"I'll stay here and lock up," Larry said.

Ed and Rhodes trotted up the walkway in the chill night. The mercury lamps in the parking lot gave them a cold light to see by. Another shower curtain ring, and then another led them toward the pool like a trail of bread crumbs. Ed's mind was trying to move, but all he could come up with were questions. What the hell was Caroline Suzanne doing with a shower curtain in the middle of the night? Maybe

she was using it as a raincoat. But why come out here in the first place? And had someone attacked her?

The trail of shower curtain rings led past the pool and through a little gate that opened onto the empty, wet desert. Ed and Rhodes looked at it from the shelter of the eaves. Something tugged at the edges of Ed's mind, but he couldn't quite say what it was.

"You think she's out there?" Rhodes asked, clearly steeling himself to run out into the rain.

"Only one way to—hold it." Ed cocked his head. A vague rhythmic noise just touched his hearing. The sound faded in and out of the noise made by the rain, which was why Ed hadn't noticed it right away. "What is that?"

Rhodes listened, shrugged. Ed concentrated. Now that he was listening for it, he could hear the sound more clearly. It was a dull, metallic thudding noise.

Bang-thud. Bang-thud.

It seemed to be coming from someplace just off the pool. Ed followed the sound to an open doorway that led into darkness. Rhodes stayed behind him.

Bang-thud. Bang-thud.

Ed wished desperately for a flashlight, a candle. Even a match. The room beyond was black as a barrow-mound. Ed's heart pounded.

Bang-thud. Bang-thud.

"What the hell *is* that?" Rhodes muttered.

Ed reached a hand into the room, ready to snatch it back if he touched something—or something touched him. He felt around the inside wall until his fingers found a light switch. Hurriedly he flicked it on.

Laundry room. Four coin-operated washing machines—two to the right and two to the left—sat just inside the doorway against opposite walls. Four pairs of stacked dryers—two pairs to the right and two pairs to the left—sat toward the back. The place smelled of laundry soap and fabric softener. All eight dryers were running, but no one was present. Someone, however, had obviously been here earlier.

Bang-thud. Bang-thud.

Goosebumps rose on Ed's arms. When he was six, his older brother Patrick had put their new puppy in the dryer and turned it on. The awful thudding noise that resulted was exactly the noise Ed was hearing now. Caroline Suzanne had screamed, and her trail of curtain rings ran in this general direction. What was thudding in the dryer?

Bang-thud. Bang-thud.

Mouth dry, tension humming in his veins, Ed moved slowly into the laundry room. Rhodes stayed in the doorway. The rain was so loud on the roof that Ed couldn't tell which dryer was making the noise. His hands were cold.

Bang-thud. Bang-thud.

Ed yanked open the first top dryer door. The drum drifted to a stop. Empty.

Bang-thud. Bang-thud.

Ed opened the second dryer, the one beneath the first. Nothing.

Bang-thud. Bang-thud.

A hand landed on his shoulder. Ed yelped, and twisted like a cat. Rhodes was standing behind him.

"Just me," he said. "Christ, you're jumpy. I'm thinking this is a waste of time. The woman isn't in here."

Bang-thud. Bang-thud.

"You go look," Ed said. "I'll catch up." He opened the third dryer, a top unit.

The banging stopped. Ed stared inside, then laughed. He reached into the dryer, pulled out a pair of sneakers, and shut the door. Beside him, Rhodes snorted.

"Told you," Rhodes said, heading for the door. "Let's—"

A pair of wide eyes gazed at Ed, reflected in the circular glass of the sneaker dryer door. Someone was standing behind him. He spun around.

Caroline Suzanne's decapitated head stared at him from inside the opposite dryer.

"Shit," Ed said softly just as Larry appeared in the

doorway with his baseball bat. Rhodes, who was near the washing machines, turned and came back. Both of them froze when they saw what Ed was looking at.

"Oh, Jesus," Larry moaned. "Jesus Mother of God. That's her head. It's her fucking head."

"Yeah," Ed said.

"Oh, man. Oh, God. I'm gonna barf. I'm gonna—" Larry stopped, noticing Ed's stony expression. "You know, you're real calm for a guy who's staring at a human head."

Ed considered this. "She wasn't that human," he said.

Rhodes opened the dryer and reached inside. The smell of blood mixed with the scent of laundry soap. Quick as lightning, Ed's hand snapped out and grabbed Rhodes by the wrist.

"What the hell are you doing?" Ed said.

Rhodes remained calm. "There's something else in there."

"Oh, Jesus," Larry said. "Oh, Jesus."

Ed glanced around, snatched up a dryer sheet. "Here, use this."

"What are you, some kind of cop?" Larry asked. He looked green.

Rhodes locked eyes with Ed for a long moment.

"Not any more," Ed replied.

Rhodes accepted the dryer sheet and used it to pluck an object from the dryer. It clinked against the metal cradle. Caroline Suzanne's head continued to stare emptily at nothing. Her dead eyes had glazed over and her features were gray and slack. The base of her neck had been cut cleanly. A chunk of her hair had been torn out, revealing pale scalp beneath. Blood glistened wetly on the dryer drum. Ed looked over Rhodes's shoulder at the thing he had taken from the dryer. It was a motel room key. The number on the crimson-soaked tag was just legible—number ten.

"Oh, man," Larry moaned. "That is fucked up."

"Was she in room ten?" Ed asked. He had been trying to fetch an ambulance when Larry had given out room assignments.

Larry shook his head and pointed to Rhodes. "*They* are."

"Where is your guy?" Ed asked sharply.

"Cuffed to the toilet," Rhodes said, but he looked uneasy.

As they ran back up the walkway, Rhodes and Ed in the lead, Larry bringing up the rear, Paris poked her head out of room seven.

"What's going on?" she asked.

"Stay inside," Rhodes said without slowing down. "Lock your door."

"What was he in for?" Ed asked, still running.

"I'm not at liberty to—"

"Bullshit! What did he do?"

They passed the windows to room ten. It was dark inside. Rhodes drew a gun from a shoulder holster.

"Is he some kind of killer?" Ed persisted. Rhodes shot him a cold look, and Ed felt the answer hit his bowels like an icy enema. "Ah, shit. Shee-*it*. On three, then. One . . . two . . . three!"

They burst into room ten. Darkness. Ed slapped the wall switch and the lights burst on. Empty. Rhodes pointed his gun in various directions, then crossed silently to the bathroom door, which was shut tight. In one strong motion, he kicked it open.

"God dammit," he snarled, and lowered the gun. Ed ran over to see as Larry, huffing and puffing, entered. Ed peered into the bathroom.

Empty. Water puddled on the floor from a pipe that had been pulled away from the toilet. The bathroom window was open, letting in the rain. Larry came up behind Ed, open-mouthed.

"Oh, Momma," he whispered.

Room three swirled with people. Alice York lay unconscious on the bed with George and Tim keeping watch beside her. Paris, Ginny, and Lou paced madly about, getting in each other's way and cursing at each other. Ed and Larry stayed by the door, the

latter clutching his bat with white fingers. Only Samuel Rhodes was missing. Ed wore his jacket to cover the fact that he had strapped his gun and holster underneath it. Several people in the room were talking all at once.

"—the *fuck* is going—"

"—someone *please* tell me what—"

"—second time I've been woken up tonight. Can't a guy get any—"

Ed put two fingers in his mouth and cut loose with an ear-piercing whistle. The room fell silent. "Okay, listen up, folks," he said. "There was an incident tonight."

"That's police talk," Larry said to Ginny, "for someone getting their head—"

"Caroline Suzanne was murdered," Ed finished.

Ginny sank to a chair. "Oh, Jesus."

"My God," said George.

"Who's Caroline Suzanne?" Paris demanded.

"The actress I was driving," Ed said.

"Where did this happen?" George asked.

"We don't know exactly," Ed replied, keeping his voice calm. "We can't find her body."

"Not all of it, anyway," Larry muttered.

"Look, as long as we stay calm, we'll be fine," Ed said. "Officer Rhodes, who's outside right now, was transporting a convict—"

"Who escaped," Larry interrupted, and Ed wanted to sock him. "He fucking *escaped*."

"*What?*" Ginny said.

Paris rounded on Larry. "Why don't you shut the hell up and let Ed here talk?"

"This is my place, 'ho," Larry said belligerently. "I'll say what I goddam please!"

"Hey, hey," Ed said, holding up his hands. "There's no need for—"

"We need to leave," Ginny said. "Now." She crossed toward the door. Lou caught her arm.

"Baby, did you hear what the man said? We're safe here. There's a policeman."

"Two of 'em," Larry said.

Paris turned her eyes on Ed, who seriously wanted to clock Larry with a heavy object. Like that stupid baseball bat. "You're a cop?" she asked.

"Was," Ed growled. "Shut up, Larry."

A knock came at the door. Everyone jumped. Larry raised his bat. Ed opened the door a crack, then admitted Rhodes, who was armed with a set of convict restraints. Ginny stepped backward, then abruptly burst into hysterical tears. Timothy stared at her, breathing fast.

"He's going to kill us," Ginny wailed. "Oh, Jesus, he's going to kill us."

Ed shot Lou a look. He returned it helplessly. Ed

cocked his head at Ginny, but Lou just looked blank. Ed silently cursed him for an idiot.

"Put your arm around your girlfriend, Lou," he said. He didn't say, *What kind of a man are you, anyway?* though it was on the tip of his tongue.

Lou obeyed with stiff, uncertain movements, as if he'd never held a woman before. "She's not my girlfriend," he said softly. "She's my wife."

His words didn't appear to comfort Ginny, who continued to sob.

"Everyone just stay in this room," Ed said, and turned to Rhodes. "Let's go."

Rhodes nodded and left with Ed right behind him. Before they could close the door, however, Paris snagged Ed's arm.

"Can you take him with you?" she asked with a sharp gesture at Larry.

"What's your problem with him?" Rhodes said.

Paris's eyes went hard. "I'm not staying here if he is."

Ed sighed and leaned back into the room. "Hey, Larry. Come with us, will you? And bring the bat."

"Why?" Larry demanded in a quarrelsome tone. "Because *she* says so? Because some cheap hooker has a problem with me?"

"Come on," Ed said. "You know the place. We don't."

"I am not trained in the hunting of convicts," Larry said in a voice that reminded Ed of Caroline Suzanne. "And I do not take orders from professional sluts."

"Not unless you're paying for it," Paris said icily. She and Larry locked eyes for a long moment. Paris looked calm, but something about her expression sent an ice cube up Ed's back.

"Fuck you," Larry said. "If you need me, I'll be in the office." And he stormed out.

"What's his deal?" Rhodes asked.

"The closet door is shut," Paris said.

"Huh?" Rhodes said.

"I know the type," Paris said. "He keeps a stack of porn by the hand lotion in his bedroom, and his address book is full of call girl numbers. Meanwhile, he's remembering that time he and a fishing buddy had three shots too many and got it on. In the morning they called it an aberration and pretended it never happened. Ha! Ten'll get you twenty he arranged circle jerks in high school, too."

"Just go back into the room and wait for us, okay?" Ed said.

"Yeah, fine. Just be careful," she said, and obeyed.

"A real piece," Rhodes said admiringly.

"Yeah," Ed said, unsure why it bugged him to hear Rhodes say such a thing. "Let's get moving."

A minute later, Ed and Rhodes were conferring under the shelter of the overhang in front of the motel lobby. The rain increased its intensity, and visibility beyond the eaves was next to zero.

"He can't get far." Rhodes had to almost yell over the noise of drumming water. "Not in this."

"What exactly are we chasing here, Rhodes?" Ed asked.

Rhodes hesitated. "Multiple homicide. Total psycho."

Ed closed his eyes with a heavy sigh. A homicidal maniac somewhere out there in the dark and rain. No roads, no phones, and a woman's head in a dryer. Who would he go for next? Alice? Little Timothy? Slowly, deliberately, Ed drew his gun. Rhodes gave him an appraising look with his oddly pale eyes.

"How about we circle 'round," Ed said. "Meet me on the other side. We'll see if he's close."

"On your mark, get set, go," Rhodes said.

Adrenaline singing in his veins, Ed dashed down the walkway, trying to look in all directions at once. Rhodes's footsteps headed in the opposite direction and faded fast. Ed's gun was heavy in his hand, an accustomed weight. He followed the walkway to the end, expecting Maine to leap out at him at any moment. His shoes tapped the sidewalk. Endless rain rushed down the gutters and eaves, and he could

barely see the parking lot. He hated not being able to see. It felt like Maine could reach through the veil of water and grab Ed's throat anytime he liked.

Ed reached the end of the walkway. The eaves continued around the edge of the building, and it was dark out back where the pool was. Less water gushed down this side of the roof and the veil had thinned. Cracked and peeling faces of a family watched Ed's every move from a billboard across the street. Happy, faded family. Mom, Dad, Bro, and Sis, all smiling and absolutely thrilled to visit Nevada. They even had a dog. Shit. Why the hell did billboard guys put up that kind of crap? No one had a family like that. Mom always drank and Dad had a boyfriend on the side while Sis dropped heroin and Bro set fires. God only knew what the dog was up to.

Ed flattened himself against the side of the motel. His breath came in little puffs. Gun low, he counted to three, and flung himself around the corner.

Nothing. Just darkness and the outline of Larry's trailer ahead of him. A dim glow as if from a nightlight burned behind its blinds. Ed thought a moment. The trailer would be a good place to hide. It was away from the motel, out of the rain, and easy to get to. Keeping low, Ed scuttled out into the open darkness. Rain instantly drenched him. Ignoring the discomfort, he zigzagged to the short steps leading

up to the trailer entrance. A tiny tin overhang gave him a bit of shelter, though he was so wet that by now it hardly mattered. Next to the trailer was some kind of vehicle—a truck?—underneath a dingy blue tarp.

Ed pressed an ear to the trailer door. All he heard was pounding rain. Raising his pistol with one hand, Ed gently tried the knob with the other. It turned easily. Breath held tight in his lungs, Ed eased the door open and slipped inside.

The smell almost made him gag. Stale air, rotting garbage, old food. Rain pounded on the metal loud enough to be deafening, as if someone were emptying a dump truck of marbles over the roof. Ed's eyes, already used to the dim light, picked out quick details. The place was narrow, barely ten feet wide. Ed was standing in the kitchen. Dirty dishes made precarious, smelly piles in the sink. The trash can was filled fit to burst, and more garbage lay scattered on the floor. Several half-empty bottles of liquor sat on the table. The linoleum was filthy, and the water dripping off Ed was probably creating mud.

Ed moved quietly into the living room, where the night-light burned in a socket near the floor. The carpet had a crunchy feel to it. More dishes were scattered across the coffee table, along with a copy of *TV Guide*. His neck itched, as if someone were watching

him. He spun. No one. He was being stupid. Maine probably wasn't here. Still, it would be stupider not to check everything.

A claustrophobic hallway led past a bathroom that was terrifying in its own right. Ed forced himself to check behind the stained shower curtain. Again, no one. It occurred to him that Caroline Suzanne's shower curtain was still missing. Was it worth tracking down? Something to think about later, maybe.

Next Ed poked his head into the bedroom. Clothes were scattered everywhere, as if the dresser had exploded. Full-sized bed, closet, nightstand, digital clock, impressive collection of fishing tackle on the wall. Ed waded through the lake of clothes, flung the closet door open, and trained his pistol inside. Nothing. Next he dropped to the floor and pointed his pistol under the bed. Still nothing. Ed straightened and holstered his pistol. He had stopped dripping, but was still wet through.

On the rumpled bed, a porn magazine had been thrown open to a scene with a man and three women. Beside it sat a phone book left open to a page of massage parlors with photos of women. *Why don't you pay us a visit?* one ad proclaimed. *I'd love to see you come.* Someone had scribbled out several female faces with a black marker. Ed couldn't sup-

press a grin. Looked like Paris knew her stuff. But what the hell was the scribbling about?

Ed examined the tackle collection. Lots of strange fishing stuff—hooks in all sizes, poles, reels. Knives. Ed took a closer look. The knives came in all shapes and sizes. Tiny, huge, curved, straight, serrated, smooth.

And the biggest sheath was empty.

Paris looked at Ginny, who huddled in the corner of room three with her arms wrapped around her knees. She was rocking herself and alternated between hiding her eyes and trying to see in all directions at once. Paris didn't know whether to feel sorry for her or annoyed at her. Lou seemed to be completely at a loss about what to do. Paris mentally rolled her eyes. If you couldn't kill it, eat it, or fuck it, men didn't know what the hell to do with it. The others sat, stood, or lay scattered around the room in various stages of unrest.

"So is that where you live full time?" Lou said. "In Vegas?"

It took Paris a moment to realize he was talking to her. She looked at him and was mildly surprised to see he was looking at her face and not her chest.

"Used to," she said. "Not anymore."

"What does that mean?"

The guy had the conversational skills of a goat. "It means I don't live there anymore."

Timothy, who was seated on the bed, reached up to pluck at the leg of George's trousers. George looked down at him.

"Go ahead, Tim," he said. "I'll be right here."

Tim shook his head emphatically.

"Okay," George sighed. "I'll stand guard." He shot the others a glance. "The toilet's plugged in our room. His mother usually does this, but . . ."

Tim pulled him to the bathroom. George leaned against the wall while Tim went inside and shut the door. Paris turned and noticed Lou was staring at her chest.

Larry Washington peered out of the office. The walkway was empty, neither cop in sight. Hefting the comforting weight of his bat, he trotted down the cement until he reached room three, when his footsteps became more stealthy. Room three. The one with the slut and her new friends in it. Shit. He should have refused to rent to her, should have told her to hit the road and start walking. Who the hell did she think she was, throwing her weight around? She was the lowest of the low, a thing even worms found repulsive. Already she was writhing through his imagination. He had seen the way Rhodes, the

good-looking cop, looked at her, and she also seemed to have some kind of hold over Ed Dakota. Maybe she'd already done them both, lay back on her bed with her thighs open and let Rhodes pound away at her until Dakota tapped him on the shoulder. "Hey, buddy—don't keep it all for yourself." "Be done . . . in a minute . . . guy." "Ooh, yeah, give me that cop's cock." Or maybe she did it doggie-style, with Rhodes behind her and Dakota getting her mouth. "You like both of these nightsticks, baby?"

Larry remembered the way Dad used to bring women home, walk them right past Mom and into the bedroom. Brassy women with bleached hair and heavy eye shadow. Women in fishnet stockings and leather jackets. Mom just sat on the couch in front of the TV, acted like she never saw anything. And Larry always heard the sounds Dad made through the wall of his own bedroom. Once, when Larry was lying on his bed moving his hand up and down to the same rhythm he heard next door, Mom burst into the room. She yanked his hand away and pinned his wrist to the mattress. Her breath was warm and sour as she bent over him.

"You're thinking about those filthy sluts," she hissed in his ear. "And you're becoming as disgusting as they are. Filthy, diseased, disgusting *sluts*."

Larry's crotch tightened. Shit, now he had a hard-

on, and it was that whore's fucking fault. No chance of a quick, guilty session with the hand lotion, either. Not if he wanted to finish this little job.

He slipped past room three and moved quickly down to room nine. A quick application of the master key, and he was in. Larry shut the door behind him. The room was dark, though Larry didn't dare touch the lights in case one of the cops noticed something. Fortunately, a bit of light edged in around the curtains. A hint of perfume still hung in the air.

Larry set his baseball bat on the bed and began searching Caroline Suzanne's belongings.

"So how long have the two of you been married?" Paris asked, more to see if Lou would raise his eyes to something higher than her chest than any real desire for conversation.

Lou checked his watch. "Nine hours and . . . seventeen minutes." He smiled. "A spur-of-the-moment thing."

Ginny didn't respond to this. Instead, she folded her arms across her chest as if she were chilly. Something didn't sit right here. A suspicion grew in Paris's head, but she kept her mouth shut. George, meanwhile, kept his vigil next to the bathroom door.

"Viva Las Vegas," Lou grinned. "Right, Gin?"

Ginny stood up. "We need to leave. Now."

"Shit, Ginny," Lou said. "I'm just talking."

"I have to get out of here. Something's happening, and I need to get out of here. Can't you feel it? This whole place is . . . wrong, somehow."

"Don't get all psychic on me," Lou warned. "You know I think that stuff is horseshit."

"I don't want to be here when they bring that man back," Ginny said, her voice rising.

"Hey, everything's going to be fine," Paris said.

"No," Ginny quavered. "We'll find no peace here." And she tried to barge past Lou to the door. He remained firmly where he was, blocking her way.

"Ginny, he told us to stay together," Lou said. Paris found his tone condescending. "You're having one of your attacks, and you're totally overreacting. Take one of your pills."

"Take one of your own pills," Ginny shot back. "You have enough of them."

"Ginny, I want you to just calm down," Lou said. "Like a good girl."

"Wha-a-a-at?" Ginny said, clearly shocked at his tone.

"You wanted me to look after you, and I'm looking after you." Lou's voice took on an edge. "Don't forget you're my wife now. Do as you're told."

"Shit, look at the time," Paris put in. "Is it the nineteenth century already?"

Ginny tried to move around Lou, but he grabbed her. George looked uncomfortable. Ginny struggled and finally pushed Lou off.

"You don't own me, Lou," she snapped.

"I own what's inside you," he retorted. "Half of it, anyway."

The remark seemed to smash through Ginny like a blow. Paris bit her lip. She'd been right. Ginny abruptly tore out of the room. After a moment's stunned silence, Lou sprinted after her. Paris shot George a glance and followed.

Outside, she saw Lou catch up to Ginny just outside their room. Ginny got the door open, but Lou snagged her by the arm and said something Paris didn't catch.

"You don't own any part of me or my baby, Lou!" Ginny yelled. She was crying.

"Yeah? Then why the hell did I marry you?"

Ginny wrenched herself away from him, fled into the room, and slammed the door. Lou smacked it with his palm. The room's front window was open, and Paris could hear Ginny crying inside.

"Ginny! *Ginny!* Don't you slam the fucking door on me!" Lou shoved at the door, and it opened. He tore inside, slammed it shut again.

"Hey, guys," Paris called. "Chill out, okay?"

Lou poked his head out the window. "We're fine,

fuck you, good-bye. No need to worry your little whore head."

"If you lay a fucking finger on her—"

"Yeah, this is me shaking in my boots!" Lou slammed the window shut. Paris took a few more steps toward their room, concerned, wondering what she should do.

The top drawer of the bureau contained a pile of lacy panties. Larry pulled out a pair and held them up. Movie star panties. These had hugged her Hollywood crotch and ass. He brought them to his nose and sniffed. Fabric softener. The image of Caroline Suzanne's severed head in the dryer burst into his mind and he tossed the underwear aside with a faint, nauseated groan. Would her ghost come back and haunt him for what he was doing?

Stupid thoughts. The rain and the darkness were getting to him. He forced himself to check the rest of the drawer, but it contained nothing of interest. Larry opened the second drawer. Nightgown, cold cream, pink satin blindfold. Jesus, actresses really used those things at night? His fingers slid under the soft cloth—

—and pulled out a fat Louis Vuitton wallet.

"Bing-fucking-o!" Larry muttered. He opened it and gave the thick sheaf of bills inside a quick riffle.

Had to be a couple-three thou in there. With that kind of money, he could blow this place easy, get to—

Voices shouted outside the room. Larry froze, then stuffed the wallet into his pocket and eased up to the window. Through a crack between the curtains he saw Lou and Ginny arguing outside their room. The slut Paris was watching a little ways away, blocking Larry's clean exit. Jee-zus! The little whore was screwing him over *again*. He'd have to do something about her. Soon. But first he had to get the hell out of this room before the two cops noticed he was missing.

His eye fell on the bathroom and he remembered the back window. With a lighthearted grin, Larry snagged his bat from the bed. Maybe things weren't as bad as he'd thought.

Ginny flung clothes randomly into her battered suitcase. Tears ran down her face, but she refused to acknowledge them. Behind her, Lou raged like a tiger with its balls in a vise. He sounded just like Uncle Matt before he started slapping Aunt Lydia around. Ginny's hands began to shake.

The whites will never find peace on our lands.

They had to get out of here. They had to leave. She and Lou would find a way around the floods. It

was impossible that *every* road was blocked. Lightning flashed, and Ginny half-expected to see a Shoshone warrior outlined in the window. What she saw was Lou.

"We're not leaving, Ginny!" he roared. "You hear me? There is no place to go! I know this sucks, but there's a flood out there, remember?"

Ginny kept packing. Bras, socks, T-shirts, jeans. Her hands were freezing.

"Stop it!" Lou snarled. "Just stop it!" He snatched up the suitcase and hurled it across the room. Clothes flew in all directions as the bag thudded to the floor. Ginny stepped back and looked at Lou. He was panting. All of a sudden Ginny felt oddly calm.

"I'm not pregnant," she said.

Lou stared at her. "Wha—?" He coughed and tried again. "What did you say?"

"I'm not pregnant, Lou. I lied."

"What are you talking about? I saw the test."

Ginny just looked at him, let her eyes bore into him. After a moment, Lou's face stretched from a mixture of disbelief and mistrust into a mask of grief and despair.

"Why?" he asked in a broken voice.

That single word sent Ginny to the edge of tears again. She had hurt him, and Lou's pain seemed to tear through her own heart like dull scissors. It had

always been that way for Ginny. All her life it seemed like she could feel other people's pain. When her sister or her friends were unhappy, Ginny cried more than they did. The sight of a lost puppy wrenched her heart. Now she had hurt Lou.

Ginny loved Lou, she really did. It was just that she loved him best when he wasn't around. Whenever he was out somewhere—with his friends, at the store, at work—Ginny couldn't think of anything except him. But the moment he reappeared, it was like someone threw a switch and she could barely stand him. And he was a rotten lover. A real minuteman who was way too proud of his dick size. Then she had heard things, rumors about what he was doing when he was supposed to be at work. She should have dumped him, washed him right down the drain. But the thought of losing him was too much to bear. Breaking up would cause him pain— and thereby cause her even more pain. So Ginny had invented a reason to get married. Lou had even believed her when she said that red on the test meant she *was* pregnant instead of not. For a guy who claimed to be streetwise, Lou could be awful gullible.

"Why would you do that to me?" Lou asked.

"Alison said she saw you at the Hawk with that fucking LaPlant girl," Ginny whispered. "Is it true?"

If he denied it right away, Ginny knew she'd believe him. She was completely ready to think Alison was a damned liar, that there was another explanation. But Lou hesitated. Hot tears filled Ginny's eyes. She ran into the bathroom and slammed the door. This wasn't how it was supposed to be. Her wedding wasn't supposed to take place in a Las Vegas chapel in front of a minister dressed in drag. Her wedding night wasn't supposed to be spent in a seedy shitheap of a motel. She wasn't supposed to be crying her eyes out over a cracked bathroom counter. Her whole life seemed to be made of wasn't-supposed-to's. Ginny Iana sank to the cold toilet seat and began to cry in earnest.

Lou Iana slapped the door. "Jesus, Ginny. What are we, like fifteen?"

No sound emerged from the bathroom. Lou tried the knob again, but it was still locked. He pounded, he yelled, he begged and demanded. No response. Anger seethed in him like lava. Who the *fuck* did she think she was? He was the hurt one here. She had fucking lied to him, deceived him from the start. Pregnant Lou's ass.

Lou still remembered the night he had come home to find her waiting in his apartment, dressed in the tight clothes he liked but she rarely wore. And

she had been all over him. All "Let's do it right here on the couch" and "We don't need condoms. I know they're always too tight for you" and "I want your big one inside me, Lou. God, it's so huge!"

He'd been pretty proud of that night. He'd just come away from screwing Jessie LaPlant. He'd blasted it twice with her, in fact, and he still managed to get it up for Ginny half an hour later without breaking a sweat. How many guys could do that?

Two weeks later when Ginny showed him the pink pregnancy test, Lou'd been so scared, he'd almost run straight from her apartment and right out of town. But he'd stuck by her and offered to do the right thing. After a while he decided it wouldn't be so bad. They could call the kid Louis—his name—if it was a boy or Callie—his mother's—if it was a girl. And he would be a good dad, better than his own old man, and show the kid how to do cool stuff like ride a skateboard and play video games.

Now he found out Ginny had been fucking with him in more ways than one. Jesus. The anger blazed.

"Fuck!" he shouted, and swiped a lamp from the dresser. It smashed on the floor and the lightbulb burst with a *pop*, plunging half the room into shadow. "Ginny! Open the door. I haven't been to the Hawk in like a year. Alison's a stupid bitch whore

who just likes to fuck with your head! Now open the damn door!"

"No," Ginny sobbed.

"How are we supposed to talk if you don't open the door? Come on, Ginny!" He rattled the knob, then kicked the lower panel. "Open it!"

"Not until you calm down." Her voice quavered.

"I am very fucking calm!" Lou screamed. "Now get the hell out here!"

Ginny didn't answer. Lou was just about to break the door down and *make* her talk to him when a tiny sound behind him brought his head around. Someone was standing in the shadows left by the broken lamp. Off to one side, the closet door stood open, even though he remembered closing it earlier.

"Who the hell?" Lou said, and stepped forward. Recognition dawned on his face. "What are *you* doing here?"

Ginny wiped her eyes with toilet paper and blew her nose. Thank God Lou had stopped pounding on the door. He sounded like a complete maniac, and there was no way she was going to let him in when he was screaming like that. What if he started beating on her? No fucking way. The current quiet was much more soothing. Maybe it meant Lou was calming down now and she could—

The door exploded with heavy pounding. The sound crashed through the tiny bathroom like thunder in a jar. Ginny screamed and almost fell off the toilet seat.

"Ginny!" Lou screamed. "Open the door!" More pounding. Ginny cringed backward and fear crashed into her.

"Jesus Christ," she whimpered. "Stop it, Lou!"

"Ginny! *Now!*" Lou howled. He sounded like a mad dog or a charging gorilla. The door shook and the top hinge came loose. Ginny was terrified. If Lou broke in, he would kill her. She knew it as certain as she knew she was a Taurus. Ginny put her hands over her ears, trying to shut out the awful noises Lou was making.

"Stop it!" she screamed. "Stop it stop it stop it stop it!"

The door shook and the top hinge flew off. It clattered into the sink. The door leaned inward, and Lou's hand edged inside. Ginny stopped breathing she was so scared.

"God! Fuck!" Lou bellowed. "Oh, Jesus—Open the door!"

Lou's arm snaked desperately around the jamb. So terrified she couldn't think, Ginny leaped forward and sank her teeth into his forearm. Warm coppery blood flooded her mouth. Lou screamed and yanked

his arm back. Ginny shoved the door back upright again and leaned against it, her heart beating so hard she could barely hear. Blood dripped down her chin. Lou gave another scream and the door shuddered.

"Ginny!" He pounded the door again, but without much force this time. Maybe he was getting tired. "Ginny, *please.* Oh God, open . . . open the . . ."

The banging stopped. Ginny heard a sliding sound, then silence. She waited a long moment, her heart still beating in her ears. Finally she said, "Lou?"

Silence.

"Lou, I'm . . . I'm going to unlock the door now."

The silence continued. Ginny slowly turned the knob. The button lock disengaged with a *clack* that made Ginny jump. Carefully, cautiously, she eased the door open and peeked into the bedroom beyond.

It appeared empty.

"Lou?"

A fist beat on the outside door, and Ginny jumped again.

"Ginny!" shouted a voice. "It's Paris. Are you okay? Ginny?"

Ginny took another step into the room. It smelled funny, like the inside of a sewer. Then she saw Lou sitting against one wall. Ginny halted, stared.

"Ginny!" Paris said, knocking again. "Ginny, open the door." A small part of her mind wondered how

many people were going to say that to her today. The rest of her was staring at the blood.

Lou raised a hand to her. It dripped scarlet. She hadn't bitten him that hard, had she? Lou's other hand was clasped across his belly. A red river ran from gashes that gaped like grinning mouths. Oh Jesus God.

"Gin . . ." Lou said faintly. "Gin . . . you . . ."

"Oh my God." Ginny put a hand to her mouth. It was Robert Maine. Robert Maine had broken into their room and done this to Lou, and she had locked him, her husband, out of the bathroom. "Oh Jesus. Oh my God!"

"Gin." Lou's lips blew scarlet bubbles when he spoke and his raised hand trembled. "Gin . . . look . . . look . . ."

And then Ginny realized the exit door was still bolted and the windows were shut. How had Maine gotten out?

"Ginny!" Paris shouted outside. "What's *wrong?*"

"Look . . ."

And Ginny also realized that Lou was pointing at the closet.

Ed was moving for the trailer door when a human shadow passed by one of the windows. Rain thrummed off the roof in a ceaseless cacophony. Ed's

heart began to pound again. He drew his pistol, slipped into the kitchen, and crouched behind the cluttered table. His foot came down on something that squished, and he smelled overripe bananas.

Footsteps on the little front porch. The doorknob rattled for a moment, then slowly turned. The door creaked open, admitting a gust of cold air. Ed waited in the semidarkness. A shadowy figure oozed into the room like a prowling bear. The blade of a hunting knife gleamed in the dim illumination cast by the night-light. Ed forced himself to keep a relaxed grip on his gun. The figure stepped into the kitchen and Ed made his move. With a shout, he leaped forward, grabbed the person's arm, and twisted it behind him. The figure yelled in surprise—a man's voice—and dropped the knife. Ed pressed the barrel of the pistol to the back of his head. The man was wet from the rain.

"Don't. Move," Ed growled, and let go of his captive's arm long enough to hit the light switch. The overhead lamp came on. Ed was holding his gun on Larry Washington.

"Larry!" Ed exclaimed, lowering the gun. "What the fuck are you *doing*?"

"I live here!" Larry yelled. "This is my trailer, man. I came to get something. What the fuck are *you* doing?"

A loud female scream cut straight through the noise of the rain.

The closet door burst open. Ginny didn't wait, didn't watch. The front door was locked, would take too long to open. Instead, she turned and fled back toward the bathroom. Her foot slipped on the blood-slicked carpet and she went to her knees. Clothing rustled behind her and Lou gave a ghastly moan. The rough carpet dug into her knees yet also felt warm and slick. Ginny whimpered and tried to scramble upright. An icy hand grabbed her ankle. She screamed and kicked backward, but the grip was too hard. It started to pull her backward. Ginny lunged forward, managed to catch the bathroom door jamb. The cold hand's grip encased her ankle in iron. Ginny hauled on the jamb with all her strength. Her ankle popped abruptly free and the sudden lack of resistance sent Ginny sprawling into the bathroom. She slammed the door. Almost immediately it shuddered as Maine crashed into it. The door made a cracking sound, and it leaned inward like it had with Lou. Ginny screamed loud and long. Maine was coming for her, coming like he had for Lou.

The bathroom window. Ginny tried to open it, but it was stuck, painted shut. She hauled on it with all her strength, but it refused to budge. The door

shuddered and cracked. Ginny snatched up the heavy cover to the toilet tank and flung it at the glass. The window shattered. The tank lid tore the screen away and dropped to the ground outside. Ginny snatched up a towel and laid it over the jagged glass teeth left on the sill. The door boomed. Its lower hinge gave way, and the door itself exploded inward. Without looking back, Ginny launched herself through the window. A cold finger grazed her calf—and then she was outside on the back walkway. Rain, the fucking rain, fell in sheets beyond the eaves. She scrambled to her feet, shouting and screaming for help. Which way should she run? Would Maine come through the window after her?

Strong arms grabbed her shoulders from behind. Ginny shrieked and spun around, fists raised. Detective Samuel Rhodes jumped back, his icy eyes narrow.

"What's wrong, kid?" he asked. "Maine in there?"

He seemed strangely placid to Ginny's mind. Ginny tried to speak, but the images of what she had seen kept flashing in front of her: Lou begging her to open the door. The gashes in his stomach. The smell of his intestines. Slipping in warm blood. The closet door. The cold hand.

Paris came sprinting around the side of the build-

ing along with Larry and Ed. They all arrived and started talking at the same time.

"What the fuck is going on?"

"Are you all right?"

"Who screamed?"

Ginny finally found her voice. "It's Maine. In our room. He cut Lou up and came for . . . came for me."

Rhodes was off and running before Ginny finished her sentence. Ginny, Paris, and the others followed. Ed and Rhodes reached the door to room six first. Ed twisted the knob and it opened easily.

"That door was locked a second ago," Paris panted.

Ed and Rhodes ran into the room. Ginny stood in the doorway with Paris beside her. Lou was still slumped on the floor. The pool of blood had grown and Lou's face was gray. Ginny's stomach twisted. Ed and Rhodes—they had *guns?*—searched the room with obviously practiced efficiency. Empty.

"Shit," Rhodes said. His tone was perfunctory.

Ed leaned down and put a hand on Lou's neck. Ginny looked at him, holding her breath. Maybe things had looked worse than they were. Maybe Lou could still be saved. Maybe—

Ed looked up at Ginny. His sad eyes crushed her tiny hope even before he shook his head. Nausea bubbled and roiled. With a cry of anguish, Ginny turned and ran out into the rain. She slipped and fell

on the slippery parking lot pavement and lay there, weeping. Then she threw up. Paris dashed out, got Ginny to her feet, and brought her back under the eaves.

"It was my fault," she sobbed, the sour taste of bile in her mouth. "I didn't open the door. I didn't open the goddam *door*."

Paris hugged her and stroked her hair, making comforting noises. "Come on, sweetie. Let's go back to the others."

As they approached room three, George and Tim looked at them through the window, their faces identically expressionless. Ed, meanwhile, turned to Rhodes, pistol still at the ready.

"Out back," he said. The two of them took off.

6

A pigskin legal case and a ten-gallon hat hit the well-worn desk. Both case and hat are spattered with rain.

"Well," mutters Judge Emmet Taylor to himself. "That was a fuckin' drive."

Taylor, a thin man with a sunbaked complexion topped by a shock of white hair, hangs his dripping overcoat on a coatrack next to the door. He sniffs the air. No coffee brewing? One o'clock in the damn morning and they want him to preside over a Hail Mary proceeding without any coffee? Someone's gonads are going to land in the snakepit for this one.

Still muttering under his breath, Taylor peers into the connecting conference room. Four men sit around the table, arguing, while Sharon, a plump, motherly-looking stenographer waits patiently next to her machine. Taylor recognizes Assistant D.A.

Greg Kerrick, Police Detective Drew Valrole, and Defense Counselor Marty Greenfruit. The fourth man Taylor doesn't recognize. Probably some stupid handwriting expert or phrenologist who wants to read the bumps on Malcolm Rivers's head and declare it was impossible for him to commit murder. Idiot new-agers. Next thing you know, the State Supreme Court would rule astrology a legitimate means of identification. "Your Honor, the defendant couldn't possibly have killed the victim—he's a Virgo."

Well, maybe that's taking it a little far. That would never happen in Nevada. California, on the other hand . . .

Taylor watches the conference room a bit longer, remembering. Greenfruit, Kerrick, and Valrole have spent considerable time in Taylor's courtroom. The trial and sentencing of Malcolm Rivers took eight months, and by the end of it, Taylor was intensely pleased with the idea that he would never have to see any of these people again. Now here they are again, and at what-the-hell-time-is-it A.M. to boot.

Fortunately, Taylor, as the presiding judge for this inane, piece-of-shit hearing, doesn't have to pretend to be anything but tired, grouchy, and royally pissed off. Greenfruit called for the hearing, so he is the one who has to make nice with everyone. Taylor is going

to enjoy this. He hated Greenfruit from the beginning, found him to be a sly, weaselly man. Greenfruit makes his living defending rapists, molesters, and cutthroats, and a fair number of his clients walk. Slicker than snot on an ice cube, as Taylor's grandad used to say.

In the courtroom, with witnesses, jurors, and reporters present, Taylor was forced to keep his temper with the man lest Taylor seem less than impartial, but in a conference room at one A.M., all bets are off.

Taylor pulls on his black judge's robe, a symbol of his authority he wears even for a simple hearing. Straightening his lapels and shooting his cuffs, he strides into the conference room, boots echoing on the hard floor. Everyone instantly stops talking and leaps to their feet.

"Your Honor," they say.

"Who the hell is that?" Taylor asks, pointing at the fourth man. He has enormous brown eyes that remind Taylor of a puppy.

"This is Dr. Charles Mallick," Greenfruit says. "My client's psychiatrist."

"The state pays for death row inmates to have *psychiatrists?*" Taylor says.

"I volunteered my services," Mallick says quickly. "Malcolm Rivers is an intriguing case that offered me

a chance to try an experimental form of therapy."

"So he'll be the most well-adjusted ghost in hell?" Valrole interjects.

"I understand your hostility, Detective," Mallick says. "You went through a great deal during the Rivers case, and it must have been—"

"Don't try any psychobabble bullshit on me," Valrole says.

"Thank you, gentlemen," Taylor says, silencing them. "It's the middle of the night and none of us wants to be here. Let's get on with it. You ready, Sharon?"

Sharon sets her fingers on the stenography machine's keys and nods.

"Allrighty, then." Taylor sits at the head of the table, and the others take their own seats. "In the matter of *Malcolm Rivers vs. the State of Nevada*, for purposes of evidenciary review as proscribed by the Supreme Court of the State of Nevada, this hearing recognizes—"

"Excuse me, Judge Taylor," Greenfruit interrupts gently. "Um . . . with due respect, we should wait until my client arrives. He has a right to be present."

"He has precious few rights, Counselor," Taylor growls. "He's twenty-four hours from his execution."

"But in order to demonstrate his mental state, Your Honor, we need—"

Veins bulge on Taylor's neck. He shoots a glance at Sharon, who after years of experience in Taylor's courtroom, knows to stop transcribing.

"His mental state?" Taylor roars. "His *mental state?* Wake up, Counselor! Right now your client is making his way from Ely Maximum Security Penitentiary! Murderers, mutilators, rapists—they've got hundreds of 'em up there. And they're all *fucking crazy!* Even your doctor friend would have to agree to that. You want me to send 'em *all* to the goddam hospital?"

"No, sir," Greenfruit says coolly. "But—"

"Then what's the goddam *point?*" Taylor booms. Detective Valrole raises a smug eyebrow at A.D.A. Kerrick.

"The point is, sir," Greenfruit begins, "that my client's time is—"

Taylor loses it again. "Do you *know* what *time* it *is*, Counselor? Do you think I have *time* for *bullshit?* I'm sure you're pleased those justices dragged me into the review of a case I already presided over, one I already *decided*—but me, I'm definitely *not* pleased. I am, in point of fact, pissed off and insulted. So when your boy gets here, do whatever you goddam well want with him. But in the name of decency, *state your goddam case!*"

He leans back in his chair, feeling spent. Assistant

D.A. Kerrick looks pleased. Dr. Mallick remains impassive in his own chair.

"Somebody get me a coffee," Taylor sighs. "Black."

Rain pounded the moonless landscape, hitting so hard that the up-spray was as fierce as the downpour. Occasional bursts of lightning took snapshots of twisted Joshua trees and scrubby bushes. Maine crashed through them, staggered once, regained his feet. The lights of the motel became fainter with every step.

"Born free," he sang. "As free as the wind blows. As free as the grass grows . . ." And he was going to stay that way. Maine had definitely had enough of fucking Rhodes telling him what to do. Rhodes was a stupid fuck. He had even left the handcuff key on the nightstand in the hotel room right where Maine could find it. What a dildo.

That reminded Maine. He fished in his pocket, pulled out the cuffs, and flung them far into the watery night. Then he swallowed the key. If Maine was caught later, he would have a handcuff key where no one would find it. All he'd have to do was wait a while and then dig for it. Fuck Rhodes.

Cold rain continued to pelt Maine as he ran-walked farther into the desert. Eventually he'd come across *something*—a house, a road, a car. But it would

have to be soon. The Cheetos hadn't done much to fill his stomach, and he was hungry. And cold. And wet.

You could go back, whispered Not-Doc in his head. *It would be pretty sweet to have that hooker sit in your lap while you squeezed her neck. And the little boy could watch while you did it. Would he know he was next?*

"Shut up," Maine said. "You always get me into trouble."

You're a filthy little faggot, Not-Doc said. *I'm gonna watch you go down on me, prove you're a filthy faggot.*

"No!" Maine shouted. "You don't exist. You aren't here."

You can't go anywhere without me, Not-Doc said. His voice was clear and crisp, easily audible above the rain. *I love you, Bobby. Let me prove it. Put the guitar down and sit on my lap. It'll feel nice, I promise. Mommy won't be home for at least an hour, so we have time.*

"No!" Maine started running through the rain, but Not-Doc's voice followed him.

"Oh Bobby boy," Not-Doc sang. "The pipes, the pipes are calling. From glen to glen and down the mountainside." *Touch this here, Bobby. Stop struggling, or I'll have to—I said, stop struggling, you little shit. Do as you're told!*

Maine slipped and measured his length on the muddy, slippery clay. He spat out grit and levered himself to hands and knees. Cold rain pelted through his hair, ran down his shirt, and soaked his muddy pants.

Oh, that's good, Bobby, Not-Doc purred. *You just kneel there like that. This'll only hurt for a second.*

"Leave me alone!" Maine tried to scream, but it came out as a whimper. "Please."

Yeah, Bobby . . . that's right, Bobby . . . that's so good . . . that's the way . . . yeah . . .

"Just stop," Maine moaned. "I just want it to stop. Don't touch me!"

What are you going to do about it, little faggot? Tell your Mommy? She'll throw you out of the fucking house for a faggot, you stupid prick. Right out on the street, you hear? With the weirdos and the crazies and their knives. They'll slice you faster than a bunch of gooks can carve up a Thanksgiving dog. So keep your little faggot mouth shut!

"I'll kill you," Maine snarled, then clapped his hands over his mouth.

Not-Doc laughed. *You go ahead and try, little faggot. Lemme show you what'll happen if you do.*

"No!" Maine howled, and ran and ran and ran. "I'll kill you! I'll kill you kill you kill you *kill you!*"

Not-Doc's nasty laugh followed him, skittering

and sliding, down a slight rise. The ground at the bottom was sodden with water, and the mud tried to swallow his feet. One of his shoes came off with a sucking sound and vanished beneath a sphincter of ooze. Maine left it behind like Cinderella, kept running, kept fleeing. Another rise loomed ahead of him, and he slipped and slid his way to the top. As he careened down the other side, he caught sight of lights through the rain. Maine sighed with relief. Lights meant people, and people meant warmth and shelter and food and money. He only had to take it.

"We're running with the shadows of the night," Maine sang. "So baby, take my hand. We'll be all right. Surrender all your dreams to me tonight."

The rain was coming down so hard Maine could barely make out what appeared to be a series of low buildings. A ranch complex, maybe? After a few minutes, he reached the edge of the grouping. More luck—the closest building was dark, apparently deserted. It had a back door that faced away from its more distant, well-lit cousins. Maine found a rock, smashed out one of the windows, and reached in to undo the lock. A few seconds later, he was trotting down a short hallway into what looked to be a roomful of giant ghosts. When his eyes adjusted to the dim light, he realized he was standing amid big pieces of furniture covered with white sheets.

The place was dry, and a bit warmer than the outside. Maine tugged one of the dusty sheets off and discovered it was hiding a restaurant booth. He was in an old diner or restaurant. Cool! Maybe there'd be a set of clean work clothes in a closet or something. Maine dried himself off with the sheet as best he could, then decided to look around. The rain wasn't quite so loud on the roof now—maybe he could look outside, get an idea of where he was.

Dust coated the window. Maine used the sheet to rub a clear space and peer outside. The first thing he saw was a neon sign. The Golden Palm Motel.

"Fuck!" Maine whispered. He must have gone in a goddam circle. Fuck a *duck!* His heart began to pound. Rhodes would find him. Rhodes would hurt him. Unless he hurt Rhodes first. Rhodes and the others. Maine's hands shook with combined fear and rage.

"Okay, okay, calm down," he told himself. "Let's find some clothes, hey?"

You won't find anything, Not-Doc said. *You're just a pissy little screwup.*

"Shut up!"

You didn't go in a circle. You came back this way on purpose because you want to kill Rhodes and all the others. Wouldn't that be nice? Watch the hooker squirm while you choke her. You could beat off over her body,

come all over her dead tits. Then you could grab the other girl, take her into the shower with you while you do her. She'd be all warm and slippery with soap and blood.

Maine had a hard-on. Panting, he brought a hand down toward it, then abruptly jerked it back up again. He wasn't supposed to do that. Not even to take a piss. But Not-Doc's words filled his mind with images, hardened his dick, made him feel like he was going to explode. His hand drifted lower, lower, lower. His heart beat faster and his breath caught in his throat. At last his fingertips brushed his crotch.

Little faggot! Not-Doc screamed. *You fucking little pissant faggot! What the hell do you think you're doing?*

Maine jerked his hand up so fast he knocked himself in the mouth. "I'm sorry," he said. "I'm really sorry. Sorry sorry sorry."

Sorry isn't good enough. I'll show you how to be sorry!

"No," Maine moaned.

A shadow moved past the glass outside, passing only inches from Maine, heading for the clear spot Maine had made on the window. Maine jumped back.

I'm coming for you, Bobby.

"Leave me alone." Maine kept moving backward, tripped over a chair, fell, scrambled to his feet. The

figure outside moved closer, stepped into the clear circle, turned. The eyes met Maine's through the glass. It was Ed, the limo driver—and he had seen Maine.

Maine spun to flee and crashed face-to-face into Rhodes. Rhodes's fist snapped around. Pain exploded in Maine's temple as the blow connected. Maine stumbled dizzily and ran in the opposite direction, making for the short hallway and the exit.

Stupid fuck they're going to catch you going to fuck you going to kill you

Maine hit the hallway. Rhodes's footsteps were right behind him. Maine could smell the cold night air that blew through the broken window. He was almost out, almost—

And then Ed was in the doorway. Before Maine could react, the limo driver's foot lashed out and caught Maine in the balls. Pain crushed him gasping to the floor. More blows rained down on him, smashing his back and sides and head and legs.

"Stop!" he screamed. "Get off me! Get off me!"

Stupid fuck.

And Maine screamed again.

Ginny Iana huddled on the cold bathroom floor of room three. Her hands were shaking. Her legs were shaking. Her entire body was shaking. Lou

was dead because of her, and she had smelled the inside of his body. Maine was out prowling around with a knife, ready to gut her and the others. She could still feel his cold hand on her ankle. Her clothes were wet.

From her pocket she pulled a little pillbox, fished out two capsules with shaking fingers, and dry-swallowed them. Lou was dead. Jesus, Maine had killed him right in their room on their wedding night. The grief and pain crushed her, ground her into the cracked linoleum. She shivered with cold.

Gentle hands pressed a white towel against her neck and her face. Ginny flinched, then relaxed. It was only Paris kneeling next to her, trying to blot her dry. The hooker noticed Ginny was shivering and removed her red leather jacket.

"Here," she said, draping it over Ginny's shoulders. "Put this on."

The jacket smelled like Chanel perfume and it was warm from Paris's body. It felt strangely intimate, smelling Paris's scent and feeling her warmth. Ginny pulled the jacket closer around herself.

Male voices shouted from outside. Ginny whimpered and pressed herself harder against the bathroom wall.

"It's okay," Paris said soothingly. "It's going to be

okay. George and Tim are out front keeping watch at the window."

"He's coming back," Ginny cried. "He's coming! He's *coming!*"

"It'll be okay, honey. Here, I'll go look." Paris rose and poked her head out of the bathroom. "What's going on out there?"

"I think they caught him," came George's voice. "Would you watch Tim for me? I'm going to go look."

Ed helped Rhodes drag the unconscious body of Robert Maine to a support column near the kitchen doorway of the diner. The convict was missing a shoe and mud coated his clothes. Larry and George watched from their position near the cash counter. Larry had his baseball bat. Rhodes sat Maine with his back to the column, splayed his legs out so he wouldn't be able to kick, and yanked Maine's hands behind the pillar itself. Ed, meanwhile, scanned the dining room for something to tie him up with, since Rhodes said he didn't have a second pair of handcuffs. Nothing suggested itself, so he moved toward the swinging silver doors that he assumed led to the kitchen. Larry, however, interposed himself.

"That's empty." He reached underneath the

counter, produced a toaster, and yanked the cord from it. "Use this."

Ed handed the cord to Rhodes, who quickly lashed Maine's hands.

"Why are we putting him in here, anyway?" Larry asked. There was a note in his voice that Ed couldn't quite read.

"Where would you prefer, Larry?" Ed asked mildly. "The office? Your trailer?"

Larry shrugged, then planted himself in front of the kitchen doors. He fidgeted there as Rhodes finished with Maine. Paris entered the diner minus her jacket and looking sexy as hell in her T-shirt and jeans. Was she really a hooker? She had never actually said so. Ed made himself look at George York instead.

"George, what was everyone doing out there in the parking lot before Lou was killed?" he asked. "I didn't catch it all."

"Ginny got upset about something and ran out," George replied promptly. "Her husband followed her. And then Paris did, too. She stood outside their room for a while. I didn't see her after that."

"What is *that* supposed to mean?" Paris demanded.

George didn't look at her. "I'm simply answering the man's question."

"No." Paris folded her arms. "You are implying I had something to do with what happened. Jesus, they've got an escaped psycho-loony convict tied up right fucking in front of you! Want him to bite your dick off to prove how nuts he is?"

"For God's sake," George said, red-faced. Without another word, he turned and strode out.

"What *were* you doing out there?" Rhodes asked.

"I told you to stay in the room," Larry added.

"Lou and Ginny were having a fight!" Paris said belligerently. "I was trying to get them back inside! I didn't have anything to do with Lou's death. Any idiot can see that—except you two."

Ed ignored the barb and glanced at Rhodes. "Can you try the radio again?"

"Yeah." He got up and left, shooting one more glance at Paris on the way. She turned her back to him. Ed moved to follow Rhodes.

"Larry," he said, "stay here and watch him. And Paris, do me a favor—go back to room three. Stay there. And try to keep the others cool."

"And where are *you* going?" Paris said. Ed thought he detected a hint of concern.

"Just do it, Paris," he said. "Please?"

Paris gave a put-upon sigh and stomped away. Larry edged up behind Ed and gave a nervous little cough.

"Uh, Ed?" he said. "I don't know if I'm comfortable with . . . you know . . . guard duty."

Exasperated, Ed turned to face him. "He's unconscious and tied to a post, Larry. If he gives you any trouble, hit him with your baseball bat." And he left.

Paris stared out of room three into the rain. It seemed like she did that a lot lately. Rain made up her whole world now. It defined where she could and could not go. It decided whether she would be warm or cold, wet or dry. It held power of life and death.

Ginny sat huddled on the couch, shell-shocked, gnawing her fingernails to nubs. Paris's jacket sat next to her. The connecting door between rooms three (Ed's room) and four (the Yorks' room) stood open, and Paris was vaguely aware of Alice York's labored breathing. Timothy sat next to her on the bed, and George York knelt in front of the TV, trying to coax a picture out of it.

"If there is no picture, first check to see that the unit is turned on and that it is plugged in to a working electrical outlet," George muttered. "Also check to see that the cable line is properly connected to the receiving socket—Figure C—on the back of the unit. If you do not have cable . . ."

"Timothy."

The voice was a new one to Paris. She turned and saw Alice's eyes were open. Timothy, tears in his eyes, took her hand. Paris moved quietly closer. Should she do something? Call someone? Ginny didn't react.

George crossed quickly to the bed. "Oh my God. Honey . . . oh my God."

"Where are we?" Alice asked. Her voice was blurred, tired. "I don't remember anything . . . except a doctor."

"You must mean Ed. He gave you the stitches." George smiled and patted her hand. "We had an accident, honey. We're in a motel now. Do you hurt anywhere?"

"A little," Alice said. "It's hard . . . to breathe." She closed her eyes again.

"Let me get you some aspirin," George said. He headed for the connecting door, and Paris stepped back to let him enter. He looked at Paris, at the window, and at Ginny. Then he grabbed the bottle of aspirin and started back toward room four.

Paris picked up her jacket. "George, can you keep an eye on Ginny for a minute?"

"She's awake," George said single-mindedly. "She needs more aspirin. Except . . . I think she's asleep again. Oh, God. Alice, please don't do this."

"Paris," Ginny said. "Don't go. Please? I feel like

there's something watching me. Watching us. It wants us all dead. It doesn't want us to find peace."

Paris didn't know what to say to this, so she ignored it. "Honey, there's something I have to get from my room. It's very important to me. I won't be gone long."

Outside, she glanced back at the window. Ginny was watching her through the glass like a forlorn ghost. A shiver ran down Paris's spine as she scurried down the walkway to her own room. She didn't notice Larry watching her from the diner door, still clutching his baseball bat.

Ed snatched two disposable cameras from the sales rack in the motel lobby and ran out the door into the night. It had become pretty obvious to him why Rhodes had been delegated to chauffeur duty— the man was insanely sloppy when it came to basic procedures. Rhodes had made no attempt to secure either crime scene, had taken no notes, interviewed no witnesses. Granted, he'd been occupied with the hunt for Maine, but still . . .

Taking a deep breath, he entered the laundry room. Raising the first camera, he snapped a shot of the overall area. Then one of just the dryers. Then one of Catherine Suzanne's staring head.

She was a person, Ed thought, his earlier remarks

to Larry notwithstanding, *but don't think of her as one. It'll make it easier. It's just a piece of evidence you need to photograph.*

Ed blasted off shot after shot, until the camera was nearly empty. After a while, he paused and pulled the camera away from his eye. A strange buzzing filled his ears and he felt a little dizzy. Hunger? He hadn't eaten in quite some time.

The dryer was empty. The head was gone.

Ed blinked. It was impossible. He shook his head, trying to clear the buzzing from his ears. The floor rocked beneath him and he swayed drunkenly. The room dimmed. Was he passing out? He tried to make for the door, get some fresh air, but he slipped and spun on the wet floor. His hand lashed out and snagged the dryer door. It came open. The sick smell of blood washed over him and he stared straight into Caroline Suzanne's slack face.

A flash of lightning illuminated room seven. Paris stood in the doorway. She reached for the switch, then pulled her hand back. A light on would tell people someone was in here. The lightning had already shown her that the room was empty.

Paris moved over to the wardrobe, reached out to open the door, hesitated. Someone could be hiding in it. Robert Maine, his panther's body coiled like a

146

spring. She told herself she was being stupid. Maine was tied up in the diner.

Except he had already escaped once.

Paris flung the wardrobe open just as a flash of lightning crashed across the sky outside. The wardrobe was empty. Only her suitcase, duffle bag, and purse on the bottom. Paris opened the suitcase, pulled aside the clothes, reached into the pocket. The money, bundles of twenties and hundreds, was still there. She stuffed it into her purse with quick fingers. Mr. Vanderschmitz's money was still in her pocket.

Lightning flashed, outlining a figure in the connecting doorway behind her. Oblivious, Paris closed the suitcase as the room dropped back into darkness. She turned to leave. Another lightning flash. A man was standing right in front of her, staring at her. Paris screamed and leaped backward. Her purse tumbled to the floor.

"Motherfucker!" she yelled.

"What are you doing?" asked Ed Dakota.

"You scared me to death, you asshole!"

"I asked you a question," Ed said. "What are you doing here?"

"Getting shit that's mine," Paris growled. She picked up her purse, slung it over her shoulder. "What are *you* doing here?"

"Excuse me?"

"What, *I* don't get to ask a question?"

Ed held up a disposable camera. "I'm taking photos. There's been two murders in the last two hours, and I thought maybe before all the evidence was—"

"That's no answer," Paris interrupted. "No answer at all."

"What are you talking about?"

Paris sat down on the bed and gave him a cool look. "You, my friend, are a *limo driver*. As in chauffeur. As in flunky to the rich and famous. So I'll ask again—what are you doing? Looking to win some beyond-the-call-of-limo-driver-duty merit badge? Tell me if I've got it wrong, but you're not on 'the job' anymore, Eddie. You don't have to be a hero. There's a real, true-to-life, active-duty copy here. If you haven't noticed."

Ed looked abashed and shoved the camera into his pocket. "Yeah, well. That active-duty cop has his head up his active-duty ass. He already managed to lose a convicted killer." He sat next to Paris on the bed. "So maybe you can find it in your heart to forgive me if I try to pitch in and salvage the situation. You think?"

Paris smiled at his intensity. He was a pretty handsome guy, with that dark hair and those pointed features. He smelled like rain and, very

faintly, of aftershave. "You, Edward, are a complicated cat."

Was he blushing? Hard to tell in the dark. "Not
really."

"I think so." She paused. "What month were you
born?"

"May."

"A Taurus. Just like me. We're a stubborn bunch,
you know. We don't like to give up." Then, without
knowing why, she leaned over and kissed him on the
cheek. "Maybe you *are* a hero."

Larry tied the kitchen door handles shut with a
length of old twine he had scrounged from the
broom closet, then trimmed the extra with the hunting knife from his belt sheath. Next to the doors was
a chest-high window for handing plates of food to
the waitresses. A pair of folding shutters framed the
opening, and Larry pulled them shut. They drifted
open. He shut them again, and again they slipped
back open. They had a tongue-and-loop for a pad-
lock, but there was no lock anywhere in evidence.

"Shit," Larry muttered. He had caught up his bat
and was heading for the front door when a voice
stopped him.

"What's wrong, buddy?" Maine asked, from the
shadows surrounding his pillar.

Larry turned in spite of himself. The bat lay heavy in his hand.

"Come on. You can tell me," Maine said reasonably. "What's in there?"

"Shut up!" Larry's fingers were white around the bat handle.

"Someone's got to clean them up, my friends, before the little harvest disappears into the mud," Maine sang. "Someone's got to collect their odds and ends when the gutters run with blood. What'd you clean up, Larry?"

"Shut *up!*"

"Tell me what's in there," Maine purred. His panther eyes gleamed in the dark. "I'm good at keeping secrets. I've got a few whoppers myself. Tell me, please."

Larry's face twisted into a demonic mask. The bat flew upward, raising itself of its own accord. "I'm warning you to *shut the hell up!*"

The kiss went no further. Instead, Paris followed Ed through the connecting door to room six and watched him take more photos. Lou Iana's body sat slumped against the wall, awash in oozing blood. The room smelled of urine and shit. Ed's camera flashed again and again.

"Where were you a cop?" Paris asked.

"Los Angeles." *Flash, flash.*

"You fired or you quit?" It seemed strange, holding a get-to-know-you conversation in a room with a dead body.

"I took a leave," Ed said.

"Why?"

Ed gestured at Lou's body with the camera. "I had enough of this. It was making me sick." He paused and leaned tiredly against one wall. "One day I got this call. A jumper. A fifteen-year-old Mexican girl on a ledge eight stories over Wilcox. Knocked up and infected with HIV. I asked her to step off. I asked her to come into my arms. And she turned to me and said, '*Cuál es la punta vivir?*' "

" 'What is the point of living?' " Paris translated. "What did you tell her?"

"I was trained to tell her about the people who'd miss her, about the dreams ahead. But for a second, I hesitated. And she saw it." He ran a hand over his face. "In that moment I honestly couldn't think of a single optimistic thing to say to her. So she jumped. Spread her arms and jumped. I only hesitated a second. One goddam second. The next day I filed for leave."

Ed gave Paris a sad smile and turned away. Paris said nothing as Ed shot Lou's body close-up. *Flash, flash, flash.* And then Ed seemed to notice something. He bent down for a closer look.

"What is it?" Paris asked.

In answer, Ed reached for the phone book, tore out a yellow page, and used it to pull something from Lou's right hand. Paris peered at it. It was a Golden Palm Motel key. A bloody tag dangled from it.

"Number nine," Paris read. "What the hell?"

"That's not right," Ed said. "This is room—hold it." He moved swiftly to the front door and yanked it open.

"What's up?" Paris asked.

"Look." On the door hung a rusty number nine. Ed put out a finger and pushed it. The number swung back into position, becoming a six. It flipped back down the moment he let go.

"Huh?" Paris said. "I'm lost, here."

Ed poked his head out the door. "Room seven on the right, room five on the left. This is room six, but it looks like room nine. Lou's key tag says room nine."

"I'm still confused," Paris said, moving up behind him. Rain fell in a steady waterfall off the eaves outside. The police sedan was still parked in front of the office up the walkway.

"Rhodes," Ed said, and took off running. Paris hurried to follow. They arrived at the car in time to see Rhodes slam down the radio handset and climb out of the car beneath the overhang.

"It's worse now," Rhodes reported. "Just static."

"Where's the key?" Ed said. "From the actress."

Rhodes blinked at him, then fished a dryer sheet from his pocket. Ed took the object from him and unwrapped it. Paris looked over his shoulder as Caroline Suzanne's room key came to light.

"Number ten," Ed said. He handed the phone book page to Rhodes. "This was in Lou's hand. Number nine. Is your guy some kind of a psycho, Rhodes? Some kind of countdown killer?"

"I'd be surprised if he knew how to count," Rhodes said, examining the key in its torn yellow shroud. "Let's go talk to him."

The trio had reached the diner doorway when a flicker of movement caught Paris's eye. She looked around in time to see Larry slink out of the office with a green money box under his arm. He was heading for the rear of the motel. Paris tapped Ed on the shoulder and pointed. Rhodes turned as well.

"Hey!" Rhodes said. "He's supposed be guarding—"

"Larry!" Ed bellowed. "Hey, Larry!"

The man froze, a guilty look on his face.

"Come over here," Ed ordered. Larry didn't move. Ed sighed. "What part of 'come over here' don't you understand, Larry?"

Reluctantly, like a child expecting a spanking,

Larry shuffled over to the diner beneath the thundering eaves, box tucked under his arm. His eyes briefly met Paris's, then he looked away.

"I told you to stay with Maine in there," Ed snarled, pointing. "Why did you go to your office? Jesus, why can't anyone do what I fucking tell them?"

"I just went . . . went to get something," Larry mumbled. "There's a psycho loose and I didn't want him to swipe the cash box. It'd give him getaway cash, you know?"

Rhodes made an exasperated noise and shoved his way into the diner. Larry nervously watched him go as Ed held out the two keys, one in each hand.

"Look, *Larry*," he said. "This was the key on . . . with . . . Caroline Suzanne. And this one was on the kid Lou."

Larry gave the keys a perfunctory glance, then returned his attention to the diner door. "Uh huh."

"How many sets of keys are there?" Ed asked.

"Ed!" Rhodes yelled. "Get in here!"

"Uh oh," Paris said. Tension tightened her stomach.

Larry, meanwhile, shied away from Rhodes's voice. Ed grabbed him by the shoulders. "How may sets of keys are there, Larry?"

"Uh . . . two," Larry said. "Two and a master."

"Ed!" Rhodes bellowed. "Hurry!"

Ed grabbed the door handle. Paris followed. Larry, however, stayed where he was. Ed paused and turned to him. "Where do you think you're going, Larry?"

"I . . . I just . . ."

Ed tore the door open and gestured impatiently. "Get the fuck inside, Larry. *Now!*"

Larry clearly wanted to be somewhere, anywhere else. He stood on the sidewalk, clutching his green money box. Paris lost her own patience. She gave him a shove from behind.

"Go, asshole!" she snapped, and propelled him inside.

7

Rhodes squatted next to Maine, who was lying on the diner floor. Maine's hands were untied, the electrical cord gone. His head was arched back. The last six inches of Larry's baseball bat were sticking out of his mouth, as if Maine were some grotesque sword-swallower. And he wasn't moving.

Larry backed away, face pale as paper. "Holy shit!"

"Jesus!" Paris breathed, then turned to stare at Larry. So did Ed and Rhodes. Larry glanced quickly at each of them, read their faces, and held up his hands defensively. Rhodes remained motionless on the floor.

"I didn't kill him!" Larry pleaded. "I didn't!"

"You lying sack of shit!" Rhodes charged at Larry and shoved him up against one wall, his forearm across Larry's throat. Larry's green box went flying. It hit the floor, bounced once, and slid to a stop.

"We need to see if Maine is still alive," Ed said.

"Are you fucking kidding me?" Rhodes said. "This bastard shoves eighteen inches of a Louisville Slugger down my convict's windpipe and you think he might still be *alive?*"

"Choked on the ultimate phallic symbol," Paris said under her breath.

"I didn't do it!" Larry squeaked. His eyes were wide.

Ed sauntered over, careful to stand, Paris noticed, between Larry and the exit. "I've never been one to leap at the obvious, Larry, but I'm having just a little trouble seeing past that bat of yours sticking out of Maine's fucking throat."

"I didn't do it!" His voice was growing hoarse. "Please! I can't breathe."

Ed said, "Rhodes, ease off a little, hey?" Rhodes grudgingly obeyed, though he didn't lower his arm. "If you didn't do it," Ed continued, "then why were you acting like a freak out there just now?"

"Motel. Manager. Murder," Paris said, ticking off her fingers. "Connect the dots, guys."

"Shut up, 'ho-'ho," Larry snarled, then gasped because of something Rhodes did that Ed couldn't see.

"Why were you trying to get away with your little green box, Larry?" Ed asked.

"I was . . . scared."

"Of what?"

"I . . . I thought . . . aw, cripes—you wouldn't understand."

"We wouldn't understand why you were scared or we wouldn't understand why you were sneaking away?"

"Both. You couldn't know."

"Try me," Ed said.

Rhodes slammed Larry against the wall again. "Why'd you kill my con, Larry?"

"I didn't kill him!" Larry blubbered. "Please! I just . . . went out . . . for a second. I don't know how this . . . I just left the bat here . . ."

"Bullshit!" Rhodes said.

"He was fine when I . . . I just . . . I went back to my office."

Rhodes backed away abruptly, leaving Larry gasping, one hand on his throat. There was a jingling sound as Rhodes held up another key.

"Look at this," Rhodes said. "Another one of Larry's keys. Number eight. The actress, the kid, my con—ten, nine, eight. Who's number seven gonna be, Larry?"

Larry was drifting toward the exit. Paris was about to call Ed's attention to this fact when George York appeared in the doorway. Rain spattered his glasses

and shone on his slicked-back hair. He started to speak, then saw Maine's body.

"Oh my lord," he whispered.

"Those aren't my keys," Larry said in a shrill voice. "You can't call them that. That's like leading the witness or something. Look!" He plunged a hand in his pocket and came up with a jingling fob of keys. Another object dropped to the floor. "*These* are my keys. See?"

"What's that?" Rhodes said, pointing.

Paris stepped forward and scooped the object up. It was a fat, black wallet with a Louis Vuitton symbol on it embossed in gold. Paris flipped it open, revealing a healthy sheaf of green cash. Larry swallowed.

"I can't wait to hear this one," Rhodes said.

"Ooh, ooh, I know how it goes," Paris said, squirming with false enthusiasm. "He's a closet drag queen with a Swiss bank account and *really* high limit on his ATM."

"Why does he run a seedy motel, then?" Ed asked.

"To meet boys, of course."

"Larry?" Rhodes said.

"Okay," Larry said. "Okay, yes, I took her wallet. Afterward. *After* she died. I confess to that, okay? But I *didn't kill her*. And I didn't kill Maine. He was alive when I split. He was sitting there saying all this shit, and then he started singing. It was wigging me

out, okay? I had to get away from him for a while. It was no big deal."

"No big *deal?*" Rhodes lunged again, and something snapped in Larry's expression. Before Paris understood what was happening, Larry had an armlock on her. The sharp blade of a hunting knife pricked her neck. She screamed once, but the sound gurgled and died in her throat when Larry increased his pressure on the blade.

"Everyone get back!" Larry shouted. His breath was moist and sour. "Get back! You aren't gonna pin this on me! I didn't do it!"

Paris licked her lips. Ed and Rhodes had both drawn pistols, though they pointed them at the ceiling—they couldn't aim at Larry without endangering Paris. The blade on her throat was cold. She could feel the corded muscles of Larry's body pressed against her own.

"Let go of her, Larry," Ed said, his voice low and calm. Paris wondered if this was the tone he had used on the suicidal Mexican girl.

"Fuck you!"

"Do what he says," Rhodes said.

George York, who was watching the scene openmouthed, suddenly jumped and spun around. Tim stood behind him, plucking at his father's sleeve.

"Timothy?" George sputtered. "What are you—?"

"Get him out of here, George," Ed said without taking his eyes off Larry.

Larry started moving toward the kitchen with Paris. The doors were tied shut with some half-rotten old twine. The dispassionate part of Paris wondered if that was recent or if they had always been tied shut and she had simply not noticed. She was strangely calm. Her life was in danger, but it felt as if she were watching everything happen to someone else.

"Let go of her, Larry," Ed said as Larry backed toward the doors dragging Paris with him. She was more beside him than in front of him now, almost facing him.

"Back off," Larry said.

Paris found her voice. "Take your greasy hands off me, you psycho!"

"Shut up, slut!" Larry screamed. "And you guys stay back. I haven't hurt anyone tonight. No one! But I don't like cheap fucking whores, and if you come one step closer, I won't hesitate to—"

With a scream of rage, Paris brought her knee up. Hard. It caught Larry in the groin. He doubled over. The knife flew from his hand and clattered on the worn gray tile. Paris grabbed Larry by the hair and smacked his face into her other knee. He grunted with pain. All the nasty little things Larry had said

161

about Paris rushed back to her, and she let the rage take her. Paris slammed into Larry like a football player. The impact knocked him backward, and Paris went with him. With mingled shouts of pain and surprise, both Paris and Larry crashed against the kitchen doors. The ancient twine snapped, and the two of them stumbled into the kitchen. It was a narrow room. A combination stove and grill took up most of one wall, and a metal worktable stood in front of it. Cookware hung from the ceiling and sat in stacks underneath the table. Shiny metal doors led to a walk-in refrigerator and a walk-in freezer.

Paris regained her balance first and leaped onto Larry's back, double-fisting the top of his head. Larry spun around in an unsuccessful attempt to dislodge her.

"Get her fucking off me!" he yelped.

Paris's fists fell fast and furious. "You *pathetic*, psychotic *piece* of *shit!*" she howled, striking him at every other word. "How's *that* for cheap? How's *that*? And *that*?"

Larry suddenly grabbed a handful of Paris's hair and yanked her forward. Hot pain tore across her scalp and she flipped over Larry's shoulder between the freezer and the worktable. The impact when she hit the floor drove the breath from her lungs.

"Slut!" he snarled, his face a mask of rage.

"Nobody talks to me that way!" His hands tightened around her throat with iron fingers. She couldn't breathe. Where the hell were Ed and Rhodes?

Paris flung out an arm, and her palm touched a handle. She heaved the object around and clocked Larry on the temple. He gave a muffled cry and fell off her to huddle in a ball on the floor with arms around his head. Paris hit him again.

"All right!" Larry groaned. "Enough! Enough!"

Paris sat up in time to see Ed and Rhodes burst into the room. She looked at the object in her hand. It was a cast-iron frying pan. How stereotypical was that? She stifled an insane giggle.

"Are you all right?" Ed said, heading her way.

"I'm fine, I think." Paris reached up and grabbed the freezer handle to help haul herself to her feet. The freezer door popped open, and something big and cold fell straight onto her. It pinned her to the floor, pressing her down from shoulder to foot. Paris looked straight into the dead face of a fat man with a white widow's peak. His cold nose nuzzled hers. She screamed and tried to push him away, but the corpse was too stiff, too heavy. It was every working girl's nightmare, to have a fat client die on top of you, and this one was cold as a sled dog's grave. The man's flesh was hard and unyielding. Paris screamed again.

And then it was gone. Ed and Rhodes had rolled the thing off her. Paris sat up, panting.

"Are you all right?" Ed asked for the second time.

Paris could only nod. The three of them stared down at the corpse in stunned silence. It wore only a white tank top and boxer shorts. Then they turned to look at Larry. But Larry was gone. The kitchen doors swung gently back and forth.

"Shit!" Ed said.

"It's the guy from the fish picture," Rhodes said. "I saw it in the office when we checked in."

"We have to catch him," Ed said. "Come on!"

The three of them rushed out the front door of the diner. George and Timothy were on the sidewalk.

"What's going on?" George asked. "Why is everybody in such a hurry?"

"Larry," Ed panted. "Did you see him?"

"He just ran around back, toward the trailer," George replied, pointing. "He had his cash box with him. Can you tell me what's going on?"

But Ed, Rhodes, and Paris were already running. They dashed around the diner and into the pouring rain. A door slammed. They dodged around the corner in time to see Larry sitting in an old farm truck about twenty yards away. A dingy blue tarp lay in the mud next to it. The truck's side windows had no

glass in them, and one turn signal dangled by a wire, but the engine roared powerfully to life.

"Larry!" Ed shouted.

George came around the corner, rain dripping down his spectacles. "Will someone *please* explain what's going on?"

"I didn't do shit!" Larry yelled from the truck. "Get outta my way!"

The truck revved once and leaped forward as Larry slammed it into gear. It fishtailed for a moment, then headed straight for Paris and the men. Instinctively they scattered. Larry spun the steering wheel and made for the narrow alley space between the diner and the office.

"Larry!" Rhodes shouted. "Wait!"

And then, not far from George, Timothy stepped out of the alley directly in front of the speeding truck. He looked at the oncoming headlights with enormous, silent eyes. Ice grabbed Paris's chest and she reached out with both hands, though she was too far away to make a difference. The truck barreled forward straight at the boy.

"No!" Ed shouted. "Tim, no!"

George was already moving. He ran toward Timothy even as Larry stamped on the brakes. The tires found little traction on the slippery mud and the truck caromed forward at a good forty miles an hour.

Tim stood in the headlights, paralyzed like a rabbit. Twenty yards. Ten. George reached his stepson and shoved him hard. Larry twisted the steering wheel. Tim flew sideways and landed hard in the mud a safe distance away. George kept moving, but Larry's frantic driving sent the truck swerving in the same direction George was taking. It bore down on him like a charging elephant. George noticed the swerve and tried to change direction. Larry yelled something incoherent and blared his horn. George slipped. He recovered his balance almost instantly, but in the delay, Larry's truck smashed full into him. Less than a second later, it crashed into the back of the office, crushing George's body and grinding it into the wall. Paris screamed. The truck stopped.

Rain bounced and pinged off the truck's roof. The horn blared again, then fell silent. George's head and arms were splayed over the grill and across the hood. Red blood dripped onto the sidewalk. A choking sound rose and died in George's throat. Ginny came around the corner and put a hand to her mouth. For a long moment, there was no sound but the rain.

"Jesus," Paris whispered. And thunder rumbled in the distance.

Ed worked grimly with the rope, lashing Larry's right arm to the office chair. Rhodes worked the left.

Ginny sat on the vinyl couch, holding a sobbing Timothy. Paris stood in the doorway, staring once again out into the rain. Larry's green cash box sat on the desk.

"It was an accident!" Larry said, clearly close to tears. "You saw! The kid ran right out in front of me! I'm not a murderer!"

"There's a dead body in your freezer, you fucking psycho," Rhodes said. He finished Larry's arm and moved down to his ankle.

"But I didn't kill him," Larry protested. "I found him like that!"

"Stiff and tidy in his underwear?" Paris said. "You have some weird ideas about what makes a good frozen treat."

"No, wait!" Larry begged. "Listen! I knew you wouldn't understand." Ed tugged the ropes to make sure they were tight. "Ow! Just listen, okay? I was in Vegas last month, and I lost everything—every cent I had. I was driving east and running on empty, so I pulled into the—ow!—I pulled into the parking lot of this motel to figure out what to do next. I came in the office, walked right in, and there's the manager. He was sitting at that desk right there, face down in a Banquet pot pie, dead. Heart attack or stroke or something. Hell, I don't know."

Ed finished with Larry's ankle and sat back on his

heels, listening. Paris and Rhodes listened as well. Ginny continued to comfort Tim as best she could.

"He had been sitting there for who knows how long," Larry continued. "So I pulled him away from the table and set him on the floor behind the desk, and that's when this auto parts salesman pulls up looking for a room. And—don't ask me why—I took his thirty and checked him in. I just took a key from the wall and gave him a room. Maybe that was wrong, but I didn't have a dime and that's what I did. And then I came back here, and I moved Larry's body—his shirt said his name was Larry, too—I moved him into the freezer."

"The freezer?" Paris said incredulously, echoing Ed's own reaction. "Why the freezer?"

"It's the desert! It was hot out," Larry said. "I thought it was the best place for him 'til his family—or someone—came along. Only no one did. I supposed I should've called the police, but more guests showed up. So I checked them in, too. And they all seemed happy. And I realized I was happy making like a motel guy. So I just . . . stayed. I mean, his name was Larry too, so it seemed like destiny, you know? Like it was meant to be."

He fell silent. Ed's knees cracked as he straightened up, not sure whether to be relieved or pissed. The poor bastard sounded convincing. It would be

easy enough to check his story, let the medical examiner determine if Larry—freezer Larry—had died of natural causes or not. But if this Larry was telling the truth, it meant they still didn't know who had killed Maine. Still could be Larry, come to that.

"This is a total crock of shit!" Rhodes exploded.

Larry cringed. "No, it's not. It's not!"

Rhodes' pale eyes flashed. He leaned down, getting in Larry's face. "Admit it, weasel. You killed him, just like you killed my con, just like you killed her husband, just like you killed his actress. *Admit it!*"

"Please stop!" Ginny cried from the couch. Tim's face was buried in her shoulder. "Please! I can't take this anymore. Neither can he. He's just a little boy!"

"It's under control now," Rhodes said, not taking his eyes off Larry. "We got the guy."

Ed crossed to the door. "I don't know what we got."

"Thank you," Larry said.

"I have to agree," Paris said with obvious reluctance. "I thought we got 'the guy' an hour ago, and then we found him gargling a baseball bat. Kinda shoots most of our theories, you know?"

Rhodes rounded on her. "Oh come on! You believe that shit? It was him! Look at him. It's him! He grabbed you with that fucking knife. He was going to kill you."

"Look," Paris said, "I don't want to sound naïve, but that story of his was so fucking unbelievable, it makes me think it might actually be true."

"You got a point," Ed said.

Ginny spoke up in a quiet, serious voice. "Maybe it's the burial ground. Read that brochure over there. A hundred years ago, the government moved these Indians here. All but one of them died because there was no water."

"And now what?" Rhodes scoffed. "They're coming back to life like sea monkeys? Gimme a break, honey!"

"Rhodes, come on," Ed said. "Easy."

"Why don't *you* take it easy?" Rhodes shot back. "You've been trying to run this show all night, pointing fingers, handing out orders. You blamed my con for everything, but then he gets himself killed, and it's obvious the weasel here did it. He had your actress's wallet in his fucking pocket! And we all saw him run down George."

Timothy moaned and put his hands over his ears.

"Please stop," Ginny pleaded, rocking him.

"You want a plan?" Rhodes said. "I got a plan. Nobody's gonna move. We're gonna stay here, just like this, in this room, 'til dawn. No one's gonna leave, and no one's gonna move." He drew his pistol and gestured with it at Larry. Larry blanched. "And if it's him,

and he tries something, I'll fucking shoot him. And if it's something out there and they come in here, I'll fucking shoot them. And if one of us tries anything—"

"We get it, we get it," Ed broke in.

Rhodes holstered his pistol and fell silent. The only sound in the room was Tim's muffled sobs. Then the lights flickered, dimmed, and came back on. Ed looked sharply to Paris and to Rhodes. Rhodes drew his gun. The lights flickered again.

"Firstly," says Defense Counselor Marty Greenfruit, "an insanity plea was refused by the court despite the fact that my client Mr. Rivers is a certifiable axis four dissociative. To this day, he remains unaware of the crimes for which he was convicted. As I'm sure you know, Your Honor, in 1986 the United States Supreme Court ruled that the states cannot execute a person who does not understand why he's being put to death."

"He signed a confession, Counselor," says Judge Taylor. As if on cue, Detective Valrole holds up a sheet of paper. At the top are the words *Confession of Malcolm Rivers* and at the bottom is a crude scrawl.

"He didn't just sign it," Valrole says. "He *dictated* it to me. He told me exactly how he killed each and every—"

"Secondly," Greenfruit interrupts, refusing to stray

from his point, "a confession was accepted into evidence despite the fact it was neither signed nor dictated by Malcolm Rivers."

Valrole slaps the table. "This is a *joke!*"

"Thirdly, we have Malcolm's diaries, found misfiled in state evidence." Greenfruit opens an evidence bag the size of a garbage sack and tosses several black notebooks onto the table. "Important to note are the spectacular changes in handwriting, style, point of view, and tone. If you would, Your Honor?"

Taylor grudgingly puts on his reading glasses and opens one of the notebooks. A childish scrawl laboriously printed across the first page reads,

My kitty dyed today. Daddy sed she burned up by accident, but I no Daddy did it on purpose. I am sad. I saw blud on her fur. It made me feel funny. I licked her fur and it tasted good. I should be punished. Punished hard.

Taylor pushes that notebook aside, opens another one. Tight, anal-retentive letters march rigidly across the paper.

7:29 A.M.: AWOKE AND SHUT OFF ALARM FIVE SECONDS BEFORE IT WOULD HAVE GONE OFF. PERFECT WEEK SO FAR.

7:31 A.M.: ELIMINATED BODY WASTES, BRUSHED TEETH WITH CREST TOOTHPASTE, SHOWERED, SHAVED. DRESSED IN BROWN COTTON SLACKS, BLUE POLO SHIRT, DARK SOCKS, LOAFERS.

7:52 A.M.: IS TUESDAY, SO MADE OATMEAL WITH RAISINS, TOAST, AND TEA FOR BREAKFAST. ATE. REALIZED HALFWAY THROUGH MEAL HAD FORGOTTEN TO ADD "BUY SHOE POLISH" TO TASK LIST FOR TODAY. BY TIME FETCHED LIST, ADDED ITEM, AND RETURNED TO TABLE, TOAST COLD, OATMEAL CONGEALED. MOST UNPLEASANT TO FINISH EATING.

The third notebook is written in a clearly feminine hand.

That idiot of a pool boy over-chlorinated the water again. That's the second time this month. My skin is so dry, it's going to take hours at the spa to remoisturize properly. I'll have to speak to Gerald and have the stupid spic fired. I don't care how cute his ass is.

The other diaries are equally diverse in both handwriting and content. Taylor is forced to admit that if they weren't in the same type of notebook, he would assume they were all written by different people.

Once Taylor is finished, Greenfruit gestures at the psychiatrist. "With your permission, sir, Dr. Mallick will elaborate further."

"Go ahead," Taylor sighs.

"Dissociative Identity Disorder," begins Dr. Mallick from his chair, "invariably arises from severe physical, sexual, and emotional abuse, usually from one or both parents. In Malcolm Rivers's case, the traumas he lived through were some of the worst I've come across, and he—"

"Like what?" Assistant D.A. Kerrick asks. "He get spanked two or three times too often?"

"Every so often, young Malcolm was given a mild day," Mallick says blandly. "His father would strip him naked, hang him upside-down by his ankles over a dish of dog food, and insert a lit candle into his rectum. He would only be released once he finished the dog food—his breakfast. He was under a time limit, of course, because the candle would eventually burn down to—"

"I don't need to hear any more," Kerrick interrupts, looking a little green. "I'll take your word for the rest."

"I have encountered patients who were beaten, buried alive and exhumed, shocked with electrical cords, burned, starved, mutilated, locked in freezers, and whose fathers arranged for them to be gang-

raped," Mallick says. "The psyche fractures in such cases. It falls apart. "

"So how do you treat it?" Taylor asks.

"There is no universally efficacious treatment for Dissociative Identity Disorder. In theory, one must attempt to move a patient toward integration, a melding of the fractured psyche. Unfortunately, Malcolm Rivers proved highly resistant to the more usual approaches, and we were running out of time with his execution approaching. So I finally embarked on a new, more experimental therapy. The first steps involved careful administration of psychoactive drugs—I can give the court a list, if it would be helpful—and careful use of hypnotic trance. Early indications were very encouraging, and Mr. Rivers moved quickly forward through the new process. I was, in fact, able to initiate the final step—"

"—with the permission of the State Supreme Court," Greenfruit interjects.

"—this afternoon. Before Mr. Rivers left Ely State Prison."

The double doors boom open with a heavy, ominous sound. A guard pokes his head in. "He's here, Your Honor."

The people in the room stir uneasily, all except for Dr. Mallick. In the corner, the grandfather clock strikes two.

Taylor clears his throat. "Any trouble?" The guard shakes his head. "Then bring him up."

"It'll take a moment, sir," the guard says. "They have to bring him up the freight elevator."

Taylor raises an eyebrow. "The freight elevator? We didn't use it during his trial."

"Yes, sir. Moving this guy around has gotten a little more complicated."

Down the corridor comes a squealing noise of steel on steel as a heavy elevator car rises to the third floor. It slams into place with a heavy, mechanical *thud*. This is followed by a squeaking that reminds Taylor of a bike that needs a shot of WD-40. The guard props the conference room doors open, and a moment later a beefy man in a white orderly's jacket enters pushing a wheelchair. The wheelchair looks solid enough to restrain a locomotive, which is good because the man restrained in it is built like a steam engine. His head is shaved and his face is oddly androgynous. An IV is plugged into his hand, and a pair of IV bags hang above him. The man's expression is placid and calm, but Taylor also notices his eyes. They are full of restrained thunder.

"You all know my client," says Greenfruit. "Mr. Malcolm Rivers."

* * *

Everyone drooped from exhaustion. Larry was still tied in his chair. Ed stood near the desk. Paris had stationed herself at the front door. Ginny and Tim sat on the couch. Rhodes sat in a chair, his pistol held loosely between his knees. Ed had opened the door that connected Larry's office to room one, then opened more doors until they could see into room four, where Alice lay sleeping. A wall clock struck two. The lights had stopped flickering, but Ed still regarded them warily. Maybe he should ask Larry about flashlights in case they went out altogether.

Tim abruptly pushed away from Ginny and moved toward the connecting door. Ginny got up to chase after him.

"No, Timmy," she said, taking his shoulder. "You need to stay in here with us. We can see into your mom's room from here." Tim shook her off and trotted off. "Timmy!"

"It's okay," Rhodes said. "Let him."

Ginny shrugged and took up her position on the sofa again. Ed wandered over to the brochure rack. Which one had Ginny been talking about? The Shoshone. He found the brochure and leafed through it. Death by drought, the bodies buried not far from the motel. Only one survivor.

"Remember that movie where ten strangers all

came to an island and they all died one by one?" Ginny said.

"*Ten Little Indians*," Paris said. "It was an Agatha Christie book first."

"Yeah, well, it turned out they weren't strangers, right?" Ginny said. "They had a connection."

"I remember that one," Larry put in from his chair. "They'd all messed with the wrong guy and he was getting revenge."

"Shut up," Rhodes said.

"I'm just saying," Ginny said, "maybe there's some connection between all of us."

Ed shook his head. "I don't think so. We're all here by coincidence."

Paris cocked her head, considering the idea. Larry chewed his lip.

"We're all in Nevada," he said finally.

"Shut *up*," Rhodes said.

"Where were you headed with your con when you pulled in here, Rhodes?" Paris asked.

"Carson City," Rhodes said.

Paris shook her head. "No connection. I was going home. To Florida. Where were you going, Ed?"

"Driving Caroline Suzanne back to L.A."

"I was born in Florida," Larry said.

Rhodes's gun snapped around to point at Larry's face. Larry flinched.

"Jesus! I'm just talking!"

"Since you've been in that chair," Rhodes said, "no one's died. So I suggest you shut the fuck up."

"No one's died since we've been in here," Larry corrected. "Since we've *all* been in here."

The room fell silent again. Thunder rumbled.

"Where in Florida, Larry?" Paris said at last.

Larry looked nervously at Rhodes, then said, "Polk County."

"You're kidding!" Paris said. "That's where I was born. What town?"

"Mulberry."

Paris pointed a thumb at her chest. "Frostproof."

"No wonder you left," Larry said wryly.

"There's a town called 'Frostproof'?" Ed said.

"They grow oranges," Paris explained. "The name kinda doubles as a slogan."

"I danced hallelujah on the day I left Polk," Larry said. "Why would you want to go back?"

Paris hesitated. "I . . . found a grove for sale. On the Internet. Oranges and limes."

"You're pulling my leg," Ed said. "An orange grove for sale on-line?"

"Hey, someone once put up a small town for sale on eBay," Paris said. "Starting bid was five thousand and it ended up going for over a million. You can find anything out there. Anyway, this farm is nine acres

and has twelve hundred trees. According to the realtor, the soil needs a few tills of phosphorus and the lanes need reeding, but it's good land." Paris seemed to realize everyone was looking at her in disbelief. "What?"

"It sounds . . . nice," Ed said.

"You think it's weird for someone in my line of work to go into citrus farming, is that it?"

"Well," Larry said, "you have to admit—"

"I grew up on an orange farm," Paris said. "I still remember how it all works."

"Everyone has to grow up somewhere," Ed said philosophically.

From far away came the sound of Tim bursting into tears. After a moment's shocked silence, everyone except Larry made a concerted rush for the connecting door with Ed in the lead. When he got to room four, Ed found Alice motionless on the bed and Tim crying in the corner. He looked terrified. Ed went into emergency worker mode. Suppressing his fear and guilt, he leaned over Alice, tilted back her head to clear her airway, and listened. He also pressed his fingers to her neck. Tim came and stood next to him, looking scared.

"She's stopped breathing and there's no pulse," Ed reported, then cocked his head at Tim. "Ginny!" Ginny took the hint and hauled the sobbing Tim

away. "Rhodes, help me get her on the floor for CPR. We can't do it on the bed."

Moving quickly, they lifted Alice onto the floor. Ed breathed twice into her warm mouth, then laced his hands together to begin chest compressions. After fifteen, he breathed twice more. Rhodes and Paris watched in silence. Why wasn't Rhodes volunteering to help, Ed wondered. Didn't Nevada require its cops to know CPR?

"Wake up, Alice," he said. "It's not time for you to go. You've got a son who needs you."

"Please, Alice," Paris said softly.

Ed continued to work. Compress fifteen times and breathe. Compress fifteen times and breathe. He kept seeing Alice's body fly through the air in front of the limosine, and it spurred his efforts. She was lying here because of him, and he wasn't going to let her die.

"Come on, Alice," he muttered. "Don't leave us. Don't do this to me."

Something caught Rhodes's eye. He leaned down and plucked something from the floor near Alice's hand. Ed kept up the breathing and compressions. It was hard work, and he broke into a sweat.

"Wake up, Alice," he gasped. "Come on! Thirteen and fourteen and fifteen and *breathe*. One and two and three and four . . ." But Alice didn't respond.

After several minutes, Ed felt a hand on his shoulder.

"It's over, Ed," Paris murmured. "You did the best you could."

Ed ran through two more cycles of compressions and breathing, then finally sat back on his heels, panting and defeated. Alice was dead.

"Jesus fuck," he whispered. "What are we going to tell Tim?"

"I think he knows," Paris said.

"This was next to her," Rhodes put in, and showed Ed a room key. Number six. Ed blinked.

"That doesn't make sense," he said. "She died because of the . . . accident."

"George was an accident, too," Paris said, "if you believe Larry."

"But why six?" Rhodes said. "They skipped seven."

The trio traded long looks.

"Aw, fuck," Paris groaned. "Oh, no."

"Yeah," Ed said. "Let's get it over with."

8

The truck's engine roared to life. Ed, standing in the rain, made "come on" motions with his hands, and Paris slowly backed it away from the office wall. Rhodes stood near the grill. It was a miracle that the truck hadn't gone straight through the wall, though the building had taken definite damage.

As the truck backed away, George York's arms and head slid limply off the hood and out of sight. Rhodes caught the body and lowered it to the ground while Paris shut the truck off and climbed out of the cab. Ed came over as well. Ginny, Tim, and Larry had stayed behind in the office.

Blood coated George's corpse. It filled his mouth and oozed from his nose. One lens of his glasses was broken. The middle of his body was a crushed ruin. Ed could smell leaking body fluids even over the rain. He took a deep breath and pried open George's

left hand. It was already cold. And empty. He did the same with the right. Also empty.

Rhodes, meanwhile, knelt next to Ed and gently peeled back George's blood-soaked jacket. With a stoic face, he searched the sticky pockets. A moment later, he pulled out a key.

"Number seven," he said.

They were back in the office. Ed had lined up the five dead keys on Larry's desk. Three of them were sticky-shiny with blood. Ed stared at them, trying to make sense out of everything. Larry still sat tied to his chair. Ginny and Tim huddled in the corner. Rhodes rummaged around in Larry's desk drawers until he produced a bottle of orange Schnapps. Paris stood in the open door and stared into the rain, as had become her habit. Water fell in front of her like a veil. She swiped at her eyes.

"This is really . . . I mean . . . it's so fucked up," she choked. "I saw what happened. I was right *there*. I saw him run out. No one could've known he was gonna do that. No one."

"No one human," Ginny said.

Rhodes rounded on her. "So is that where we are now? It's the Shoshone spirits getting their fucking *revenge*? Why not blame the fairies or the leprechauns?" He slugged down a mouthful of

Schnapps. "Hell, maybe it's the ghost of the guy Larry shoved in a baggie!"

"Only one Shoshone survived the drought," Ginny said. "Maybe they mean for only one of *us* to survive the flood."

"Aw, fuck that!" Larry said.

"Listen," Ed said, catching both Paris and Ginny in his gaze. "I want you to take Ginny's car and get out of here. Both of you and the kid."

"Where are we supposed to go?" Ginny asked. Her voice quavered.

"How much gas do you have?"

"Half a tank, I think."

Ed checked the wall clock. Behind him, Rhodes sat on the edge of the desk, staring at Larry and sipping from the Schnapps bottle.

"It's almost three," Ed said quietly. "You can drive until dawn on that. Just keep moving. When you get to the flooded part, turn around and go the other way, or something." He ran a hand over his face with a sigh. "I should have sent you away sooner. I just don't understand what's happening here anymore. And not only that"—he lowered his voice—"Rhodes is making me nervous."

Paris nodded once and headed for the connecting door. "You stay here, Ginny. I'll go get our stuff. Tim's, too."

"What are you doing?" Rhodes demanded.

"They're leaving," Ed said.

"What? You can't let a bunch of suspects run out after five people—"

"Do you really think they're suspects, Rhodes?" Ed said with note of belligerence. "I don't. And if it's not them, then they're safest where *we* aren't."

Rhodes wiped Schnapps from his upper lip. "There's a thing called procedure, Eddie, and you know damn well—"

"When exactly did procedure start mattering to you, Schnapps boy?" Ed interrupted.

"I'm telling you they're not going!" Rhodes's voice grew shrill.

"I say they are," Ed snapped. "So back the fuck off!"

Rhodes's pale eyes glared icy daggers at Ed. Ed stared back, unmoving. Finally Rhodes kicked the desk. "Fuck!" He retreated to the sofa with the Schnapps bottle.

A few minutes later, Paris reappeared, laden with bags and suitcases. She set them down just outside the main door under the overhang near the police sedan. Rhodes glared at her as Ginny led an unresisting Tim out the door. The boy looked dazed and only half-aware. Ed's heart broke to look at him. No child should have to go through anything like this.

"This is bullshit!" Larry called from his chair. "I wasn't allowed to leave."

"Shut up, Larry," Rhodes said.

"At least don't leave with my truck keys," Larry said. "I know you still have them."

"Yeah, like I want to be seen driving a truck that won the Yeeee-Ha Hick Award," Paris said. She dropped the keys on Larry's desk next to the cash box and went back outside.

"Ready, Tim?" Ginny said. "On three we'll run to my car, then drive up to get Paris and our stuff. One . . . two . . . three!" They dashed away. Ed went out under the eaves and stood next to Paris, out of Rhodes and Larry's sight.

"Take this," Ed said, and handed her his .38 snub-nose. "I'll be okay without it."

Paris nodded, then suddenly kissed Ed on the cheek for a second time. He turned and changed it into a full lip-lock. Paris's mouth was warm and gentle on his. Ed's hand reached up to touch her damp hair just as Rhodes opened the office door.

The explosion knocked Ed off his feet.

Ed was vaguely aware of being shoved backward and slamming into the wall of the motel. Glass shattered. Larry screamed from inside the office. Paris cried out, too. Ed was lying on his back on the damp sidewalk, staring up at the metal overhang. A warm

trickle ran down his cheek. His brain couldn't encompass what was going on. Paris had kissed him. Rhodes had opened the hotel door. Now he was lying on his back. He turned his head. Debris was raining down over the parking lot. Some of it clattered and pinged off the overhang.

Ed sat up. Paris moaned beside him. Rhodes was nowhere to be seen. Out in the parking lot, Ginny's car was a raging inferno. Ed's mind finally cleared and he scrambled to his feet. Beside him, Paris did the same.

"Are you all right?" he demanded.

"Shit!" Paris said, staring at the burning wreck.

"Hey!" Larry yelled from inside the office. "Hey! I got fire extinguishers!"

Ed turned and dashed into the office. Every window had been shattered by the shockwave. Glass cracked and crunched beneath his feet. Rhodes was pulling himself to his feet, looking dazed. The office was a terrible mess. Rhodes opening the door had allowed the shockwave to blast straight into the room. Larry had fallen sideways, and his chair had partially broken. His bonds had come loose. Rhodes shook his head as if to clear it, then ran over to Larry and helped him free of the chair, practicality momentarily overcoming suspicion.

"Where are the extinguishers?" Rhodes demanded.

"Back room," Larry said. "Come on!" They raced away. Ed went back outside. The car continued to burn. Paris stood with her arms tightly crossed.

"Is there any way Ginny and Tim could've . . ." Paris began, and trailed off.

"I don't see how," Ed said, feeling sick. "Jesus."

"We're never getting out of here," Paris whispered.

Larry and Rhodes rushed out of the office with two red canisters. They ran to the car, then halted uncertainly. The intense heat was keeping them back. Finally Larry moved in, spraying white powder ahead of him. Rhodes joined him. Rain sputtered and hissed on the superheated metal. Smoke billowed into the sky. After a few minutes, the fire died down. The extinguishers ran out of juice, but the rain continued their work until only a few flames flickered inside the ruined shell. Rhodes and Larry both stared into the car for some time. Rhodes said something to Larry, and they came back to the eaves.

"There's no trace of them," Rhodes said in disbelief. "No bodies, nothing. Where the hell are they?"

"Maybe it got so hot, they were cremated," Larry said.

Ed shook his head, feeling dazed again. "There'd be *something* left. A belt buckle. Teeth. Something."

Rhodes pointed accusingly at Ed. "This was your idea. 'They're safest where *we* aren't,' remember that?"

A sledgehammer of guilt slammed Ed in the stomach. He turned away, jaw clenched. Rhodes was right. He had urged Ginny and Tim to leave. Ed was responsible for three deaths now.

"Maybe you wanted them to leave for a reason, Ed," Rhodes continued. "Maybe you *wanted* them in that car."

Ed couldn't speak. The image of Tim and Ginny being torn to bits by an explosion wouldn't leave his mind.

"Where's your gun, Ed?" Rhodes said. Paris's hand fell to her purse. Rhodes stepped forward and frisked Ed with quick, practiced movements. Something jingled in Ed's jacket pocket. Rhodes reached in and pulled out a pair of keys. Ed's mouth fell open and his mind spun.

"Rooms five and four," Rhodes breathed, holding them up.

"You fuck!" Larry said. "You tried to frame me!"

"Those aren't mine. Someone put those in my pocket." Ed turned to Paris, who looked unhappy and confused. "They're not mine!"

Rhodes produced a pair of handcuffs from his pocket. "I forgot I had an extra pair in the car," he said, and roughly spun Ed around to click them into place. "Give me his gun, Paris. Now. I know you have it. You grabbed at your purse when I asked where it was."

"The keys aren't mine!" Ed protested again. The cuffs were cold and tight on his wrists.

"Where's the gun, Paris?" Rhodes said.

Hesitantly, uncertainly, Paris opened her purse and handed it over. Rhodes spun the action once, checked the safety, and shoved it into his pocket.

"The office is a loss," he said. "Let's get in the diner."

Ed's mind whirled as Rhodes hauled him roughly down the walkway. He hadn't put those keys into his pocket. He knew that for a fact. Someone had put them there, but who? Any of the others had the opportunity to do it, he supposed. Paris had kissed him. Rhodes had searched him. Even Larry had come close enough to him after the car blew up.

Or maybe it was the Shoshone. Ed swallowed. The darkness and rain around him seemed full of glittering eyes and cold, dry fingers. Arms raised to the sky begged for water, thirsted for revenge.

Paris reached the diner first and opened the door. She paused in the doorway. "Oh no. No fucking way."

"What? What is it?" Larry asked, but she had already run inside. He scurried after. Swearing under his breath, Rhodes hustled Ed into the diner as well.

It was dim inside, lit only by the blue-white mercury lights from outside. Rhodes and Ed joined Paris and Larry, who were standing just inside the door.

The diner was completely empty. Maine's body was gone.

"Oh my God," Paris said.

Leaning neatly against the pillar was the top of Larry's baseball bat. It was broken in just the right place so a man could fake his death by sticking the cut-off end in his mouth. Larry crossed to it and picked it up.

"Too bad you didn't remember those extra hand-cuffs earlier," Paris observed. "Otherwise we might have been able to tie him up with something besides a toaster cord."

"What the *fuck?*" Rhodes finally exploded.

"You checked his pulse, right Rhodes?" Ed said. "When we found him with the bat. Tell me you checked his pulse."

Rhodes said nothing.

"Unlock his cuffs, Rhodes," Paris said. "Ed didn't blow up the car, and you know it. Although how Maine got his hands on a car bomb, I can't imagine."

Rhodes didn't turn his eyes from the empty place once occupied by Maine's body. After a long moment, he held out a handcuff key. Paris took it and released Ed. He rubbed his wrists in relief.

"If Maine is alive and free," he said, "that puts a whole new light on everything."

"It puts a whole fucking *sun* on it," Paris growled.

"Do you think he somehow arranged for . . . what happened to George?" Larry said, a strange note of hope in voice. "It would mean that it wasn't my . . . that I didn't . . . you know."

Ed shrugged. "Dunno. We could check it out, I guess."

"And look for what?" Rhodes said. "A handy dropped confession? Maine's initials carved into the tire tracks?"

"Can't hurt to look," Ed maintained, and turned to leave.

"You aren't going anywhere without me," Rhodes said, and drew his gun. "I still have suspicions about you, Dakota. You too, Washington. I want you both where I can see you."

"So I guess *I'm* not a suspect," Paris said. "Gosh. That makes me feel all happy and bouncy inside."

The wind had picked up outside as all four of them made their way around the diner to the muddy rear courtyard. Ed braced himself. Even after years on the job, dead bodies still made him shudder. A part of him was glad that he wasn't so hardened to human suffering and pain, though at the moment it made life really hard. Life. It seemed like his whole life now centered around this shitty motel. Did he even have a life before he had come here? And once all this was over, would he have—

George York's body was gone. No crushed torso, no broken glasses, nothing. Not even a trace of scarlet on the truck's radiator grill. The four adults stood motionless, stunned.

"What the fuck is going on here?" Rhodes said hoarsely.

"There should be something." Ed knelt in the cold rain and ran his hands over the muddy spot. "An impression, some blood, *something*."

A door slammed in the wind behind them. Everyone spun, startled. Lightning flashed and cut across their faces. As one, they turned and ran to the motel, pounded up the walkway to room six. Ed flung open the door.

Lou's body had vanished. The carpet and wall were perfectly clean.

"The laundry room," Larry said. And they ran again.

All eight dryers stood wide open, like gaping mouths. Ed edged up to the one in the top left corner. It was empty. And clean.

"No blood," he said incredulously. "Not even a drop. But it was everywhere."

"There's this stuff on TV," Larry said. "They claimed it can get stains out of anything, and really fast."

"Someone's collecting bodies," Rhodes said.

They ran back to the ruined office and through the connecting doors into room four. The bed was neatly made. Alice's body was gone. Paris wrenched the front door open.

"Motherfucker!" she shouted to the world. "I give up! What the hell do you want? Answer me, you sick bastard! Whoever the hell you are—what do you fucking want?"

Ed put a hand on her shoulder. "Paris . . ."

She whirled on him. "I'm gonna be thirty next week and I want to go home and grow oranges!" she snarled. "Got a problem with that, *Edward*?"

For a long moment the only sound was the drumming of the rain. The lights flickered, dimmed, then came back on. Then Larry said, "It's your birthday next week?"

No response from Paris.

"It's *my* birthday next week," Larry said tentatively. "May tenth."

Paris blinked. "Me, too."

"Me, too," Rhodes said.

"Yeah," Ed said.

Thunder boomed. Ed caught Larry's eye, jerked his head toward the connecting door. Larry nodded in understanding.

It only took a few seconds for everyone to reach the wrecked office. All the drawers on the desk had

been knocked open and records had scattered everywhere like paper birds. Water dripped from the ceiling. The picture of the man with the carp—the man Larry had found dead—lay on the floor, its frame cracked. Larry dug around in the mess until he came up with his green box. He opened it, revealing cash and photocopies of everyone's identification.

"George and Alice York," he said, paging through them. "Caroline Suzanne. Robert Maine's prison card. Edward Dakota. Ginny and Louis Iana. All with the same birthday—May tenth. What are the odds? It must be ten trillion to one."

Something nagged at the edge of Ed's mind. He recognized the feeling. Back in his cop days, it meant he had missed a clue, an obvious one. Experience told him that if he chewed on it for a few minutes, it would probably come into focus. But what was it? The room numbers? They had already figured out why the killer had gone out of sequence—the six accidentally transformed into a nine. The birth dates? Maybe. He took the pile of copies from Larry and leafed through them again. George Allen York. Alice Newman York. No ID for Tim, but he was—had been—just a kid. Caroline Norma Suzanne. A bad ID photo made worse by the photocopying. Hmmmm . . .

"What is it?" Rhodes asked, peering over his shoulder.

With a crash, a section of the ceiling gave way and water cascaded into the office. Paris leaped aside with a yelp. The four people dodged into the connecting room. Rain poured into the office, soaking the papers and flooding the carpet.

"God, it never lets up," Larry shouted, sounding both pissed and scared.

"Between the truck and the explosion, I'm surprised the whole goddam building hasn't collapsed," Paris said. "Maybe we should—"

The lights went out.

"Motherfucker!" Paris shrieked.

Rhodes jerked the front door open. The neon sign had gone black, and the parking lot lights shed only dim illumination.

"Where's the transformer, Larry?" Rhodes asked. "The fuse box?"

"In back. By the laundry room." He trotted toward the door and pointed into the semidarkness. "Back there. On the other side of the building. I'll come with you."

"I'm not staying in here," Paris said.

The itching at the back of Ed's mind grew stronger. He looked down and noticed the ID copies were still in his hand. He laid them out on the bed, though he could barely see them.

"You coming, Ed?" Larry asked. Ed didn't answer.

He was concentrating so hard that he barely noticed when the others ran off. Ed finally hunted around in his pockets until he came up with the limo keys. The key chain had a small flashlight on it. Ed shined the beam on the photocopies, illuminating one after the other.

Cold stole over him and gooseflesh rose on his back and arms. He swung the beam back and forth over the row of paper in disbelief. This couldn't be true. The coincidence was too big, too much. But there it was.

"Ginny and Louis Iana," he breathed. "Virginia and Louisiana. Caroline Norma—North Carolina. Paris Nevada. George York. Samuel Rhodes—Rhode Island. Robert Maine. Larry Washington." He pointed the beam at his own ID. "Edward Dakota."

A strange buzzing pulsed in his ears. Ed swayed dizzily on the bed. He had felt this way before. Was he getting sick? He fumbled in his pockets, trying to find his pillbox.

"Malcolm Rivers was raised in a roadhouse in northern Nevada. He was repeatedly beaten, molested, and tortured by his father and his father's customers."

"Who's there?" Ed said.

"His mother died of a drug overdose when he was twelve. Soon thereafter, Malcolm's father decided he should take her place in his bed."

Ed twisted around, trying to locate the source of the voice. The room began to brighten around him. He blinked, now able to make out someone. A man seated at a table. He looked familiar.

"Malcolm's father rented him out to customers at the roadhouse, often six or seven times a night. His price would drop the day he turned eighteen, so his father told everyone Malcolm was underage until he was almost twenty. You can imagine the impact all this had on young Malcolm's psyche."

Ed swallowed, tried to speak, and failed. He cleared his throat and tried again.

"That you, Doc?"

A thick wire lay sparking in the mud behind the motel. It smelled like ozone. Paris grimaced and forced herself to keep running with Larry and Rhodes. She was so tired. When had she last slept? Or eaten? She couldn't remember. The adrenaline surges that had been crashing over her all night long were taking their toll, and she was finding it harder and harder to concentrate. Rhodes and Larry were looking pretty beat themselves. Right then she would have done Pat Robertson for free if it meant getting a bed for the night.

They reached the laundry room and went around to the back. Here the wind blew cold rain under the

eaves and straight into their faces. The tiny bit of light shed by the parking lot lamps didn't reach back here, either. The place was darker than the inside of a dead black cat, as Paris's grandmother liked to say.

Larry located the electrical box by touch. He and Rhodes fiddled with it, but the darkness combined with the slashing wind and rain to defeat them.

"I can't see anything," Rhodes said loudly. "Get me a flashlight!"

"I've got one in my trailer," Larry yelled back. "But there's a downed wire in the courtyard and I ain't going back there. I like my balls to stay raw, not fried."

"There's a downed wire?" Rhodes said. "Then why the hell are we fucking with the circuit box?"

"The mercury lights are on an independent circuit," Larry said. "That's why they're in a brownout. If we can figure out what's wrong, we might be able to get them working. The motel will be blacked out, but we'll still have light from the parking lot."

"I still need a goddam flashlight!"

"And I'm still not going back to my trailer."

"You got a flashlight in the cruiser, Rhodes?" Paris shouted.

Before Rhodes could answer, Larry said, "It's a cop car. Of course they've got a couple. Good thinking!"

"Hold on!" Paris said. "I'll go get one."

"Wait!" Rhodes said, but Paris ignored him. She

dashed down to the parking lot—or tried to. The best she could manage was a fast trot. Her legs felt like they were growing roots and planting themselves. God. She wanted dry clothes, a hot meal, and a soft bed, in that order.

Better get used to this, she thought. *You want to be a citrus farmer, remember?*

She did remember. As a kid, there had been plenty of sleepless nights when the frost warnings came in. Countless times had she and her brothers spent the dark hours running up and down the grove lanes, lighting smudge pots in a desperate attempt to keep old Jack Frost from painting the oranges or their delicate blossoms. One bad frost would ruin an entire crop and teeter the farm on the edge of bankruptcy.

One bleary winter morning, she had come into the house, coughing and blackened by smoke, and she realized how much she hated this life. Fertilizing, pruning, reeding, weeding, harvesting, packing, selling. And school in between. Her parents never let up, either. Always talking about how you had to work hard to stay afloat. Do this, do that, and above all, keep working. Screw that. Paris wanted to be her own boss, do what *she* wanted. So when she was seventeen, she had run away to Las Vegas. Lots of bright lights, a big city, a real happenin' town.

Six hard months later, she came to realize what

she had thrown away—a stable home and people who cared about her. Las Vegas, on the other hand, was harsh and uncaring. It was full of pimps who wanted to hook her on drugs and thieves who tried to steal her shoes and street people who stared and muttered. It was full of casinos who didn't want to hire her because she was a dirty, underage runaway. It was full of fear and dread and loneliness.

Finally Paris had tried to call home and got no answer, not even the machine. Something made her trek down to the library and get on one of the public-access computers to check recent news stories in Frostproof, Florida.

The story about the house fire jumped out at her. No survivors. House destroyed. Half the grove decimated. Paris fled the library in tears. Two days later on her eighteenth birthday, she broke into a house while the owners were at work, used their shower, stole some decent clothes from their closet, and got a job as a working girl.

Now, more than ten years later, it was time to backtrack. Her family was gone, but she could get a farm going again, start a new life among the roots of her old one. She was looking forward to walking among the groves again, smelling the fruit and blossoms, listening to the crickets on a sultry summer evening. How could she have hated such a life? Sure, fighting frost

and working outside under a hot, humid sky was difficult, but it beat letting people paw over her for money and licking Reddi-wip off fat businessmen. Maybe she'd even find the right guy, have a couple of kids, and show them the beauty of it all.

First, though, she had to survive a night at the Golden Palm Motel.

Paris yanked open the driver's door of the police sedan and the interior light came on. The car was still parked under the overhang by the office, so she didn't have to go out into the rain to reach it. She plunked herself down behind the steering wheel. The seat was uncomfortable—something was poking her in the back. It occurred to her that she could try the radio again, try to raise some help.

The radio had been ripped out. A few multicolored wires dangled like broken fingers from the housing.

"What the . . . ?" Paris said. Had Maine done this after his escape? Probably. Shit! Okay, deal with that later. Flashlights first. She rummaged around inside the car. No flashlights on or under the seats. On the floor near the accelerator, she found a long, sharp piece of metal like a rat-tail file. It didn't look like any kind of police equipment she had ever seen. On the other hand, she wasn't a cop.

No use checking the back seat for a flashlight—

Rhodes wouldn't have put one back there with a prisoner. That left only the trunk. She leaned over and opened the glove compartment, searching for the trunk release switch. A bunch of papers fell out. She found the trunk release and pressed it. There was a *thunk*, and the lid rose behind her. Then Paris grabbed the papers to stuff them back into the glove box. A name caught her eye: Robert Maine. His prison papers. Maybe there'd be a clue about how to find and catch him in there.

The first page was just a prison transfer form, with name, prison address, crimes committed, and other vital statistics. No real help there.

The second page was a prison transfer form for Samuel Rhodes.

Paris's heart thudded into her throat. She read the paper again, trying to make sense of it. Samuel Rhodes. Ely State Penitentiary. Five feet, ten inches tall. Black hair. Blue eyes. A hundred and sixty pounds. Doing time for double homicide.

Rhodes wasn't a cop—he was a con. A murdering con. Stunned, Paris leaned back into the seat and felt something poking her again. She twisted around to see what it was. There was a small hole in the seat, a puncture ringed with dried blood. Paris's skin crawled. Slowly she inserted the piece of metal she had found into the hole. A perfect fit.

In a flash, she knew what had happened, as if she had been there.

Samuel Rhodes is sitting in the backseat next to Robert Maine. Both of them wear prison-issue coveralls and boots. In the front seat sits the real cop. They're driving through the desert. The sun is high, the temperature is up, and the AC is going full-blast. Maine is probably bobbing his head, singing something insipid.

"Be quiet back there," orders the cop.

Maine grins and starts humming instead. Rhodes, meanwhile, crosses his ankle over his knee. From the sole of his boot he extracts a small round spike he made from a scrap he picked up somewhere. Between the AC fan and Maine's humming, the driver doesn't hear a sound. Rhodes carefully positions the point of the spike in a seam he has found in the protective armor plating between him and the driver. He lifts his foot and rams the spike through the seat.

The car swerves as the officer writhes in agony. Maine whoops with joy. The car screams left, then right, finally leaving the pavement and bumping to a stop on the shoulder. The

officer has slumped over the steering wheel, blood streaming down his back.

"You are my sunshine, my only sunshine," Maine sings gleefully. "You make me happy—"

"Shut up," Rhodes snaps, "or you're next."

Rhodes kicks at the passenger door for several minutes until it finally gives way. Together, he and Maine drag the dying officer from the car. Maine reaches down and, with a quick, practiced twist, breaks the man's neck. Rhodes removes his clothes and takes them for himself.

"What am I supposed to wear?" Maine asks.

"You're in it."

A while later, rain thunders down on the car as it pulls into the motel parking lot. The fuel gauge reads EMPTY.

"Now what?" Maine asks.

Rhodes steps out of the rain and into the motel office. "You the manager? Officer Samuel Rhodes, Corrections. I'm transporting a convict."

Paris stood behind the car, trunk open before her. Inside lay a fit, middle-aged man wearing white briefs. Blood had dried around the wound in his back and his head lolled at an unusual angle. Paris clamped her lips together to keep from screaming.

She slammed the trunk shut and ran back toward the laundry room. Larry was in danger, and she had to tell him—

Rhodes would be standing right there, and he had a gun. Two of them, since he had taken Ed's. Jesus. Paris tried to keep her breathing under control, school her features into nonchalance. She was walking toward one cold-blooded killer, and there was another one running loose in the darkness. Rhodes was a convict, too. Was that why Maine had gotten loose? It would have been easy for Rhodes to cuff him in such a way that he could break free of the toilet. And wasn't it convenient for Maine that Rhodes had forgotten about his spare handcuffs so Maine would have to be tied with electric cord? And Ed had complained that Rhodes wasn't following proper police procedure. Shit, for all Paris knew, Rhodes had been committing the murders, with or without Maine's help. It would have been easy enough for him to plant the keys on Ed, direct suspicion away from himself.

And now Rhodes had a pair of guns.

"Fuck," Paris said, and turned the corner. She could barely make out Larry and Rhodes. They were still poking at the junction box, trying to see by the flame of a cigarette lighter. Rhodes looked perfectly normal, not at all like an escaped killer.

"Larry," she said. "Hey, Larry."

Larry and Rhodes both turned. "What?" Larry said. "You find a flashlight?"

"No. I couldn't"—her voice quavered and she cleared her throat—"I couldn't get into the trunk."

Rhodes's eyes met hers, pale blue and icy cold. A flicker crossed his face, and a tense fist clenched in Paris's stomach.

"You couldn't open the trunk, huh?" Rhodes said quietly. "You couldn't figure out the latch?"

"Nope. Didn't see a thing." She was lying badly, but couldn't seem to take the quaver out of her voice. "You got any ideas, Larry?"

Larry flicked the lighter and turned back to the box. The wind had died down a little, so the eaves afforded some shelter from the rain. "Nothing unless you want to dance across some electric mud to get to my trailer."

"Come with me and we'll look together," Paris said.

"Nah," Rhodes said. "Larry and I will stay here and keep trying."

"But—"

"Yep. I'll just stay here a while with my bud, Larry." Rhodes clapped Larry on the shoulder. "Why don't I just do that? In case someone shows up and wants to hurt him."

Paris felt sick. "I think I'll . . . I'll check the office for a flashlight. Or maybe Ed will think of something. He's probably there."

"Probably," Rhodes agreed. "Tell him I've still got his gun. Paris."

Paris couldn't stand it anymore. She turned and ran for the office. Her earlier fatigue had vanished. She had to find Ed, find him fast. Rhodes was armed and dangerous, and Paris was out of her depth.

Water continued to flow from the ceiling over the dark office floor. Paris stood in the doorway, barely able to see inside.

"Ed?" she called. "Ed, are you here?"

Footsteps on the walkway behind her. Too scared to look, Paris ran into the office. A door slammed in the distance. Something caught Paris's foot, and she sprawled facedown across the flooded carpet. Water went up her nose. She scrambled to her feet, slipped again, got her balance, and ran for the connecting door. In the dark room beyond, she could barely make out a series of papers lined up on the bed like dead ghosts.

"Ed?" she said hoarsely. "Ed?"

Shadows moved outside the window. Paris ducked, then ran into the next room. It was pitch-black. "Ed?"

"Paris!" whispered a man's voice ahead of her.

"Ed! Ed, it's Rhodes. He's—"

"I know, sweetie." A cigarette lighter flamed to life, illuminating Rhodes's face. His pistol was pointed straight at her. "I know all about Samuel Rhodes."

Paris's blood froze. "Oh God."

"I just want my life back," Rhodes said. "That's all. I'm just like you."

Paris slowly backed into the room behind her, the one that connected to the office. Rhodes stayed with her. Paris's eyes never left the gun.

"You're not just like me," she said. "You're a killer. You were doing time for a double fucking homicide!"

"My wife and her boyfriend were running away with my kid. If I hadn't shot them, I would never have seen my son again."

"What about the guy in your trunk? Was *he* running away with your kid?" Paris continued backing through the room until she was standing in the office, hoping for a chance to break and run. Rhodes, however, glided smoothly forward, lighter in one hand, gun in the other. "What about all the other people you fucking killed tonight?"

A flicker moved in the corner of the office. Paris didn't let her eyes stray from Rhodes.

Rhodes came into the office and took two more

steps toward her. "That's far enough, honey. I'm warning you right now—I've got a temper problem. I'm no pussy like Larry. Nothing's gonna stop me from getting out of here, got it? The sedan's on empty, but the truck is full. All I need are the keys. You had them last—what did you do with them?"

"Don't you remember?" Paris said. "You were right there."

Rhodes pointed the pistol at her face. "Don't fuck with me. If I have to hurt you—"

"Where the hell is Ed?" Paris demanded. "What did you do to him?"

"Where are the keys to the fucking truck?"

"Ask the pussy."

A crack resounded through the office. Rhodes's face jerked in surprise, then went slack. He collapsed to the floor, revealing Larry holding a red fire extinguisher. He kicked Rhodes in the head, apparently for good measure.

"Asshole," Larry muttered, then said to Paris. "I'm sorry I called you a 'ho. Let's get the fuck out of here."

Holding hands to stay together, they fled the office and ran around to the back toward Larry's battered truck. Sparks jumped and snapped from the fallen wire, and they slowed down to give it a wide berth. The rain fell and fell and fell.

"That was a pretty good move, guy," Paris said.

"Yeah." Larry opened the truck door. "Gimme the keys."

"I put them on your desk next to the cash box, remember?" Paris said. "Didn't you pick them up?"

"No. I was tied to the goddam chair." Larry closed his eyes. "Fuck. They're probably buried in junk by now and we'll never—no, wait. Shit!"

"What?"

"I got spares."

"Where?"

"That's the shit. They're in the file cabinet. In the office."

"Oh." Paris swallowed. "Okay."

"So we're going back in there." He sounded like he was saying it more for himself than for her. "Right?"

Paris nodded.

"Okay." Larry sniffed. "Let's go."

9

Rhodes still lay slumped on the flooded floor. Thick fluid, black in the dim light, dribbled out of his ear. Larry ran to the back corner, yanked open the file cabinet, and snatched out a set of keys. He tossed them to Paris, who stood silhouetted in the doorway, and warily approached Rhodes's still form.

"What are you doing?" Paris asked.

"We need a gun." He knelt and reached for Rhodes's pistol. "I should've grabbed his before we left."

"He's got two," Paris said. "The other's in his jacket pocket."

Larry found Ed's pistol and tossed it in Paris's direction. She stretched a hand for it and missed. It thudded to the floor. Larry was already reaching for Rhodes's other gun.

"Larry," Paris said, "let's just forget—"

Rhodes sat up with a snarl and snatched his gun. He pressed the barrel against Larry's thigh and pulled the trigger. Paris screamed. The shot boomed deafeningly through the little room. Larry cried out in agony and rolled away. Rhodes, still sitting on the floor, took more careful aim and fired again. The bullet tore through Larry's chest. Blood gushed and spurted from a severed aorta. Larry choked, and his eyes held Paris's as they glazed over. He died.

"No," Paris whispered.

Rhodes started getting to his feet. Before she could lose her nerve, Paris scooped up the pistol Larry had tossed in her direction. She leveled it at Rhodes, but her hands trembled wildly.

"I will kill you where you sit," she yelled, "so lose the gun. Now!"

With a blank expression, Rhodes fired into the ceiling four feet from Paris. Water trickled like blood from the hole. Paris shrieked. He shot the ceiling again—*bang!*—two feet from Paris. One foot—*bang!* He aimed directly at her.

"All right!" she sobbed. "All right. Shit." She threw down her gun.

Rhodes struggled to stand, obviously still dizzy from the blow he had taken. "Give me the truck keys."

Paris didn't move. Tears coursed unchecked down her face, but she didn't move.

"I'm not interested in you, honey," Rhodes said, "but I'm not fucking around. Give me the keys!"

Paris stood motionless for a long moment, then turned and fled. A shot rang out from behind her and she braced herself for the pain, but none came. She raced toward the back of the motel, then changed course when she remembered the downed wire. A shot cracked through the night, and chunks of wall plaster sprayed her face. Jesus, where the hell was Ed?

Paris flew down the walkway, looking for a place to hide. A long piece of metal from Ginny's ruined car lay on the cracked cement in front of her, and she snatched it up like Larry's baseball bat. Another shot rang out, and she dove into the vending machine nook. The darkness hid her movements, she hoped. It stupidly crossed her mind that she could smash open the machines with the metal club and get all the snacks she wanted now. She crouched in the darkness, her own breath loud in her ears. The rain, always the fucking rain, poured over the walkway.

Careful, shuffling footsteps came up the walkway. Paris peeped around the corner and made out a dark figure coming toward her from the direction oppo-

site the office. Paris crouched lower and raised the metal club higher. If it was Rhodes, he'd doubled back around. If it was Ed, he was about to get his head knocked in.

Someone was breathing behind her. Paris spun around, club at the ready. It was Ed. How the hell had he gotten in here? His face was sharp and pale, his eyes black holes in his head. He looked like a demon. Panic seized Paris and she turned to run from him just as Rhodes's footsteps reached the vending nook. Paris flattened herself against the wall between two machines before Rhodes fully entered the place. Ed faded into the shadows. Rhodes stood in the entrance and looked around slowly, deliberately, like a snake trying decide whether or not to strike. Paris held her breath, knowing he'd hear her if she made the slightest sound. Rhodes's feet shuffled against cement as he turned in place, looking, seeking. The metal club grew heavy in Paris's hand, and she realized her sweaty hands were losing their grip. One finger slipped away, then another.

Come on, you bastard, she begged silently. *No one here. Move on!*

Rhodes coughed once and spat on the concrete flooring. Another finger came free. Paris's arm was shaking with the strain of not letting go. Rhodes blew out a heavy sigh, then turned and walked away.

Paris heaved a quiet sigh of her own and grabbed the club more firmly.

"Ed?" she said to the shadowy corner where he'd been hiding. "You there?"

And then Ed was beside her. He looked even worse—hair disheveled, face drawn. He grabbed her free hand and hauled her out of the vending nook and around the corner to the back. His hand was ice-cold. They were in the area between the pool house and Larry's trailer. The pool house had an irregular roof whose eaves stuck out in L-shapes that formed four rippling curtains of cascading water. Nearby, the downed wire hissed like an angry serpent. Paris pulled her hand free of him.

"Please get away from me," she said.

"I'm not going to hurt you, Paris," he said.

"Why the *fuck* should I believe you? Where the hell have you been?"

Rhodes appeared around the corner. Paris cried out and raised her club. Rhodes raised his pistol, barely visible through the four watery cascades.

"No!" Paris shouted.

Ed shoved Paris back. Rhodes fired. Ed grunted and slammed against the pool house wall. Blood spurted from his shoulder. Paris shrank back, terrified. Her mind, fatigued and stressed from too many hours of fear and pain, refused to work. She couldn't

think, couldn't run, couldn't do anything but stare.

"How's *that*, you fuck?" Rhodes yelled.

And Ed . . . chuckled. Paris looked at him, unable to comprehend what she was hearing. "What happened to you?" she demanded. "Where did you go? You know something."

"Stay here." Blood continued to flow down Ed's shoulder as he staggered to his feet.

More fear rippled through her. "Why? Where are you going?"

He smiled at her. "Just stay here."

"Ed . . ."

Ed turned to face Rhodes and started advancing toward him, breaking through the first cascade. Water washed blood from his streaming shoulder and puddled it at his feet. Rhodes aimed the pistol again.

"Stay where you are and toss me the fuckin' keys!" he barked.

Ed took another step forward. Paris watched, paralyzed. What was he doing?

"I didn't do all this," Rhodes said shakily. "You can't blame me for this! It's bigger than me."

"Slightly bigger," Ed said. "Yes." He stepped through the second cascade. Rhodes waved the gun.

"Stop!" he ordered.

"No!" Paris cried. "Ed!"

Ed stepped through the third cascade. Only one

more watery veil lay between him and Rhodes. Rhodes fired. The muzzle flashed bright as lightning and sounded loud as thunder. Ed grunted as the bullet plowed into his torso, but he kept moving. He broke through the last cascade. Rhodes fired twice more at point-blank range. Ed jerked twice, then flung himself forward and landed on Rhodes. They rolled in the mud, locked together like lovers. Paris ran toward them, trying to make sense out of what was happening. Rhodes realized he was rolling toward the puddle that contained the sparking downed wire. He pushed away from it and back into Ed. Ed managed to grab Rhodes's gun. Their arms trembled in a contest of strength. The gun moved toward Rhodes, then toward Ed, then toward Rhodes. Blood poured from Ed's wounds. Paris stood over them with her club, looking for an opening to use it, but the rain and the darkness made it hard to sort out who was who.

Ed bellowed once and the gun fired. Paris raised her club. Rhodes flopped sideways, a gaping hole in his chest. His sightless eyes stared up into the cold rain. Ed rolled away, leaving the gun behind. Paris dropped the club and knelt next to him in the mud. He was gasping for air and bleeding fast and furious. The strength drained from Paris's body and she felt helpless and alone.

"Oh God," she said. "Tell me what to do, Ed."

He managed to look up at her, a hopeless shadow in his eyes. Paris's heart twisted. There had to be something she could do. He couldn't just die like this, in the uncaring mud and rain.

"Let's get you into the truck," she said. "We'll drive you to the hospital." She tried to move him, but he pulled away. "Ed, you need to go to the hospital!"

Ed chuckled again. It was a weak, ironic sound. Tears sprang to Paris's eyes.

"How can you laugh? What's so fucking funny?" she sniffed.

"You had to be there," he gasped.

"Ed, please," Paris said, "let me help you."

Ed shook his head. The life was draining from his eyes as fast the blood was draining from his chest. "Only one . . . can survive," he said. "Only one."

"What the hell is that supposed to mean?" she demanded. "Some Shoshone burial ground thing? I don't buy it, Ed. No fucking way. The Shoshone ghosts are—"

"We're the ghosts, Paris," he coughed. "We just didn't know."

"Ed, don't you leave me here," Paris cried. "Don't you leave me, too."

* * *

Ed Dakota stared unblinking up into the dark sky. He could feel the holes in his body, sense the air and water rushing into them, through them. Raindrops fell into his eyes, making his vision blurred and watery. Paris didn't know. Of course she didn't—none of them had, including him. Until he heard Doc's voice again.

"Doc . . ." he rasped. "Was it . . . supposed to hurt this much?"

When he had seen the figure back in the motel room, the lights had told him that something other-worldly was happening. It had grown brighter and brighter, washing out the walls, the windows, the IDs on the beds, until there was nothing but light. Ed heard nothing but his breathing, as if he were under water. The light grew brighter until it hurt Ed's eyes. He tried to fling up a hand to block it out, but his arm wouldn't move. He felt something tugging at his wrist, restraining it.

"What's going on?" said a voice.

"Please be quiet, Detective," came the answer. The voices swirled together, in and out, up and down, like a Doppler effect on LSD.

"He can hear what we're saying?" said an older man.

"Of course he can, Your Honor. It's just hard for him to react right now."

The light cleared with an abrupt rushing noise. Ed

looked around, bewildered. What the hell? He was in a dark-paneled room with a white ceiling and fluorescent light. A long conference table stretched ahead of him. At the other end sat a group of men in suits. Three he didn't recognize, including the thin, older man who sat at the head of the table. He wore a judge's robes. A motherly woman sat in the corner, tapping a little machine. Something was humming inside his head. Voices? Someone was talking, whispering, but the men in the room weren't saying anything. Where the hell was he? How had he gotten here? Some weird Shoshone trick?

Ed tried to stand up and realized he was fully restrained. His wrists and ankles were cuffed to the arms of . . . a wheelchair? A wide leather strap held his upper body firmly against the back of the chair, and an IV was plugged into the back of his hand. Beside him sat a rumpled man who had dark hair, enormous brown eyes, and a goatee.

"Doc?" Ed said. "Dr. Mallick? Where am I?"

"He recognizes you," the judge observed.

"Of course," Dr. Mallick said. "We've spoken many times. Haven't we, Ed?"

"Yeah . . . I suppose." Ed shook his head, trying to make sense of this. He felt like he was standing halfway through a doorway, one foot in two different rooms. Doc. He had talked to Dr. Mallick often, and

yet he . . . hadn't. Ever since that girl had committed suicide, Ed had spent his days shuttling actors and rich big shots around in a limousine. He didn't talk to doctors. Except . . . no. He *did* talk to doctors. *A* doctor, anyway. All the time.

"You came to see me right after you had some trouble at work, remember, Ed?" Dr. Mallick said. "You had a few blackouts."

Ed blinked, trying to dredge up some reason from all this. A half-memory came to him. White coats, latex gloves, being strapped to a gurney, yelling his throat raw. A prick on his arm. "Am I in the hospital again? How long have I been blacked out?"

"What's the last thing you remember, Ed?" the doc asked.

"I was at a motel. There was . . . a storm . . . I couldn't . . . we couldn't . . . get out," Ed said. Rain pattered against the dark windows. Always rain. "We couldn't get out."

"What happened at the motel?"

Ed tried to bring a hand to his forehead but the restraints held him back. "What's with the cuffs, Doc?"

"They're for your protection," Dr. Mallick said smoothly. "What happened at the motel?"

"People were . . . dying. The bodies . . . disappeared. There was this family . . ."

"The Yorks," Dr. Mallick supplied.

"And this convict came in . . ."

"Rhodes."

Ed shook his head, confused. "No, he's the—" A cold feeling ran over him and he turned to Dr. Mallick. "How do you know him?"

"I know them just like I know you," Dr. Mallick said. "Ed, last you remember, who was still alive?"

"Paris," Ed answered. "Larry. I don't know about Maine. He disappeared, and the baseball bat was just lying there. But all the other bodies disappeared, too. Even Miss Suzanne's head."

The judge picked up a black notebook and paged through it with an astonished look on his face. He set it aside and checked another, and another.

"I know that one," Ed said. "It's mine. Isn't it?"

"Ed Dakota," the judge read from each cover. "Paris Nevada. Larry Washington. Samuel Rhodes. Timothy York. George York. Caroline Suzanne. And there are others."

"Ed," said Dr. Mallick. "Ed, I need you to look at something." He opened a folder and pulled out a photograph. It showed a man built like a refrigerator who outbulked Ed by a good eighty pounds. His head was shaved and his face was strangely androgynous. He had gray eyes. Ed looked at the photograph for a long time.

"Do you recognize this man?" Dr. Mallick asked.

"No," Ed said.

A murmur rippled across the room. Even the stenographer paused in her work. Dr. Mallick waited for quiet.

"Edward, this man's name is Malcolm Rivers and he has had a very troubled life. He was convicted four years ago for murdering eight people at a roadside motel in a terrible rage."

"He did *this*," said one of the other men. From a rain-spattered folder, he flicked a series of photographs across the table so they landed one by one in front of Ed. He got brief glimpses of each one. A decapitated head staring from a dryer cradle. A young man with his abdomen slashed open, intestines visible. A woman on a bed whose filmy eyes stared at nothing. A man with a crushed torso and cracked glasses. A charred, blackened body sitting in a ruined car. A man with three gaping bullet wounds. Ed stared at them, feeling horrified and sick.

Dr. Mallick swept the photographs away. "Detective Valrole, *please!*"

"What am I doing here?" Ed asked in a small voice.

"Edward, some people live terrible lives. Their childhoods are filled with pain and torture—beatings, rape, psychological abuse. In some cases, the child simply can't imagine that such horrible things

would happen to him, so he decides it must have happened to someone else. His brain creates other people—a series of alternate personalities—for it to happen to, and the child forgets the trauma ever took place. And if the trauma is repeated, the other personalities take over again so the child doesn't have to experience that particular pain. This process is called dissociation."

Mallick paused to take a sip of coffee. "Most of the personalities are unaware of their counterparts. From their point of view, they have blackouts—periods of total amnesia—during the times other alters are in control of the body. A skill that one personality learns isn't necessarily shared by the others. In one of the most famous cases, a woman named Sybil was unable to perform simple multiplication because when she was a child, a personality named Peggy always took over during math lessons in school."

"What does this have to do with me, Doc?" Ed asked.

"Sorry," Mallick said. "Sometimes I wander into lecture mode. Edward, Malcolm Rivers lived such a life. His father abused him horribly, and his mother allowed it to happen. He felt betrayed and abandoned. Then his mother abandoned him further by dying, another terrible trauma. Her drug overdose was actually a form of suicide. The last thing she

said to her son was, 'What's the point of living?' "

The words slashed through Ed like a knife. *"Cuál es la punta vivir,"* he whispered.

"Yes."

"Why are you telling me this?" Ed rasped.

Dr. Mallick's voice remained gentle. "Because you, Edward, are one of Malcolm Rivers's personalities."

For a moment the world stopped. Even the raindrops froze on the black windowpane. Ed's mind spun, unable to take in this idea. It was impossible. Utterly insane!

"Look at this, Edward," the doc said, and placed the handle of a mirror in Ed's cuffed hand. Ed turned it so the glass reflected his face. A gray-eyed man with a shaved head stared back at him. Terror tore through Ed. He yelped and flung the mirror away. It shattered on the floor.

"Jesus Christ!" he yelled. "Why am I—Jesus! What the fuck is going on? *Where is my face?*" He caught a glimpse of himself in the dark window. The terrified reflection of the big, bald man struggled against the wheelchair restraints. A beefy man in orderly's scrubs hovered behind him, tense and ready to do . . . what?

"Try to stay calm, Edward," Dr. Mallick said. "Everything will be fine."

"What is going on?" Ed screamed. "Where is my face? *What are you doing to me?*"

"Edward, there's a reason I am doing this, if you just let me—"

"*Why am I tied down? Let me go! Where is my face?*"

The other people in the room were frozen still as statues. They stared unabashedly. The judge's mouth had fallen open.

"Please, Edward," Dr. Mallick said. "You know I'm telling the truth. The fact that you see a real reflection in the mirror instead of a hallucinatory version of how you *think* you look tells me that you're starting to accept the truth. You know who you are and you've begun to accept it."

But his calm words had no effect on Ed's panic. "Where is everyone?" he screamed, straining at the cuffs. "Who are these people? What happened at the motel? Where's Paris?"

"The motel doesn't exist, Edward. It's only a symbol for the roadhouse where Malcolm grew up. The people you met there don't exist, either. Malcolm and I created it together, using drugs and hypnotherapy. It's a place where all of his personalities—all of *you*—can confront each other face-to-face."

Ed stopped fighting the restraints. His breath continued to come in short, frightened gasps. Tears were gathering in his eyes. He didn't want to cry. If you cried, Dad would tie you up, make you—no, that

wasn't right. His dad was dead, had been for decades. Ed didn't have a dad anymore.

"You've been sharing a single body with ten others, Edward," Dr. Mallick said. "You've been living an episodic life."

"You're a liar!" Ed burst out.

"Consider what you know," Dr. Mallick continued relentlessly. "Everyone at the motel named after a state. Everyone with the same birthday. The blackouts."

Ed pulled at the restraints again, wanting to clap his hands over his ears. "I was a *cop*. A cop in the rampart division of the LAPD for six years! I live in Hollywood, in a studio apartment." He became more frightened, more frantic. "The elevator smells like cat piss! The six button doesn't work."

"This is complete bullshit," said the detective. "It's an act. I've seen it a thousand times before."

Ed rounded on him. "You don't believe me? Ten-eleven Vine. Check it out! Go ahead—*check it out!*"

"You don't live there, Edward," said the doctor. "You don't live anywhere. Malcolm is in the final stage of a medical treatment, one that forces co-consciousness. One that brings all his identities, including you, together. The motel is a scenario suggested to awaken memories in Malcolm's core. It's not a real place, Edward."

"It's real!" Ed snapped. "I was *there!*"

"There are inconsistencies in that place," Dr. Mallick said. "Didn't you think to wonder how you could leave Las Vegas and drive west toward Hollywood and end up at a motel with a call girl who was driving east toward Florida? I knew there would be violence at the motel, and with it, the number of identities would be reduced."

Ed became still. "Reduced?" His voice was shaky.

"Only one of the alters you've met tonight committed these murders four years ago, Edward."

"Maine," Ed whispered. "But he disappeared."

"The bodies disappeared because they never truly existed. Once Malcolm's mind let go of them, they vanished."

"Oh, God."

"In nineteen hours, Malcolm will be put to death for the murdering personality's actions, unless I can convince that man"—Dr. Mallick pointed at the judge—"that the murderer and all the other alters are gone."

"So you're *killing* us?"

"I'm helping you integrate," Dr. Mallick said. "It's an experimental therapy, but Malcolm's execution is coming up quickly, and there wasn't time for more conventional methods. Each death is actually an integration, Edward."

"I don't want to integrate," Ed said. "I don't want to die."

"If the therapy doesn't succeed," Dr. Mallick said, "you will all surely die with Malcolm tomorrow. But if we can show the judge that only one personality—a harmless personality—remains within the body, then he might stay the execution and Malcolm will go to a hospital instead so we can finish his treatment and make him well again."

"I don't . . . I don't believe it."

"I need you to."

Ed stared at the doctor, feeling utterly shattered. This couldn't be happening. He was Edward Dakota, ex-cop and now limo driver. His favorite meal was sloppy joes and tater tots. He hated housecleaning but did it anyway because he hated having a cluttered apartment even more. His dad had been a . . . a . . .

Ed faltered. What had his father done for a living? He couldn't remember. What had his childhood home looked like? He couldn't remember that, either. What was the name of his junior high school? His first girlfriend? He didn't know. Tears ran down his cheeks.

"I am trying to integrate a man's mind, Edward," said Dr. Mallick. "To repair a life fractured. And to purge a killer. I need—Malcolm needs—a sin-

gle identity to survive. There is only one body."

The strange buzzing noise droned in Ed's ears. It rose and pulsed and Ed heard his own heart beating. The light faded and he could smell old motel mildew. Was someone screaming?

"What . . . what do you want from me?" Ed said.

"Only one can survive, Edward," Dr. Mallick said. It was too dark to see his face. "Edward . . . stay with me. I need you to understand . . ."

His voice faded entirely. Another scream slashed through the darkness. Ed was standing in the dark motel room again. Rows of ID copies lay on the bed. And then he was outside in the chill rain. He gazed about the courtyard, stunned, emotionally drained. The wind blew water into his face, and he put up a hand to touch himself. He had hair and a small nose and a lithe build.

He turned his back on the motel. Ahead of him stretched the blackness of the desert. It wasn't real. He could just walk away, survive.

More screams, and a shot. Then another shot. Suddenly he didn't care what the doctor said, didn't care about the conference room. Paris was screaming in either fear or pain, and he had to help her . . .

"Stay with me, Ed," Paris repeated. "Come on, stay with me!"

Ed lay on the muddy ground, feeling his life pour out of him. The storm had lightened considerably, almost stopped. Tears ran down Paris's face, mingling with the rain. He lifted a hand and brushed her cheek. She clasped it, and her hand was warm. Only one could survive.

"I . . . saw you," he said softly, and managed a weak smile. "I saw you . . . in an orange grove."

He exhaled once more, and died.

10

The sky lightened and dawn rose slowly over the Golden Palm Motel. The rain . . . stopped. Paris held Ed's slack hand as the tears dried on her cheeks. It felt strange not to have water pouring over her. Ed's wounds had stopped bleeding and now only oozed slightly. A little ways off, Rhodes lay dead. She was a hooker surrounded by corpses.

No. She wasn't a hooker anymore. Ed had said he saw her surrounded by orange trees, and she got the feeling that this was the reason he had walked toward Rhodes, let Rhodes shoot him. Ed had let himself die so Paris could have her dream.

A fresh tear slid down on the dry salt that streaked her face. Ed's hand was growing cold. All right, then. Ginny had said only one would survive. Maybe it was the Shoshone, maybe it was something else. But Ed had ensured Paris would be that

survivor. She wasn't going to throw that away.

Paris gently set Ed's hand down, then dragged his body into the motel, unable to bear the thought of vultures dropping from the sky and tearing at his flesh. She pulled him onto one of the beds, kissed his cool cheek once, and covered him with a sheet.

"Thanks, Ed," she said. "I don't know why you did it, or what you meant by all the things you said, but thanks."

Then she went into Caroline Suzanne's room, took a nice hot shower, and rummaged through the actress's possessions. All Paris's clothes were wet, but Caroline was about Paris's size. Paris didn't think Caroline would mind if Paris took a few things. She put on a pair of blue slacks and a cream-colored blouse, then gathered up her own things. The orange grove money was still in her purse. So was Caroline's fat Vuitton wallet, the one Larry had dropped and Paris had picked up in the diner. Paris opened it and counted the cash inside. Just over two thousand dollars. She supposed it was stealing from Caroline's estate, but Paris was sure she needed the money more than Caroline's heirs, whoever they were. Caroline herself was beyond needing it at all.

Paris went outside around back and climbed into Larry's old truck. The clouds had broken up and moved off, revealing a glorious blue sky and a warm,

friendly sun. Rhodes's body was already gathering flies. She wondered if it would vanish like the others had and abruptly she didn't care.

The truck started on the first try. It wouldn't be safe to drive it very far, but Caroline's wallet would let Paris buy something better once she cleared the vicinity around the motel. Ahead of her, the bright orange sunrise made her squint, and Paris was grateful for the warm light.

In the hearing room, Malcolm Rivers sits restrained in his wheelchair. He is smiling serenely and squinting a little, as if he is staring at something bright. Judge Taylor swallows hard and twists brown hands in the lap of his black robe. Assistant D.A. Kerrick, Defense Counselor Greenfruit, Detective Valrole, and Sharon the stenographer all look as stunned as Taylor feels. It chilled every part of Taylor's body to watch Rivers's face change, look somehow younger and more masculine, speak in a voice that didn't match his body. Taylor has seen any number of strange things, both in his courtroom and out, but Rivers outranks them all.

"The question, Your Honor," says Dr. Mallick, "is whether to convict the body or the mind. Malcolm Rivers's body committed those murders, that is true. But the person who remains inside did not. You wit-

nessed the destruction of ten souls tonight. Nine were innocent, one was guilty. The violence that existed in him has been executed."

There is a long pause. Then Kerrick says, "Your Honor, the prosecution would like to state that Malcolm Rivers belongs at the state hospital, not the death house."

"Won't that position cause some tension with your boss, Mr. Kerrick?" Taylor asks. "I happen to know Mr. Bywater was very . . . adamant about Malcolm Rivers's execution."

"Better tension for me than death for him," Kerrick says.

Taylor rubs his eyes. In the window behind him, a rising sun chases the clouds away. "I need time alone to consider my decision."

Paris drives onward in her new—well, new to her—yellow pickup truck. The desert sands have fallen behind her. Right now she is zipping through the cool forests and snow-capped mountains of northern Arizona. After that, she'll skate through New Mexico, Oklahoma, and a few more southern states before turning south to Florida. She can almost smell the oranges.

Despite last night's lack of sleep, she feels crisp and alert. The mountain breeze washes through her

hair with long, cleansing fingers. She is free of her old life, free of death, free of terror. Her only worry is that the farm might sell before she gets there, and that is a small worry indeed after last night. For the first time in a long time, things can't be better.

Everyone except Malcolm Rivers stands as Judge Emmet Taylor re-enters the conference room. Rivers, of course, is still in restraints. The bags under Taylor's eyes are heavy and his face looks ancient, as if ten years have passed instead of a single night. His mouth is dry and his hands are shaking from all the coffee he has drunk during the evidenciary hearing. The single piece of paper, the paper that will decide a man's life, lies flat and heavy in his hand. The air in the room seems tight and rigid, and Taylor feels like he has to push his way to the head of the table.

"You may be seated," he says, and everyone sits. Malcolm Rivers remains in his wheelchair, a slight smile on his face. His eyes track back and forth, though there is nothing much in front of him. He is making a soft purring noise, and Taylor realizes it is the sound of a car accelerating. Malcolm's cuffed hands hold an invisible steering wheel. Everyone else politely, almost painfully, ignores this behavior.

"We have heard several arguments here this morning, both for and against the execution of Malcolm

Rivers," Taylor begins. "Mr. Rivers killed eight people that we know of. No one disputes this fact. Whether he confessed properly or not, the evidence brought forth at his trial proved beyond the shadow of a doubt that Mr. Rivers slaughtered his victims with malice and cruelty, ending their lives and bringing unthinkable pain and suffering to their families and friends. The victims bore no relationship to Mr. Rivers, nor did he interact with them in any way before he killed them. He had no reason to cause their deaths except as a way to expunge his own terrible anger. The manner of his victims' deaths also indicates that Mr. Rivers carried out his murders with forethought. He did not kill eight people in a motel by accident or in a fit of jealous rage or out of fear for his own life. This means that by the laws of the State of Nevada, Mr. Rivers committed first-degree murder, a single instance of which commands the death penalty. Mr. Rivers committed this capital crime eight times in a single night. The law has therefore declared his life is forfeit.

"However, there are certain circumstances that require this court's attention. Mr. Rivers's childhood was terrible beyond imagination, so terrible it shattered his mind. Only part of his mind committed eight atrocious murders, and the defense has argued that the rest of Mr. Rivers's mind was unaware of what

was happening, that Mr. Rivers's left hand does not deserve to die along with his right. And Dr. Mallick—along with Mr. Rivers himself—has rather dramatically testified that the only person left inside Mr. Rivers is not the person who committed these crimes.

"Does Mr. Rivers's childhood mitigate what he did? Does it excuse the behavior or merely explain it? Is it fair and just to kill a man who seems to be unaware of his crimes? How do we tell a man that the monster who killed his wife is alive while she is dead? These are the most difficult of questions. I can't answer all of them. Like all men and women in my position, I can only make the decision I think best for this single case after hearing arguments presented by both sides."

Taylor unfolds his paper and readjusts his reading glasses. Everyone in the room stops breathing except Malcolm Rivers. He makes more soft motor sounds.

"In the matter of *Rivers vs. Nevada*," Taylor reads, "it is the recommendation of this court that Mr. Rivers's execution be stayed. He will instead be transferred to State Psychiatric Services under the care of Dr. Mallick."

A heavy sigh whispers through the room. Dr. Mallick gives a relieved smile and shakes hands with Marty Greenfruit. Kerrick looks a bit dazed, as if he is facing an execution of his own. Taylor makes a

mental note to have a word with D.A. Gary Bywater about that.

"And now, lady and gentlemen," Taylor says, "it is a bright, clear Friday morning. I am going to take a three-day weekend and see if I can get some sleep despite all the coffee. We are adjourned."

Malcolm Rivers makes more vroom noises as the orderly pushes his enormous wheelchair out of the conference room and into the freight elevator. Dr. Mallick follows with a relieved expression. A beatific smile remains frozen on Rivers's face. At the service entrance to the courthouse waits a corrections van. The orderly pushes the chair down a ramp, then looks uncertainly at the van. Rivers came in a different vehicle, one equipped with a hydraulic lift. The van has no such equipment and indeed doesn't even look big enough to hold the wheelchair, let alone with Rivers strapped in it. The orderly looks to Dr. Mallick, who smiles and reaches around to undo Rivers's restraints. The orderly stiffens.

"It's all right," Dr. Mallick says. "He's harmless now. The only personality left isn't violent."

"He still needs to be restrained, sir," the orderly says. "State law."

"I know." Dr. Mallick releases Rivers's wrists and ankles, then fits him with a set of shackles that

restrain Rivers's hands in front of him. "There. That'll satisfy the law. Are you ready to go, Malcolm?"

Rivers stops making motor noises and suddenly stretches, as if he is getting out of a car for a rest break. Dr. Mallick gently herds him into the back of the van and climbs in with him. The orderly looks as if he is about to say something, then shrugs and shuts the van door. A uniformed corrections officer with a handsome face and bright-red hair looks over his shoulder from his position in the driver's seat.

"Everything set back there, Doc?" he asks, and starts up the van.

"Right as rain, Seth," says Dr. Mallick. "Let's head out." He turns to his patient and beams. "Malcolm, I'm so proud of you and everything you've done. You've made amazing progress." *And proved my experimental theory*, he adds with silent exultation. "We're taking you to a hospital, and I'll visit you almost every day. We'll talk about whatever you want and help you get completely well. Is that all right?"

Malcolm Rivers turns his head and looks out the window of the—white van? yellow truck?—with a peaceful smile. The voices no longer scream inside his head. Sunlight flickers on his face, warm and gentle. This is a fine place, a beautiful place. Why had it taken so long to get here?

The vehicle moves forward. It is definitely a yellow pickup truck. Paris's truck. Orange trees rush past both sides of the road beneath a calm Florida sky. Paris sings happily to herself. It is an Irish love song her mother used to sing. Paris didn't realize how much she's missed green trees and green grass until she's come back to them. This is beauty. This is home.

Dr. Mallick notices that Rivers's car sounds have changed to soft singing. He leans forward, trying to catch the words, see if any clues about Rivers's current mental state are to be had. Up front, Seth drives the van carefully and competently through light morning traffic until they clear the city. The desert is already drying out from last night's rain, and soon it will bloom in a riot of short-lived flowers.

"Merrily, cheerily, noisily whirring," sings Malcolm, "spins the reel, swings the wheel, while the foot's stirring."

Mallick doesn't recognize the words, but it sounds happy enough. He gives a relieved sigh and checks his watch.

Paris grinned up at a giant real estate sign at the side of the road. The word SOLD marched across it in bold, congratulatory letters. A narrow lane led off the road and into the grove, the grove that was now hers.

Eight hundred orange trees, four hundred lime. Each tree was peppered liberally with little green fruit. She reached out and brushed her fingers over a pebbly young orange. The grove smelled just like home.

Paris left the truck parked in the lane and went walking among the lush green trees, already making plans. She'd bought the grove free and clear, along with the equipment to care for it, but she would need to buy fertilizer, hire workers, and pay household expenses until the harvest came in. That would mean mortgaging the place. But that was all right—one good harvest would pay that off.

From her back pocket, Paris pulled a serrated gardening fork. She knelt in the grove and scooped out a nice-sized clump of dirt and grass. She set the fork aside and crumbled the clump of earth between both hands, savoring the feel and analyzing its composition with long-dormant skills.

There was something sticking out of the depression she had made. An old coin? A piece of litter? Puzzled, Paris reached down and gently pried the object out. It was a key. Dangling from it was a tag. Number one.

A small sound rustled behind Paris. The color drained from her face and she spun around on her knees. Timothy York stood right behind her. He was holding the garden fork.

"Hello," he said, and touched her shoulder with an icy hand.

At his touch, memories flashed through Paris's head. Her muscles sagged, her body went weak. It felt like she was a small stream suddenly overrun by a raging river, and she couldn't separate herself from Timothy—or was her name Malcolm? She remembered being a small child finding a dead kitten, knowing Dad had done it, feeling the murderous rage. She remembered the roadhouse, Dad's customers, and the things they had done to him behind closed doors while Mom counted the money so she could buy drugs. She remembered flaming candles and every blow that had landed on her back, sides, face, and head. And she remembered the rage.

Suddenly she was back at the Golden Palm Motel, looking at it through a child's eyes. Timothy looks from Larry's speeding truck to his stepfather, calculates, then runs in front of the truck.

Malcolm Rivers crashing his huge body into a man wearing glasses, crushing him against a wall just like Dad used to slam Malcolm around . . .

Timothy climbs into the backseat of Ginny's car after refusing to sit up front, then slips out the back door and runs just as she is turning the car key.

Malcolm throwing a handcuffed young woman into

her car, dousing her with gasoline, lighting a single match just like Dad did to the kitten . . .

Timothy stands at his mother's bedside. Her breathing is harsh and labored. He puts one hand over her mouth and pinches her nose shut with the other.

Malcolm shoving a pillow down over a motherly woman's face, pressing hard while she struggles and thrashes just like Malcolm did when Dad laughed and put a pillow over his face . . .

Timothy stalks Caroline Suzanne as she trudges through the rain under her shower curtain, phone glued to her ear.

Malcolm raising his knife behind a blond woman talking on a cell phone like the one Mom always used to call her dealer . . .

Timothy steps out of the shadows behind Lou as he argues with Ginny through the bathroom door. The knife is heavy in his hand.

Malcolm slashing over and over at a young man who huddles trapped and screaming against a door, crying just like Malcolm did the first time Dad left him alone with a customer . . .

Timothy shuffles toward a bound Robert Maine, dragging Larry's baseball bat behind him. Maine's eyes widen in fear.

Malcolm smashing a man across the back of the

head, then breaking the baseball bat and shoving it down his throat like Dad used to shove other things down Malcolm's throat . . .

Timothy makes a face at his mother. Out of the corner of his eye, he sees oncoming headlights. Mom imitates his face. Timothy scoots backward on the seat. Mom steps back into the road.

Malcolm throwing a struggling woman out into the road in front of a roaring semi, just like the ones Dad's customers sometimes arrived in . . .

Timothy stands above the paralyzed Paris and raises the garden fork. She tries to scream in defiance but can't make a sound.

"Only one can survive," Tim says.

"You killed everybody," Paris whispers. "We thought it was Maine, but it was you."

Tim shoves Paris hard with impossible, amazing strength. She flies backward and slams into a tree. Little green oranges pitter to the ground all around her. The wind is knocked from her lungs and she gasps for air. Tim advances on her, gardening fork held high, just like Dad held it. There is nowhere for Paris to run.

"Tim," she says. "Tim, we never hurt you. We only wanted to help you."

Then Tim tosses the garden fork away. It vanishes into the grass. Tears are running down his face. Paris

presses against the rough bark of the tree, heart pounding.

"I'm sorry," Tim says in a strange, flute-like voice. "It's like when I licked my kitty. I should be punished. Punished *hard*." He pulls his belt from the loops around his waist. "You have to do it. Please. Only one can survive."

Paris swallows and manages to edge away from the tree. He wants her to kill him? She can't. She won't.

"It's all right, Tim," she says soothingly. "You don't have to be afraid of me. I'm not going to—"

Tim moves fast, blindingly fast. In a flash he is behind her and the belt is around her neck. It is a thick leather belt, just like the one Dad used both to beat and choke him with. Paris claws at her neck, tears at her throat, but the belt is an iron band. The last thing she hears is Tim's voice.

"Only one can survive."

Malcolm Rivers twists toward Dr. Mallick. Blackness lies behind his eyes. Dr. Mallick, in a half-doze, notices the movement and rouses himself.

"What is it, Malcolm?" he asks gently. "Is something wrong?"

"Only one can survive! Only one can survive!" Malcolm holds his shackled wrists out before him.

The chain dangles between the cuffs like a belt.

"It's all right," Dr. Mallick says. "Malcolm, you don't have to—"

Malcolm lunges.

Several busy moments pass. The van lurches, sways, and swerves off the road. It crashes into a ditch. A small flock of birds flutters frantically out of the way, circles once, and flies off. Everything is quiet except for the tick of heated metal from the van's engine. Then the voice of a small boy sings from inside the van.

> "As I was going up the stair,
> I met a man who wasn't there.
> He wasn't there again today.
> I wish . . . I wish he'd go away . . ."

ROMANCE FROM GEORGINA GENTRY

COMANCHE COWBOY   (0-8217-6211-7, $5.99/$7.50)
Cayenne McBride knows that Maverick Durango is the perfect guide to lead her back home to her father's Texas ranch. And when the fearless half-breed demands that she give up her innocence in exchange for his protection, Cayenne agrees, convinced she can keep her virtue intact . . . until she falls in love with him.

WARRIOR'S PRIZE   (0-8217-5565-X, $5.99/$7.50)
After spending years in Boston at a ladies' academy, the Arapaho maiden Singing Wind returns to Colorado. Ahead of her lies a dangerous trek into the Rocky Mountains . . . where a magnificent warrior dares to battle for her body, her heart, and her precious love.

CHEYENNE SONG   (0-8217-5844-6, $5.99/$7.50)
Kidnapped by the Cheyenne warrior Two Arrows, Glory Halstead faces her captor with the same pride and courage that have seen her through hardship and bitter scandal. But as they make the brutal journey through the harsh wilderness, Glory and Two Arrows discover passion as primal and unyielding as the land they are destined to tame. . . .

Available wherever paperbacks are sold, or order direct from the Publisher. Send cover price plus 50¢ per copy for mailing and handling to Penguin USA, P.O. Box 999, c/o Dept. 17109 Bergenfield, NJ 07621. Residents of New York and Tennessee must include sales tax. DO NOT SEND CASH.

YOU WON'T WANT TO READ
JUST ONE—KATHERINE STONE

ROOMMATES   (0-8217-5206-5, $6.99/$7.99)
No one could have prepared Carrie for the monumental changes she would face when she met her new circle of friends at Stanford University. Once their lives intertwined and became woven into the tapestry of the times, they would never be the same.

TWINS   (0-8217-5207-3, $6.99/$7.99)
Brook and Melanie Chandler were so different, it was hard to believe they were sisters. One was a dark, serious, ambitious New York attorney; the other, a golden, glamourous, sophisticated supermodel. But they were more than sisters—they were twins and more alike than even they knew . . .

THE CARLTON CLUB   (0-8217-5204-9, $6.99/$7.99)
It was the place to see and be seen, the only place to be. And for those who frequented the playground of the very rich, it was a way of life. Mark, Kathleen, Leslie and Janet—they worked together, played together, and loved together, all behind exclusive gates of the *Carlton Club*.

Available wherever paperbacks are sold, or order direct from the Publisher. Send cover price plus 50¢ per copy for mailing and handling to Kensington Publishing Corp., Consumer Orders, or call (toll free) 888-345-BOOK, to place your order using Mastercard or Visa. Residents of New York and Tennessee must include sales tax. DO NOT SEND CASH.

ROMANCE FROM JANELLE TAYLOR

ANYTHING FOR LOVE   (0-8217-4992-7, $5.99)

DESTINY MINE   (0-8217-5185-9, $5.99)

CHASE THE WIND   (0-8217-4740-1, $5.99)

MIDNIGHT SECRETS   (0-8217-5280-4, $5.99)

MOONBEAMS AND MAGIC   (0-8217-0184-4, $5.99)

SWEET SAVAGE HEART   (0-8217-5276-6, $5.99)